Dear Vincent

Enjoy the book!

Timothy Sarratt

THE DEVIL YOU KNOW

Timothy Lassiter

authorHOUSE®

AuthorHouse™
1663 Liberty Drive, Suite 200
Bloomington, IN 47403
www.authorhouse.com
Phone: 1-800-839-8640

First published by AuthorHouse 10/24/2007

ISBN: 978-1-4343-3160-1 (sc)

Printed in the United States of America
Bloomington, Indiana

This book is printed on acid-free paper.

My thanks to Jennifer and Dawn,
whose help and knowledge made this book what it is.

To my friends, my family, whose continued support
gives me the strength and courage to follow my dreams.

To my Alison, whose love and support
makes me the man I am.

And finally, to my daughter,
whose every breath is an inspiration to me.

CHAPTER 1

Nicholas Grenier sat in a comfortable black, leather-backed chair, tapping the fingers of his right hand against the dark stained, wooden right arm of the chair. The rhythm was a cadence he had once observed on television, when watching the Marine Corps drill corps performing during a live event. He remembered how mesmerized he had been by their presentation, watching hundreds of individuals moving as one, astounded by the precision and dedication it must have taken for each man to become one mind. For some reason the beat from the cadence had always stayed with him, and had become a part of him, part of his nervous tapping when he was made to wait anxiously. When Nick became aware of his nervous tapping he stopped abruptly and looked at his watch. Thirty minutes had elapsed since he had been escorted into the doctor's office and told to wait, and there was no sign that his waiting would end anytime soon. Nick hated this room. As he looked around, examining every piece of furniture, he could not comprehend how anyone could become relaxed here. Everything in the room was perfectly placed, as though the room itself were lifted from the pages of a home decorating magazine. Every picture on the wall was perfectly level, each inkblot suggestive in it's own way, drawing the attention of the viewer. Nick could not bring himself to look at them, avoided them whenever he entered the room, afraid of what images his mind might interpret from the pictures.

Turning his attention away from the walls, Nick looked down at the floor, scanning the Persian carpet for a spec of dirt or a stray thread; hoping to find any evidence that anyone had voluntarily stayed longer than the required period of

1

time. Finding nothing, his eyes wandered to the coffee table centered perfectly in front of the couch. Nick was certain that if he measured, he would find it no more than a millimeter off center. The magazines on the table were fanned out in a precise pattern. Shaking his head, Nick looked up to the ceiling and sighed. The room felt so sterile. Nick found it ironic that it was this room's very esthetic perfection that made it feel so barren. It was akin to being alone in an alien environment, a place where there was no trace of human contact. It was so strange that people would consider this room, in it's confining perfection, to be a place where they felt comfortable enough to retreat into the deepest, darkest corners of their hearts and minds to release their innermost pain. Nick had found it particularly ironic that the person who led each patient down this path, Dr. Nancy Tanner, owner of this practice; was herself neurotic, cold, and often times just as sterile as the room itself. Her need for perfection was evident in her appearance; she belonged to this room. Nick's sessions with Dr. Tanner often left him angrier and more emotionally uncertain than when he arrived. Their sessions together were always argumentative, neither being able to back down from his or her position. Yet, there was something about their sessions that did eventually make him feel better, even if it was two to three hours later. Though she seemed to be completely unyielding, she did provide him with another perspective to his troubles.

Nick was derailed from his quiet introspection by the sound of the metal switch in the door as the knob turned and the door opened inward. Dr. Tanner stepped in through the door carrying a yellow legal pad in one hand, then turned to close the door behind her. She then turned towards him, adjusted her dark green framed glasses, and smiled.

"I'm sorry to have kept you waiting," she said, making her way to her chair. "I ran over time with another patient."

Nick made no attempt to hide his annoyance, shifting in his chair as though doing so would give him better physical leverage as he mounted his verbal assault.

"Can I ask you a question?" he asked, regarding the woman as she slipped her slender body into the chair across from him. "Why do you bother to make appointments when you are never on time? I mean, every time I come here you are running at least thirty minutes late. Do you realize that's thirty minutes of my life that I am never getting back?"

"Well," the doctor said with a sigh. "Perhaps you should arrive thirty minutes late so that I don't waste any of your precious time."

"Ah, I thought you'd say that," Nick said with a smile, having already anticipated her response. "However, if I were to arrive even ten minutes late for my appointment, your secretary would make me reschedule. Trust me, I know."

Dr. Tanner simply smiled. This frustratingly argumentative approach was how all of their appointments started. Nick would always pose a question, something biting that he was certain would provoke an argument or a debate. Lately, she had come to wonder what would happen if she simply did not play along, if he would become more agitated if she just conceded his point. However, Nick had been careful during their conversations and so far she had not yet had the opportunity to test this thought. Their sessions were very much like a chess game, each topic strategically brought up to evoke a certain response and each response a careful counter.

"How has your caseload been lately?" Tanner asked eager to push on. Nick had been referred to her by an old friend, his superior, Lt. Brenda Hollings. Shortly after a particularly difficult case, the first homicide case for the young detective, Hollings had suggested that Nick go to see Tanner. As the doctor understood it, it had been more of an order than a suggestion.

"Work is work," Nick replied. "Someone commits a crime, and it's my job to figure out the who and the why."

"Have there been any homicides lately?" Tanner asked, carefully watching the detective's facial expressions. Nick was a detective assigned to the Investigations Unit of the New London Police Department. Since he started with the unit there had been three high profile murder investigations, as well as many street murders that fell under his watch. Nick had been instrumental in solving them all.

"Not since the last time we talked," Nick answered, adjusting his position in the chair.

"Has your stress been any better?" Tanner asked, probingly.

"No better, no worse," Nick answered flatly. "There is not much stress in solving a burglary case. In fact, I don't even bother with them anymore; I strictly handle the homicide cases."

"Are you sure that's a wise choice?" Tanner asked, obviously concerned. "We've talked about your anger, especially about you suppressing it. Lately your cases have not left you with the time to unwind or with an appropriate outlet for release, and so your anger and frustration build until you are at the point where you are about to have a nervous breakdown."

"My anger," Nick began. "Comes from seeing abused women and children. My anger comes from drunk drivers plowing into a family only to be the sole survivors of the accident they created. My anger comes from kids gunning down other kids in schools so they can prove that they're men, something they wouldn't know the first thing about because they never had appropriate role models in the first place. My anger comes from pompous, arrogant, anal retentive doctors who think that they can listen and nod and have any clue about the horrors I see on a daily basis."

"What do you do with your free time?" Tanner asked, unfazed by his remark. Nick turned and looked up at her with an incredulous look on his face.

"What free time?" he asked.

"Do you do anything for fun?" Tanner asked, although she knew the answer to this question. It seemed to be a recurring theme in their sessions lately. However, Nick had always skirted the issue, hesitant to discuss his personal life, and the doctor was now determined to make him look at it.

"I catch the guilty," Nick answered, immediately aware of how corny the answer was.

"When was the last time you went out on a date?" she asked. Nick looked down at the floor, a feeling of longing and remorse washing over him.

"I don't have time for that sort of thing," he answered in almost a whisper, a biting twinge of pain and regret surging up in his chest.

"You mean you don't take time for that sort of thing," Tanner insisted. "Is there a woman in your life?"

"There was," Nick answered, allowing himself to run away in a sudden flood of memories. "I worked with her. Because of me she was kidnapped by a killer I was pursuing. We found her before he could hurt her, but..."

"But what?" Tanner asked, prodding him along. "Do you believe her abduction was your fault?"

"No," Nick answered, a hint of uncertainty in his voice. "Not really. I just couldn't live with myself if someone I loved was hurt or killed because of me."

"And so you cut yourself off," Tanner said, continuing the detective's thought. "You throw yourself into your work, which you know is literally consuming you alive, and just let life pass you by."

Nick said nothing, just continued to stare at the floor. This was not an area he felt comfortable discussing, and he wracked his brain searching for an exit strategy.

"I want you to go to the window and tell me what you see," Tanner said. Nick looked at the doctor for a moment, trying to determine whether or not she was serious. When he could not distinguish any mocking tone or suspicious glance, he rose from his chair and walked over to the window. He stared out for about thirty seconds, and then turned back to Tanner.

"I see a car parked in a handicapped space without displaying the proper tags," Nick answered. "I see two teenagers jay walking across the street, not that it really matters. I see two cars with expired registration, and interestingly enough I see a man standing outside the bar across the street, keeping watch."

"Keeping watch for what?" Tanner asked, slightly amused and yet mildly disturbed at the same time.

"Probably keeping watch for his boss inside," Nick answered, as he made his way back to his chair. "My guess is that a small time drug dealer works out of the bar, he's probably making one of his usual stops and the man outside is keeping his eye out for the police. You should really move your office to a more upscale part of town."

"That's quite amazing," Tanner said. "You must be a very good police officer."

"Thank you," Nick answered.

"I'm not sure that was meant simply as a compliment," the doctor stated. "Do you realize that in thirty seconds you were able to notice everything that was illegal or wrong, but you were incapable of noticing an attractive woman, a nice car, the arrangement of the garden below, or the beauty of the weather? In fact, you were incapable of noticing any beauty at all."

"And so you think I'm incapable of noticing beauty," Nick surmised.

"No, that's not what I said," Tanner responded, shaking her head as she corrected him. "But I am concerned that if you continue on this way that someday you won't be able to find happiness in anything. I'm afraid that your anger will consume you. You need to go out, live life and enjoy yourself. Ask a woman out on a date, go to a sporting event, join a club, do something."

Just then Nick felt a slight vibration around his waist. A slight smile formed around the corners of his mouth as he was able to instantly appreciate the irony of his work intruding just when Tanner was telling him he needed to have something more than work in his life. He ignored the pager that was rattling on his belt and thought about what Tanner had just said. She was unaware that anything was happening, and continued on with her observations. Then, thirty seconds later his pager vibrated and starting beeping. This stopped Tanner, a look of mild annoyance washing over her. There was a rule that all cell phones and pagers had to be turned off, but Nick never followed the rule, knowing that the moment he did would be the moment he was needed most. A moment later, his cell phone began to ring, along with the pager that was vibrating and chiming. Nick pulled the cell phone out of his pocket and simultaneously unclipped his pager. The cell call was from his boss, and the pager read, HOMICIDE: GET YOUR HEAD OUT OF YOUR ASS AND CALL IN.

"Can I ask what is so important?" Tanner asked, already knowing the answer.

"Death," the detective answered, simply. "And it's calling my name."

CHAPTER 2

Detective Grenier spent no more than five minutes making his way out of the psychologist's office. Nick was acutely aware of Dr. Tanner's unhappiness as she watched him leave. He could not help but wonder if she felt as though they should have made better progress in the amount of time they spent together. The detective had to be honest with himself, he was making it harder than it had to be. He was being unyielding in many ways. Perhaps it was his lack of desire to go to therapy in the first place that was making if difficult for him to open up, but Nick could not help but feel as though Dr. Tanner still did not thoroughly appreciate the place being a police officer held in his life. She did not understand that his work was the only reason Nick got out of bed in the morning. Ironically, it was also his work that was causing him to have to see a therapist. As Nick made his way to the door, Tanner insisted that he make another appointment before he left. Nick tried to make her understand the importance of time, but she insisted, arguing that a dead body was not going anywhere. Finally, not wanting to argue anymore, Nick made an appointment with the receptionist and hurried out the door. When he stepped out into the summer air, Nick looked around at his surroundings and was amazed at how right Tanner had been. When he had looked out of her office window, he had allowed himself to see nothing but what any good police officer would see. It had never occurred to him there might be something beyond that, something everyone else saw and probably took for granted. It was a beautiful summer day, warm and sunny with no humidity. There were blue skies above with the occasional large, pillow-like, cumulus cloud drifting lazily across the sky. He wondered then and there if she was right, if perhaps he was becoming too carried away with his job. Nick had not even attempted to pursue any type of relationship since his short-lived one with Anna Meaders.

Thinking about this caused his mind to wander for a moment. He was lonely, that he knew. He wanted a relationship, but was very uneasy about getting into one. He knew that his excuse of not wanting to put someone at risk was just that, an excuse. Though he was a little concerned, there were very few serial killers like his first, The Nemesis. There had been more to that case and even though Nick had solved many other murder cases since then, none of them had compared to the complexity of his first homicide. He knew that the real issue holding him back from pursuing a relationship was more a fear of himself. He dealt with some very horrible crimes, and he did not want to bring that life home with him. He could not imagine a woman who, after hearing about his day, would want to remain with him for any length of time. To compensate for his loneliness, or perhaps to force it out of his mind, Nick threw himself into his work, putting in more hours than were necessary to solidify cases, tracking down leads and rigorously preparing himself for the assault he would endure on the witness stand when the cases finally went to court.

Nick was the lead detective of the Investigations Unit, and though he worked alongside other detectives, he did not have a partner. Nick worked alone; it was the only way he knew. The chime of his cell phone jogged his mind back to the present. He pressed the call button and placed the small receiver to his ear.

"Where the fuck have you been?" asked a female voice. Nick recognized it immediately as being the voice of his superior officer, Lieutenant Brenda Hollings. She had brought him in on The Nemesis investigation and put him into the Lead

Investigator position. After the case was over, he had decided to stay on and the two had been working well together ever since. Hollings understood things about Nick, things most other superiors could not, and it made for a good working relationship.

"I've been at the fucking psychiatrist that you insisted I go to," Nick answered. She was his superior, and in front of anyone else he would show all the respect due her and her position. However, there was also a casual side to their relationship.

"Oh yeah?" Hollings answered. "Has she certified you as crazy yet?"

"No," Nick answered with a laugh. "But there is still plenty of time."

"Maybe I should talk to her," Hollings added. "There are plenty of things I could tell her."

"Well, I've got an appointment for next Friday," Nick informed her. "You could go for me. Now, what's so important?"

"We've got a multiple murder in Salem," Hollings said. "Man and woman shot dead in their RV. Our officers were first on the scene and say it looks like a murder/suicide but I want you to go out there and have a look. You'll figure it out for sure. I don't want to write off a case as a murder/suicide and have it come back to bite me in the ass if someone else ends up dead."

"What is it you want me to do?" Nick asked.

"You know what I want you to do," Hollings answered. "I want you to do what you do, see the crime, feel it out, whatever."

Nick knew exactly what Hollings meant, he knew it before he asked. Nick had an uncanny ability to understand a crime scene, especially a murder scene and know what had happened and usually why. It was one of the reasons that Hollings had given him the lead detective position ahead of other detectives who had been in the department longer, and it was why Nick stayed with the New London Police Department. He had expected his previous assignments to keep him in Hartford, but after his first homicide, it did not end up that way.

"What if that's all it is, a murder/suicide?" Nick asked, wanting to clarify his position on the case.

"Well, then you just hand it off to Mitchell and Wilkins," Hollings answered, referring to the other two ranking detectives in the Unit. "They're already on the scene. I sent them right over to make sure no one screws up the scene. I can't stand those beat cops who want to show off and end up touching something they should have left alone."

"What's the address?" Nick asked, getting into his car and starting it up.

"You know where Witch Meadow Lake is, right?" Hollings asked. Nick knew the area intimately, having camped on those very grounds many times. In fact, Nick lived only a few miles from the scene of the crime, and as he pulled his car onto the road and veered across the lanes of traffic to head south on Route 82, he felt no concern about the murder he was going to. Hollings had said the first officers on the scene said it looked like a murder/suicide, and they were probably right. Murders, deaths, shootings, stabbings, they happened everywhere. Serial killers, however, were rare even though they tended to eat up all of the media attention. Connecticut had had only one serial murderer before the case Nick took over a year ago, and none since. As he headed down the rural Route 82, he allowed his mind to wander back to his brief appointment with Dr. Tanner. He was still bothered by her observation, by the fact that Nick took no time for himself. He did not like how quickly she came to her observations of him, especially when they turned out to be right. As for expanding his social life, that was easier said than done. Nick knew that he was not unhappy with his life, but he also knew that he was angry. He was also worried about becoming desensitized; he had seen it happen too many times.

He thought about this and other things as he made his way down the well known back road. He opened the windows in his car, and though it was July, there was very little humidity and it was actually pleasant to be outdoors. According to the weatherman, tomorrow the humidity would return to close to 100% and everyone who did not have air conditioning running full blast would wish that they did. Nick eased off of the gas a little as his car shot over the road, running through the little, quiet towns of Bozrah and Montville and then finally entering Salem. It took him all of twelve minutes to get from Tanner's office in Norwich to the crime scene in Salem. After showing his badge to the campground's gatekeeper, who was obviously irritated at the police for forcing him to close his campground on such a fine day, he weaved his car through the narrow, dusty path to the numbered address that Lt. Hollings had given him on the phone. In front of the huge RV were two squad cars and an unmarked car, most likely that of Detectives Mitchell and Wilkins. There were no officer's outside, no one marking off the crime scene. Nick quickly called Hollings to make sure that there were additional officers on the way, and slipped his cell phone back into his pocket. Nick turned around quickly and spotted curious neighbors inching their way forward to see what they could see. Nick yelled at them sharply, warning them about coming any closer than his car, then he saw another cruiser coming down the path towards him and turned back to the RV.

"Well," the detective said aloud to himself. "Here we go again."

CHAPTER 3

Nick took a quick look at the immediate area, examining the RV and the surrounding lot. Bags of garbage were heaped in a plastic garbage bin on the far side of the rig and it looked to the detective as if the family vehicle had been parked there for a while. The lot had all the signs of a family setting up for a long stay. The scuffed and worn WELCOME mat lay partially overturned, folded over in the far right corner from wear. A clothes line stretched from one side of the RV to a six foot wooden pole to which was bolted the power and water hook-ups. Clothes hung sloppily off of the line as though they had been hung days ago and removed one at a time when needed. A man in a blue-grey suit stepped out the door and down the wooden steps to meet up with Nick before the detective examined the scene.

"Get me up to speed," Nick said to Wilkins as they shook hands briefly. Detective Peter Wilkins was now the most senior detective in the Investigations Unit and had the most time in service. When Nick was given the position of lead detective he was concerned that Wilkins would be impossible to work with. Nick had seen this very thing happen with Wilkins' partner, Mark Anderson, who before he left was in line to be the next lead detective. Anderson's bruised ego made him unable to work with Nick, leading to his transfer. Nick knew that his presence on that first case could cause a major rift in the unit, but the lieutenant kept everything together in the end, and Wilkins had proven himself a major asset in the unit. So far, there had been no hard feelings about Nick's unusual promotion over the other detectives.

"We've got two dead bodies," Wilkins said, jumping into his narration. "One male, J.B. Todd, the other female, Karen Thompson. It looks as though the male died from multiple gunshot wounds, three from the looks of it. As for the woman, one shot to the temple, looks self inflicted."

"What does the J.B. stand for?" Nick asked, following the detective into the RV.

"Fuck if I know," Wilkins answered. "He looks like a hick."

Nick planted both feet inside the trailer and was instantly assaulted by the smell of burnt tobacco. The smell was everywhere, having permeated every object and even seemed to be oozing from the walls. Nick looked down at the floor at the bodies of the man and woman. The man was lying face up with three large blood stains on his shirt. In the middle of the stains were small black circles which Nick knew to be gunpowder burns. Nick turned his attention to the woman lying to the left of the male. The entire right side of her head seemed as though it had been caved in. There seemed to be no sign the bullet exited on the other side of her head. Nick just shook his head and sighed.

"Who moved the body?" Nick asked, nodding his head in the dead woman's direction.

"How'd you know she was moved?" asked a male officer.

"I did," a young officer spoke up. The young man was pale and Nick could tell immediately that he was not used to seeing dead bodies. "I thought...I needed to make sure that the guy underneath was really dead."

"It's alright," Nick said, understanding the confusion and shock that go along with viewing a dead body for the first time. "What's your name?"

At that moment, Wilkins chimed in, introducing the young officer who rolled the dead body with his partner as patrol cops from Colchester who answered the call at the same time as the New London officers had. Wilkins then introduced Nick to the two New London officers who were the first to arrive on the scene. Nick looked back at the Colchester cop and his rookie partner and smiled.

"If you don't mind, why don't you and your partner go out and secure the scene," Nick said, knowing that the younger officer had to get outside and get some air. The older officer just nodded, appreciating the detective's concern. As the two officers approached, Nick raised his hand for a moment. "Put some tape up around this thing but stick around, I need to talk to you guys about jurisdiction."

The other officers answered in the affirmative and stepped out of the trailer. Nick then turned his attention back to the dead bodies. There was something so peaceful about these bodies, something that he did not usually witness at a crime scene. At most of the homicide scenes he visited, dead bodies often showed surprise or agony in their faces. The shock of being shot, or the agony of pain after being stabbed while the life slowly slips away, were all expressions he was used to seeing on the faces of the victims. However, there was no shock in these faces. The man's face seemed confused if not a little angry. However, the woman's face seemed at peace, perhaps a little welcoming. *Perhaps she had been eager to leave this life*, he thought to himself. It was that thought that started a strange scene in his head. The scene was not strange to him though, he had witnessed this kind of experience at every crime scene. He could see the victims, before they were victims, events happening as if their lives were in rewind.

"Why all this attention over a murder/suicide anyway," asked the male officer from New London. Nick closed his eyes, frustration clouding his mental view of the events. He turned his head in the direction of the two officers.

"Who the hell are you again?" Nick asked, allowing his annoyance to become evident in his tone.

"Officer Peter Socha," the man said, caught off guard by the sudden anger that was seeping from the detective. "This is my partner, Officer Jennifer Kelley."

"Pleased to meet you," Nick said with a smile and a nod. "Now shut the fuck up before I throw you out on your ass."

The officer was immediately quiet but there was a sense of petulance about him, as though he had just been scolded by an adult. The junior officer's feelings did not matter to Nick as he resumed his examination of the dead bodies. The image of the two before the murder materialized before him again, and he kneeled down watching it as if the images were really there. The male officer opened his mouth to say something, but Wilkins raised his hand and shot the young man a look that immediately silenced him. Nick watched the scene as it slowed and then began to run forward. He watched as the man and the woman yelled at each other. He could not hear their words, and he did not know whether this scene before him was some deep intuition or just part of his imagination run wild, but he had a good idea of what had happened here. He had a feeling that a scene similar to this happened every night, and it had for a long time. The detective watched, grieved, as he saw the man hitting the woman, pushing her, throwing her to the floor. He could feel his blood boiling as the man beat on her, hitting her in the face; going from his open hand to his fists.

"Things got out of control," Nick said aloud, not directing his comment towards anyone in particular. "He did not usually get this violent."

"How could he...," but the young officer was cut off again.

"He's punching her, kicking her," Nick said, his voice cracking with empathy and rage. "She was terrified, more terrified than she had ever been. She gets away from him. She gets the gun out of the drawer."

Nick pointed out past the officers and into the kitchen.

"She points it at him," Nick continued. "I don't know what she was telling him, but he did not believe that she would shoot him. He laughed at her, even egged her on."

Nick caught his breath suddenly. Everyone inside the RV had his full and undivided attention.

"He noticed it," Nick said. "A crack in her determination. He rushes her for the gun. He's standing over her, hitting her and she fires. Three times. He backs away and then falls to the ground, dead. She comes forward, screaming. She falls here, to her knees."

Nick pointed to a spot right in front of the very place where the man lay dead.

"She puts the gun to her head and fires," Nick continued. "She falls on top of him. Jesus, they die together."

"How could you know that he beat her?" Socha asked. Nick pulled a pen from his pocket and leaned over the dead woman. He fished the pen point underneath the sleeve of the woman's shirt and lifted it up, revealing a large bruise.

"Damn," Socha exclaimed.

"You'll find bruises like these all over her body," Nick said, rising from his position over the bodies. "Some will be fresh, some will be slightly yellowish. Those are older and were healing."

"That was..." the female officer began in astonishment.

"Freaky," Socha interrupted. Nick, however, was not listening. He stared down at the corpses, as the sorrow within him began welling up. A part of him just wanted to start beating his fists against the male victim. Nick knew that he needed some kind of outlet, some release. This was not the release Dr. Tanner had been talking about. This was simply the anger and sorrow at two lives lived so briefly, so violently, so painfully, and finally, so pointlessly.

"Some boys take a beautiful girl, and hide her away from the rest of the world," Nick said, repeating the lyrics to a song that suddenly seemed so appropriate. There was a pause for a moment as everyone in the room looked over at the detective.

"I want to be the one to walk in the sun," the female officer said softly, finishing the verse. Nick turned to Officer Kelley and smiled, nodding his head.

"That's all she really wanted," Nick said, realizing that there was someone in the room who had some kind of understanding of the pain that filled this home. "She just wanted to be the one who walked in the sun."

"Can someone tell me what the hell I'm missing?" Socha asked, stepping between the detective and his partner.

"Yeah," Nick answered, his frustration with the arrogant patrol officer getting the better of him. "You're missing the five year old witness to this nightmare."

"What witness?" Socha asked, confused.

"That one," Nick said, pointing to a picture on the wall of the two victims, smiling together as though they were a happy family. Between the two adults was a little girl, smiling, probably laughing as she was suspended in the air by the two adults. "She's somewhere in this house, and she saw everything."

CHAPTER 4

Detective Grenier walked to the back end of the camper, through a short and very narrow corridor that could barely be called a hallway. Nick was followed by Wilkins and the two patrol officers. At the end of the corridor, Nick saw that there was a small doorway on the left and the right. To the left was a tiny bathroom, and to the right was a small bedroom. As Nick came to realize, this was not the traditional camper. In fact, it seemed to be more like a trailer or mobile home. Adjusting his idea of the size of the home, he concluded that this family had either been here for a while, or they had plans of staying for some time. Nick walked through the doorway into the bedroom, where he found his other detective, Andrew Mitchell taking digital photographs of the entire room. Mitchell had been the junior most man in the Investigations Unit. He and Detective Mitchell has struck an immediate friendship upon Nick's arrival in the unit, as they were both junior men having to prove themselves. As before, Nick was concerned when he was given the position of lead detective that this immediate friendship with Mitchell would dissolve. When Nick had been called in to help on The Nemesis case, Mitchell had been the first, and for some time, only person who he could talk to. Somehow, they had been able to maintain their friendship, even after Nick's promotion, and there had not been any hostility from either Wilkins or Mitchell since.

Nick walked into the room and stayed behind Mitchell, keeping his hands in his pockets. He was not wearing any latex gloves, and though it was certain that this case was a murder/suicide, he knew that the crime scene unit would have to collect their own evidence, and the last thing he needed as a lead detective was to leave his prints on something vital. Nick watched the detective snap photos, able to see exactly what images Mitchell was shooting in the display screen. Out of the corner of his eye, Nick noticed the other three attempting to make their way into the room. Nick held up his hand, stopping them in the doorway. Making a full turn, Nick was amazed at just how small the room was. A double sized bed lay directly in the middle of the room, taking up most of the available space. There was a twelve inch border of walking space between the edge of the bed and the wall. Nick knew that somewhere in this room, a frightened little girl was hiding.

"That's about it, detective," Mitchell said, scrolling through the photographs he had taken of the crime scene. "I think I have taken every picture that we could need to wrap this case up."

Nick nodded, and then raised his outstretched index finger to his lips, indicating he wanted everyone to be quiet. Nick moved to the corner of the room, the only place where there was enough room for him to bend down. He unclipped his detective's badge from his belt and placed it face up on the floor, then pushed it to the edge of the bed, just slightly under.

"Hello under there," Nick started as if talking to the bed itself. "My name is Nick, and I'm a policeman. I know that you're scared, I was wondering if you would come out so I can help you."

There was no sound and no movement. Nick listened carefully and could not even hear breathing. All eyes were focused on the bed, waiting in hushed anticipation.

"I know you're scared and not sure what you should do," Nick said, trying to sound as calm and non-threatening as possible. "I know that your mommy told you to hide and not to come out, no matter what. You are a very good girl to do what your mommy tells you. I bet your mommy also told you that policemen are supposed to protect you, and that you have to do what they tell you. I am here to protect you, I promise. That's my policeman's badge on the floor. You can take it if you want and see that I am really a policeman."

There was another pause, everyone waiting with baited breath. After about thirty seconds, five little fingers hesitantly slid out to the edge of the bed, felt for the badge, then grasped it and pulled it back under the bed quickly.

"Oh shit," Mitchell whispered without thinking.

"I bet you're a big girl," Nick began. He was building a trust with the girl, he could feel it. She had felt safe enough to take the badge, now he just had to make her feel safe enough to come out. He knew they could not just go under there and bring her out, as she was like a cornered animal. "I bet you can even read. Can you read the word Protect on there? It's the word that starts with a P. That means that I have to protect you, no matter what. Do you believe me?"

"Yes," came a soft little voice after a moments pause.

"Do you know what a policeman looks like in his uniform?" Nick asked. "Have you ever seen one?"

"Yes, I saw them at the parade," the little girl answered. "At the fourth of July."

"That's right," Nick said. "They were in the parade. I have four other policemen here who want to protect you too. Two of them are in uniforms just like you saw in the parade. They want to meet you and take you somewhere safe. I bet you like ice cream, right?"

"Yes," the voice said her interest suddenly peaked and obvious in the tone of her voice.

"Well, I bet we could take you to get some really good ice cream," Nick said, resorting to bribery. "But first I need you to do something for me so I know that you are safe. I need you to put that gun in your hand down and slide it out on the floor."

Nick waited, terrified that the mere mention of the gun would remind the girl of why she had it and how she got it. There was silence again, and Nick knew that he could not let her mind go back to that nightmare.

"All the ice cream you can eat for the gun," Nick said. "Sounds like a good trade to me."

All of a sudden, the little hand came out pushing a .38 snub-nosed revolver by the handle. The little hand backed away from the gun, but remained visible. Mitchell bent down with a gloved hand and gingerly picked the revolver off the floor, removing the danger.

"Thank you, sweetheart," Nick said. "You are a very brave and good girl. Now, if you want to come out, I'd like to go find some ice cream."

The little girl, no more than six, cautiously emerged from underneath the bed. Her hands were stained with blood, and there were a few streaks of tears down her face, a stark contrast to her angelic features. Officer Kelley gasped and exclaimed something that Nick could not hear, then burst forward and gathered the little girl up in her arms. Holding the girl tight to her body, Nick watched Officer Kelley quickly make her way out of the room with the little girl, covering her eyes so that she would not see the gruesome scene that lay ahead. Nick rose to his feet as Mitchell checked the weapon. There were only two unfired bullets in the weapon that holds six. He sniffed it, and then pulled back as he caught the distinctive smell of burnt gunpowder.

"It's been fired recently," Mitchell stated. "With two rounds left, I'd say this pretty much makes it the murder weapon. I'd better bag it."

Nick watched as Mitchell made his way past the other detective and officer towards the door. Officer Socha walked and shook his head in disbelief.

"Damn, if that girl had stayed quiet, it could have been hours before we would have known she was missing," Socha exclaimed. "And with a gun..."

His voice just seemed to fade off with his train of thought. Mitchell looked back into the room, a disgusted look spread across his face. He had seen the rage in Nick's eyes before he had left the bedroom, and now looking back, noting the nod of his lead detective's head, he closed the door slowly behind him. Once Nick heard the click of the door latch, he grabbed Socha by the shirt and shoved him hard against the wall.

"I ought to beat the living shit out of you," Nick exclaimed, able to contain his anger no longer.

"What the fuck are you doing man?" Socha cried out, trying to push himself off of the wall. Wilkins had come up quick and pressed all of his mass against Socha, pinning him to the wall.

"That girl could be dead because of you," Nick shouted. "What the fuck is wrong with you? Haven't you heard the phrase, securing a crime scene?"

"How the fuck was I supposed to know she was in here?" Socha asked, frantically. "There was no evidence."

"Didn't you notice that the murder weapon was missing?" Nick asked in disbelief.

"I, I..." Socha stammered, trying to find an excuse. It was becoming clear to him that he had really messed up, and now he was searching his brain for the reason why he had not noticed the weapon missing.

"I, I," Nick said mockingly. "Shut the fuck up. Do you have any ambitions beyond traffic duty?"

The officer could do nothing but nod at this point, his anger and embarrassment at the situation he had put himself into having momentarily taken away his ability to speak.

"Then remember this image," Nick said, warning him. "Think of that girl with a hole in her head just like her mommy and remember that it was your fault because you were too busy trying to act like a big shot in front of cops from another town than securing the crime scene. Next time you are at a crime scene, think to yourself, 'Did I do everything to make this scene secure, or is Detective Grenier going to beat the shit out of me because I forgot something?' Just keep that in mind and get out there and start interviewing the neighbors in the area."

When Wilkins released the terrified officer, Nick could see his hands shaking. He knew that Socha probably wanted to take a swing at him, and the detective was preparing himself for it. However, the officer just inched himself away from the wall and passed the detectives. He turned just as he reached the door, there was a look of his face that made Nick think he was going to cry.

"That won't happen again, detective," Socha said softly. Just then the door handle turned and the door opened to the image of Officer Kelley.

"The girl is in my squad car with the park owner's wife," she said, tossing Nick his badge back. "Thought you might want this back. The crime scene guys are here."

She took a look at her partner, then back to the two detectives. There was a tension in the air and a look on Socha's face that she had never seen before.

"What's going on here?" she asked.

"Nothing," Nick said with a smile as he clipped the badge back on his belt. "Just some professional advice."

CHAPTER 5

The rest of the day was taken up in the actual investigative process. Though there was no doubt at this point that the case was a murder/suicide, there were still a lot of unanswered questions. Nick needed to understand why this happened. He was certain that Todd had beaten his girlfriend before; there were plenty of bruises to prove that. Nick was thankful to see that there did not seem to be any signs of abuse on the little girl. His heart ached for the girl though; seeing her mother dead, having to pry the gun from her dead hands. The detective could not imagine the amount of therapy that would be needed to make this little girl feel whole again, if that were even possible. Unable to continue thinking about the sheer horror of the case, Nick set everyone to their tasks and began his own part. Nick needed the camp neighbors closest to Todd and Thompson interviewed, as well as the camp owner. Hopefully, it would be through these lines of questioning that he would get the answers he needed to feel comfortable enough to put this case to rest. Though the medical examiner's office had removed the bodies, Nick could still see the images of the man and woman lying there, and he could not help but wonder what Karen Thompson thought this day would be like. *Where did she plan to be at the end of the day?* He was certain that a cold metal slab in the morgue did not enter into her thoughts.

After his "friendly advice" to Officer Socha, he set the patrol officer to the task of getting information from the neighbors. Socha was able to find out that arguments and fighting between Todd and Thompson were a regular part of campground life. The people who had been camping next door to the victims were a retired couple from Vermont who were spending two weeks driving through southern New England. They, like everyone else, talked about how the couple argued every night, the arguments escalating to shouting matches. When asked why they did not say anything about the noise, everyone had the same answer: It wasn't any of our business. None of the neighbors seemed interested in getting involved in anyone else's affairs, and everyone swore that they knew nothing about the physical abuse. Socha was certain that each and every member of the campground was lying. He said they all had the same reaction, none of them being shocked when they heard about it, all of them just shrugging and saying they had no idea. When asked about the relationship with the little girl everyone swore that Todd acted indifferent towards her, as though he could not be bothered with her. However, every neighbor was certain that Todd did not hit or abuse her in any way. When Socha briefed Nick on his findings, the officer seemed to share his opinion that there was no violence towards the girl, though no one seemed to be sure. In the end, Nick was impressed with the amount of detail Socha put into his work; their earlier confrontation having changed his attitude and perspective of the young officer.

Nick spent his time interviewing the campground owner and his wife. They seemed like a nice older couple, though Nick could not help but feel they knew just as much, if not more, than the neighbors around the crime scene. They made no attempt to hide the fact that they knew there was arguing and verbal abuse, though they feigned shock and ignorance when told about the long history of physical abuse. Nick questioned them about the daughter, trying to see if they had the same impression as everyone else as to the nature of the relationship between Todd and the girl. Neither of them felt there was anything more than a man who was dating a woman with a daughter from a previous relationship. They said that though he was never mean to the girl, Todd never paid any type of attention to her either. Nick found out that the wife of the campground owner actually babysat the child for the mother. The mother had just found a job in the last couple of weeks, and the wife had offered to watch the girl for free as she understood that the mother did not have the money to pay for real daycare. It seemed that the mother repaid the family in other ways, baking desserts, doing household chores on the weekends, and anything else that they might need. As for Todd, he had paid for the lot on the campground for six months in advance, and the only real concern the owner showed came when he realized that he might have to give up the money that was paid.

"I tell everyone," the owner said, as if his words made it legal. "All transactions are final."

"Yeah, well," Nick said shaking his head. "We'll see about that."

By the end of his questioning, Nick was certain that the owners held the same level of complicity as everyone else in the park. They knew about the abuse and they did nothing about it. It infuriated the detective, thinking that this poor woman probably felt as though she had nowhere to go and so stayed and continued to be abused with no hope that there was any other way. Had just one of these people showed the slightest interest or concern, life could have turned out so differently for this woman and her daughter. It just seemed like such a complete waste.

Officer Kelley stayed with the young girl and worked to find her relatives and inform them of what had happened. After hours of phone calls, Kelley had found the little girl's maternal grandmother in upstate New York and had been forced to place the call. The woman was devastated at learning of her daughter's death, and seemed totally ignorant of the fact that she had met Todd and moved to Connecticut. The last bit of information the mother had was that her daughter had moved to Boston to find a job and make a go of it there. After a two hour phone conversation, the grandmother indicated she would come and get the child. She indicated that she would not be in Connecticut until the following morning. Apparently, the grandmother felt as though she had to get her home ready for a six year old to live in, and was unable to leave until she felt she had accomplished this. This information put all of the officers in a bad mood, knowing that if the grandmother could not be there until the morning, legally, the girl would have to be placed in foster care. Nick tried to pull some strings, but though it was just for one night, child services demanded she be put through the system. Reluctantly, Officer Kelley filed the paperwork for foster placement, and Lt. Hollings came down personally to pick up the girl. Watching his lieutenant drive away, he could not help but be furious with the system he was a part of. This girl, who had watched the most horrific thing anyone could imagine, would now be bounced between people she did not know until her grandmother, who she apparently did not even remember, was able to pick her up. *This girl is going to be in therapy forever*, he thought to himself.

After so many hours on the scene Nick wanted nothing more than to just leave and go back to the police department. He met with Detective Wilkins, who had been assigned to work with the crime scene investigators who were processing the scene, for a period of time. The CSU techs came to the same conclusion as everyone else; Thompson had shot Todd and then turned the gun on herself. After going through the scene, they could find nothing but circumstantial evidence of physical abuse, and they found nothing that indicated the girl had been victimized. That would have to be flushed out by a psychiatrist.

The only interesting news came from Detective Mitchell five hours after the initial finding of the gun. Mitchell had taken the gun straight to the forensic lab, wanting to deal with someone face to face and make sure that there would be no questions as to the chain of custody of the weapon. There was some interest when that particular revolver turned out to match the same weapon used in six different robberies all over New England. Nick immediately assigned Mitchell to do all research on J.B. Todd to see who he was and how he got the weapon. If the police were able to put six open robbery cases to bed, then maybe there would be some feeling of accomplishment after such a horrible case. Unfortunately, Nick could not help but feel as though nothing would really make them feel good about this case. Closing a case was only a physical part of the job, it still lingered with the detectives involved; every case did.

Nick drove back to the New London Police Department where he spent the rest of the afternoon and early evening filing paperwork in regards to the case and reviewing updates from his detectives. At one point, he found himself alone in his darkened office, the sun setting in the windows behind him and the light waning from the room. All of a sudden, the telephone rang.

"Detective Grenier," Nick answered, only then aware of the time.

"What in the hell are you still doing in the office?" asked his lieutenant. "It's almost eight o'clock at night on a Friday. You should be out at a bar, picking up chicks."

"There was paperwork to do," Nick explained quickly, hoping to steer his superior away from the subject of dating. "How did the girl get on with child services?"

"Yeah, there was a problem with that," Hollings started. "Little Michelle never made it to the foster care center. I stopped by the house and Don took one look at her and told me she was staying as long as it took her grandmother to get here."

Nick smiled in the dark as he let out a sigh of relief. He could picture her husband telling her that she was not letting the girl go. Don Hollings was the quintessential family man, he loved children and though they had three of their own, there was never too many children in the Hollings house.

"That was before little Michelle informed me that you promised her all the ice cream she could eat," Hollings continued. Nick laughed out loud.

"Oh yeah," Nick said. "Sorry about that. It couldn't have been that bad. How much ice cream can a little girl eat?"

"How about twenty dollars worth," Hollings answered. "She's going to puke everywhere later and I'm going to make you come over and clean it up. Now what's going on with the case, any new information?"

"Not really," Nick answered. "There was the thing about the gun, and Mitchell is tracking down Todd's past as we speak. I'm thinking that when Todd was casing the bank in Boston, he met Thompson and that's how the relationship started. He shows interest in her, she needs a man in her life. I don't know whether or not she knew about his criminal activities, but we'll find out."

"God I hope not," Hollings said with a sigh. "Not that it matters that much now. So what's your thinking on the case?"

"Well," Nick began, leaning back in his metal desk chair. "There is no big secret here; it was a murder/suicide. I don't even think that Thompson meant to kill Todd; I think things just got out of control. I'd like to arrest everyone in that park, they all knew what was going on and did nothing, but beyond that, there are no more avenues to investigate. I feel comfortable enough about handing this over to Mitchell and Wilkins until the last pieces of evidence come in. If other states want in because of the robberies, they can have it."

"My feelings exactly," Hollings answered. "We have more than enough crime to deal with here. This one seems pretty much solved. The grandmother will pick up Michelle tomorrow and all the living victims will be pretty much gone. Now, why don't you get out of there?"

"I'm just finishing up, and then I'll go home," Nick promised.

"You are the only thirty year-old single man I know who does nothing on a Friday night," Hollings stated. "You're a pretty good looking guy, for a white boy. You should be out there hitting on the ladies."

"I'm not very good at that kind of thing," Nick said.

"You don't have to be," Hollings answered. "They'll come to you. You know why you're in counseling right now?"

"Because you're making me go," Nick answered.

"No," Hollings responded, picking up on the sarcasm. "It's because homicide is your life. It's all you know, it's all you do. You need to get out there and join the land of the living."

"So you're telling me that if I go out and pick up a woman you'll stop making me go to counseling?" Nick asked.

"I'll think about it," Hollings answered, though she had no plan on doing so. "Don't Mitchell and Wilkins go to a certain bar every Friday?"

"Yeah," Nick said. "All the cops in the area do. It's down in Mystic, maybe I'll join them."

"No maybe's about it," Hollings said. "Think of it as an order. One that I will be checking on Monday morning. Now get out of there before I have you arrested."

Nick laughed and said good night. Hollings was right; his life did revolve around death. There was no reason it had to be like that, and he was going to sink further into depression if he did not get out of this pit. He thought of what she said; join the land of the living. Perhaps that was just what he should do.

CHAPTER 6

The Blue Wall was a quiet little pub located on the edge of Groton and Mystic, Connecticut, known by every cop in the southeastern part of the state because it catered especially to police officers. Though open to everyone, every night you could expect to find no less than fifty off-duty officers enjoying the evening there. The bar was run by a retired Hartford police officer who had moved down to Mystic to live on the water. After less than a month in retirement, he found himself deliriously bored and started looking for something to occupy his time. Within six months he had purchased the building and bought out the previous owner, who was drowning in debt because of a lack of clientele. After a brief period of remodeling, Blue Wall was opened and anyone in law enforcement was offered a discount. The offer brought in so much business that the owner finally decided to make the discount a rule with the bar. Nick had been in the bar a few times when he was a more junior officer but had not been back for many years. When he entered, the detective was amazed at how much the place had grown and changed since the last time he had been here. Looking around, the first thing to grab his attention was the bar. Every seat was taken and men and women were standing around, talking and placing orders. Looking beyond the bar, he saw how the building had been expanded to add booths, tables, and a game area where pool tables, dartboards, and small basketball hoops had been set up.

Getting swept up in the momentum of patrons entering and exiting the bar, Nick fell in and was pushed through the door and up into the bar itself. Nick looked around for anyone he might know, hoping to spot Mitchell or Wilkins somewhere.

He milled around the bar for a few minutes, declining to place an order when an attractive young waitress carrying a round tray passed by. As he quickly made his way around the bar, Nick scanned the faces of the patrons, looking for his detectives.

"Detective," he heard someone call out. Nick looked up and saw Mitchell's head above the rest of the crowd, beckoning him over. When Nick approached he saw Mitchell sitting with Wilkins and two other detectives from the Investigations Unit. "I didn't expect to see you here tonight."

"Yeah well," Nick started. "All work and no play, right?"

"Meaning Hollings ordered you to get out of the office," Wilkins chimed in.

"I guess I couldn't do any more damage to that case today," Nick said, laughing along with the other detectives. "It's pretty much wrapped up anyway."

Nick ordered a beer and sat with the detectives as they discussed other cases, some still open and some long since solved. Though he was with people he knew, Nick did not feel at ease. He watched the faces of every person at the bar, watching their expressions, their body language, even deciphering their conversations; as if waiting for someone to commit a crime. *This is a police bar, you idiot,* he told himself. *No one's going to be that stupid.* Unfortunately for Nick, this was the predatory nature within him, and though he had learned to channel it all through his police work, he had not yet learned how to turn it off. As he scanned the crowd, Nick's eyes subconsciously recognized a familiar face. He backtracked quickly, searching for the face again until his eyes fell on Socha. The young officer was sitting alone at a small counter overlooking the billiard tables. Nick grabbed his beer and made his way over to the officer.

"You drinking alone tonight?" Nick asked. He had meant the question to be friendly, but it came out sounding more like a taunt.

"Screw you," Socha replied. "I'm off the clock; I don't have to put up with your shit."

"Hey man," Nick said, raising his free hand. "That didn't come out right. I didn't mean anything by it. This place is not exactly my kind of scene either."

"Oh yeah, I know," Socha said with a roll of his eyes. "We've all heard about the great Detective Grenier. The cop who doesn't sleep or eat until he solves a crime. The cop who has never failed to close a case. Everybody, take notes so that we can be like Detective Grenier."

"Man, you don't want to be like me," Nick responded with a chuckle. "I solve cases the way I do because I have no life. You're going to be a detective someday, and you're going to do things your own way. Hell, it may even be a better way."

Socha looked up at the detective skeptically for a moment.

"That's not what you said earlier today," Socha said, remembering the hostile scene at the crime scene.

"Yeah well, you were being a cocky little shit," Nick said bluntly. "You were trying to show off and it was fucking up my investigation. You had to be knocked down a few rungs. It happens to all of us."

"It happened to you?" Socha asked, unconvinced.

"More than once," Nick said with a smile, as if reminiscing. "Besides, once you got down to interviewing the neighbors, you did a really good job. Your gut feeling about all of them was right on, all of them knew about the abuse and none of them did anything about it."

"That was pretty obvious though," Socha responded. "Anyone would have figured that out."

"Hey, don't dismiss those feelings," Nick warned. "It's those instincts that can help you blow a case wide open. It's that little warning in the back of your mind that tells you someone is lying, or hiding something. Learn to trust your instincts and you will be a great cop."

"Thanks," Socha said, nodding his head. "I'll keep that in mind."

"I'll give you a perfect example. See that woman over there," Nick said, gesturing to a woman sitting alone at the far end of the bar. "She's been sitting in the same seat for as long as I've been here, nursing that apple martini. She's talked to a few guys who have approached her, but not connected with them. She wants to connect with someone, she's just waiting for the right person. Why don't you go over there and buy her a drink?"

"I don't know..." Socha started, watching the woman.

"Would it make you feel better if I made it an order?" Nick asked with a smile, taking a page from his lieutenant's book.

"Well," Socha said, sliding off of his stool. "If it's an order."

With that, Socha walked away. Nick watched as the officer walked to the other side of the bar and struck up a conversation with the woman. Within minutes, the two were smiling and seemed deep in conversation. Nick was pleased to have had the opportunity to talk with Socha. The detective was not happy with the way he had left things with the junior officer when he left the crime scene earlier, and now felt as though he had sufficiently cleared the air. Nick then turned his attention to the rest of his beer and drained the contents as he tackled the decision to stay or go. When his glass was empty he placed it down on the small counter and pushed it away from him. Within seconds, he saw a beer placed back to the side of him, a beautiful woman pushing it over.

"No thanks," Nick protested. "I didn't order another."

The woman stared at the detective for a few seconds, an expectant look on her face as though he were supposed to recognize her. Nick strained for a moment, looking at the woman until he suddenly realized.

"Officer Kelley?" he asked, shocked. He barely recognized Socha's partner in her street clothes. There was nothing flashy about her appearance, something soft and subtle, but Nick could not help but feel immediately attracted to her.

"Please, my name is Jenn," she said with a smile. She had noticed the awestruck look, then the gleam in his eye. "That was a really nice thing you did just then. It should also make him much easier to work with. That alone is worth buying you a beer."

"Isn't it supposed to be the other way around?" Nick asked. "Aren't I supposed to be buying you a drink?"

"I think that's only if we are on a date," Jenn answered, a mischievous smile on her face. "Are we on a date, detective?"

"Not if you're calling me detective," he answered, smiling back at her. "Call me Nick."

"Alright, Nick," she said. "This is going to sound stupid, but I have to say it. The way you worked at the crime scene today was amazing. Especially when you honed right in on the little girl, I don't know how you did it. Even I missed that fact."

"What I did just comes naturally," Nick said, shaking his head. "It's something you will learn to do too. However, the way you handled yourself with the little girl, that's what was really incredible. You took that girl up like you were her mother, and don't think I didn't notice how you instinctively covered her eyes when you took her out of there."

Jenn looked down at the floor, slightly embarrassed.

"Thanks, I..." she started. "She just didn't need to see that. Not again."

Nick nodded silently for a moment. They were both there together, in their minds, back in that cramped trailer with the stench of tobacco clogging their nostrils, the gruesome scene burned into their minds.

"It pisses me off, you know?" Jenn said suddenly.

"I know," Nick responded. "I'd lock up every one of them if I could. They are just as guilty as Todd, every neighbor who knew about the abuse and did nothing."

Jenn looked up at him suddenly, confused.

"No, I meant the victim, Karen Thompson," Jenn said. "There's no excuse for staying with a man like Todd, allowing yourself to be used as a punching bag every night. Especially when you have a child."

Nick watched Jenn for a moment, as the true meaning of her words began to sink in.

"Well, I guess we'll never really understand," Nick said, desperately searching for a way to brighten the mood. "So, do you come here often?"

Jenn looked at the detective quizzically for a moment and then laughed.

"That was the cheesiest thing I've ever heard," she said, her face bright and beautiful with her smile. "I'm sure you can do better than that."

"How long have you been partners with Socha?" Nick asked, feeling as though he needed to come up with something meaningful after his amateurish last question.

"Six months," Jenn answered. "Don't tell me that all we can talk about is work. Ask me something else."

"What do you do outside of work?" Nick asked, at this point feeling utterly stupid. This was the part of being social that Nick felt he was not very good at. He could walk up to and talk to anyone; he was comfortable enough with himself for that. However, here, one on one with a beautiful woman who he found himself attracted to, who he would like to get to know better, this was where he began to stumble.

"I work out a lot," Jenn answered with a smile. "I'm also going to school to get my law degree."

"You want to be a lawyer?" Nick asked, feeling a sudden rush of relief as he realized that he had stumbled onto an entirely new line of questioning.

"Yeah," Jenn answered, smiling. "I want to be a district attorney. You know, prosecute the criminals and send them to jail forever."

"How much longer do you have in school before you get your degree?" Nick asked.

"Just a year," Jenn answered. "Actually a little less, then I'll sit for bar exam. I'm already talking to people in the D.A.'s office, you know, getting my foot in the door and meeting people who can put in a good word for me when the time comes."

"Well," Nick started. "I'm sure you'll have no trouble there."

They continued to talk about her legal aspirations, and even discussed some cases that they had worked on, talking about how they would have done things differently. Though it seemed to Nick as if they had only been talking for a short time, they had continued talking for over an hour. Nick only became aware of the time when Jenn looked down at her watch.

"Oh damn," she said with a start. "It's already ten thirty. I really have to be going."

Suddenly, Nick found himself stammering over his words, worried he had said something wrong. He started searching his memory for anything he might have said. Jenn sensed his concern and put her hand on his arm.

"I've got a class first thing in the morning," she explained with a smile. "Or I'd stay longer. I would like to get together again if you're interested, though. You know, talk about a case or go out or something."

The young woman quickly wrote her number down on a cocktail napkin and pushed it over towards him.

"I mean it, really," she said. "It was amazing working with you today and I really enjoyed talking with you. If you ever need help on a case or something, you know."

She was pushing, maybe a little bit too much, but he found himself reassured by it. He found his concern melt away as he realized that there was a connection and they both felt it. They smiled at each other for just a moment and then she turned and walked away as Nick rose from his place on the stool. He watched her walk out of the bar, then picked up the napkin and looked at the number for a few minutes. Dr. Tanner told him he needed to get out more, he needed to do something that wasn't related to his work. Jenn may not have been a total separation from his work environment, but maybe this was a step in the right direction.

CHAPTER 7

Why can't I just fall asleep? The little girl heard the voice inside her head ask; her voice, her words, and squeezed her eyes shut tight in a vain attempt to make her body fall asleep. She relaxed for a moment, and attempted to push all the ominous thoughts from her mind, forcing herself to think of nothing. She wanted to be asleep as soon as possible. She wanted to fall asleep immediately. If she had any chance of getting through this night unscathed, she would have to be asleep before her uncle got home. She was a smart little girl, a smart girl who had to endure this pattern of fear for too long. Being the smart little girl that she was, she had learned that on weeknights there was a chance that her uncle might leave her alone. She knew that if she was asleep when he came into her room, he usually would not attempt to wake her. On these nights, he would usually just stand in the doorway watching her, as if he were watching her breath; looking for any movement or indication that she was not fully asleep so that he could make his move. She had also learned how to pretend to be asleep, and she was becoming very good at it. Some nights it worked, some nights it didn't. Even now, she was not sure what was worse; when he came in, or when he stood there in the doorway watching. She remembered the first time, the first time he hurt her. However, for some reason, she remembered the first time she pretended to be asleep more vividly. She remembered praying for him to leave, wishing she were deaf so she could not hear his steady hard breathing from the doorway, with the bittersweet smell of drink wafting her way, making her nauseaous. She could remember cautiously sneaking peaks at him, wondering why he was still there, wondering why he would not just go away. She remembered hearing her heart beat, a rhythm that always seemed in time with the slow steady ticks of the second hand of her mother's old alarm clock. Time would go by so slowly, and when he was with her, it seemed to slow even more. She could remember what the sickly neon glow of the clock hands looked like looked like through her tears of her pain and humiliation. On those nights, she would watch the clock, just watching and waiting for it all to end, wishing she were anywhere else but next to him. She remembered screaming for her mother to come and help her, even if her screams were only echoing through the darkness of her mind.

The little girl shook her head back and forth as though she were shaking the terrible memory away. She tried to focus again, tried to empty her mind and think about nothing. She closed her eyes and tried to focus on the blackness again, imagining her mind were a newly erased blackboard. Unfortunately for her, the more she tried to focus on nothing, the less relaxed she was and the more awake she remained. *Tell your mother,* said the voice in her head. She couldn't, she knew she couldn't tell her mother, it would break her heart. The little girl could still remember her father leaving; no, she could remember her mother telling her that her father was leaving. She could remember that he did not come home; that he never explained it to her. One day he came home from work, and the next day he didn't. She could remember her mother crying for days on end. She could remember her mother locking herself in the bathroom for hours at a time, only to come out and go straight to bed without a word or acknowledgment. This was immediately followed by a new type of grief. There were times when everything seemed all right, and then out of nowhere she would begin to cry again. There was no foreseeing what could and would set her off. Just looking at something that brought back a memory of married life would cause a total emotional breakdown for her mother, typically making her useless for the rest of the day. There were the days that she would be making dinner and start crying for no apparent reason. Then there was the day when the little girl's aunt, her mother's sister, came and told her that she could move in. There was the look of hope on her mother's face, and the little girl could remember feeling a sense of adventure as she moved in with her aunt and uncle. She could remember how grateful her mother was, how happy she was when she got the second job. She remembered the promises her mother made, how she would make a better life for the two of them. How could the little girl tell her mother what was happening now, just when she had begun to get her hope back?

Sleep. Sleep! The little girl screamed the words in her head, as if ordering herself into unconsciousness. She heard a car drive down the road and listened carefully, trying to gauge whether it would keep going or if it would slow and pull up the driveway. If it was her mother she would be safe, if only for the night. Her mother would come, crawl into bed with her and they would fall asleep together, her mother stroking her soft golden blond hair. If it was him, she would pretend she was asleep. She would curl up in a ball and concentrate on her breathing so as not to rouse his suspicions. She wondered if he knew she pretended to be asleep those times. Immediately, she knew that he didn't; she knew that he was too far gone. *If he knew*, she thought with a shudder. The little girl knew what would happen if her uncle learned that she was only pretending to be asleep. He would come in every night and wake her, whether she was truly sleeping or not. He would crawl into bed with her too, but not like her mother did. There was nothing loving about him, nothing at all. He was vicious, scary, painful, mean, abusive, strong, overbearing, and overpowering; but there was nothing loving. If he knew that he had been outwitted by an eight year old girl, there would be nothing but pain. The little girl found herself shaking with the thought of him, but she could not stop herself. *Then there was the weekend.*

The little girl hated the weekends. The weekend were the two days of the week every child was supposed to love the most. When everyone else was out playing, staying up late, watching television; she was avoiding the house, going to bed early while her aunt was still awake, and staying away from her uncle. She was sure that her aunt knew nothing about what was going on. She was sick most of the time and would go to bed right after dinner almost every night. The little girl would try to sleep over at her friend's house during the weekends, but that was not possible every weekend. She had one friend in particular, Courtney, who she loved spending time with. Courtney was her best friend and her family was so nice. There was something so completely different about them, something she did not understand, but it was something she loved basking in. They were always smiling, always laughing, always comfortable. The little girl had never had that feeling in any place she could remember; not before her father left, and certainly not now. Courtney's family ate meals together, played games together, watched movies together, went out together. Whenever the little girl could get invited over, it was as though she were just another member of the family. It was like, being warm all over, like being in a blanket. Everybody laughed and joked. They prayed at dinner, but that didn't bother the little girl too much, not enough to keep her from wanting to spend as much time with Courtney and her family as possible. The little girl had prayed; she used to pray all the time. She used to pray that her father would come back; she used to pray that her mom would stop crying. Then she started praying that her uncle would stop touching her, she prayed that he would stop climbing into bed with her, she prayed that he would go away. Her prayers went unanswered, though. Her uncle was still there, still touching her in bad places, still kissing her in ways that were wrong. God was not out there, he was not listening; there was nothing. On the weekends, her uncle would not stand in the doorway. On the weekends, he would come right in and slide under the sheets with her. On the weekends, he hurt her the worst.

Another car drove by and the little girl tensed as she listened. The engine sound stayed the same, the headlights became steadily brighter and then diminished just as quickly. Then the car was gone. The little girl let out a sigh of relief. *Why don't you just hide*, said the voice inside her. The little girl almost laughed out loud at this thought. Where was she going to hide? Where in this house could she go that he would not find her? She couldn't run away, this she knew for sure. *I'm eight years old*, she thought. *I have no money, no way to get around. Nobody is going to hide me, take me in.* There was Courtney, of course. She knew that Courtney's family would take care of her if she ever needed it. Realizing this sparked an entirely new line of thinking for the little girl, a moment of hope. Could she run away to Courtney's house? No, she knew that her mother would come looking for her and that would be the first place her mother would look. Then the little girl would have to explain herself, and that was the very thing she was trying to avoid. Could she tell Courtney's parents what was happening? She knew that they would believe her, but what would happen after that? Would they be able to keep her and her mother, the little girl was pretty sure they could not. Would the little girl be taken away from her mother? No matter what she thought of, the same results came to her. Her mother would find out, and that would ruin everything she had worked so hard for. Then she heard a car again, she listened closely while watching the light in the window. This time the car did slow down, this time the light from the headlights panned around the room as the car made the slow, gentle turn into the driveway. The little girl wasn't even breathing. She sat up on the edge of the bed and waited for the car engine to die and the headlights to go out. Then she ran to the window as softly as possible and peered through the split in the curtain, keeping her hands behind her back so as not make them move in the slightest. Through the window, she could see what she feared the most. Her uncle's car was resting in its usual place in the driveway, the driver's side door swinging open and her uncle climbing out. The little girl raced back to her bed, curled up in a ball and started to pretend she was asleep; and waited.

She heard the front door open; she heard the screen door slam shut. She listened intently for his footsteps, for any noise that might give her some clue as to where he was in the house. She would crack her eyelids occasionally, squinting out into the darkness. She knew that he was not there yet, the bedroom door had not opened, the room had not yet been bathed in the soft light from the hallway. There was no towering shadowy figure standing there, silhouetted by the hallway light, appearing dark and menacing. She heard nothing. The little girl listened closer, straining to hear any sound, but there was none. She wanted to get out of bed and peer out through the crack underneath the door, but she knew better. There was no way that she was going to climb out of bed, not with him in the house. There was a cough, somewhere off in the house, but not close. The little girl's eyes were open now, staring into the darkness as though her focus would help her to hear more clearly. *What is he doing? What is he waiting for?* She had no doubt that he would end up at her door eventually. He usually checked the house to make sure that her aunt wasn't awake and that her mom was not home. Then he would make his way to her door. However, tonight, she could not hear anything. Every minute that passed seemed as though it were an hour. Every heartbeat pounded through her so that she could hear every beat in her head as loud as a drum. Then she heard the dreaded sound, his footsteps like the ominous beat of a drum, coming down the hall.

You're asleep. Be asleep. She closed her eyes and started concentrating on her breathing. She needed to breathe normally and rhythmically, so as not to give any indication that she was actually awake. She curled up on the edge of the bed, but tried not to tense, tried to make it seem natural. She heard her uncle at the door, his hand on the doorknob and she fought to keep control. *Don't tense, keep breathing. You're asleep.* Though her eyes were closed she could still sense the change of color from pure darkness to soft light as the bedroom door swung open. The little girl heard nothing, just waited. *Keep breathing, keep relaxed.* Her uncle was in the doorway, just standing there watching her. This was the worst time for her, the waiting. Will he come in? Will he just give up and go away? She realized that she was hearing something from the doorway, and as she listened closer, she came to know what it was; his breathing. He was breathing hard, while he watched her sleep. The little girl cracked her eyelids and squinted out. She could barely make him out, standing there. He was shaking a little, and for a moment, the little girl wondered if he was afraid to come in. What she wouldn't give to have him be afraid of her, for the roles to be reversed, even for just one night. Then there was a noise, and she jumped. His arm had slammed into the side of the door, his clumsiness causing the door to swing away and slam the wall hard. He noticed the sudden movement on the bed and knew that the little girl was awake.

"My precious little one's awake," her uncle said softly as he entered the room. The little girl had no defense, knew that there was no way to stop what was coming. However, she closed her eyes again and pretended to be asleep. She stiffened though, when his rough hand touched her head. He must have noticed that too, though he said nothing. He stroked her hair for a moment, and then his hands passed down her back and down to her leg where it rested there over her pajamas. She never opened her eyes, not even when he spoke.

"It's time to play our favorite game," he whispered in her ear. The bitter sweet smell that seemed to hover over him was unusually strong this evening, and it made her want to gag. "It's time to play *my* favorite game."

CHAPTER 8

The killer stared up at the beautiful cathedral, thinking about what lay waiting for him inside. This was the night, the beginning of something he had been dreaming about for so long. Now those dreams were about to become a reality. Tonight, he would start the greatest work he had ever done. Tonight, the world would start to see what justice really was. The killer just stared at St. Patrick's cathedral in Norwich, Connecticut; going over the plan in his head. He had been studying this particular event for weeks now; studying plans and layouts of the cathedral, familiarizing himself with the schedules and routines of every person who lived and worked there, and memorized the placement of everything inside the cathedral itself. He knew that his focused study and determination had made it so he could do tonight's work blindfolded. *This is it*, he thought to himself. *This is the moment when everything will change.* This moment was filled with such excitement for the killer, such anticipation that he was almost afraid it would get the best of him and that he would make some tiny mistake. The killer pushed that thought out of his mind. He knew that he had studied this one event too long and hard to make a mistake now. There would be no miscalculations; this would be the most shocking event in this state for a long time. What would make it even more shocking is the full understanding of what had been done. It would take some time, people would not understand at first. The killer would have to have patience, but the public would understand in the end. That was all that mattered to the killer; that the people understood that he was on their side. That he was doing this for them.

The killer clung to the shadows of the large, historic house that sat across the street from the cathedral. His legs were twitching in anticipation, but he hardly noticed. He pushed his left sleeve up just a little and covered his right hand over his watch while pressing the glow button at the same time. He read the time, 9:58p.m., still two minutes to go. In his mind, the killer could see where everyone was on the grounds. He could see where the nuns were, most of them in bed or on their way. He could see where the few priests who lived one the premises were, and most importantly of all, he could see where his prey was. His prey was making his way back into the cathedral for one last moment with God, one last moment of thanks for his deliverance from harm. The killer could feel his anger and rage boiling up inside of him as he thought about it. His prey did not deserve the blessings that were given to him, and the killer knew that those blessings were definitely not given to him by God. They were given to his prey by scared old men who were afraid of the truth. The killer was not afraid of the truth, instead was driven by it. He checked his watch again, 9:59p.m., only fifty seconds before his work began.

The killer detached himself from the side of the old home and walked quickly across the street, separating himself from and merging with other shadows along the way. He was dressed in black from head to toe, and was not concerned with being seen. Even if he were seen, it would be impossible for anyone to recognize him. A black hood covered his head and hair, and black face paint concealed his features. Forty five seconds and his switch device would activate and cut the power to the cathedral from the main line. Forty seconds and the killer would make his move. He ascended the steps of the cathedral, taking them one at a time but moving quickly nonetheless. Thirty five seconds and he inserted a pick into the lock of the enormous wooden doors of the cathedral. He twisted the pick a little and inserted a pin. In a flash, he heard the click of the lock and felt the heavy latch give a little under the pressure of his fingers. Thirty seconds and he was in the small lobby, making his way between the huge wooden doors and the locked glass doors that gave access to the cathedral itself. Twenty five seconds and he jammed the pick into the second set of locks, leaving the glass doors unlocked. Twenty seconds and the killer was inside the cathedral. He made his way deeper inside, slipping behind the columns to keep from being seen. Fifteen seconds and his eyes locked in on his prey. This was going to happen just as he had planned. In fact, for a moment, the killer could not be certain if this was real or just his mind running loose with his fantasies again. This is just what he had imagined, the anticipation, the flood of adrenaline and pleasure, the certainty of his mission. Ten seconds, his prey was on the move. Nine seconds, the killer was closing the distance. Eight seconds, he was moving in the shadows, far enough away that his prey could not see him. Seven seconds, his prey stops and takes a long look at the pews and the altar. Six seconds, the killer is practically blind now, his anger and hate having reached critical levels. Five seconds, the killer now detaches himself from the shadows and starts running towards his prey. Four seconds, and his prey is still unaware of what is going to happen. Three seconds, the killer takes a deep breath and jumps onto one of the pews, giving him enough speed and leverage to launch himself into the air. Two seconds, everything is right on plan, nothing can stop what is about to happen. One second, his prey looks back, suddenly aware that something is happening. Then the killers watch chimes an electronic beep. The lights go out suddenly, but the killer is not concerned. He knows where he is, he knows everything.

CHAPTER 9

Father Michael Allun made his way out of the dark, narrow hallways into the main gallery of St. Patrick's Cathedral; just as enraptured by the opulence and magnificence as he had the day he was first assigned here by the church six months ago. There was a feeling of history here, deep history. He, of course, knew the history of St. Patrick's just as well as every other clergy member did; but there was something else, something inspiring. It was more than the scene of the crucifixion that lay at the front of the gallery; it was more than the heavy thick pews that sat in perfect alignment on either side of the enormous space. It was not the richly elaborate adornments that were scattered throughout the space; it was something deeper, something that existed in the very foundations. When Father Allun first stepped foot in the cathedral, he felt it immediately and knew that this was where he was meant to be. He understood the irony of his feelings, this assignment at a strange new parish in a new state; he should have felt more alone than ever before. However, there was something that called out to him, not the voice of God, but something inside of him, instinctively telling him that he was home. It was not Boston, where his career began, but then again, Boston was no longer home; St. Patrick's was.

As he made his way forward, Father Allun raised his hands and touched the side of every pew as he passed. There were no sounds emanating from anywhere in the gallery, even his own footsteps were quiet as he moved forward. It had become a nightly ritual for the young priest, making a last walk through the cathedral, making one last communion with God before the night was over. It was only at times like this that the young man of twenty six felt closest with God, only when it was quiet, when there was no one else around, when it was just the two of them. That was when he could speak to God, and when God would speak to him. That was when he could confide in the only being that would ever truly understand him. This place, here in front of the altar was the only place where Father Allun could share his emotions; his pain, his pride, his love. This is the only place where he could share all of those things that the Catholic Church told him were sins. Every man shared the same emotions that Allun had, even the other priests. However, unlike the priests, Allun did not feel as though sharing these emotions was something to be ashamed of. This was who he was; this was who God had made him. It was that thought, that moment of sheer clarity that helped the young man to understand himself and his purpose. It was that moment that made him a better man than those around him, and a better priest.

Father Allun reached the front of the cathedral and stood directly under the altar, staring up at the image of Christ on the cross. Standing there, staring up at the image that was as much a part of him as his own limbs, Allun imagined the emotions that went through the masses when they came and stood where he was standing. So often, it was the sensation of love, of understanding, of compassion, of guilt, of fear. All of the emotions that years of catholic school had instilled in so many people. *We are sinners, we are not perfect nor can we ever be. Everything we do will be wrong in some way or another, but you must continue to strive to be perfect, though you will never be. And above all, you must confess.* Confession, thought Allun with a sigh. This was his confession; this is where he could be totally honest and faithful with God. He found it so ridiculous, sitting in a wooden box, where men, women, and children came to confess their sins, whether perceived or real. This place where one could be totally anonymous and tell a person who would not judge you that you had sinned. Father Allun could see what the purpose of it had been, and how it served the masses and the church. Now he saw it as nothing more than an outdated ritual that had little to no meaning. It was now a place where the "faithful" told their little sins and hid their real ones. He heard the lustful thoughts, the minor law breaking, the lies, and the anger; told the offenders to say the appropriate number of prayers and sent them on their way. However, he knew that there was more, there always was. The parishioners never talked about the hurtful lies, the abuse, the stealing, the embezzling, and the extramarital affairs. All of these things were never mentioned, though many times widely known about. Confession had become useless, something that was forced on children and guilty wives. There was no truth to it whatsoever, but then again, it fit right in with the church that he had come to understand; there was no truth in anything. Father Allun purged these thoughts from his mind and stood there transfixed on the scene before him, allowing himself to be alone with God. It was then, standing before the altar, that he did the thing that he did every night, the thing that would have him excommunicated from the church were anyone to see him. Father Allun lifted his arms and crossed one leg over the other, and standing there, imitated the crucifixion.

Standing there, he imagined himself as Christ. It was only at times like these that he felt secure enough to do this. Only when he knew that he was alone, when all the other members of the clergy had gone to bed long before could he experience his true religion. It was so infuriating to know that he was only able to feel complete when he was alone here. If seen, the other priests would have assumed he was making a mockery of Christ and the crucifixion. He would have been deemed crazy or worse, though he could not imagine what his colleagues would have considered to be worse. They would have demanded that Allun explain himself, though they themselves could never truly understand. They did not experience God the way that he did, and they never would. The other priests were nothing more than sycophants, their only true love being the power they yielded. They only cared about money, stature, politics, and of course Rome. However, Father Allun felt nothing for these things, and felt nothing for these other priests but pity. He was so far above them, that if caught, explaining himself would have been a waste of time. They had no comprehension of the energy and power that emanated from this place. They had never sought out anything remotely existential in years. Perhaps as they grew older they forgot about the truth and could only see what existed here, on the worldly plain. Father Allun hoped that was not the case, he could think of no worse prison for his mind than ending up like them.

I am like You, he thought to himself and he stared up at Christ. If his thoughts could be heard he would be guilty of blasphemy. He did not, however, mean his thoughts to be at all disrespectful. He could understand just how much Christ had given of himself. He understood what being nailed to the cross truly meant. Christ had given himself for humanity; given himself in a way that no one else had ever been able to do before or since. Allun tried, desperately tried to give of himself. He tried to do good work, tried to bring people to the church; however, his efforts of the last few years had become less and less motivated by the church. He found it more and more difficult to give himself over to the Church when it was the Church that would never understand him, never accept him. They would never appreciate him for who he truly was, and they would never comprehend his thinking. And so the young priest had contented himself with just helping those around him, any way that he could. However, standing here, basking in the warm energy that flowed from the altar, certainty filled his mind and heart and he knew that he was not wrong. Father Allun was loved by God, and he was accepted. Finally, the dull ache in his arms became a searing pain the longer he kept them outstretched. He stood there imitating the altar until he could no longer take the pain. This was his penance; this was what he had to do to know that he was accepted and loved, and that he was not like them.

Father Allun let his arms fall back to his side and turned, making his way back to the offices in the rear of the building. He was finished for tonight; tomorrow was another day and he would begin the process again. However, tonight he had let all of his emotional and physical pain go; he was free for the moment. As he walked slowly back down the aisle, passing the pews, the lights went out suddenly. Father Allun stopped in mid stride and was certain that just before the lights had gone out he had seen something behind him, just over his right shoulder. He turned quickly, seeing nothing though until he was struck on the back of the head with something hard, then little flashing white lights erupted in front of him and he felt a wave of light nausea wash over him as his muscles seemed to go flaccid and gravity took the young priest down to the ground.

CHAPTER 10

Father Michael Allun awoke in the darkness lying face down on a cold tile floor. He blinked several times, trying in a vain attempt to clear his vision, only realizing finally that there was nothing to see. He tried to move but his arms were secured behind him. Moving his fingers around, he could barely feel the metal shackles that bound his arms behind his back. He strained several times, only to find his predicament unbreakable. His arms were sore and he had an incredible headache. In the distance, he heard the soft trickle of running water. The sound was annoying and only added to his fear as he attempted to guess where he was. He knew for a fact that he was not on the grounds of St. Patrick's Cathedral. He would have known if a place like this existed, he would have found it long before now. Allun felt as though he were going to roll over as he realized that the tiled floor sloped down at a soft angle. He screamed out into the darkness repeatedly begging for help, only to hear the echo of his own voice in return. Using his legs to turn himself over, Allun managed to get himself up into a seated position and inched his way backwards, trying to gauge the dimensions of the room he was being held in. He was too weak to keep this up for very long, and quickly gave up trying to find a wall. Instead, he turned his thoughts inward and attempted to remember what had happened to him last.

He had been in the cathedral. That was the first thought that came to him, the first thing he remembered. He had been in the cathedral communing with God. He started to remember what he had been thinking about; the hypocrisy and the ridiculous concerns of the people around him. He had been thinking about himself, he had been thinking about the similarities between himself and Christ. He then attempted to remember what had happened after returning from the altar. He was finished for the evening, he was about to make his way back to his quarters. He remembered retracing his steps as he made his way through the gallery. Then the lights had gone out, the cathedral had lost power. He remembered that just as the power had died, something had caught his attention from the corner of his eye. There had been something coming at him, just over his left shoulder. That was when he had felt the searing pain in his head, which was the last thing he had remembered until he woke up here. *What am I doing here? What is going on?* At this point, he was not sure if he was asking these questions aloud or not.

Time seemed to pass very slowly. With only his inner thoughts to keep him company, his emotional fortitude was starting to wear down. He had called out to God for answers many times, both aloud and in his mind. There had been no answer though, so far there had been nothing. The constant trickle of water in the background was becoming incessant. The sound echoed off every wall, making it all the more annoying. He could not get the sound out of his head, he could not think clearly. Time was beginning to fade into nothing as he lay there, searching for answers.

Allun thought he might have drifted off into sleep a few times, but was not sure. Soon, his entire body started to hurt and all he could feel was an aching pain in every muscle. The tile floor was cold and uncomfortable, and the cold was beginning to seep into his skin. Out of nowhere, he heard a light tapping that as it continued, became louder and louder. It took a few seconds, but he soon recognized the sound as footsteps, and screamed out for help, re-energized by the hope of rescue. It did not occur to him that the person coming might be his attacker; he was just desperate for help. Suddenly, he felt something grab him, first by his shirt pulling him up to his knees, then by his hair dragging him forward. He screamed in pain as he was forced to push himself forward on his knees. Allun's assailant tossed him down to the floor again roughly and walked away. The priest continued shouting, asking all sorts of questions of the man. No answers were forthcoming, no sounds other than the footsteps and the running water. Allun tried to lift himself to his knees, but slipped and fell back down against the tile, slamming his head down hard. The pain that had eased to a constant ache was now sharp again.

Suddenly, there was the sound of twisting metal, as if a valve were being turned on. The shriek of metal seemed to fill the cavernous space, causing Allun to wince in pain. Then water began to sprinkle down hard from above; first cold, then warm, then comfortable. Allun lay there under the spray of water, the warmth filling him, re-energizing him for a few moments. As he lay there, the water went from comfortably warm, to hot, to unbearable. His skin was starting to burn under the extremely hot temperatures and soon he was shouting again, begging his assailant to turn the water off. Allun twisted and jerked, trying unsuccessfully to inch his feeble body away from the burning torrent of water. It was no use though, the rain of water was everywhere, and Allun was bound too securely to move more than a few inches. Then, without warning, the water temperature went from searing heat to frigid cold. Immediately, the severe temperature change irritated his already sensitive skin and all Allun could do was curl up into the fetal position and wait for the water to stop. While the water continued to soak him, the cold temperature lowered his body heat. Then, just as it started, the water ceased and the young priest was left shivering violently on the cold tile floor. He did not attempt to speak, and the man in the shadows did not make any noise. The only sound to be heard was the continuous trickle of water. After a while, between slipping in and out of consciousness, Father Allun cried. He did not care now if anyone could hear him; all he knew was that mentally and emotionally, he was totally alone.

Allun awoke with a start, thinking he heard something off in the distance, his hypersensitive mind taking over. He listened for what would seem like an eternity, and then drifted off again, no matter how hard he tried to fight it. His clothes were still soaked from the cold shower and he was beginning to feel sick. He had no idea now what time or day it was. He had no idea how long he had been there. There were no windows, no sign of light at all. Though his eyes had become accustomed to the darkness, he still could not see anything. He would roll face down against the ground and still could not see the tile floor. After a while he began to smell something. It was something he could not place at first, but the more he took the delightful scent into his nostrils, the more certain of it he became. It was food, more specifically, it was grilled meat. His belly roared like a lion and suddenly all he could think of was getting something in his stomach. The last time he had eaten anything was at dinner, hours before he made his final walk through the cathedral, and at this point he had no idea how long it had been since his last meal. He was dehydrated, becoming malnourished, tired and cold Allun knew that if he were to survive this, he would need to eat something soon. As if sensing his thoughts, the footsteps came again and then there was the sound of something metal hitting the floor directly to his right.

"Eat!" demanded a strange voice to his left. The voice was digital, as if processed through a computer. At this point Allun did not care about the voice, did not even think about his imprisoner. He lied down on the floor, inching along on his belly like a worm until he came upon the plate. He put his face directly into the food and bit off a large chunk of what he could only assume was meat. It was tough and cold and there was a strange taste to it. As Allun tried to force it down his throat, his body rejected it from the taste and he spit the food up and onto the floor. Allun coughed repeatedly as the taste began to permeate his mouth and breath. Allun bent down again over what he assumed was the plate and inhaled deeply. He gagged and pulled himself away immediately, attempting to keep himself from retching. Whatever the food was or had been, it had long since gone bad and was rancid. Allun rolled over completely and vomited hard, causing his body to fill with pain as his muscles violently contracted trying to force the food and smell from his body. Once finished, Allun used all of the energy he could muster to push himself away from the stench of the food and his own vomit and sought out the sound of the trickling water. At this point, it did not matter to Allun whether the water was clean or rancid; he had to get something in his mouth. He found a slope on the tiled floor that seemed to be the lowest point and felt around with his nose until he found what he was sure to be a drain and slurped up the small amounts of water from the floor. He could not suck up nearly enough of the water and was left expending more energy.

"Why?" he screamed out into the darkness, and then passed out again from his pain and exhaustion.

When Father Michael Allun awoke, he was no longer lying on the cold, tiled floor wearing soaked clothes stained with his vomit; he was tied naked to a wooden chair. Allun jerked violently, trying in vain to loose himself from his restraints. There were cords of rope that bound his arms, legs, torso, and neck to the strange chair. The more he jerked, the more the pressure increased on the rope that went around his neck. Allun sat there, his eyes going back and forth wildly looking for anything in the darkness. However, like before, there was nothing to see. There was something strange about the chair that he was bound to. He could feel some kind of break or opening underneath his buttocks, and suddenly he was filled with terror. Something within him knew that this chair was used for torture, though he could not imagine what kind.

"Where is your God?" asked the digital voice from some dark corner.

"God is everywhere!" exclaimed Allun. "What do you want from me?"

"I want you to repent," answered the voice, this time from far behind the chair. Allun jerked back, turning his head to see if he could see anyone behind him.

"I have nothing to repent for," the young priest answered. "And if I did, I repent directly to God, not to some crazed lunatic. Not to you!"

"You have much to answer for," the voice said, this time from a totally different area of the darkness. Allun was now totally disoriented. His terror was feeding his paranoia. "Over the course of our time together, you will confess and repent for all of them."

"What is this?" Allun demanded. "Who are you?"

"This is an inquisition," answered the digital voice. There was a pause for a moment, and then Allun felt something warm and moist against his face. It was the breath of his attacker. Allun tried to jerk his head away, but was kept in place by the rope around his neck. "And I am your judge."

With that, Allun's terror was complete. He knew in that instant the rest of his life would be filled with pain, and more importantly, he knew that his life would not end soon enough. Suddenly, there was a slow, rhythmic vibration from beneath him as the sound of metal grinding against metal pierced his ears. Then, Allun felt a searing pain from against his skin and the sound of the grinding metal was replaced with his own endless screams.

CHAPTER 11

On Saturday Nick went back to work, but he did not immediately return to the Investigations Unit in New London, instead he drove up to Hartford. Before becoming a homicide detective, Nick had worked undercover for the Narcotics and Vice squad in Hartford. His undercover career was abruptly ended when a major drug sting exposed him as a police officer. Being forced out of his undercover life so quickly had been very hard on the detective, and had brought him to the brink of quitting the police force. Nick hated to admit it, but had it not been for The Nemesis case, he might not even be on the force anymore. Even after his first homicide investigation Nick continued to feel conflicted but decided to keep up with his contacts in the drug world. This had been a major part of his life that he had dedicated more than three years to. He had created a separate life, one that was not so easy for him to give up. Hollings knew about his contacts and about his Saturday outings, and though she was concerned about the impropriety of a homicide detective spending off duty hours with criminals, it had proven beneficial on more than one occasion. The information that had been passed from Nick's old contacts had helped Narcotics Units all over the state make large busts of big time dealers and raids on drug labs. All in all, these little tidbits of information had helped local law enforcement in many cities to lower the number of drug related crimes and fatalities over the last year. When Nick had first started going back to Hartford, most of his contacts would not speak with him. Some were shocked by the fact that this man they had known for three years had been a police officer all along; while others simply felt that they could never trust him again. In the long run, almost all of them realized that it was good to have someone on the inside, a friend in high places and they came around.

Nick spent most of the day in Hartford, showing his face around, picking up little tips here and there; but mostly warning his contacts to keep their peddling to small time. Nick made it clear that he could help the dealers if they got caught only if they weren't doing any hardcore dealing, like doping teenagers or putting huge amounts of drugs on the street. Selling a dime bag on the corner was one thing; supplying ecstasy to teenagers at a party was something else entirely. Nick could not and would not stick his neck out for that, and he made sure everyone knew it. He was not a wide eyed optimist; Nick never believed that he could stop the drug trade entirely. The detective knew the world too well to believe that anyone could do that. So long as there were junkies out on the street, so long as there was always a demand for that high that made you feel on top of the world, or totally removed from the abysmal life that one was left with; there would always be the dealers. So long as there were dealers, there would be drug labs. *Ying and Yang*, Nick thought to himself. He knew that you couldn't have one without the other. The detective was never certain where he stood on the legality of some drugs. He always felt that it was a waste of time and resources to chase marijuana dealers and users around town when backroom chemists were devising new, cheaper, and ultimately deadlier forms of crystal meth and ecstasy. However, Nick knew that any type of drugs bred violence, and he had dedicated himself to his job and done it well for many years.

Nick hooked up with everyone he could find. He had learned a long time ago that you don't get anything for nothing, and knew that if he was going to get any useful information, he was going to have to give something up on his end. Nick dropped hints about where local busts might be made, alluding to the fact that it would be best if his informant wasn't around at the place or time. This was a common procedure, common enough so as not to piss off the local law enforcement when they conducted a raid. Everyone was supposed to be working on the same side, and so long as Nick passed on all of the information he was given, no one had anything to complain about. After he had gone through his list of contacts, Nick drove home with his hands-free device firmly planted in his ear, relaying all of the information he was given to his friends in Narcotics Units across the state. There was always a territorial issue with law enforcement, and though everyone was after the same goal, each department wanted to look better than the next. As with everything else, the criminal world had gone high tech. Cell phones and the internet kept the criminal underworld connected and the police had to be just as connected to make any headway in this war. Nick didn't want any gripes with any departments, didn't want to hear anyone complain about being out of the loop, and so gave up his information to everyone. Nick had no problem with it, narcotics wasn't his world anymore, homicide was.

There had been one prevailing thought on his mind the entire day; Jenn. He had the napkin in his pocket; all day trying to decide when the best time to call her might be, or even if he should call her at all. If he called her now, he would run the risk of sounding desperate. If he didn't call her all weekend, he ran the risk of appearing uninterested and ruining any chances he had of asking her out. It was ridiculous, and he knew it. He could understand the most heinous killers, but could not put himself in the mind of a woman. After coming up with no clear solution, Nick decided to put these worries on the back burner and continued on back towards New London, stopping by Hollings' home to check in on the child Michelle. The little girl was getting along well, especially now that she had so much attention. Hollings and her husband doted on her for the short time she would be there, and Michelle had found new playmates in the lieutenant's children. All in all, Michelle seemed very happy considering what she had gone through. Nick couldn't help but wonder whether or not the little girl could remember the last time she had been this happy. After about an hour Nick left the Hollings household, though being he had been asked repeatedly to stay for dinner. Hollings was worried about the amount of time Nick spent alone, as was obvious by her demand that he see a therapist. However, Nick pleaded other business and left, stopping by a few electronics stores on the way home, buying new gadgets that he didn't need but felt as though he must have. After spending three hundred dollars, he left and finally arrived home as the sun was setting. He ate a quick dinner and then made the call that he had been deliberating over all day.

"Hello," said a woman's voice. Nick wasn't immediately certain whether it was Jenn or not.

"Hi, is Jenn there?" he asked, listening carefully.

"Who's calling?" asked the woman.

"Uh, it's Nick, Nick Grenier," he responded, kicking himself for sounding so unsure.

"I don't know if I know a Nick Nick Grenier," answered Jenn playfully. Nick couldn't help but sigh under his breath. "I know a Nick, and a Detective Grenier, but I don't know... Oh God, don't tell me your parents gave you the same first and middle name did they?"

"Give me a break," Nick started. "Are you always this hard on men who call you?"

"I don't get a lot of calls from interesting men," Jenn answered. "So I have to make it memorable."

"I can't imagine why," Nick responded.

"Men are intimidated by my beauty," she said.

"I'm sure they are," Nick answered in a noncommittal way. He was still worried about sounding desperate. "Well, in a way of not appearing intimidated, I was wondering if you would like to go out and do something tomorrow."

"I'd love to," Jenn answered. "I'm teaching a class at ten, but I'll be free anytime after that."

"You go to school and teach?" Nick asked, remembering their conversation the previous evening.

"I teach a self defense class for women," Jenn explained. "It's in Mystic; you should come down and see it sometime. I think you would be impressed."

"Maybe I'll check it out tomorrow," Nick said, trying to remain casual.

"Maybe we can go out after," Jenn responded, mocking his cool attitude. She gave Nick the directions and after making a little more small talk, they hung up. Nick was satisfied with their first telephone call and spent the rest of the night playing with his new electronic toys and watching television. He went to bed around two in the morning, reminding himself that Jenn's class started at ten. He would show up fifteen minutes late so as not to appear over eager. Nick felt as though he had just gotten to sleep when the telephone woke him. Nick looked up at the clock next to his bed which read 7:12 a.m. He picked up the phone next to the clock.

"There better be a really good reason for some someone to call me at seven o'clock on a Sunday morning," he said into the receiver.

"It's Hollings," his lieutenant answered. "And I always have a good reason."

"Your husband is going to start wondering if we're having an affair if you keep calling me at these strange hours," Nick said sarcastically.

"Yeah, I'm sure he's losing sleep over it," Hollings answered. Nick was certain that she was looking over at her husband in bed, who was most likely snoring away in a deep and restful sleep. "There's been a murder in Norwich and I've offered to send you up there to give them your opinion."

"Remind me," Nick said, sitting up in his bed. "How is a murder in another city our problem?"

"The Norwich chief of police called me and asked for a favor," Hollings answered. "They wanted our best detective to give them an opinion on a murder that was called in an hour ago. Since you are my best detective, and because I love being owed favors, I told them that you would be up there immediately. That's how it has become your problem."

"Lovely," Nick said, swinging his legs over the side of the bed. "Let me get a shower and get some coffee and I'll be on my way."

"Skip the shower and the coffee," Hollings said in a manner that sounded more like an order. Immediately, Nick's interest was piqued. "Get up there now. You'll understand why when you get there."

"All right," Nick conceded. "Should I get dressed, or should I go with what I'm wearing now?"

"This conversation is heading somewhere that I don't want to go," Hollings said. "I'm going back to sleep and the last thing I need is an image of you in your Dragnet pajamas that are two sizes too small. It's Sunday, it's my day to sleep in."

"Rub it in," Nick muttered. "Let the Norwich chief know that I'll be there in thirty minutes. What is the address?"

Hollings relayed the address.

"The lead detective is a guy named Kevin Smith, hook up with him and give him your impressions, you know what I mean," Hollings said. "And Nick, this one's a bad one."

CHAPTER 12

Without being given the time to shower, Nick threw on some jeans and a tee shirt and a Boston Red Sox ball cap on his head and headed up to Norwich. He knew the street that Hollings had provided, but did not know the particular building. He arrived approximately twenty minutes after leaving his home, and followed the directions precisely, as he assumed there were most likely police roadblocks already established. As he had expected, two blocks away from the crime scene he no longer needed the directions as the police cruisers and television vans that lined the street were more than enough indicator for him. Nick sighed as he counted the number of news vans parked on the curb of the street and was thankful that this was not his case. He hadn't seen so much press interest since The Nemesis case. He knew that this was not going to be good. *Just give them your honest opinion*, Nick told himself. *Then get the fuck out of there.* Nick drove down the street, which had become one lane due to the congestion on either side. He was stopped at a police roadblock and a young uniformed officer stepped up to the driver's side of his vehicle and tapped on the window. Nick lowered his window and flashed his badge.

"Detective Grenier," Nick informed the young man. "I've been called in by the lead detective, a Kevin Smith."

"You've been cleared, detective," the officer said. "Go through and park your car over by those squad cars, then you're going to have to walk up to the scene."

"Where's the scene?" Nick asked, still unclear as to what building the address belonged to. The officer looked at him strangely for a few seconds.

"The cathedral," the officer answered.

"Are you shitting me?" Nick asked in disbelief. "That's like a block and a half away. Are you telling me that everyone has to walk that far?"

Nick was thinking of the crime scene unit, walking in the morning humidity, lugging their cases full of chemicals and tools all the way to the cathedral. However, the young officer took Nick's comments as attitude and fired back.

"What the hell do you want from me," the officer began, extremely annoyed. "A golf cart to ferry you back and forth?"

"Excuse me?" Nick asked, shocked by the officer's response. The officer looked down for a moment, as if recollecting himself, and then back up at the detective.

"I'm sorry, detective," the officer said. "The press has been trying my last nerve. We've moved the roadblock this far out so that they wouldn't know where the crime scene was yet, but it's not exactly working."

"Don't let them bother you," Nick said, understanding the officer's frustration. "In fact, don't even talk to them, don't say anything. And if any of them try to get passed you, arrest them. If they give you any shit, tell them your following orders."

"Whose orders?" the officer asked, amused as he considered the detectives advice.

"It doesn't matter," Nick answered. "Everyone out here is higher than you; it will take them forever to figure it out. By the way, how will I know which one is Detective Smith?"

"He's hard to miss," the officer answered. "He's the big ass Indian dude."

"Indian?" Nick asked

"You know," the officer said. "He's a Mohegan."

"I believe we are supposed to refer to them as Native Americans," Nick said, becoming annoyed. The officer's bad attitude was rubbing off.

Without waiting for a response the detective rolled up his window and drove on. Suddenly, Nick felt very tired. The lack of sleep from the previous night, combined with the thought of viewing what he had been informed was a gruesome crime scene was beginning to weigh on him. He didn't want to be a part of this; he didn't want to touch a murder that was not in his jurisdiction. No matter how limited his involvement, he knew that the moment the media saw him, they were going to look to him for answers. That was a position he simply did not want to be in. Nick parked his car and made the walk down the street, toward the cathedral. Only then did it begin to sink in the reason for the mass media blitz. There had been a murder, a gruesome murder, in the cathedral. This was definitely a case that he didn't want. Nick walked along the sidewalk, approaching the cathedral, looking for anyone who fit the description of Kevin Smith. The foot traffic in and out of the cathedral was intense. Both plainclothes and uniformed officers were walking in and out, pulling on and off paper booties. Nick saw a car door open and a large man climbed out, and Nick knew immediately that this man was Kevin Smith. The detective was well over six feet tall and from what Nick could tell, a solid block of muscle. His head was shaved down to a small growth of stubble over his scalp.

"Detective Grenier," the tall man called out.

"Detective Smith," Nick said, offering his hand.

"Call me Kevin," he said, extending first a tall cardboard cup of coffee, then his right hand. "I thought you could use this. I really appreciate you coming up, detective."

"My name's Nick," Grenier answered, taking the coffee. "And I'm glad to help. What have you got here?"

"Altar boy came through this morning, preparing for mass," Smith began, walking up the steps of the cathedral to the large wooden outer doors. "He was replacing candles, replacing bibles, whatever it is they do on a Sunday morning. That was when he found our victim. He blew chunks all over the place and ran out screaming. A nun found him and after spending five minutes trying to get a coherent story out of him, she called 911. No one entered or exited until the first squad car arrived on the scene. It was patrolling this neighborhood and was the first to respond."

Nick processed all of the information as he stopped at the top of the steps and took a pair of paper booties to cover his feet.

"Have you questioned the responding officer?" Nick asked.

"Yes," Smith answered. "His reaction to the scene was the same as the altar boys. He was pretty messed up; he goes to church here. After getting his statement I sent him to set up the barricades and roadblocks."

Nick nodded to himself, immediately understanding the attitude of the young man he encountered at the roadblock. He had been the officer who had been the first to respond to the scene, and he was most likely still embarrassed and annoyed by his reaction.

"Who's the victim?" Nick asked.

"His name is Father Michael Allun," Smith answered. "He is the local hero priest. He's been here for about six months and he's already done more for the church and the community than all the other priests combined."

"Yeah," Nick said. "I've seen him on television. I've heard about the good work he's done. He has pretty much been the face of community service in this area."

"Yeah, well, someone didn't think so," Smith said as he too, wrapped the shoe coverings over his feet. "I've got to warn you, this is bad, really bad."

The two detectives passed through the great wooden door and into a small lobby that separated the wooden outer doors from the inner glass doors. They then passed through the glass doors into the main gallery. There, in the middle of the aisle separating the pews on the right and left, hung the deceased Father Michael Allun, upside down, tied to a very crude wooden cross. Immediately, Nick's heart sank. The cross and body twisted ever so slightly, never more than four or five degrees in either direction, but more than enough to get a full idea of the amount of torture the victim had endured. Nick could do nothing but shake his head in disbelief. He had never in his life seen something so bad.

"I didn't have them cut him down," Smith said. "I wanted you to see him just as he was left."

Nick said nothing; he couldn't take his eyes off of the image in front of him. Allun was covered in blood, his face his body, arms and legs. He was naked, his arms bound to the arms of the cross, his right foot over his left and also bound at the bottom of the wooden beam; all bound by thick rope. Nick couldn't see what had killed him, could not distinguish any types of wounds through the blood drenched skin. There was blood all over the floor, so much so that it did not dry, just formed a large pool underneath the suspended body. The scene was becoming far too much for Nick, and he knew that he had to click over to police mode. He hadn't gotten that feeling yet, the feeling that started to cause a mental image of the crime in his mind's eye. His senses were overwhelmed and he had to step back, mentally. So, allowing himself to separate a little from the crime, Nick looked at the body through a more scientific method.

Nick started with the cross. It was heavy duty wood that seemed to have been burnt through. The more he stared at it, the more Nick knew that if it had been burned it would have lost any structural integrity. The wood must have been burnt merely on the surface with something like a blowtorch. This was when the detective started making mental notes. The wood was made to look burnt. The body was covered in blood, obviously the killer had no problem torturing the victim; however, the killer didn't nail his hands or feet to the cross. The killer didn't crucify Allun. There was something in that thought, something that should have told him about the killer but he just couldn't figure out what it was. Nick finished with his cursory visual examination of the body and turned his attention to the binding of the victim. Nick could now see how the rope which fastened the body to the cross was all one length, binding the arms, the legs and the entire body to the wooden cross. Following the rope as it snaked around the legs, Nick realized that it was secured to the cross around notches in the wood, and then followed it up to the ceiling. It was only then that he was able to understand the severity of the image. The rope vanished into the high rafters of the cathedral gallery.

"My God," Nick exclaimed.

"God had nothing to do with this, detective," Smith said softly. He had experienced the same sickening awe and wonder by the scene, and knew immediately that it was not something that could be verbally shared. It had to be visually witnessed. "A monster did this."

"How high is it?" Nick asked, ignoring the detective's remark. There were no monsters in the world; Nick knew this for a fact. This was a criminal, a man; nothing more. However, this particular criminal had a deep anger for the victim, the church, or both.

"Nearly forty feet," Smith answered. "One of the crime scene guys had a laser that measures distance, it was thirty nine something."

"How the..." Nick stammered as he quickly reminded himself that he was in a church. "How did he get up there?"

"I have no idea," Smith said. "But I pity the tech that has to go up there and dust for prints. So, what do you think?"

"I think you should have your boys cut him down," Nick said, turning to face Smith. "And we should talk outside."

CHAPTER 13

Detectives Grenier and Smith stepped out into the warm morning air, discarding their shoe coverings and tossing them into a special bag placed outside the door by the CSU. Nick spent a few moments processing what he had seen. He knew that Smith was standing there, waiting for Nick to give him some insight on the murder, and suddenly the detective felt under an enormous pressure to give the right answers. He tried to concentrate on what he had seen, allowing himself to remember his first impressions. It was difficult for him at first; having to push away the expectant look on Smith's face and focus on what he was there to do. The crime scene was just what everyone had warned him it would be, bad. However, it was extremely difficult to give anything but a theory when there was so much that he didn't know. He knew nothing about the type of death Father Allun had suffered, or how long he had been tortured. *How long had he been tortured?* That question stuck in Nick's mind, and suddenly he realized that there were questions he could ask that would help him understand the crime even before the autopsy report was available.

"What are you thinking about?" Smith asked, sensing a sudden change in Nick's demeanor.

"That kind of damage had to have been inflicted over a long period of time," Nick stated. "Do we know what Father Allun has been up to for the last couple of days?"

"It's funny you should ask," Smith started. "We've been unofficially looking for Father Allun for about fifteen hours now. He was supposed to be present for a fund-raising event yesterday morning, and then he was expected for a big meeting with the diocese yesterday afternoon. He was not present for either event."

"When were the police notified of Allun's disappearance?" Nick asked.

"Concerns were floating around since his absence from the fund-raising event," Smith answered. "As you know, Allun is a high profile figure around here and he has never missed an event in which he has previously promised to attend. When he missed the meeting with the diocese, the chief of police was alerted *unofficially*, and an investigation was initiated; *unofficially*."

"An investigation was initiated," repeated Nick. "So I take it some questions were asked around here. When was the last time Father Allun was seen?"

"He was seen by a nun around 9:45 Friday night," Smith answered. "The nun was heading towards the rectory, and Allun was making his way into the cathedral, they exchanged pleasantries and she headed on. Apparently, Allun was fond of making a walk through of the gallery before turning in."

"So from what we know, he could have been missing from anywhere as early as 9:45p.m. Friday night," Nick commented. "I think we can assume that he was abducted. Any idea as to where and when he was?"

Smith looked down at the ground, as if preparing his thoughts. Nick was unsure for a moment whether or not he was thinking about his answer or was trying to decide how much to hold back from Nick.

"What is it?" Nick asked, sensing the other detective's dilemma.

"We are pretty certain he was abducted from here on Friday night," Smith said, as if ashamed for holding back on the other.

"What the hell are you not telling me?" Nick asked.

"Look," Smith began. "You need to understand, the church is a big part of this community. St. Patrick's and the Norwich Diocese is one of the only ones that have been able to avoid scandal while the church in Boston was dealing with the sexual abuse scandal. The church is really concerned about the way this murder looks."

"Don't talk to me like I don't know this community," Nick began, offended. "I grew up here; I understand just how old this church is and how important it is to this town."

Smith looked back down at the ground, as if still trying to decide what to do.

"You know what?" Nick started. "This is not my case, you asked me up here for my advice. I have absolutely no problem leaving you holding the bag."

Nick turned and began making his way down the steps of the cathedral. He was pissed; he knew that Smith was holding out on him. It was insulting for Nick, not to mention infuriating, as he knew that he could be at home sleeping or reading the newspaper. He didn't need to be here, trying to force little bits of information out of another city's detective. At the same time, there was something about this crime that Nick could not get out of his head. This was a particularly heinous crime, and he could not help but feel as though there was a message behind it.

"I'm sorry," Smith said as Nick walked away. Nick stopped for a moment and looked back. "You're right. There is more, and I do appreciate you coming up here. It's just...I'm under a lot of pressure to keep this quiet."

"Keep what quiet?" Nick asked. Smith didn't answer immediately. He just turned and waved at Nick, inviting the other detective to follow. Nick followed behind the larger man as he made his way around the side of the cathedral to a large metal box with thick pipes leading out of it. Nick recognized it immediately as the electrical box that led in from the street.

"On Friday night at exactly 10:10p.m., Connecticut Light & Power received a call from a priest informing them that the power was out," Smith explained, opening the thin metal door to the electrical junction. "CL&P did a computer check of the electrical grid and found it up and running. After talking the priest through cycling the breakers, they sent a crew down to check it out. They found this."

Nick inched closer and could clearly see the remnants of a burnt out box and the thick line leading into the pipe cut. Between the two breaks in the line were multiple new wires with metal grippers on either end.

"What you see now is the patchwork the electrical company did to keep the church running until they can get a crew out Monday morning," Smith said. "The diocese wasn't happy about it, but as long as they could still conduct mass, they were satisfied."

"They're not conducting mass now," Nick commented. He stuck his finger out and was about to touch the burnt plastic before he stopped himself. "Well, we know one thing for certain now."

"What's that?" Smith asked.

"We know that this was definitely premeditated," Nick answered. "Whatever this device is, its job was to slice through the power line and incinerate itself in the process, leaving no evidence. I'll even bet that it was set to a timer."

"So whoever killed Father Allun was planning this," Smith said, following Nick's line of thought. "He was out to kill Allun."

"And probably embarrass the church," Nick added. "You don't go to all the work to string a body up like that without wanting to leave a message."

"What's the message?" Smith asked.

"That's for you to find out," Nick said with a smile. "This is your case. However, in my opinion, you have a killer who is angry at Allun, the church, or both. This is a very emotional crime. Your killer kidnapped Allun, held him for possibly over twenty four hours, tortured him, and finally killed him. Your killer displayed his body in a very public manner, which indicates to me that he might have something against the church and is trying to discredit the church by leaving the body naked. I think your killer most likely knew Allun, was close to him in some manner or another as is evident by the fact that he knew Allun's ritual of coming through the cathedral before going to bed. In any case, all of this is preliminary, and I'm sure that we'll know more when we get the autopsy report back."

"Which should be this afternoon," Smith said. He smiled at the look of surprise on his fellow detective's face. "One of the medical examiners is a parishioner, he volunteered to do the autopsy today and get a report to us in a few hours."

"Then I say cut the body down and let him get to work," Nick advised. "I'd be interested in seeing his report when he's finished. I could come back up here this evening if you still want some help."

"Yeah, I'll give you a call," Smith said, slightly confused. "Does that mean you're leaving for now?"

"I got things to do," Nick said. "Besides, you don't need me for this. Anything comes up, just give me a call. If not, I'll see you later this afternoon to go over the autopsy report."

"You make it sound as if you've got a hot date or something," Smith asked, his smile spreading from ear to ear.

"I do," Nick answered smiling back, and then made his way down the sidewalk towards his car.

CHAPTER 14

Nick walked slowly back through the old neighborhood of Norwich towards his car, unable to stop thinking about the murder scene he had just come from. The brutality of the crime made it more than obvious to the detective that this was a very angry killer. There was something deeply emotional behind this, something that caused the killer to use the maximum amount of pain possible. On the same note, his technique indicated that he was patient and methodical. Whoever this killer was, he was smart and kept his emotions in check, no matter how much anger boiled underneath. Nick wondered if the killer's only release was in the grotesque nature of Allun's murder. But deep down, he was certain there was more to it than that. The killer positioned the body to send a message to someone; perhaps even to strike back at someone. That led Nick to believe that this may not be an isolated incident. This may be not be the last he heard of this killer. He kept reminding himself that this was not his case, not his responsibility; but that did not relieve his building interest in the crime. *I need to see that autopsy report*, he thought to himself. A lot of the detective's questions would be answered once the medical examiner examined the wounds and the particular method of death. No, this was not his case, but Hollings had sent him here to consult, and he wasn't going to let this thing go until he knew the killer was apprehended.

Just as he made it to the end of the second block where his car was parked, he ran right into a mob of reporters. This was not the place where they had been delegated to assemble, but here they were nonetheless, and there was no escaping them.

As soon as they saw the detective they began firing away at him with their questions.

"Detective, can you tell us who the victim is?" asked a young female reporter Nick did not recognize.

"I'm not a part of this investigation," Nick answered, unsure of whether his answer was a lie or not. He was not officially a part of the investigation, though his presence could lead the press to certain assumptions.

"Then what is your involvement in this case?" asked another reporter from one of the local stations.

"My family lives here in Norwich," Nick answered, attempting to be as vague as possible. "I just came down to see what all the commotion was about."

"Can you give us any details about the crime?" asked the first female reporter.

"No," Nick answered. "You probably know more about it than I do. Suffice it to say, the Norwich Police Department seems to have everything in control and you should probably direct your questions to them."

"Are you saying you have no part of this investigation whatsoever?" asked a male voice from the back of the pack.

"That's what I said," Nick answered, trying to push his way through the crowd.

"Then do you deny that Lt. Brenda Hollings was contacted early this morning by Chief Robert Thaxton of the Norwich Police Department and was asked for some assistance regarding this murder?" the male voice fired back. Suddenly, Nick stopped walking as all eyes were on him. The reporters stopped shuffling around him and simply pushed their microphones and dictaphones in his general direction. Nick looked through the crowd, searching for the person who asked the question, yet at the same time realizing that the longer he hesitated in answering the question, the worse it looked.

"I don't know anything about a conversation between Lt. Hollings and Chief Thaxton," Nick answered apprehensively. "This is the first I'm hearing of it."

"Then Lt. Hollings did not contact you around seven this morning and tell you to come to Norwich to assist in a homicide?" the reporter asked. It was then that Nick found him. With the movement around them stopped, Nick could clearly see the reporter and stood in shock for a moment as he stared into the eyes of a former colleague.

"Lt. Hollings asked me to come up and offer the assistance of the New London Investigations Unit, more than that I don't know," Nick answered, realizing that the reporter already knew as much or more than Nick did, and was hoping to catch the detective in a lie. "However, as I said, the Norwich Police Department has the investigation under control and I would forward any further questions on to them."

With that, it was clear that they would not be getting any further information, and the mob quickly began to disperse and head back to their cars and news vans to get the information into story form. As Nick watched them walk away, he homed in on the nosey reporter and followed him over to the Channel 30 NBC news van.

"Hey Anderson," Nick called out. The other man stopped and turned around. "What the hell are you doing? You're a reporter now?"

"Since my retirement, I was lucky to find an organization that appreciates my long service to the police department," Anderson answered with a smile. It was a jab at Nick, and what's more, this was his way of getting back at the New London Police Department.

Mark Anderson had been a detective in the Investigations Unit for many years. In fact, he was the senior detective in the unit when Nick was called in to help investigate The Nemesis. Anderson and Nick had never gotten along; Nick had never investigated a homicide before that case and Anderson was in line to be lead detective. Anderson had questioned Nick's instincts and opinions regarding the murders and had quit the department halfway through the investigation. Nick had assumed that Anderson simply transferred, and was shocked to see him here working for the local NBC network.

"Look," Nick began. "I didn't push you out of the department."

"Oh please," Anderson said with a wave of his hand. "That's all water under the bridge. Everything happens for a reason. I'm making three times the money here than I was on the force, and my knowledge has really come in handy at putting me ahead of other reporters when it comes to crime stories."

"So we're good then?" Nick asked, uncertain. Nick extended his hand in friendship, though he felt that there was something malicious lurking below the surface of Anderson's fake smile. The reporter took Nick's hand and shook, softly at first, then exerting a little pressure. Anderson drew Nick close and spoke directly into the detective's ear.

"My beef is not with you," Anderson answered. "It's with that bitch Hollings and those traitors Wilkins and Mitchell. Hollings wanted me out from the beginning, and the other two should have stuck up for me and didn't to protect their own asses."

"That's not what happened and you know it," Nick responded, returning Anderson's tight grip. Nick could feel his face flush as anger inside of him began bubbling up to the surface. He pulled his hand free of the reporters and stepped back. "You were out of line and you know it. The only person you have to blame for what happened is yourself."

"You're a tool, a means to an end," Anderson said, laughing at the detective. "Hollings used you to oust me and to make herself look good. Wilkins and Mitchell are using your success to hopefully advance their careers, and now I'm using you to get my revenge. You're Hollings' golden boy and when you fuck up, which you will eventually, I'm going to be there to turn it into a major story. Wherever you go, whatever case you investigate, I'll be there watching. To be honest, I kind of feel sorry for you, stuck in the middle like this. Kind of."

"Fuck you," Nick spat. "You watch all you want, but I'll be watching you too. You step over the line just a little bit, and I'll bury you."

Nick turned from the reporter and walked away. He knew that his anger was going to boil over any minute now and he was going to say something that he would regret. As he walked away, he could hear Anderson taunting him.

"Oh, that hurts me detective," Anderson said, laughing. "After all we've been through. Are you sure that I can't get an exclusive? How about just a quote?"

CHAPTER 15

On the drive home, Nick put on a homemade CD and turned it all the way up, trying to push the steady current of thoughts out of his mind. His cell phone rang continuously during the twenty minute drive back to his house, but he chose to ignore it. He didn't want to think about the crime scene he had just come from, nor the confrontation with Mark Anderson. Anderson was pissed and he would be using the only weapon he had against the department and Hollings specifically. He would watch from the sidelines and taunt the department, using his police knowledge as his weapon. He would smear them in the media, making them look bad whenever things were going well, and God forbid someone really make a mistake. Anderson would use the media to destroy them all. *Thankfully, this isn't your investigation,* he thought to himself. That thought only brought him back to where he didn't want to be; thinking about the crime. The only thing the detective could do was block it out, block out his interest, block out his need to assist in the investigation. He had done his job, and that was that. He had been called out to consult, and he had consulted. Sure, he would go over the details of the autopsy, make sure that Smith was on the right track, and then he would wash his hands of the whole thing.

Nick arrived at his home and quickly ran inside, stripped, and jumped into the hot shower, acutely aware of the time and his date with Jenn. He was eager to see her, eager to do something that might take his mind off of the case. Nick got out of the shower ten minutes later and dried off, then dressed. He dressed casually, but still nice, making sure not to seem as though he was trying too hard. Nick dressed in jeans and a soft pink button down shirt. Nick drove off, making his way to Mystic where Jenn's class was being held. He knew the area of Mystic fairly well, knew the street the studio was on, though he had never heard of the gym the studio was in. However, he found the address with little difficulty and walked inside. Nick asked the woman at the front desk where the class was and informed her that he was meeting with the instructor, and then she informed Nick that he was expected. Nick did not know what to make of her comment, but followed her instructions to a studio room in the back of the building. Nick opened the door and found himself the center of attention. Twenty women turned from where they stood around a large, blue gym mat with Jenn centered directly in the middle of the group.

"And here is our victim now," Jenn said with a smile. "Ladies, this is Detective Nicholas Grenier. I hope he will be kind enough to be our guinea pig for today's class."

The initial wave of uneasiness that Nick experienced walking in the door immediately shifted into dread as he realized what he was being asked.

"I'm afraid I'd make a poor demonstrator," Nick said, immediately recognizing just how poor his excuse was.

"Oh come on," Jenn continued. "The ladies here would love to have a demonstration by a homicide detective. Ladies, what do you say?"

Suddenly, the twenty plus women of the class erupted into applause, pleading with the detective to join the class. Nick shook his head and backed away from the mat.

"Really ladies," Nick protested. "I'm just here to observe."

"Well, I really can't blame him," Jenn started. "I'd be afraid of being beat up by a woman too."

All eyes shifted back to the detective and there was some low moaning around the room as all the women waited for

Nick's reaction to the challenge to his masculinity. Nick sighed, and with a defeated smile on his face, slipped his feet out of his shoes and made his way across the studio to where Jenn was standing. Again, the ladies applauded the detective and parted way for him to take his place. He looked at Jenn and saw her smile, not the satisfied smile of someone who had just won herself a victim, just a caring almost loving smile. Nick smiled back and reached out to take her outstretched hand. With near blinding speed, Jenn wrenched his hand back with the slightest of ease and before he knew it, Nick was flat on his back with the entire class standing over him just looking down.

"You see ladies," Jenn said, offering to help Nick up. "That's all it takes to surprise an attacker."

Over the course of the next thirty minutes, Nick wondered many times what had possessed him to take her up on her offer to observe her class. She had conned him with her beautiful, disarming smile. Every time Nick got up, every time she warned him to brace himself, he was never truly ready for what was to come. By the end of the class, every muscle in the detective's body burned with pain. There were muscles on the inside of his leg that he didn't even know that he had, aching at the slightest movement.

"Ladies," Jenn said as the class reached its end. "Let's all thank Detective Grenier for being our attack dummy for the day."

As the class applauded one last time, Nick couldn't help but wonder what kind of dummy she was referring to. He smiled and held up a hand, and as the women exited the studio, he did his best not to wince or limp with every step he made toward the wooden bleachers that lined the far wall. Nick eased himself down onto the bench just as Jenn said her goodbyes and reminded everyone about the next class. She turned her attention to the bleachers and smiled as if feeling the detective's pain.

"I've heard of painful first dates," Nick started. "But this one takes the cake. Is this some kind of screening process?"

"I had no doubt you could handle yourself," Jenn said, climbing up the bleachers, and sitting directly behind him. She immediately began massaging his back, kneading away the pain in his muscles. "But if it makes you feel any better, you're the first 'first date' in a long time."

"I can see why," Nick said, nearly moaning as her hands melted away the aching tension. "Not all of those moves are taught in the academy; where did you learn it?"

"Most are adaptations of my own design that stem from different forms of martial arts and self defense," Jenn answered. "Many martial art forms include fluid, but time wasting moves that prepare you for your next attack. However, here I try to teach women how to incapacitate quickly and with the least amount of effort, increasing their chances of getting away."

"Well," Nick began as he rotated his shoulders around in an attempt to test their pain level. "You definitely have some interesting moves. I bet you could teach a class to the police department. Anyway, was that our date because I don't feel I gave it my best."

"You were a good sport," Jenn said, slapping him on his back. "You've earned yourself a coffee and a few more hours."

"Lucky me," Nick answered sarcastically.

"Don't worry," she said. "It'll be painless."

Jenn took Nick down the street to a small coffee shop where they spent hours talking. Nick lost himself in their conversation, feeling at ease with someone for the first time in a long time. Nick knew that he did not open up to people easily, including his colleagues. They all knew him, they were close in a professional manner, but no one really knew what made him tick. Even Hollings, who probably knew him best of all, really didn't understand him. Perhaps it was that she could not bring herself to understand him, but then again, she did not need to; she just needed him to do what he was born to do, catch killers. But now, sitting here with her, he found himself smiling, even laughing. He found himself so at ease with Jenn that at one point he thought that if she asked, he could tell her everything about himself. He asked about her career, about the college classes she was taking and how long it would take her to get her law degree. She had her whole life mapped out; she knew where she would apply for work and the chances of her getting hired. She seemed to have it all planned.

"So," she started. "Tell me what you thought about my class today."

Nick looked at her cautiously for a moment before he answered.

"I thought it was very educational," he answered. She stared at him for a minute, as if probing his expression to ascertain whether or not he was telling the truth.

"It's alright," she said. "You can tell me what you really think. It won't hurt my feelings."

Nick sat up straight in his chair and sighed. She knew that he was being diplomatic, trying to be polite and hide his true feelings. She, however, has asked him and he was not going to lie to her.

"There's a reason we tell people not to fight back, you know," Nick said. "I'm all for self defense and empowering women, but we all know that the more you submit the more likely a victim is of making it out of an attack alive."

"I remember a case where a woman was blitzed in a parking garage when she was leaving a shopping mall around Christmas, her arms full of presents," Jenn began, her eyes drifting above his head as if she were recalling her own memory. "Her attacker threw her in her car and kidnapped her, driving her all over the state, threatening to kill her, and finally abandoning her on the side of a deserted back road in the woods of northeastern Connecticut in the freezing cold of December. She barely made it to the police station without freezing. I remember that she wondered whether or not she could have avoided the hours of emotional torture she received if she had only been able to incapacitate him in the beginning long enough to get away."

"At least she came out of it alive," Nick said. He had dealt with the same type of cases himself, and he knew that there was some truth to Jenn's argument.

"Try telling that to a rape victim," Jenn shot back, staring at him. All Nick could do was sigh and nod his head. He didn't need to concede the point; they both knew that she was right.

"Well," Nick said. "This conversation went downhill fast."

"Sorry," Jenn said, shaking her head. "I'm kind of a fanatic when it comes to this issue."

"You make a good advocate," Nick admitted.

"You still haven't told me that much about yourself," Jenn reminded him. "What have you been doing with yourself all weekend?"

Nick smiled at her, wondering if he really wanted to tell her the story behind his Sunday morning. She watched intently as he struggled with himself. Finally, he looked up at her where he found her staring patiently, waiting for him to begin. The detective didn't want the date to end, and he didn't want to hold anything back from this woman. He liked her, and she liked him, and he knew that he had to start somewhere.

"Let's take a walk."

CHAPTER 16

Nick walked with Jenn around Mystic talking about the case earlier that morning. He did not have any planned route, nor did he have any exact idea where he was going, but he just walked on discussing the details of the murder. To her credit, she did not interrupt him, listening as he went on. She did notice how he steered away from some details, particularly when it came to the body and the way in which it was discovered. Jenn did not press him on these issues, deciding that he would reveal whatever he was holding back in his own time. She could sense the great struggle that existed within him. There was something about this case, someone else's case for that matter, which made it nearly impossible for him to let go. They walked down past the Mystic Seaport, not even stopping at the tourist attractions. They continued on down the streets of Mystic, towards the drawbridge that crosses the Mystic River, and two blocks of shopping stores that lined the main street. They bought ice cream cones at a small shop and stopped finally to look out over the water. It was only then that Nick realized that he had been talking the entire time. To his amazement, she seemed to have stayed with him and his story.

"Sorry," Nick started, looking down at the water. "You must have been wondering when I was going to come up for air."

"Not at all," she protested. "It's amazing to listen to you talk about a crime scene. I know that I've only seen you at one scene so far, but you have a passion about it that is very contagious."

"Thanks," Nick said. "I think. I don't usually talk about it like this. In fact, I don't usually talk about it at all. You're the first person that I've felt comfortable discussing this kind of stuff with. I guess that's why I didn't realize that I was monopolizing the conversation."

"Like I said, don't worry about it," she repeated. "So, where do you go from here?"

"I don't know," Nick answered with a shrug. "I promised that I would give Detective Smith my insight after he received the autopsy report. He should be calling any time to let me know when it's done."

"The M.E. is doing the autopsy today, on a Sunday?" Jenn asked incredulously.

"I know," Nick said. "The M.E. is a parishioner and I gather there was some emotional history for him. Unfortunately, there is already an enormous amount of media attention and I think Norwich wants to look as though they are deep into the investigation by tomorrow morning. Once the identity of the victim is made known, there is going to be a media frenzy."

"Does Detective Smith plan on making it known that you are helping with the investigation?" Jenn asked.

"I kind of made it known myself," Nick answered, thinking back to his confrontation with the mob of reporters early in the day. "Why do you ask?"

"I just think that if this investigation doesn't go anywhere," Jenn stopped for a moment, as if considering her words carefully. "It's just that with the media attention, if the police don't find the killer quickly, they'll be looking for someone to crucify."

Nick looked over at her suddenly. It was only then that Jenn realized what she had said.

"Sorry," she said quickly. "Wrong choice of words."

"Detective Smith is competent," Nick said, understanding her concern. Nick was a very visible member of the Investigations Unit, especially after the Nemesis case. Jenn was right; Nick knew that he had to limit his visibility regarding this case.

"He'll catch the killer. My meeting with him this afternoon will be my final involvement in this case."

They walked back through Mystic the way they had come, absently heading back to the gym. Their conversation strayed from work and Jenn seemed to focus on other things, and Nick quickly realized just how much of the conversation he had monopolized earlier. He could only imagine what she was thinking of him now, realizing just how much energy and thought he put into his work. Nick could kick himself for not allowing himself to separate from work for just a short period of time. Nick spent the rest of his time focusing only on her, being attentive to their conversation and not mentioning work again. He hoped he could salvage something from this date. There was something about her, something calming and certain. He liked her more and more, and with every step closer to where they started their day, he was more certain that he wanted to see her again. He only hoped that she was feeling the same way. As they reached the shopping plaza that housed the gym, Jenn pointed across the parking lot towards her car.

"I'm sorry about earlier," Nick stated, not really knowing what to say. "I shouldn't have gone on and on about the case. I just get into these things, and I have to admit, you are the first person that I could really talk to about it."

"Don't be sorry," Jenn answered, as though his concern had been for nothing. "I was interested, or else I wouldn't have asked. It's amazing to listen to you talk about a crime scene; you really have an understanding that few people share. Besides, it has to help to have someone on the inside who knows what you are talking about."

"That's for sure," Nick admitted. "Though murder conversation has to detract some from a date."

"Is that what this was?" Jenn asked playfully. "A date?"

"I'd like it to be," Nick answered, certain of himself.

"Then that's what it was," she assured him. "And really, don't worry about it. I had a good time."

"Good," Nick answered, relieved. "I'd like to see you again."

"Me too," Jenn answered. "Why don't you give me a call later?"

"I'll do that," Nick promised. Just then his cell phone began to ring. Nick pulled the clip off of his belt and stared down at the number.

"I hope that's not another girlfriend," Jenn said with a smile.

"No," Nick answered. "Large, bald Native Americans are not my cup of tea."

"You have to go?" she asked as they reached her car.

"It appears so," Nick answered with a sigh. "But the sooner I get this over with, the sooner I can let this case go."

They said goodbye and Nick watched as she climbed into her car and drove away. All in all, he felt as though this had been a good date. His phone started ringing again, and the detective pressed the SEND button and placed the phone to his ear and listened.

"The report is done," Smith informed him. "I'd like to go over it with you. There's some pretty fucked up stuff here."

"Are you being followed by the media?" Nick asked.

"Not yet," Smith answered. "They feel somewhat comfortable having set up shop outside the police station and the crime scene, but you never know."

"Then why don't we get some coffee and pick through the report," Nick suggested. "I have a feeling we could both use some caffeine at this point."

"Good idea. Eating right now is out of the question," Smith said. "I thought the scene itself was bad, but this report only makes it worse."

CHAPTER 17

Before driving back up to Norwich, Nick had suggested a
small diner overlooking the main street of town. During
the course of the drive he could not help but think about the
time he spent with Jenn; how at ease he felt talking with her,
how at ease he felt overall. He hoped that she felt the same
way. Nick hated to admit it, but his Dr. Tanner, had been
right; he was lonely. Nick shook his head a moment after that
word popped into his head. Nick wasn't necessarily lonely, he
was simply alone. He had been alone since he let Anna walk
out of his life. He had never experienced something like that,
something that felt so right, yet he knew down deep it was
somehow wrong. But with Jenn, he did not get that feeling at
all. This was someone who understood him, or at least wanted
to. There was something about her demeanor that allowed
him to open up, so much so that he did not realize when he
was going too far. Looking back now, he did not feel as though
he had scared her off. It was something in the way she spoke
to him before they parted company, something that assured
him that they would see each other again. When Nick reached
the diner thirty minutes after talking with Smith, he expected
to find the other detective sitting in a booth already. It turned
out that Nick was the first to arrive and so he found a table
and ordered one of their special roast coffees. The thought
of food made his stomach growl, reminding him that he had
not eaten all day. However, he knew that Detective Smith was
right about the crime scene photos and was not certain that
he would be able to eat anything after seeing the case file.

At that moment, a concern popped into Nick's head. It
was something that had been skirting the periphery of his

imagination, a concern that until now he had been unwilling to look at seriously. Usually, Nick got a sense about the case; a vision would pass over him, it would pass before his mind's eye. He would see the crime; he would see it in a detail that could not be captured by crime scene photos and autopsy reports. It was something that only the killer could see; something only another killer would understand. There were two competing forces within Nick; a killer and a cop. Like genetic traits passed down from one generation to the next, the detective had learned that he had inherited both of these traits from his close relatives. The Nemesis case had forced him to accept a horrible truth about his family's past; his grandfather had been a police officer while his grandmother had been a killer. His grandmother had killed a man in self defense, a man who had raped her and killed three people. Though she was a victim, there was something about killing the man who had brutalized her that scarred her psyche; something she had passed on to Nick. Over the course of Nick's career, he had learned to use this gift to his advantage, and had seen some remarkable results. So far, he had not investigated a crime that he had not been able to solve. But now it was gone; the sense had not surfaced, the vision had not come. Now Nick was getting nervous.

A few minutes after the waitress brought his steamy cup over, Detective Smith appeared at the opening to the dining room. He whispered something to a waiter, who turned and pointed in Nick's direction. Smith then nodded and made his way to where the other detective was seated.

"Didn't wait, good thinking," Smith said, as he approached the table. He leaned over and turned the cup around gingerly with his fingers until he could read the writing that indicated which roast. "Even better. You picked the place that has the best coffee in town."

"This is the only place that serves coffee in town," Nick remarked. "It's the only place that brews more than one flavor. All the other places just serve coffee flavored tar."

"Harsh," Smith replied. "True, but harsh."

Smith dropped the file down on the Formica table and it made a slapping sound as it came to rest. Nick eyed the file for a moment, just half a second. His heartbeat accelerated slightly as he quietly anticipated the information that lay within. That was all he allowed himself though, remembering for the hundredth time that this was not his case. After the Norwich detective placed his order, Smith caught Nick up on the details that had transpired since he had left the cathedral that morning.

"I must congratulate you on how well you handled the press," Smith said, admiringly. "You made it clear that Norwich was handling the case, made us look competent, and yet didn't give anything away to those vultures. I could learn a few things from you."

"You might have a problem with one of the reporters," Nick said. "The NBC guy's name is Anderson, and he used to be a cop."

"Yeah, I saw him grilling you," Smith said, blowing the steam off of the surface of his drink. "What's the deal with him?"

"He's out for blood," Nick answered. "He feels short changed by the department, and won't think twice about exacting his revenge by slaughtering the career of the first cop who crosses his path."

"Thankfully you crossed his path before me," Smith commented with a sarcastic smile.

"Just watch your back," Nick advised. "Now are we going to go over the autopsy report or what?"

Smith pushed the file across the table and Nick turned the chart around to face forward, opened it up and lifted the first page off the small pile of pages and pictures inside the manila folder. Nick brought his cup to his nose and took a deep wiff as if bracing himself before diving into the details of the report.

"I have to tell you, CSU lifted literally thousands of prints," Smith said. "There is no way they can eliminate all of them, though they will run them all through the database and we'll see who has a criminal record. However, that process is going to take days."

"Is there any good news?" Nick asked, not lifting his eyes from the report.

"Not really," Smith answered honestly. "Father Allun did a lot of work with the underprivileged, as well as ex-cons. Maybe one of them had a beef with him and killed him. It's not much to go on, but it's a possible angle."

"Unlikely is how I would put it," Nick commented gingerly sipping his coffee. "Jesus, this guy really worked him over. Broken fingers, shattered skull, sodomized, multiple broken bones, broken jaw, over one-hundred stab wounds and lacerations, and third degree burns."

"Like I said," Smith interjected. "Jesus didn't seem to be on his side."

Nick slid the report to one side and then looked at the crime scene photos. He glanced back and forth between the photos and the report, matching the picture with the description in the report. It did not take much time at all for the detective to realize that there was a picture missing, though the description was carefully marked in the report. He looked up into Smith's smiling face.

"I know what you're looking for," Smith said. "I just wanted to see if you are as good as they say you are."

"Do you want my help or not?" Nick asked, making no attempt to hide his annoyance. Smith unfolded his arms and placed a picture down on the table in front of the other detective. Nick centered the image before him and leaned over, his head almost touching the table. In the picture was a small, round piece of what looked like plastic with an indiscernible image on the top of it.

"It was found on the inside of his right thigh," Smith said as Nick stared at the picture. "It was just below the surface of the skin."

"Any idea what it is?" Nick asked.

"Not until five minutes before I got here," Smith answered. "I had forensics put a rush on it. I got some preliminary information, though they are not finished analyzing it yet. It's a piece of red wax. The lab guys took a sample of it to analyze, and they are going to take a digital snapshot of the image in the middle, enlarge and enhance it. We should have a better idea of what it is and what it means by tomorrow morning.

Nick sat back and put all the pictures in order, slipped them back into the file and finally placed the autopsy report on top and closed the file.

"Well, what do you think?" Smith asked.

"I doubt this is someone with a simple grudge," Nick answered. "This isn't someone who Allun simply pissed off. This is someone with a deep down hatred. It may not even be with Allun himself; it may have something to do with the church. I can't say more than that now, at least not anything that would be useful or even close to accurate. For that I would need to study the file for a little longer."

"There's not much in there," Smith warned. "Not much more than you already know."

"You never know what little clue might be the answer to the riddle," Nick said. "Do you mind if I borrow this file overnight?"

"I thought you might ask," Smith answered. "That's your copy. Keep it for as long as you need. I really appreciate your help."

"I'll give you a call if I think of anything," Nick said. He rose from his place in the booth and reached into his back pocket for his wallet. Smith raised his hand to protest.

"Let me cover the drinks," he said. "It's the least I can do."

"Well, that's kind of you," Nick stated. "I hope I can repay the kindness."

"There's only one thing you can do for me detective," Smith said, looking Nick square in the eyes. "Find that little clue I'm missing."

CHAPTER 18

After their meeting, Nick took his copy of the file and went home. He knew that every impulse in his body would tell him to start working on the case immediately, but Nick also knew that the thing to do at this point was to have some separation. Forcing himself to try and come up with the answers was not going to do anyone any good. His flashes of insight would come when they did, until then, there was no need to dwell on the issue. Nick needed to devote himself to something else for a while, so when he got home he placed the file on the side table in his living room and decided that there was only one other thing to concentrate on; food. Food was the only thing in the house that really held any interest for him, except for his rigorous exercise routine. Ironically, it was because of Nick's love of food and cooking that he had to work out as hard as he did. Nick had first purchased his exercise equipment as a way of keeping from getting depressed during a quiet, unsure period of his career. He had built himself a routine, that now, he was unable to break himself of. Now, because of the elaborate meals he prepared, he was forced to stick with his rigorous schedule.

Nick entered the kitchen and turned on the television as he began removing the necessary ingredients from the refrigerator and pantries. As he began to prepare his meal, his mind slowly wandered back to the events of the day. The detective had a bad feeling that Anderson would not waste any time making good on his promise to get his revenge. As soon as Nick switched the channel to the local NBC station, he found that his suspicions were well founded. The thirty minute program had just started and the first story they aired was the murder in St. Patrick's Cathedral. Anderson's face flashed up on the screen, obviously on location not far from the cathedral itself. Nick watched all twelve minutes of the report, listening intently as he devoted his true intentions to slicing the vegetables. There were two reports, one which focused on the crime itself, the second devoted to the shock and outrage of the community. As it turned out, Anderson was the first reporter able to find out the name of the victim. Using his vast resources of contacts in the police department, Anderson was able to scoop all the other channels with Allun's name and let on that the manner of death was "particularly gruesome". Something burned in the back of Nick's mind, a thought, the spark of an idea, as the detective continued to listen to the report. Having to check himself, he knew that now was not the time to think about the case. *Separation*, he reminded himself as he continued with the ingredients for the dinner.

As Anderson continued talking about the case, elaborating on the little information that had been divulged by the police department in a vain attempt to make it look as though the he knew more than he did, Nick could not help but notice that Anderson waited as long as possible before releasing the name of the victim. Though he could not be sure, Nick guessed that Anderson was able to get the name fairly early in the day, probably not long after the Nick left the crime scene. However, Anderson waited until now to reveal the information to the public, giving the police as much time as possible to notify the next-of-kin. Nick smiled to himself, realizing immediately that Anderson was playing smart, realizing that this was no petty pissing match he had with the police department. He was calculating and patient, and he was going to have his revenge. Had Anderson revealed the name of the victim before giving the police every opportunity to notify the next-of-kin, he would have burned any bridges he had left with the department. The backlash would have hit the fan so hard and fast that any contacts he had on the inside would dry up instantly for fear of being found out. At the same time, in the eyes of the police department, Anderson would become public enemy number one. The police would go out of their way to exclude him, even going so far as to give clues and leaks to other channels. Anderson could not risk that, he had to play the game if he was going to get his own revenge.

Nick knew in that moment that Anderson would be patient, determined, and focused while manipulating things his own way. Anderson would continue to make himself look good to his viewers, while sullying the image of the department. That thought elicited one word that echoed throughout Nick's mind, *sociopath*. This word, and its implications, stopped the detective cold for a moment. His mind instantly conjured up the criminal psychology classes he had taken before becoming a police officer. *Sociopath*, noun, "someone with a sociopathic personality; a person with an antisocial personality disorder". Nick knew that there was only one place to go from there, and that was a *psychopath*, another noun, "a person with an antisocial personality disorder, manifested in aggressive, perverted, criminal, or amoral behavior without empathy or remorse". No, Nick thought to himself, realizing that that was a huge leap from the angry, frustrated man that he saw on the television screen. Anderson was angry and vengeful, and some of him might even have a right to be; but, he was too smart to take this anger to the extremes. His actions regarding the release of the victim's name backed that up. Nick returned his attention to his dinner and ten minutes later was seated at the small kitchen table eating his meal and mulling over the rest of the nights' news.

There was nothing terribly interesting about most of it. The weather was to stay the same; warm, some humidity but becoming seasonably cooler. Fall would begin to set in to New England, the leaves would change color and fall from the trees and soon there would be those picturesque scenes from calendars all over. For now though, summer still had Connecticut in her clutches and was not going to let go easily. As for sports, the Boston Red Sox were doing a great job of diving headlong into another losing season, with little hope of making it to the post season, much less the World Series. The only hope for local sports fans rested with the New England Patriots who would be warming up for pre-season action very soon. The only other piece of news that interested Nick was the second report done by Anderson, capturing the feelings of the community over the murder of the beloved pastor. Anderson may not have been a reporter for long, but he knew how to pull at the heart-strings of the community and of the individual. According to the report, this was the first time that the cathedral had closed and not held a mass in over sixty years. Anderson's report was less of an indication of the mood of the masses as it was an attempt at creating the mood he desired. He was successful at making the people he interviewed feel the emotion he wanted of them; grief, shock, anger, and rage. Every time an interviewee shed a tear, or clenched a fist, Anderson was able to turn that emotion against the one entity he felt was responsible for this tragedy, the police department.

Nick finished his dinner, cleaned up the used dishes and cookware, and went into the living room where the case file was waiting for him, almost beckoning him. The detective could have laughed at himself when he picked up the file and made his way around the room to the stereo system. He had so wanted to get away from the case emotionally, think of something else for a while. However, by turning on the television, by listening to Anderson's report, he had kept himself from that time away that he so desired. He did not have the willpower to leave it alone, to separate himself from a case for even five minutes. This was something he should be working on with his therapist; not trying to get in touch with his feelings. Nick powered up the stereo and checked the CD tray. In the tray lay a homemade CD of classical music he had possibly downloaded illegally from the internet. He was not sure of the legitimacy of this software program that he was using to download the music, nor did he make any attempt to find out. When it came to downloading classical music, Nick knew that all of the composers were long since dead and was quite certain that they were not going to make a fuss about royalty rights. Unfortunately, this logic did not extend to any of the newer music he downloaded.

Nick turned off the lights and cautiously made his way to an old leather armchair in the corner of the room. He depressed the small plastic slide of the lamp that connected the circuit and illuminated the bulb, causing the room to be illuminated in the soft golden glow around the immediate vicinity of the armchair, then steadily dissipating into darkness further out into the room. Nick eased himself into the old leather chair which had belonged to his grandfather. The chair, old, worn and yet still beautiful as only a leather piece can be, fit it's occupant like a glove, an experience Nick had never known until the first time he sat here after his grandparents had passed away, leaving the home to him. Nick picked up the stereo remote control and pressed play, and then quickly scrolled through the list of songs until he found the number he was looking for, knowing the number by heart. He pressed the repeat button twice, causing the player to remain on that one song, then turned his attention to the case file. Pachelbel's Canon in D major began to filter through the speakers. This was a piano solo version, one of the most beautiful versions Nick had ever heard of the piece, and one that never failed to calm the detective and ignite the more intuitive and creative centers of his brain.

Allowing the music and the comfort of the chair to wash over him; Nick began by looking at the crime scene photos. In fact, it was more a matter of watching them, as if some movement in the glossy, black and white images was going to jump out at him. But that was exactly was he was hoping for. He let his unconscious mind process the photos, putting his detective's brain on pause and letting something else happen; letting anything happen. Nick often wondered what an untrained eye saw if allowed to observe a crime scene. Would emotion immediately overtake the mind and cloud the judgment of the observer? Or perhaps, would the observer see something casual, something overlooked by the trained and detail-oriented mind of a police officer? When questioning suspects, Nick had always been amazed by the casual details picked up on by a witness, or the smells and textures so accurately memorized by the victim of a crime. Nick needed to see the scene with fresh eyes; with no preconceived notions of what happened there. He needed to look at the background and not focus on the victim or how he was displayed, and perhaps, that would ignite the visions that had guided him to the truth every other time. He needed a spark.

As he stepped out of the role of the police detective, and simply observed the photos as if gazing at art in a gallery, Nick was immediately struck by the photographer's talent. There was an artistic characteristic to the photos, one that would usually go unnoticed due to the focus on the victim. However, when Nick looked past the victim to the immediate surroundings, he could see why the photographer stood where he did, why he angled the camera in the way that he did. The photographer had already taken the normal profile shots that he was taught to take in school, and then had turned his attention away from the immediate vicinity of the victim. When he had done so, his artistic side had taken over and Nick could now get a better sense of the scene itself. This had been exactly what the detective needed, as he found himself now staring at a picture of a line of pews at the front of the cathedral. The camera had been aimed downward from a forty five degree angle from above. Nick focused on the empty pews, allowing his mind to wander a little bit. He wondered how many people had sat in those pews over the course of their existence. Most likely these were not the original pews, though there was an antique quality to the look of them. *How many people had sat there, their heads bowed in prayer? How many people had risen from those pews, filled with hope for even just one more day?* As these thoughts filled his mind, Nick allowed himself to see people, families coming and going, sitting and standing, praying and holding hands as they rose to leave. That was when it hit him. That was when Nick saw the first clue that he had been looking for. There was something about this image, about the pews. Though the intent of the photographer had been to capture the uniformity of the pews, one perfectly set in front of the other, he could not have known that one of them was off center.

Nick couldn't take his eyes off of the image, amazed that he had not seen it before, amazed that no one had seen it before. One of the pews was askew, not quite in line with the others. As Nick examined the photo closer, he noticed a pale mark on the marble floor, the perfect outline of where the pew had originally been for so many years. Something had moved the pew, and though Nick could not see where the victim had been hanging from this angle, he couldn't help but feel as though this is where the killer had attacked Allun. Now only if he could see the image in his mind, if he could see how it had played out, then he would have some answers. Nick read the autopsy report over and over, looking for anything that might help. Unfortunately, nothing jumped out at him as it had in the photos. He was getting tired and the music had drifted now to the back of his mind and was nothing more than white noise. He was fading quickly, and though he knew he should keep reading the file, he was too tired to fight the inevitable. Nick allowed his eyes to close, and just as he did a pale blue image appeared in his mind; then another and another. They were flashes of an image, one that he could not entirely make out, but he quickly realized the images were in time with each strike of the piano keys as the music played on in his living room. The music was slow, and each image only lasted as long as the sound of each note. It was like an echo, an unearthly echo, reverberating from the sound of the note, filling his mind with the crime scene. Nick did not fight these images though, and he soon began to understand more and more. Each image was the next step in the order of events that had happened that Friday night; each one another step forward like an individual slide on a reel. Nick allowed the images to begin rolling in faster and faster succession like a movie beginning to role. There, on the brink of his subconscious, between the light and the dark, Nick smiled to himself and let the vision run.

CHAPTER 19

The moment Nick gave himself to the vision, he began to feel as though he were floating away. He felt no sense of time or space, no sense of direction, and barely a sense of movement. He could see nothing; there was only darkness, and the feeling that something was tugging on him like a current pulling him downstream. Nick was unsure of what he would be seeing, if he would see anything at all, and where it would come from. They were the individual images again, and like before, with each flash came the next step until the flashes were so close together that it became a moving scene. Nick watched in amazement as a figure that looked like Father Allun made his way down the row between the pews. There was something very different about this vision. In his previous visions at other crime scenes, Nick would be standing at the scene, witnessing the events unfold in his mind while the actual crime scene lay before him. This time it was different though, now in his own home, without the luxury of the crime scene, and he hoped he would be able to remember as much of the vision as possible to aid him when he woke.

Father Allun continued to make his way to the front of the gallery to where the altar stood. As he passed, Allun touched each pew, caressing the side corners as though he were admiring perfection. *Perfection*, rang a voice in the darkness that the detective could only believe was his own. *The Lord is perfection.* Nick was uncertain what the thought meant, or even where it had come from. Nick let the thought pass and continued to watch the events unfold before him. Allun reached the front of the gallery and stood directly in front of the altar and the image of the crucifixion that stood just above him. Allun simply stood there staring, and Nick began to wonder whether or not the priest was praying or in some type of silent meditation. Then Allun raised his arms and turned his head down and away just slightly. Nick felt as though he were holding his breath as Allun mirrored the image that stood before him. Nick's mind was busy trying to process this image and understand its meaning all at the same time. Was he mocking the crucifixion? Was he mocking Christ? Did he think of himself as Christ? All of these questions slipped through his mind as he watched, both shocked and amazed. Nick desperately wished that he knew what Allun was thinking and feeling, yearning to know what was going on in the mind of the man. Whatever it was, Nick knew that it was something deep and profound, and he knew that he must learn more about the priest.

As Nick continued to watch, he found himself both moved and compelled, though by what he could not be sure. These were all pieces to a puzzle that Nick needed to put together. There was no way that he could leave this case alone now. There were too many questions that needed answering. Finally, Allun lowered his arms and stared at the altar and the image of the crucifixion one final time before turning and heading back the way he had come. As he walked back down the row, the scene seemed to change. The background of the gallery, everything that was not immediately surrounding the priest faded away. Nick's mind knew instantly what was happening. This is when the power was cut, and any moment now, the killer would strike.

Suddenly, from the far corner, Nick could see the outline of an individual, starting very small at first but growing as the figure approached the priest. Nick knew immediately what it was. Someone was coming, and they were coming closer and faster. It was the killer; Nick had no doubts. There was no visible movement from where Father Allun had been standing, no attempts to move away. Allun must not have been able to hear his attacker coming, and in the darkness, he definitely could not see him. As the figure approached, Nick could make out a type of outline of the attacker. The body seemed toned, lithe, and moved quickly and without hesitation. There was no face though, no definition or features, giving the attacker the appearance of the Grim Reaper. When the attacker approached but was still more than ten feet away, he moved in a way that Nick had not expected. It seemed as if he was about to step up on the pew, but the moment he did so, the image of the attacker disappeared completely. The figure simply vanished, and after two seconds, all was dark. The final image Nick saw was that of a mass of light, and Nick could barely make out the image within it, but before everything went dark he could make out the image of the attacker atop of the priest. Then the figure turned his head back, as if looking at the detective. Figure had no face and no place for eyes, but that only served to make the scene all the more haunting. It was as if the attacker knew that Nick was watching, a silent understanding that they were not alone.

Nick awoke with a start. He shifted quickly in his leather armchair, trying to get his bearings. He was home again, bathed in the golden warmth of the lamp on the small table just to his left. The music was still playing, and Nick reached for the remote to shut it off. He closed his eyes and rested his head back for a moment. He felt as though he had been holding his breath for five minutes. The vision did not replay itself, but Nick did not need it to. He knew that he was not going to forget what he had seen. Father Allun had been attacked, and now Nick knew that it was a blitz attack. The killer knew that Allun would be in the gallery there, alone; just as Allun had known that he would be alone in the gallery. The sisters had told Smith that Allun had a nightly ritual of going into the main cathedral space, though they had been under the impression it was time that he spent communing with God. Nick now knew that it was a time he spent involved in something far different. Had someone from the church walked in on him and witnessed what Nick had seen in his vision, they most likely would have had a far more shocking reaction than even Nick had. Strangely enough, there did not seem to be any hesitation on the part of Allun, so he must have known that he would be alone. The killer knew that Allun took his time. This meant that the killer knew Allun, and that Allun possibly knew his attacker. Though he had never really believed it, Nick was now certain that this was not some random attack, that this was aimed directly at Allun. It was not an attack on the church itself. That narrowed the field down considerably. Nick reached into his pocket and fished out his cellular phone, then dialed a number and waited.

"Shit man," answered Detective Smith without any of the normal pleasantries. "Don't you ever sleep?"

"Sometimes," Nick answered vaguely. "I notice you're still awake."

"Yeah," Smith answered. "It's a little hard to sleep after a scene like that. Besides, I need some personal time before I dive back in. I feel like I might be missing something that's staring me right in the face."

"I know what you mean," Nick said. "I need you to make a call and make sure that the crime scene remains secure, that means nobody goes in or out. That includes church staff."

"That would mean posting a couple of uniforms in and around the cathedral," Smith said. "It would be very difficult for me to get my boss to go for it for more than a couple of days. I mean with the overtime and all."

"I don't think we'll need them for that long," Nick said.

"Did you come up with something?" Smith asked.

"I'm not sure yet," Nick answered. "We'll see in the morning. What about you?"

"Actually, the analysis came back on that wax," Smith said. "It's old, I mean really old, like a couple hundred years. The lab is going to try to narrow down exactly when and where it was made by breaking down its components, but I'm not holding my breath. But shit, who goes out of their way to stick a couple hundred year old wax, with some weird picture on it, into a dead priest."

"Are we sure he was dead when it went in?" Nick asked.

"CSU said there was very little blood on it," Smith answered. "That means post mortem. Any thoughts?"

"Not off the top of my head," Nick answered. "Though I think I know someone who can help us with this. Can you meet me at the cathedral at ten tomorrow morning?"

"Sure," Smith said. "Does that mean I can get some sleep now?"

"Yeah," Nick said. "There's nothing more we can get from this case tonight. I'll see you tomorrow morning."

With that, Nick signed off and rose from his chair, switched off the light and made his way upstairs. He plugged the cell phone into its charger and cleaned up for bed. Finally, after climbing in, he thought about the next day. Tomorrow he was going back to Norwich to get some answers, but first he needed to see Hollings and warn her of what was to come.

CHAPTER 20

Conscious of his tight schedule, Nick left for the New London Police Department early the next morning, hoping to get in and talk to his lieutenant without much of a fuss. Unfortunately, he was not so lucky, as he found a team of reporters from all of the major stations camped out in front of the police headquarters when he pulled his car into the lot. These were not the primary reporters, but since Nick's involvement on the case was splashed all over the place, the press was now not willing to miss anything and was staking out both departments. Nick opted not to get entangled with the crowd and snuck in through the back door. He made his way through the department, feeling as though all eyes were on him. Something was going on, as if some rumor was circulating around the water cooler regarding Nick, and unfortunately everyone else knew except him. The detective made his way up the stairs to the Investigative Unit and found all eyes focused on the lieutenant's office. Nick approached Mitchell and asked what was going on.

"It's about time you got here," Mitchell stated. "They've been waiting for you."

"What do you mean it's about time?" Nick asked. "I'm half an hour early. And who's they?"

Mitchell pointed to Hollings' office, but Nick could not see through the half closed vertical blinds that had been drawn over the windows.

"Governor Haisley is here," Mitchell said. "He's been here for over an hour and I believe he's making the lieutenant nervous. They've been paging you and calling your home and cell the whole time. Don't you check your messages?"

Nick reached down instinctively around his waist and felt for his pager and cell phone. His pager was absent and when he extracted his cell phone from his pocket, he found that it was turned off.

"Oh shit," Nick replied and made his way to the office door. Hollings' secretary, a woman they all called the "gatekeeper", sat with a disapproving look cast over her face. She just nodded as he approached, indicating that Nick had her approval to enter. Nick knocked on the door and stuck his head in.

"Detective," Hollings said, her face a mask of disapproval just as harsh as her secretary's. "I'm so glad you could join us. I was about to send out a search party."

"Sorry I'm late, I was getting an update on the case in Norwich," the detective lied. This seemed to placate Hollings and please the governor at the same time. No one lost face when a subordinate was busy working and covering everyone's ass. The Governor rose from his seat and extended his right hand, which Nick accepted eagerly with a firm grip.

Nick appraised the governor for a moment. Haisley was a formidable man; a man that had climbed the rungs of the political ladder, throwing other people off along the way. Governor Haisley came from a rich family in the south and that was all anyone knew about his past. He came to Connecticut after serving in Vietnam and immediately established himself as a man with political ambitions. Though he never announced himself publicly, he went to work as a high school teacher who was voted to head the school board in Hartford in an astonishingly quick amount of time. The first year he ran for mayor of Hartford, he won and began an active and unrelenting campaign against drugs and violence in the capital city. He was re-elected three more times before he was asked to join the campaign of a relatively unknown business man as lieutenant governor. Haisley accepted, to the shock of most of his friends and family, and was reported to have won the election for the business man who became the next governor of the state. However, controversy marred the new governor's first term, with allegations of insider trading and financial corruption becoming more and more rampant everyday. Finally, his term nearly in ruins, the governor resigned his office, passing the reigns over to Haisley. It was rumored throughout the capital that Haisley was immediately supposed to pardon the ex-governor who would then live out the rest of his days in quiet seclusion. However, Haisley did not pardon his previous boss, and was very vocal about harsh punishments for anyone who was complicit in the scandal. The ex-governor was found guilty and sent to jail, while Haisley enjoyed the increasing respect and approval of the voters who called him a man of the people. Looking at him now, Nick couldn't help but wonder if Haisley had stirred up the scandal as a way to embarrass the then governor and save himself the hassle and financial burden of having to get himself elected to the highest office of the state.

Haisley looked older to Nick than the last time they had met. The governor did not look older in age, just wiser and stronger than before. The man had gained some weight, which only made him seem all the more domineering. However, for his favorite police detective, he was all smiles; like a loving grandfather.

"Nick, my boy," the Governor said, pulling the detective close and wrapping a large arm around his shoulders. "It's been a long time. The lieutenant was just telling me what a good job you've been doing since your transfer became official."

"I've been fortunate to work with some really great detectives," Nick said, turning on the charm. "And I've learned a lot from Lt. Hollings."

"So modest he is," Haisley stated, removing his arm and returning to his seat in front of the lieutenant's desk. "But don't be too modest, or you'll never get promoted. So what's the news on the priest murder?"

"There are some really solid leads," Nick stated. "Detective Smith is right on target with his investigation and seems to have the case in hand."

"I see," the governor said, noting the fact that Nick was making it clear that Smith was in charge of the investigation. "I have to tell you, though; I'm concerned about this Smith's lack of experience in these kinds of cases."

"From what I understand, Governor, this is a murder investigation," Nick said, trying to dispel the governor's belief that this was anything more. "Detective Smith has solved many homicides from what I've been told."

"That's not what I mean and you know it," Haisley said, casting a discerning eye upon the detective. "It's the type of homicide that concerns me. It's the savage nature and more importantly, the media attention that concerns me. This case is big news, and I don't want to see us look bad."

"He's doing everything that I would do," Nick assured him. "As I said, the investigation is right on target."

"Then there shouldn't be any disruption if you take the lead on this case," the Governor said, not missing a beat. "I want you to head up the investigation. I want someone who has the trust of the community and the media."

"With all due respect sir, we can't just..." Nick started.

"No, with all due respect to you son," interrupted the Governor. "I'm not really asking you. I like you Nicky boy, I always have. Your manner of solving cases is, different, but I tolerate it and go out of my way to support you because you always get results. This is a high profile case and I've already got the archdiocese breathing down my neck. We need resolution on this matter, and we need it quick. In short, we need a win. Do you understand?"

Haisley looked the detective square in the eyes, and Nick knew exactly what the Governor wanted from him. The tension was mounting in the office as the two men stared at each other, and what was only half a second felt like an hour.

"We understand, Governor," Hollings said, walking around from behind her desk. "Don't we, detective?"

"I understand," Nick answered, breaking his silence. "This case will be wrapped up neatly and quickly, you have my promise."

Suddenly, the Governor was all smiles again. He grabbed Nick again and this time engulfed the detective in a giant bear hug. Then he turned and shook hands with Hollings and gave his assurance that they would have his support, as if immediately falling into the role of a campaigning politician, then headed out the door spewing broad congratulations upon the detectives in the squad bay.

"Jesus," Hollings started. "For a minute there, I thought it was going to come to blows."

"Nothing to worry about," Nick said, brushing the incident aside. "Just our way of measuring each other's dicks. It's a guy thing."

"Is this something you men do often?" Hollings asked.

"Only when one alpha male encounters another," Nick said. "If we take over the investigation, we send a signal to the community and to the press that there is no confidence in the Norwich Police Department."

"I know," Hollings agreed. "That's why we aren't going to take over the investigation. We are going to work side by side so that no one loses face."

"Speaking of losing face," Nick said, altering the subject slightly. "I think we have a problem."

"If you mean Anderson," Hollings said, already reading the mind of her detective. "You'd be right, we do have a problem."

"He's a reporter now," Nick informed her. "And he's all over this case."

"I know," Hollings said. "I put in a good word for him with the station chief. I thought that it would cool his jets a little and let him be more appreciated as a reporter with insider knowledge, than as a detective with limited ability."

"Well, now he's out for blood," Nick said. "Your blood."

"Then we better make sure we don't give him any ammunition," Hollings stated. "How's the case? Is what you said about the leads true?"

"It is," Nick said. "Though I don't know what they mean yet. However, we've got a good idea where to go next."

"Then perhaps you better get going," Hollings said, indicating their meeting had come to an end.

CHAPTER 21

Nick returned to the scene of the crime with an agenda. There were facts that he had picked up on from the case file the night before that he wanted to review for himself when he got back to the cathedral. There were also things that he had seen in his vision that he wanted to compare with the actual crime scene in an attempt to separate fact from fiction. Nick walked around the massive gallery that was the inside of the cathedral, retracing the steps Father Allun had taken in Nick's vision. The detective walked up and down the aisle between the two rows of pews that faced the altar, even going so far as to touch the corners of the pews as he passed, just as Allun had done. Nick then confronted the altar, staring into the down-turned face of Christ on the cross. He looked for something, anything that might captivate the attention and provoke the response that it had in Allun. However, Nick was not getting the same feeling and he was not prepared to re-enact the scene of Father Allun mirroring the image before him. Should someone walk in, Nick knew that this was not something that he was prepared to explain away. Though not altogether satisfied, Nick knew that he was not going to find any more understanding of the events preceding the attack, and turned his attention to the other reason he was here.

Nick walked down the aisle again, examining the footing of the pews along the floor until he found the spot he was looking for. It didn't take long for him to find the pew that was out of line and the detective quickly got down on his hands and knees and examined the pew itself. This was the one that was in the picture, the pew that was not in perfect alignment with the others. Nick withdrew a dry erase marker from his pocket and removed the top, then drew an outline of the pew footing on the floor. After returning the marker to his pocket, Nick tried to move the pew with what he deemed to be less than casual force. With one hand he attempted to push the pew back, but was met with the resistance of the sheer weight of the object. Nick sighed, then rose from his place on the marble floor and dusted off his pants. He then took several paces down the row to another pew and attempted to lift his side. Realizing that the pew was far heavier than he had imagined, Nick tried again, bracing himself and pulling with all of his might. Nick was barely able to lift it an inch.

"Hey, there," Smith called out from the entrance of the gallery. "What are you trying to do, throw your back out? You have to lift with your legs."

"I tried that already," Nick answered back. "Why don't you bring those guns over here and help me lift this thing."

"Why are you trying to lift it?" Smith asked curiously. "You need to prove who is stronger?"

"No I have no doubts about that," Nick answered with a sly smile. "How much can you bench?"

"More than you," answered Smith, warily. He reached over and lifted Nick's arm effortlessly, then let it drop. "Why?"

"Because I need your help," Nick answered, gauging the circumference of his arms to be less than half that of the other detective's. "Try and lift this pew."

Smith bent down, squared his shoulders and aligned his back and heaved, lifting the side of the pew less than six inches off of the ground. Finally, after trying to hold it for a few seconds, he eased the pew back down into place.

"Man, that thing's got to be four to five hundred pounds all together," he said, straightening himself.

"Yeah," Nick muttered in agreement. "But to move the end a couple of inches would take what, two to three hundred pounds of force, right?"

"I guess," Smith said with a shrug. "Why all the fuss?"

"Take a look at this pew here," Nick said, leading the other man down the row. "See how it's not quite in line with the others. You don't think that could have been by common parishioner foot traffic. I think this was where Father Allun was attacked. Allun paused here as he was walking back from the altar; he stopped when the power went out. The killer ran at him from a right angle to this point."

"But how did the killer navigate pews in the dark?" Smith asked.

"He didn't," Nick continued. "He jumped up on this pew, using it to catapult him up onto Allun."

"Which explains the few inches of misalignment," Smith said, finishing Nick's thought. "Yes I guess it's possible, but how could you possibly know that for certain."

"I don't," Nick answered. "But these kinds of guesses usually turn out to be right."

"Well," Smith began. "You didn't have to call me down here just to show me this. I would have believed you over the phone."

"There's more," Nick said. "I met with the Governor this morning. He wants New London to take over the case. We don't want to take this out of your hands, but Haisley is concerned about negative press."

"So you called me down here to boot me off in person?" Smith asked, his irritation showing through. "Let me bow down and show you my appreciation."

"We're not taking over," Nick promised. "But to appease everyone, my lieutenant wants us to work together. This is still your case, and I am still consulting. This way, everyone feels like they got what they want."

"What do you want?" Smith asked, eyeing the young detective suspiciously.

"I just want to catch the wack-job who is responsible for this," Nick answered. "And I want to keep my eye on a certain reporter who is out for police blood."

"Who, that reporter for NBC?" asked Smith. "He sure didn't make any effort to make us look good last night."

"Nor will he," Nick answered. "In fact, he's going to try and squeeze us every chance he gets. He and I have history."

"Well, maybe you two lovebirds should get some couples therapy," Smith suggested sarcastically. "In the meantime, what do we do about the case?"

"We go and see a doctor about a wax problem," Nick said with a smile. He then turned and waved for Smith to follow him out of the cathedral.

"Just as long as it's not earwax that we're talking about," Smith said as he followed along.

"I have a friend who works at Yale University," Nick said. "She's a forensic specialist, very well known in her field."

"You don't mean Dr. Sarrucci?" Smith asked.

"You know her?" Nick asked.

"Yeah," Smith answered. "She testified for the prosecution at a couple of homicide cases I've worked on. You?"

"She and I have been good friends since high school," Nick answered. "Well, at least we'll all know each other. Hopefully that will help us to get some answers sooner."

The two detectives climbed into Nick's car and made their way out of Norwich to the backwoods towns to meet up with Dr. Sarrucci and, Nick hoped, to start to shed some light on this case.

CHAPTER 22

Dr. Jessica Sarrucci was one of the foremost experts in the forensic world, having developed and refined many techniques that were now common practice in forensic analysis. Sarrucci had testified in countless court cases, many of which were high profile, and had become quite the celebrity in her field. Now, she had settled to a quite life of teaching as a professor at Yale, though she still lent her expertise as a consultant to both prosecutors and defendants alike. On top of being a world famous forensic scientist, she was also a life long friend of Grenier's going back to elementary school. Sarrucci lived in a small, quiet town outside of Norwich. It took Nick less than fifteen minutes to drive out to his friend's house. Once there, he and Detective Smith made their way up the porch, only to be greeted at the door by Sarrucci herself.

"Well, if it isn't the infamous Detective Grenier," Sarrucci said sarcastically as she opened the door. "It's about time you came out to visit me."

"I'm a busy man," Nick responded. "It's tough maintaining my infamous status."

"It's no trouble for you at all," she said with a knowing smile. "You and the word infamous go hand in hand. Who have you brought with you?"

"Detective Kevin Smith," Nick began as he turned to his colleague. "This is Dr. Jessica Sarrucci."

"You look very familiar to me," Sarrucci said, examining the man who was a giant compared to the petite scientist. "I was a state witness at one of your cases, wasn't I?"

"Yes ma'am," Smith answered respectfully, surprised at Sarrucci's memory. "It was the case where a Chinese immigrant family was murdered."

"I remember," Sarrucci said. "It was a horrible case. Please call me Jessica, calling me ma'am makes me feel very old."

Sarrucci showed the detectives into her living room and offered them both something to drink. They both declined, and after reminiscing a little about old times, they sat down in the living room. Immediately, Nick and his old friend jumped into school stories, and Sarrucci told Smith about the many times Nick got himself into and out of trouble as a teenager. Soon it felt as though they were all old friends reminiscing about more innocent days. But the real reason they were all here was always a dark cloud in the background. Nick tried to skirt the issue for as long as he could, but eventually they ran out of stories and were left with the thick case file which seemed to Nick like a lead weight. He could tell Sarrucci was already interested as she stole glances at it every now and then. Finally, Nick set the case file down on the table in front of her.

"So detectives, what do you have for me?" Sarrucci asked.

"I'm sure by now you've heard about Father Allun's murder," Nick began. "Detective Smith caught the case, and I have been called in to consult. There was some information discovered by the crime scene team that I thought you might be able to help us with."

Sarrucci opened the file gingerly and removed all of the reports, and spread the photos over the table in the order they were detailed in the autopsy report. She put the forensic reports to the side for a moment, and concentrated on the autopsy report. She read the report for five minutes, going over the details and the photos together; but to Nick and Kevin Smith who were barely able to contain their anticipation, it felt like forever. Smith himself was in awe of Nick; to have such a valuable resource to consult whenever he needed was an advantage any detective would love to have. That, combined with his unique ability to see through crimes, made it obvious to Smith why Nick had an unblemished record of solving murders. Finally, Sarrucci placed the report down in front of her and sighed.

"Well," she started. "You have a sick, angry killer out there. This was a very emotional killing. Your guy wasn't satisfied with killing Allun; he had to torture him first. Your killer is filled with pain and anger, but I'm sure that you've heard all of this from your own people. I'm not sure what I can tell you that might be different or more helpful."

"We were actually more interested in your views of the forensic report," Smith said, turning the scientist's attention to the report just to her left. "Particularly, the report about a piece of wax found in the victim's thigh."

Sarrucci gathered up the report and began reading again. This time, the detectives could sense her mounting interest as she continued to read on down the page.

"Seven hundred years old?" she asked incredulously.

"That's what our forensic experts said," Smith answered. "And I think they're pretty good, after all, you trained them."

Sarrucci looked up from the report for a moment and smiled.

"I've trained most of the forensic examiners in this state," she answered. "How good they are after they leave school depends greatly on how they treat their job. If they treat it as just a job, then they are not going to be very good. If they treat it as a career, as an extension of their lives, then you might just have some very good people."

"Back to the wax," Nick said, trying to bring the conversation back on point.

"I wish there was a picture of it here," Sarrucci said, flipping through the images she had already viewed.

"Underneath the report," Nick said. "There's an actual size image and a digital enhancement so that you can more accurately see the image on the wax."

Sarrucci found the two pictures and held the first in one hand and the report in the other. She then placed the photo down and took up the enhanced image. The moment she brought the picture up to her face she gasped, and placed the photos side by side. She looked back and forth between them for a moment, then back to the report.

"Your people are certain about the age of the wax?" she asked without looking up. "Seven hundred years?"

"They couldn't be exact, but they said between six and seven hundred years," Smith answered. "The test was repeated and confirmed by two forensic examiners and their supervisor."

"What is it?" Nick asked insistently.

"This all makes perfect sense now," she said, as if having a conversation with someone else in the room. "My evaluation of your killer is all wrong."

"How do you know?" Nick asked, unable to contain himself. "I need you to explain this to me."

"The wax is a stamp," Sarrucci began. "It was used to seal official documents for hundreds of years. Each stamp had a seal, crest, or an image that represented the family name of the person who had written the document. I'm shocked that wax from the period survived this long. It must have been kept preserved by someone familiar in the techniques of preservation and conservation."

"The stamp?" Nick asked. At this point he could not care less about the wax. Sarrucci's response to the report led him to believe the stamp was the important clue.

"The stamp is the personal seal of Tomas de Torquemada," Sarrucci answered. "Torquemada was the leader of the Spanish Inquisition."

Nick and his fellow detective sat back a little, as if crest fallen. Sarrucci found their response to be very anti-climactic, as she was nearly jubilant over the finding.

"It's obvious you two need a refresher course in the history of the medieval age," Sarrucci said. She rose from her chair and began talking as if teaching her students in a Yale lecture hall. "The Spanish Inquisition was started in Spain by the Catholic church. The Church was concerned about the growing numbers and power base of the Jews of the period. They weren't only scared of how many Jews were moving into Europe, the church was also concerned about the possibility of large groups of people converting to Judaism. The Spanish Inquisition is made more famous than other inquisitions because of the wide use of torture at the time."

Sarrucci looked back at her two students and smiled. Both were captivated by her words and she could see the gears turning in their minds as they took her words and applied them to the case at hand.

"Any person could denounce their neighbor, enemy, and even family member as a heretic and the church would 'investigate'," Sarrucci continued. "Now when I say investigate, I use the term loosely, as they did not really check into the past of the accused to see if there was any substance to the allegations. The Church felt that the only way to convert the heretic and purge the evil thinking that was Judaism was to torture them, and let me tell you, they came up with some pretty interesting ideas. The accused was not just burned at the stake publicly, for there was no assurance that they would confess and repent before death. No, the monks needed to be sure that the accused would repent. They devised devices that caused so much pain, while keeping the victim alive that he or she would confess to anything to stop the pain. There was the Judas chair, which was a chair with a pyramid shaped device that could be inserted into the rectum or genitalia, painfully stretching the particular opening. There was the head vice, which should need no explanation. There was the glove, which was a device that crushed the bones in the fingers and hands. There was The Pear, which was like the Judas chair except that there were little spikes that shot out once the device had expanded fully in the orifice of choice. For those stubborn individuals who would not confess easily, there was disembowelment. The monks would cut a small opening into the abdomen and methodically pull out the intestines, keeping the victim alive for as long as possible. Finally, after the accused had 'confessed' and repented, they would be burned at the stake. The sad part is this wasn't confined to just Spain; millions died."

"Jesus Christ," Smith said absently as his mind processed the graphic visual images that he translated from Sarrucci's words.

"It's funny you should say that," Sarrucci said as she sat back down. "Jesus was a Jew. I wonder what they would have done to Him."

"Wait a minute," Nick said, scrambling forward to pull the photos in front of him. He flipped through the images as he spoke. "The Judas chair, the head vice, the glove, burning. The killer did to Allun everything that was done in the inquisition."

"Yes," Sarrucci said. "And I'll bet that your killer tried to make the torture itself as historically accurate as possible. If he used authentic wax from the period, I'll bet he re-created the devices in remarkable detail."

"But where would you get this kind of information?" Nick asked. "I can't imagine you can just go online and find it."

"My guess is he got the information from the same place he got the wax," Sarrucci said. "This wax has probably been stored in some Catholic archive, and I wouldn't be surprised if it was in the main archive in the Vatican City. How your killer got his hands on them is a mystery, but if anyone could have, it would be someone affiliated with the Church, closely affiliated."

"Jesus," Smith repeated under his breath.

"Detectives," Sarrucci began, making sure she had both of their full attention. "This killer is highly educated, methodical, and exacting. The precision, determination and time needed to fully torture Father Allun without giving into his pleas would take a great deal of mental fortitude on anyone's part. Also, your killer is trying to send a message, he is making a point to someone; someone who was certain to see how Allun ended up. Lastly, your killer means business, and he will kill again."

CHAPTER 23

Nick and Smith drove back to Norwich, neither man speaking as they contemplated the weight of her words and what it meant for their investigation. Nick felt forced to rethink his entire evaluation of the motive in this case. So far, Nick had been flirting between the ideas that the murder was motivated by hatred for the Church, or against Father Allun directly. Now Nick was uncertain of whether either idea was true, or that both were. The motive seemed so unusually nebulous to the detective and on top of all of that, he was haunted by Sarrucci's final words. *He will kill again.* The silence from his colleague was equally chilling. He couldn't help but wonder what was going on in the mind of the other detective.

"What are you thinking about?" Smith asked, as if reading the mind of the other detective.

"I can't get her words out of my head," Nick answered. "I'm particularly bothered by the fact that she thinks the murder of Allun is a message for someone."

"So what do you think?" Smith repeated.

"We need to focus the investigation on some very specific points," Nick began. "First, we need to find out everything we can about Father Allun, and I mean everything there is to know. I want to know where he comes from, what school he attended, where he grew up, and every assignment he has had with the church since he was ordained. Second, I want to know the schedule of every person who works for and with the church, where everyone was the day Allun was attacked and abducted, where they were through the weekend, and when Allun was found hanging in the cathedral. Finally, we need to find out where the wax came from and try to find the stamp. If we can find out where it came from, we might be able to find the killer."

"It sounds like you suspect someone in the church," Smith said.

"I don't know," Nick answered. "I think we'll have a better idea after we talk to someone in the diocese itself."

"You think they're just going to let us go into the church and poke around?" Smith asked. "They're going to fight us every step of the way, even if they aren't hiding something."

"So you think they're hiding something?" Nick asked, smiling.

"I'm not an idiot," Smith replied. "Sarrucci said the type of death and manner in which Allun was displayed was a message for someone. If that's the case, it was for someone who would see him like that, someone in the Church. However, if that is the case, they are not going to be forthcoming."

"I'm sure the Church doesn't want to be labeled as interfering in a police investigation," Nick commented.

"We're talking politics here," Smith reminded him. "The Church isn't just St. Patrick's Cathedral. The Church is everything Catholic right up to the Vatican. They will protect themselves and their power no matter what, not to mention the fact that the Church may not be involved whatsoever. You know there is this thing called innocent until proven guilty. I tell you, the more I think about this case, the more it gives me a headache."

"I know what you mean," Nick said. "As for the Church, I don't care about their guilt or innocence; I just care about finding this killer. Sarrucci said that he'll strike again, and she's not usually wrong. The Church holds some clues; we just have to find them."

The two detectives sat in silence for a few minutes, thinking about the same thing. They needed a way in, a way to convince the diocese to allow them unfettered access to everyone working in and with the church.

"Walk softly and carry a big stick," Smith muttered under his breath.

"What?" Nick asked, confused.

"We need to have a secret weapon before we go in there," Smith answered. "We need to know everything that they could possibly tell us about Allun before they tell us."

"Catch them in a lie before they tell it," Nick said, following the detective's logic.

"That's if they tell a lie," Smith said. "I feel as though we are being particularly tough on the diocese before they've done anything wrong."

"I know what you mean," Nick said. "But you have to admit, they're reputation for cooperation isn't that good."

Nick drove Smith down to the New London Police Department where they spent the next few hours gathering any information they could on Father Allun. Michael Allun was born to privilege in Boston. His parents were bankers who inherited the family business from Allun's grandparents. The family business was three generations strong, and even in this time of economic decline, the bank seemed to still be going strong as more branches were popping up all over New England. Allun's siblings ran the business, though everyone in the family profited from it, and Allun received a percentage of the banks earnings every month. Simply put, Allun was worth a fortune. After high school Allun went to Notre Dame, and was ordained as a priest the year after he graduated. He was immediately posted back in Boston, but after a year and a half, was asked to fill a post in the Norwich diocese. Just before he moved, Allun took a three month vacation.

"Take a look at this," Smith said as he entered Nick's office. "Before he took up the post in Norwich, the good father purchased a round trip flight to Rome, returning three months later."

"He went to the Vatican," Nick said, leaning back in his chair. "If the stamp was in the Vatican archives, what are the chances that he was able to take it out of there?"

"From what I hear, not very good," Smith answered. "Just being a priest doesn't give you unfettered access to the Vatican city. Just to view the items in the archive he would have had to pull a lot of strings, and to actually get a historic item out of there would have been next to impossible. Besides, wouldn't it have been the killer who would have brought the stamp?"

"I don't know," Nick answered. "It's the only theory that comes close to fitting the facts at hand. I did find something interesting though. Apparently, Father Allun owned a home in Norwich."

"But the priests told us he lived there at the cathedral," Smith said. "They said he lived there on the premises."

"They lied," Nick answered. "Or they didn't know. Either way, we need to get into his home and have CSU tear the place apart. We also need to find his car."

"How do you know he had a car?" asked Smith.

"Well, he had to get back and forth somehow," Nick answered. "It should be relatively easy to get DMV to do a search for any vehicle registered to a Michael Allun."

"This whole case seems very strange to me," Smith said, looking down at the floor and speaking as though to himself. "Why would Allun want to move from the Boston diocese his hometown, to Norwich where he knew no one? Why was he reassigned so abruptly? According to the information we obtained, he did not ask for a transfer. He was doing very high profile work for the church in Boston, and everyone seemed pleased with the results. Here is a priest whose family name runs deep in the roots of the city, politically and socially, who is doing good work and bringing positive credit on a diocese that is still in desperate need of good press after the sex scandals of a few years ago. Why move him so suddenly? Why move him at all? It just doesn't make sense."

"Nothing in this case makes sense, yet," Nick answered, shuffling some papers into a manila folder and placing it on top of the actual case file. "But I think it's time we went and got ourselves some answers."

"Who are we going to be asking the questions of?" Smith asked, suddenly interested.

"Anyone who has answers, whether they know they do or not," Nick answered. "We're going to talk to the priests."

"How are we going to play this?" Smith asked, following Nick as they headed out of the Investigation Unit and down the stairs to the parking lot.

"Why good cop, bad cop, of course," Nick answered with a smile.

"Excellent," Smith said, smashing his balled up fist into the palm of his open hand. "Who gets to be bad cop?"

"I do," Nick answered without hesitation. "You've got to be the hero. You live there, you work there. The priests need to count on you to be sensitive and compassionate to their needs. Trust me; it'll only help you out in the end."

"Yeah alright," Smith answered, acting as though he were sulking. "It's just that, I never get to be bad cop."

"Don't worry," Nick said with a smile. "I'm sure you'll have your chance before this is all over."

CHAPTER 24

It was already after two in the afternoon when Nick eased the car off of Interstate 395 and drifted through Norwich, making his way back to the cathedral. Unfortunately, the detective's work was far from over. After identifying the house owned by Allun, Smith spent much of the ride north talking to CSU and the district attorney's office, getting all necessary warrants and documents ready to give them permission to search the house and collect evidence. Smith also called the Department of Motor Vehicles to start a search for any vehicle registered to Michael Allun. Nick remained silent throughout the drive, listening as Smith conducted police business on his cell phone and happily reminding himself that this was not officially his case. Though he was pleased to work it, he was also happy to leave all the real grunt work to Smith and his people in Norwich. Nick finally pulled the car into the parking lot of the St. Patrick's Cathedral and shut off the engine. Both detectives eased out of the car, and Nick looked around briefly before making his way inside. The police perimeter had already shrunk from this morning and was now just the building itself. All side roads were open and the only evidence of a police presence were the two squad cars parked in front of the cathedral and the two uniformed officers talking at the top of the steps. Both detectives showed their badges, and entered.

Nick and Detective Smith made their way through the dark hallways that were off to the side of the main gallery to the offices that lay off to the back of the building. They were met by a secretary, possibly a nun though neither man could tell for sure as she wore regular clothing. They were told to have a seat and she would announce them. As the minutes dragged on, Nick began to understand what was going on. The priests knew why the detectives had called for this meeting, and rightly assumed that the detectives were here to get information on Father Allun, as well as access to the victim's living space. He knew the priests would demand a timetable for opening the church, and Nick was not ready to make any promises; not when everyone was still a suspect. Nick hoped that they would not be prepared for the fact that he had done his own digging and would have more ammunition on his side than they did. After waiting for just over five minutes, the doors opened and an older man dressed in black stepped through the threshold.

"Detectives," he said formally. Both rose and stepped up to the priest. "I am Father Jeffrey Thomas, personal assistant to the bishop. My colleagues and I have assembled to give you any help that you need. Please follow me."

The detectives followed the older man through the door and into a conference room, where Nick immediately realized that he and his partner were outnumbered. Nine priests sat around a long, rectangular conference table and stared up at the two police officers as they were shown to their seats. Father Thomas made his way slowly around the other men to his own seat at the head of the table, and sat down.

"Now," Father Thomas began. "What can we do to help you in your investigation?"

"You can start by giving us all the information you have on Father Allun, his personnel files and anything else that might help us get a better idea who he was."

"Who he was?" asked one of the priests. "He was a priest of this church and a faithful servant of God and of the community."

Nick smiled as if prepared for the line.

"He wasn't always a priest," Nick answered, staring the other man down. "We are looking for any information pertaining to any prior assignments he might have had with the church, groups and charity events that he helped with, and any personal information that you might have on the man."

"We had a feeling that you were going to need that information," Thomas said, pushing a thin file forward. The file was slid along the table by each member of the clergy until it stopped in front of Nick. The file was much thinner than the preliminary file Nick had begun back at the Investigation Unit. The words, *Cover up*, rung in his mind. Nick sifted through the file quickly as he shot off other questions.

"It says here Allun began his work in the Boston diocese, but was transferred here shortly after," Nick said, as if reading the information off of the page. In fact, he had memorized it from his own file as had he planned the sequence of questions that were about to unfold. "Why was he transferred so soon after his first assignment? Was the transfer his idea or the diocese's?"

"The expansion of the Indian casinos has caused an explosion in the population of Norwich," Thomas began without missing a beat. "The majority of the people who are moving to Norwich are poor immigrant families who do not speak much English and have little or nothing to start off with. These people turn to the church for help. Bishop McAllister thought our diocese could use more help and requested a young, energetic priest who could reach out and connect with our changing community."

Nick took a deep yawn as he continued reading, not bothering to look up from the information he was given.

"Sounds like it came straight from a pamphlet," Nick said. "How long did it take you to come up with that press release?"

"Detective, please," Smith said softly, immediately falling into the role of the good cop. "I'm sorry, please continue."

"As to your second question," Thomas started, immediately turning all of his attention to the more respectful detective. "We priests do not question the orders of the Vatican."

"Nor should a priest who is so young and naïve," muttered one of the others. Both detectives picked up on the condescending tone of the priest, as well as the soft chuckle bellowing from around the table. Nick understood immediately; Allun wasn't liked.

"I think that we've shown our intent to be honest and forthcoming by answering all of your questions," Thomas started. "Now I was wondering if we could get some answers of our own."

"Two," Nick muttered, again without looking up from the file.

"Excuse me, detective?" Thomas asked, his annoyance beginning to show through his priestly demeanor.

"We've asked two questions," Nick stated, staring directly into the eyes of Father Thomas. "And you've answered two questions. You said 'all of your questions' as if we've been sitting here for hours interrogating you all. I just wanted to set the record straight, but please, ask your questions."

Father Thomas frowned for a moment, but regained his composure quickly.

"We would like to know when we can open the church again," Thomas began. "The people of this community look to us for spiritual guidance, now more than ever. We can't sit here shut down indefinitely."

Smith spent five minutes placating their concerns as Nick threw in some grunts and groans to show his annoyance at having their schedule dictated to by the church. As planned, Smith showed he was in charge of the case and made it sound like he was making the decisions without actually giving them any clear idea when the church would be able to re-open to the public. The priests also asked when Allun's body would be released so that they could hold a public service. With his eyes firmly glued on the pages of the personnel folder, Nick had to silently acknowledge how well Smith was playing his part. He was bending over and taking it from them while making it sound like he was in charge of everything. The clergy members were feeling like they were back in charge of the situation when Nick felt as though it was time to step in and shatter their confidence.

"Please don't worry," Smith said as Nick slowly closed the file so as not to attract any attention. "The police department is not blind to your needs, nor out of tune with your concerns. We want to catch this killer with as little disruption as possible to the church and the community."

"This is bullshit!" Nick shouted, bolting out of his chair and throwing the file down in front of Thomas. Smith was out of his chair in a heartbeat, his thick frame colliding with the smaller detective's.

"Detective," Smith started with a more commanding tone. "These are priests. Show some respect."

"Why should we show them any respect?" Nick asked, yelling his question at Thomas directly. "They're lying out of their asses. For one thing, we already know Allun's move was ordered by the Boston diocese. There was no request from this end. They think we're stupid cops who couldn't find our way out of a paper bag without their help."

"If you don't like your assignment to this case," Thomas began. "I'm sure calls can be made as high up as the Governor's office to move you onto something you might be more interested in."

Thomas sat there with a superior smile that made Nick teeter between wanting to laugh in the priest's face or knock his teeth out. However, Nick knew that he now had the upper hand, and reached into his pocket to retrieve his cell phone.

"Really?" asked the detective, pressing numbers into the pad of his phone. "Well let's see what he says then, shall we. I only spoke to him this morning when he officially assigned me to this investigation."

Suddenly, all eyes began looking nervous and flittered back and forth between the detective and Father Thomas.

"Yes, this is Detective Grenier and Father Thomas of the Norwich diocese calling to speak to Governor Haisley regarding the Allun murder," Nick said into the phone. "Sure I'll hold."

Nick then turned his attention back to Father Thomas.

"I mean, you could be right," Nick said, patronizing the older man. "He might give a shit more about what you think than the public's overwhelming desire to catch a killer. I might just be stone cold wrong. Let's just see."

"That won't be necessary," said a deep voice from behind the detective. Nick turned to find a much older man casually dressed in jeans and a University of Connecticut sweatshirt standing in the doorway. "Nick, it's good to see you again. It's been a long time."

"It certainly has, Bishop," Nick responded, a flood of emotion and memories surging to the surface as he laid eyes on the man for the first time in nearly ten years. "You're looking well."

"Why don't you and your colleague take a walk with me," the bishop began. "Let's see if we can answer your questions without bothering the Governor."

Nick just stared back at him for a moment, then focused quickly on the older man's words and pressed the END button on his cell phone, cutting the call short.

"I think we can do that," Nick said, and turned his head to the side to signal Smith that they should follow the bishop who was already making his way down the corridor, leaving the astonished priests alone in the conference room, wondering exactly what was about to happen next.

CHAPTER 25

The two detectives followed closely behind Bishop Andrew McAllister as he made his way through the narrow halls that led from the offices out to the open manicured gardens on the cathedral grounds. McAllister stopped for a moment, inhaled deeply and smiled. He then continued on, making his way over to a cast iron and wood bench on one side of a stone path. Nick and Smith took a seat on the bench directly across from the bishop, all eyeing one another; all waiting for someone to speak. Nick wondered briefly how many meetings McAllister had out here in the privacy of the gardens, away from inner workings of the church and the gossip and politics of its clergy. McAllister seemed older to Nick, older and wiser like a grandfather would look. There was nothing infirm about the bishop. In fact, there was something even more commanding about him than there had been the last time they met, ten years before. Nick was amazed to see McAllister looked at him in just the same way he had then; there was no anger, malice or judgment in the older man's eyes. Though Nick had chosen a different road than the bishop had wanted him to a decade before, Nick had always felt as though he had betrayed the old man in some way, though McAllister did not judge him. There was only the loving concern that there had always been. It was in the moment that Nick realized he couldn't look the other man in the eye.

"So I take it from your little comments earlier that you know each other," Smith said, feeling as though they would all sit there in silence unless he took the initiative.

"Nick used to be a member of the congregation when he was younger," McAllister said, never taking his eyes off of the younger man. "He had a crisis of faith ten years ago that I tried to counsel him through."

"That was a long time ago," Nick said, conjuring a fake smile to hide his discomfort with the conversation topic.

"Not so long that you don't still carry the pain with you," McAllister observed. "You see Detective Smith, the man you see here is not the man that I knew as a teenager. The hard exterior of this man has been reinforced through many years of pain, not unlike your own past."

Nick looked up at Smith, not expecting this change in the conversation's focus.

"It pleases me to see the two of you working together on this case," McAllister said. "I think you could learn a lot from each other."

"We need some answers regarding Father Allun," Nick started, switching the conversation back to the reason they were gathered there. "If we are going to catch this killer, we are going to need to know everything there is to know."

"Allun was a very driven priest," McAllister said. "He was also one of the most passionate believers I had ever known. He was a man with a vision, and whether it was right or wrong, he was going to see his vision through to the end. However, if you want to know everything there is to know about Father Michael Allun, you are going to need to do most of the digging yourself. He was a private man, and I don't think anyone truly knew everything there was to know, save God."

"Why was Allun transferred here?" Smith asked.

"Much of Allun's vision had to do with his advancement through the ranks of the Catholic Church," McAllister answered. "He could have done good works for years and years in Boston and never get recognized or singled out for his efforts with so many priests vying for attention. However, here in a smaller diocese, he was able to make himself much more visible through his efforts. He knew that positive media attention would help secure his path to advancement, and a man with his resources was able to do many high profile 'events'. That was how he had become such a beloved figure here in a short period of time. We were his little experiment, so to speak."

"What do you know about Allun's little vacation to the Vatican before coming here?" Nick asked while processing the information McAllister provided. He felt as though the bishop was speaking in riddles, as if every answer only bred more questions.

"From what I understand, Allun went to Rome to smooth things over with the powers that be," answered the bishop. "He had caused problems for the diocese and was not particularly liked when he left Boston. Allun went directly to the Vatican to make sure his career was still on its way up. Whatever happened there, he came back more certain of himself than ever."

"I couldn't help but notice a certain level of contempt from his colleagues here," Smith observed. "He didn't seem to make any friends here either."

"It was no secret why Allun was here," McAllister said. "I don't think the other priests prescribed to Allun's way of thinking. However, if you are thinking that someone in our diocese disliked him enough to kill him, I can't help but think you are mistaken. The priests here are at the end of their careers. They are looking for a quiet place to do God's work and be respected until they die. The only ambitious man left here is Father Thomas, who wants my job when I get promoted or die. Allun was no threat to Thomas, as he had no intention of being a lowly bishop."

Nick couldn't help but smile at the term "lowly bishop". However, he was beginning to get a better understanding of his victim.

"If you really think the murderer is related in some way to the church, I would begin my search in the Boston diocese," McAllister suggested off hand. "There was much more animosity there."

Just then Smith's cell phone began to ring, and he rose and excused himself for a moment and walked a few steps away.

"You were really tough on Father Thomas in there," McAllister noted. "Did you really call the Governor's office?"

"I can't lie to you," Nick said, shaking his head. "It was a bluff. If he had insisted on talking to the Governor, he would have been happily disappointed. The highest person he would have talked to on that call was my lieutenant."

"So you can't lie to a bishop but you can lie to a priest?" McAllister asked with a playful smile across his face.

"Father Thomas started it," Nick fired back.

"Yes he did," acknowledged the bishop. "It's unfortunate that a priest's job lately has more to do with protecting the church than guiding its congregation. Allun was a strange man, with some very wild beliefs, but while he was here, he did help a lot of people. That's something that must not be forgotten in the course of your investigation."

Nick sat up straight all of a sudden and looked hard at McAllister.

"What are you trying to tell me?" Nick asked. It was just at that moment that Smith walked back over and interrupted the two men.

"That was CSU," Smith informed his colleague, selecting his words carefully in the company they were in. "They need us to head over."

Bishop McAllister rose and shook hands with both detectives, all the while maintaining eye contact with Nick, letting the detective know that he realized he had not answered his question.

"I hope you remember everything I've said here," McAllister said as they parted. "And don't hesitate to call me if you need any 'guidance'."

Nick was confused, but was more interested in what McAllister was not saying. It kept him from following up with any further questions as he began to follow Smith towards the parking lot. Suddenly, Nick remembered one last question and stopped. When he turned, he found McAllister standing just where he had been, watching the detectives walk away.

"How hard would it have been for Allun to get into the archives at the Vatican?" Nick asked. For a moment, McAllister appeared to be genuinely caught off guard by the question.

"Next to impossible," the bishop answered. "There is a particular order that handles materials that go into the archives. I couldn't even get in to see the holy relics."

"So then it would have been literally impossible for him to remove something from there, right?" Nick asked, following up.

"Absolutely," McAllister answered. "The only person who could remove something permanently would be the Pope himself. Why do you ask?"

Nick smiled and turned on his heel, catching up with Smith who was only a few steps ahead. They left the bishop standing there, contemplating the question long after they left the grounds. They both headed to their individual cars, as this was where Smith had left his vehicle when they met up earlier that morning.

"What did you think of his answers?" Smith asked, unlocking the driver's side door of his car.

"I think everything he told us was true," Nick answered back over the hood of his own car. "It's what he didn't tell us that I am particularly interested in. He left a lot of things out purposefully."

"Well, then it's a good thing we are so good at reading between the lines," Smith said. "That was CSU by the way. They said they have found some things at Allun's house that we might find particularly interesting and they want us to tell them what to bag and bring back for analysis from his house."

"Well my friend, it appears our day is far from done," Nick said, then climbed in his car and turned the key in the ignition. Both he and Smith pulled out of the parking lot and headed off to Allun's house, both contemplating individually the meaning of the bishop's words.

CHAPTER 26

Nick drove quietly through the backstreets of Norwich, absently navigating the roads of his hometown as he made his way to Father Allun's home. His mind was not on the case at hand, nor was it there in the car. He was thinking about the town itself, he was thinking about the decay of this quiet town that he had once called home. There had been a dramatic change over the course of the last ten years, and it had begun with the arrival of the first Indian casino. There were two Indian casinos in Connecticut; one, about ten miles outside of Norwich and the second just on the outskirts of the town itself. The development and expansion of both casinos had caused a surge in the population of Norwich and the surrounding area. No one could have been prepared for the number of people who would come to the area to seek jobs. It was this sudden population explosion that was causing the town to sink lower and lower into despair. As Nick pulled into the quiet neighborhood where Allun had secretly lived, he felt that he was entering one of the last havens left that held any history to the town Nick remembered.

From the view of the untrained eye, the town might seem as though it were actually prospering. New stores, shopping plazas, and restaurants were popping up all the time, but to those people who knew what the town had once been like, it was obvious that everything new was the real problem. The casinos were hiring employees right and left, working them long and hard while providing stability and benefits. However, the low salaries these employees were taking home caused a strain on the local businesses, as no one could afford to pay the prices for goods. Businesses had been forced to adapt by lowering their prices, and in doing so, had to cut the salaries of their own employees to keep from going under. The ripple effect was endless, and no one went untouched by it. The town also found tourism on the rise as more and more people came to the casinos, so restaurants and motels began popping up overnight, each trying to undercut the prices of their local competitors. Quality gave way to the urgency of demand, and it was the image of the town that suffered. Sadly, these were just some of the issues that plagued the town, and while it tried to keep up with the expansion, the influx of immigrants, both legal and illegal, and the decline in personal lifestyle; no one could see the city as it began to sink in on itself. To Nick, it was like seeing a loved one after a long separation; only then could one see how old and frail the other had become.

Nick pulled his vehicle over to the side of the road, across the street from the address Detective Smith had provided him. This was a beautiful quiet neighborhood, not unlike the one that Nick had grown up in. In these quiet neighborhoods, with their neatly manicured lawns and perfectly tarred driveways; it was easy to forget what was happening to the rest of the town. Standing here now, watching the bustle of law enforcement and crime scene personnel, Nick could understand what the appeal had been for Father Allun when he purchased his home here. The activity around the house had caused a commotion in the neighborhood, with Allun's nieghbors standing in their lawns watching. Nick crossed the street and made his way up the driveway to the front of the house. Smith was standing in the doorway with a crime scene kit in his hand, extending it out to the other detective.

"You know the drill," Smith said with a disappointed look on his face. "I'm kind of wondering now if we should have come here ourselves before alerting CSU."

"Doesn't matter now," Nick said. "What's done is done. I just hope there is something to find here."

"The bishop gave us some direction," Smith said. "It's a start."

"Some direction?" asked Nick as he donned his protective shoe coverings and latex free gloves. "He hinted around and pointed us in a hundred directions. He didn't give us one solid thing to go off of."

"Don't start getting down on me," Smith said. "This is only day two, the investigation is still in its infancy."

"And we have no real clues," Nick reminded his colleague. "We need to find something solid and we need to do it quickly."

The detectives spent hours stepping around the crime scene technicians as they looked for anything that might point them in the right direction. While CSU dusted every surface in the house for fingerprints, Nick and Smith concentrated on the personal things in the bedroom and the study. However, there was very little evidence that Allun actually lived there. Everything was neat and orderly, all magazines and knick-knacks perfectly aligned and in their place, and even CSU was frustrated with the lack of prints they found.

"CSU has pulled only three sets of prints so far," Smith informed the other detective. "It's ridiculous. Why pay for a home and not live here. There's got to be something we're missing."

"There is," Nick assured him. "This house was a haven for Allun, but it was also a liability. He stayed here as little as possible, and yet everything is perfectly neat and I can't find a trace of dust. There are even vacuum cleaner tracks on the carpet; and rather fresh I might add."

"What are you getting at?" Smith asked, failing to follow the detective's logic.

"If Allun really didn't stay here that often, why did he need to have it cleaned regularly?" Nick asked, looking around the rooms. "He was trying to keep up appearances. He was using this house for something else, something that didn't jive with his professional life."

Just then, a member of the crime scene unit stepped into the master bedroom.

"You need to come downstairs to the garage," the young man said. "I think we found what you were looking for."

The two detectives followed the younger man down the steps and through the long hallway to the inside entrance to the garage. Nick stopped and smiled as he inspected the door.

"Three deadbolts, two chains, and the lock in the doorknob," Nick said. "All locked from inside the garage itself."

"It looks as if he were trying to keep something locked up inside," Smith said.

"Or trying to keep someone within the house from getting into the garage," Nick said. "Whatever it is, this is what we've been looking for. The clues to his murder are here, I guarantee it."

The crime scene investigators worked at the locks, and finally decided to cut the chains and use the battering ram to knock the door open. On the inside of the door, there was another set of deadbolt locks. Nick couldn't help but notice the lengths Allun had gone in order to keep this room safe. Already, Smith was inside and examining the room, and when Nick rose from his cursory examination of the door he found himself unprepared for the sight that awaited him. Going from the prim and proper perfection of the rest of the house made stepping into the garage seem like the fictitious world of a movie set. The entire space had been closed in, and thick weather and sound insulation had been installed over all of the walls and over the area where the garage car doors had been. A row of simple desks and card tables had been assembled to create an "L" shape. Like in a studio, computers, digital video cameras, and digital voice recording equipment filled the desk space, with large flat screen monitors positioned in the corner of each desk. In front of the row of desks, a raised platform stage had been erected, and on the stage were two different themes.

"Heaven and hell," Smith said as he brushed past Nick to step up onto the stage. "It seems as though there was a lot more to our Father Allun than we thought."

The first theme on the staged platform was that of a simple, clean bedroom. There was a double bed on a standard metal frame in the middle of the platform. The walls, which were nothing more than heavy partitions, were painted white with a perfectly positioned picture on each wall. There was a dresser, painted white, to the left of the bed. Standing there, looking in, it seemed like a normal bedroom. However, the theme on the other side of the partition let the detectives know that there was nothing normal going on in this makeshift studio. The partitions on the second side of the stage were painted a dark red, almost crimson color. Leather straps hung down from the ceiling and lined the partitions. On the shelves that hugged the walls were more sexual toys and devices than Nick knew existed. Most of the devices had a sado-masochistic theme.

"Where the hell would someone get all of this shit?" asked Nick in a state of shock over all of the sexual instruments. He picked up one in his gloved hand and examined it, attempting to figure out what it did.

"S&M 'R Us," answered one of the crime scene techs who opened a drawer in the dresser of the makeshift bedroom to find it filled with personal lubricant.

Nick stepped off of the stage and looked around at all of the recording devices. From his vantage point, he noticed cameras on tripods and some positioned in the corners overhead.

"So he's taping himself having sex with someone?" Nick asked. "Or multiple people?"

"I just hope to God it's not kids," Smith said, examining the hanging straps as if wondering what a person would look like bound in them. "This town doesn't need that kind of problem."

"Uh, detectives," called one of the techs from a corner of the garage far from the stage. "I think you better take a look at this."

Nick and Smith made their way over to a large metal safe that stood upright against the wall. Inside were six shelves, the first three containing homemade DVD's while the last three shelves contained VCR and Beta. Each had an initial and a name, followed by a date on it; and Nick noted that the dates went back at least ten years. The detective stepped back from the safe and looked around the room.

"The safe was unlocked, I take it?" Nick asked the tech.

"The door was partially open," the tech answered. "I didn't even test the handle."

"So the killer finds this room, sees what's in the safe and kills Allun," Smith surmised. "That makes sense."

"How did he get in here?" asked Nick, shaking his head. "And if the killer had keys, then why go to all of the trouble to lock up the garage door and not take the time to close the safe completely?"

"Then what's your theory hotshot?" Smith asked sarcastically.

"I don't have one yet," Nick said. "But I think we're going to have to watch all of these tapes to figure out what was going on here. The killer might be on any one of these."

"Shit," said Smith. "I don't know if I can do it. I don't want to see what I think we're going to see."

"I don't think we have a choice," Nick answered. He then turned to the tech. "Collect all the movies and send them over to the Investigations Unit in New London. I want you to take all the hard drives and I want them examined. It's very possible that there are 'sessions' on the drives that haven't been put onto disks yet. Same goes with the video and audio recording equipment."

Nick watched as the techs began to follow his instructions, and then turned to Smith.

"There's nothing else we can do here tonight," Nick said. "CSU will be working late and they certainly don't need us standing over their shoulders. We'll meet back in New London tomorrow morning to start going through this crap."

Smith agreed and both detectives headed out of the garage to let the crime scene team begin their work. Just as Smith reached the door that led to the rest of the house, he stopped and turned back for one final look. He knew that he was not in control of this case, that in fact, this case was in control of him. Every time he and Nick looked for more answers, they were confronted with more and more questions. He sighed.

"And the hits just keep on coming."

CHAPTER 27

As Nick and Kevin Smith sifted through the videos and notes kept by Father Michael Allun, it became clear to them that the process was going to take a long time. A day turned into two days, and then two days became five and before they knew it a full week had gone by since Allun had been abducted and they still had very little clues. The detectives went from having no information to having too much. Allun had been meticulous in his record keeping, and though it would prove helpful in the end, the detectives were having difficulty processing what they had. Allun had been performing a bizarre experiment, having sex with women and men to reach some sort of existentialism during the heightened state of arousal. Allun's computer notes almost seemed scientific, and his theories and hypotheses strangely made sense to the detectives in a perverse sort of way. However, that clear scientific approach to the victim's thought process was lost when Nick and Kevin viewed the videos. The tapes showed consenting adults of all different ages, all different races and sexes, giving into Allun's charm and allowing him to push their sexual boundaries further and further. Never was Allun abusive or rough with his partners nor did they seem to be uncomfortable with what he was asking; in fact, there was a real feeling of caring for each that was obvious to the detectives as they sat in an interrogation room that had been converted to give the officer's more space. The one thing Nick had noticed was that in none of the videos did the partner seem to know that Allun was a priest.

Through the whole process of viewing tapes and cataloging information, the detectives were acutely aware that time was against them. The media attention on the case was reaching a near fever pitch as the reporter, Mark Anderson, had been stirring up the pot, turning public opinion against the police. Lt. Hollings' first response was to keep quiet and not give into the reporter's constant baiting. However, after a full week had gone by, Hollings knew the department was going to have to come up with something fast. Nick and Smith tried to put the pressures of the media out of their minds as they continued to wade through the evidence. Kevin was certain the killer was one of the people on the tapes, and though there did not seem to be any coercion or force to perform in the acts, the Norwich detective was certain that Allun was killed because of the *experiment* and the killer could be linked back to one of these people. The names on the video labels turned out to be last names and first initials, and during most of the sessions, Allun called his partner by name giving the detectives a little more help. Nick agreed that Allun was killed because of his tapes, but was not ready to pin the murder on one of Allun's partners. Nick was even less in agreement when Kevin stated they should be focusing on the male partners. He believed that the killer had to be a male because of the strength needed to overpower Allun; and though Nick agreed with his thinking regarding the sex of the killer, he felt as though there were more possible suspects out there than just these men.

"I hope you two have some good news for me because I've just been called up to the chief's office," Hollings stated as she breezed into the room. "I've been 'invited' to a telephone conference with the governor, who is very anxious to find out if we have made some progress and can make a statement to the press."

The lieutenant could tell by the expressions on the two detective's faces that they did not have an answer that would get her out of the hot water she was about to step into.

"You've got to be kidding me," she started. "You've been investigating this case for five days now, three of which you have been sitting here watching this shit, promising me that the leads would come from these tapes. Now you want me to go upstairs and say we have nothing yet."

"We don't have anything," Nick fired back. "We have tons of information and so far thirty or forty possible suspects; we just have too much information."

"In case you haven't heard, Anderson's kicking our asses all over the airwaves," Hollings stated, her frustration mounting. "Now he's got community leaders doubting the police and the chief is pissed. He backed my play to keep quiet and now it's about to blow up in our faces."

The tension was getting thick in the room and Nick knew that they weren't making any progress sitting here talking about what was happening outside these walls. Nick pushed out his chair abruptly and rose.

"All right, let's stop and think for a moment about what information we do have here," Nick said, pacing back and forth in front of them. "We have forty or fifty willing sexual partners, all consenting adults, taped either with or without their knowledge."

"You saw that setup man," Kevin said. "There's no way they didn't know they were being taped."

"I agree," Nick said, pressing on. "But I don't think they knew of or were a part of Allun's little experiment. In fact, I don't even think they knew he was a priest. None of his partners were even remotely shy about being with him, and though they seemed a little over eager sometimes to give into his charm, I don't think they were drugged in any way."

"What are you getting at?" Hollings asked impatiently.

"I say we make a statement to the press," Nick stated. "In fact, I think we should hold a press conference."

"And tell them what?" asked Kevin. "That he was having elicit sex, with partners of both sexes and that he had been videotaping the entire time. Do you know what kind of shit-storm that will create? The media will attempt to coerce anyone in this department to smuggle out a copy of one or more tapes, and with the money they will be willing to pay, it will happen sooner or later. This would be a nightmare."

"I agree with Detective Smith," Hollings said. "I don't see how letting any of the information we actually know out will help our case at all."

"I don't think we should tell them anything about Allun's experiment," Nick said with a smile. "I think we should do just the opposite. Allun didn't break any laws; he was a consenting adult having sexual relations with other consenting adults. Kevin thinks that he was killed by one of his partners, but I don't agree. There is no reason for one of them to kill him, especially when doing so would bring more attention on Allun and would likely expose everything in the process."

"I don't know of many criminals who look that far ahead when committing a murder," Smith said.

"Our killer knows about what Allun was up to, but was not a partner," Nick stated with certainty. "The seal of Torquemada wasn't left in his thigh accidentally or by pure chance; it was left there for a reason. It was to note the similarities between what was done in the crusades and what Allun was doing now. You read the notes; Allun was using sex to bring himself and his partners closer to God. Sometimes he used the emotional, caring aspects of making love, and other times he used pain. No matter the methods, the similarities are undeniable. The killer knows about Allun's private life, and so do we."

"Which brings me back to my original question," Hollings began. "What are you getting at?"

"We give the press false information," Nick said. "We tell them Allun was a great person, someone of unimpeachable

TIMOTHY LASSITER

character who we believe was killed by someone he had tried to help. We push the issue about Allun's good works, and tell the vultures that we are looking into anyone he tried to help while helping the community."

"To what end?" Kevin asked, unsure of his colleague's thought process.

"To draw out the killer," Nick answered. "The killer knows what Allun was up to privately, and I promise you that he will contact us if he thinks we are on the wrong track with our investigation. Remember what Sarrucci said. We have an angry killer who is trying to send a message. If he thinks we haven't gotten that message, he is going to let us know. Giving out this information now will buy us some time to do more investigating and will hopefully draw out our killer."

"This is risky, Nick," Hollings said. "If the press finds out that we were withholding information, they are going to have our heads."

"It's the best plan we've got right now," Nick offered.

"It's the only plan we've got," Kevin said under his breath.

"What will you do while you're waiting for the killer to contact us?" Hollings asked sarcastically. Nick could tell that she wasn't totally sold on his idea, but it was growing on her. At this point, she needed something to tell the brass.

"In the meantime, we will use DMV and criminal databases to track down every one of his partners and find out what they know and where they were during the murder," Nick answered. "We keep our information confined to myself, Smith, Wilkins, Mitchell and you. I realize we can't afford to leave any stone unturned, and I could be wrong about the killer, and this will give us enough time to check all of the leads we have right now."

Hollings sighed and looked down at the floor. Nick knew what she was thinking, and the fact of the matter was, there were no suspects that stood out from the others. In fact, the partners could barely be called suspects. Nick admitted that he could be wrong about the killer, but he really did not believe that he was. In fact, his belief that the killer was not one of Allun's partners was one of the first things that really felt right since his vision of the murder five nights ago. His theory made sense, and it fit together with Sarrucci's interpretation of the evidence.

"I'm not going to authorize this myself," Hollings said finally. "I'm not going to put my neck out on the line only to get it chopped off if you turn out to be wrong. Brief Wilkins and Mitchell and make a plan for tracking down Allun's partners while I talk with the brass. When you are interviewing the partners, be sympathetic. Make sure they know that they are being ruled out as suspects and that any information they give us will be destroyed. If they think their encounter with Allun will be broadcast on the news they'll be less likely to work with us."

Hollings left the room and headed up to her meeting, leaving Nick and Kevin with the unpleasant task of getting Detectives Wilkins and Mitchell up to date and giving them instructions on how Hollings wanted things handled. The four detective's first step was to run the names and faces through any databases available to law enforcement. Nick knew that this would provide probably seventy five percent of the personal information they needed to track down thier addresses. From there, they would question each person and eliminate them as a suspect. Thirty minutes later, the plan was finally set and everyone knew what their jobs were. Just before the four detectives split up, Hollings' secretary knocked and entered the room.

"The lieutenant just called," the gatekeeper said. "She said to set up your press conference."

CHAPTER 28

Detectives Grenier and Smith stood side by side behind a wide podium in front of almost one hundred television reporters, cameramen, and newspaper reporters with bright lights glaring up from the back of the conference room. All eyes were focused on the detectives and there was an anticipatory energy that filled the space as the men and women eagerly awaited any new developments that they could get onto the five o'clock evening news. This would be the lead story for the night, and everyone knew it. It would run in the two to three evening newscasts that usually started at five or five-thirty and continued on until the national news came on at six-thirty. There was rumor that the story might even be mentioned on the national news, though it had received very little coverage nationally because of the lack of information released by the police thus far. All of the reporters felt that the news conference was the direct result of the pressure that had been applied on the department by the stinging broadcasts of Mark Anderson. Every reporter was clambering to keep up with Anderson. He already had a leg up on everyone else, having come from a law enforcement background and his first hand knowledge of police procedure gave him a natural advantage. Most other reporters believed that he was being fed information on the case from friends he had who were still on the force. Whatever it was that gave him his advantage, everyone now knew that the police could be bullied, and every network was going to use this to their advantage.

Nick and Kevin had spent over an hour preparing for the conference. The chief of police had preferred to just make a statement, but after Hollings explained the plan to the chief and Governor Haisley during the telephone conference, the Governor overruled the chief and the press conference was given the green light. This was still officially a Norwich case, and Nick wanted Detective Smith to be able to maintain the image of control. Nothing had been said between the two men, but Nick found that more often than not, Kevin deferred to Nick's experience and expertise. In front of the cameras though, Hollings wanted to minimize the potential damage to her unit, and was all too happy to allow Detective Smith to be the focus at the podium. Though the press conference was being held in New London, that fact was simply dismissed because of the size of the Norwich Police Department compared to the facilities in New London.

"I'd like to start by making a few official comments, then I will discuss the investigation thus far, give you the information we are able to release at this time, and finally I will open the floor to your questions," Smith began. The moment he opened his mouth to speak, a hush fell over the audience and all the attention was on him. Smith shuffled some papers around, as though slightly unprepared, then cleared his throat and continued. "Father Michael Allun was a great community leader, and we want it known that this department has maintained a tight lip about the case so as to minimize confusion and to maintain our focus. Though he was only in Norwich for a brief time, Father Allun's work was of great benefit and he will be deeply missed by his community. That being said, there have been some reports that the police have been mishandling the case, or to put it bluntly, that we have been lazy in our investigation. It's for precisely that reason that we have not made statement until now, when we can show you exactly what the focus of our investigation has brought to light so far.

The Norwich Police Department, in partnership with the New London Police Department has been able to narrow the scope of our investigation and we now believe we know why Father Allun was killed. We have several suspects with possible motives and whose alibis are shaky at best. Though I cannot elaborate on that portion of the investigation, I can tell you this. We are now relatively certain that Father Allun's murder was directly related to his work in the community. As you know, Father Allun selflessly devoted himself to both the Church and to his community, first in Boston and more recently here in Norwich. We believe that his killer is someone who was either a direct recipient of the charitable works of Father Allun, or someone who had worked closely with him on a more personal or spiritual level. Having said this, we are asking for the community's help. As I've said, we have several suspects in mind, but we need to establish a more conclusive history. We are asking for any information relating to any conversations Father Allun might have had with anyone regarding stalking or receiving threatening phone calls or messages. Any information that anyone might have could help us to arrest and convict this sick criminal.

Again, Father Allun was a devoted priest and selfless giving man whose only concern was for his community and the people in it. He gave so much and asked for nothing in return. If anyone has any information, we hope that you will come forward to help us solidify our case and find justice for a man who has given us so much. Now, Detective Grenier will take over for a moment and fill in any details that I might have missed."

There was a slight pause as Detective Smith stepped away from the podium and Nick stepped up. The reporters welcomed the break to catch up on their shorthand and make the necessary notation of a new person speaking.

"Thank you, Detective Smith," Nick started. "I would like to start by thanking the Norwich Police Department for allowing us to participate in this investigation. We are all very eager to bring closure to this case and see the person responsible brought to justice. I'd also like to personally thank the Norwich Diocese for its complete openness and patience with the police department as we try to close this investigation quickly and restore a feeling of safety and security to the people of Norwich and its surrounding communities. It is because of the unfettered access the Church has provided to the grounds, church records and files regarding Father Allun's work with the Church that we have been able to safely say that this murder was not committed against the Church as a whole, nor were there any religious overtones to this attack.

This murder was not against Catholics, or any religious group or denomination. This was an attack against a good man who was killed by a person who wanted more and more. We don't believe that this murder was especially premeditated; it was a hasty, amateurish, spur of the moment crime. The killer is just that, an amateur who is most likely poor or of limited means and has been relying on the Church, and the charitable works of Father Allun in particular, to get by. The killer is not very well educated, probably did not complete or might not even have attended high school. Most likely, he is an addict of some sort that has let the emotions of the moment take over and is now praying that the police do not put two and two together. Anyone who comes forward with any information can be assured that their identity will be kept confidential and is only being used to solidify the evidence already available. We will now take your questions."

Hands flew into the air immediately, almost before Nick could get the last word out, however, it was Mark Anderson who began asking questions without waiting to be called upon.

"Detective, if this killer is such an amateur, how is it that your department is having such a difficult time closing the case?" Anderson asked. A hush fell over the crowd again as everyone waited for the detective's response. Though they did not know what Anderson had against the police, they were sure getting good entertainment and he was keeping the police on their toes. Nick smiled, though, knowing this question was coming.

"As you know, having been a detective, it doesn't take the most intelligent criminal to get lucky and not leave a ton of incriminating evidence," Nick said. "No matter what you see on television, homicides are never solved in an hour. Mr. Anderson knows that well enough, having left his share of unsolved cases with the police department before he left."

That was it, Anderson was immediately deflated. Every reporter in the room turned their eyes to Anderson, who stood there nearly shaking, unable to speak. The biggest critic of the police during this case had been silenced by his first question.

"What information are you expecting to get from people in the community?" asked another reporter, seizing the moment.

"Just as we said," Detective Smith said, stepping up for a moment. "We are only looking for information that corroborates the evidence at hand. We are looking for any evidence that Father Allun was being stalked or was being threatened in any way."

"When will St. Patrick's Cathedral be reopened for Mass?" asked a third reporter.

"The cathedral is officially no longer a crime scene and can now hold Mass anytime," Kevin answered as he stepped up to the podium. "In fact, I believe that a candlelight vigil is being held tomorrow evening in remembrance of Father Allun."

"How can you say that there is no religious overtone when Father Allun was found murdered in the cathedral?" Anderson called out, having regained his composure. Nick assumed the microphone to answer the question.

"Father Allun was found in the cathedral because that was where he was attacked," Nick answered. "There is nothing more to it than that."

"But the way he was found?" Anderson stammered. Nick looked over at Detective Smith with a confused look on his face.

"The way he was found?" Nick asked, his brow furrowed. "He was found murdered. I'm not sure I understand your question. However, I can assure you that it was not against the church, it was against Father Allun personally."

The press conference wound up with a few more questions that Kevin fielded easily and then the detectives excused themselves and the reporters quickly scattered to get their stories into the stations for the earliest opportunity. Hollings came out from where she had been standing in the background and approached the detectives.

"Well, you bought yourself a little more time," Hollings said in a hushed voice, still unsure of whether the press conference was the right move at this point in the investigation. "And you managed to make everyone look good in the process. The press will be kept at bay for at least a day or two as they wait to see if any information comes in from a concerned citizen. I'm pleased with the way you put Anderson in his place, though that may come back to bite us in the ass. So what's the plan now?"

"Wilkins and Mitchell are running the names we have through the database," Nick answered. "I still don't believe that the killer is one of them, but we don't have anything else to do until our bruised killer's pride gets the better of him and he calls in to set the record straight."

"Not to mention the fact that you could be wrong and the killer could be one of the people on the tapes," Kevin said, a firm believer that the simplest answer is usually the correct one. He then looked back at the reporters running around, standing in front of cameras to do their stories. "I just hope we haven't tied the noose that they are going to use to hang us."

CHAPTER 29

Within five minutes of the press conference ending, Lt. Hollings received calls from both the chief of police and the governor's office. Everyone seemed pleased with the way in which the media had been handled, especially the Norwich Diocese. Nick had bought them a little bit of time, though how much time he did not know. The media would be pushing the community angle, focusing on the charitable events performed by Father Allun. This would give the police a little time to work without the media pressure. However, this brought Nick right back to where he was before. He did not know who the killer was, he had no suspect, and as he stood over the printer as it spat out names and addresses of people he was certain were not involved in the murder, he knew he was losing precious time. Hollings was now in full agreement with Detective Smith and wanted Detectives Mitchell and Wilkins to help them perform door to door interviews with Allun's partners in the hopes that some leads would come from them. Nick protested, knowing that no one was going to just offer up information regarding their sexual encounters, especially after they found out it was with a priest. Nick was left with the hope that his plan to draw out the killer through the press conference would work the way he had planned. He and Kevin had really laid it on thick, making it sound as if Allun should be a nominee for sainthood. Whether the killer was a sexual partner of Allun's or not, that should have inflamed him enough to make him want to set the record straight.

Nick looked over to the empty desk that Kevin had been occupying since the two detectives began working together.

Smith sat at the desk, reclined slightly, lost in his own thoughts. It was then that Nick realized the Norwich detective hadn't said two words since leaving the press conference with him almost thirty minutes ago. Smith looked pensive, and even slightly upset, as he sat there twirling a government issue black plastic pen between his fingers.

"What are you thinking about?" Nick called out from where he stood ten feet away. Smith just continued twirling the pen around staring off into space. "Detective?"

Smith snapped back to reality quickly, accidentally dropping the pen on the desk in front of him.

"What?" he said with a start. "What's up?"

"You haven't said two words since we got back here," Nick said. "I was wondering what you were thinking about."

"I don't know," Kevin said, as if almost floating back to the place where his mind had been. "Something I...I just can't put my finger on."

"What's that?" Nick asked.

"If I knew what it was, I would be able to answer you," Kevin answered, looking slightly annoyed.

"Yeah, sorry," Nick said, suddenly realizing the stupidity of his question. "We'll start the interviews tomorrow. There's no need to go out tonight, we would be out until midnight."

Smith was gone again, his mind trying to figure out why the alarms in his brain were going off, trying to figure out what had set off his mental confusion in the first place.

"Hey man," Nick said, walking over to the desk. "What's bothering you?"

"I don't know," Kevin said, sitting up straight at his desk. "I feel as though there's something I've overlooked. Something was said at the press conference that has stuck in my craw, and I just can't figure out what it is."

"Well that's a problem," Nick said, unsure of what a craw was, but understanding the feeling Kevin was experiencing.

Usually, that was when Nick needed some peace and quiet to let his right brain work the problem. "Do you want to go over the press conference again, we have it on tape."

"Or we could just watch the news," Kevin said with a smile as he put the problem aside for a moment. "I'm just going to head home. There's no reason to start the interviews tonight, it's just going to take all night."

Nick just smiled and nodded in agreement, realizing the other detective had not heard a word he had said since coming back from the press conference.

"You're probably right," Nick said with a little laugh. "What do you say we meet back here tomorrow morning?"

Nick walked Kevin to the double doors of the investigations unit, and after the other detective had exited, he turned back to collect his paperwork and clean up his office somewhat. As he made his way back, he saw Hollings standing in the doorway to her office, just watching over everyone as they worked. Nick walked over and stood beside her.

"What's up with Smith?" she asked, keeping her gaze on the squad bay in front of her.

"He's got something stuck in his craw," Nick answered, wondering if his lieutenant would be more familiar with this phrase than he was.

"I hope he gets it out before it gets infected," Hollings stated, though Nick could not tell whether she was being sarcastic or not. He just decided to let it go. "What's the plan now?"

"Tomorrow we'll start pounding the pavement," Nick answered. "We'll talk to Allun's sexual partners, everyone we can find that is. I still think it's going to be a waste of time. None of them are the killer, and none of them is going to be very honest about their relationships."

"I think you're wrong on this one," Hollings said. "And it beats you guys sitting here and doing nothing, just waiting for a clue to fall into your lap."

"I bet you twenty bucks the killer makes contact with this office before Monday," Nick said with a smile.

"You're on," Hollings said, extending her hand out and shaking with the detective. "You better bring cash because I don't accept checks or money orders. Did you see Dr. Tanner today?"

"Ah shit," Nick said, shaking his head. He had forgotten about his standing Friday appointment with his psychologist. "I'll have to reschedule."

"Why'd you miss it?" Hollings asked as though Nick had done it on purpose.

"Probably because I've been sitting around waiting for clues to fall into my lap," Nick said sarcastically.

"Well, you better call her office and reschedule smartass," Hollings said, not missing a beat. "In the meantime, what are your plans for the rest of the night?"

"I don't know," Nick started. He was about to tell her that he was going to go home and work the case in his mind a little when his cell phone started to ring. Nick unclipped it from his belt and looked at the number displayed on the message window. It was one that was vaguely familiar to him. "Hello?"

"I was starting to think you might have fallen off the edge of the world or something, but then I saw your press conference," started Jenn, her voice playful. "What's the matter with you, you don't return your messages or something?"

"Sorry about that," Nick said, a sense of relief flooding over him suddenly. "I've been busy with this case. What's going on?"

"I want to see you, that's what's going on," Jenn answered. "You looked way too serious during that press conference. I thought I would let you take me out to dinner or something."

"That's very big of you," Nick said with a laugh. "Where do you want to meet?"

"Why don't you pick me up at my place," Jenn suggested. Nick immediately realized that this was a good sign; it meant their relationship was indeed moving forward. "I'll be ready in thirty minutes, and don't be late."

"Yes ma'am," Nick replied, then took down her address and hung up the phone. He turned to Hollings, who was staring at him, expecting a detailed account of the telephone call. "I'm sorry lieutenant, I'd love to stay and chat, but it looks like I've got a date."

Nick winked at his superior, who could only smile and turned to walk away. *This was going to be a good night*, Nick thought to himself. He was going to have a good time with Jenn, and he was going to get some kind of insight as to how she felt about him. And to top it all off, Nick was certain the killer would make contact before Monday; he had to, Nick had more than just twenty dollars riding on it. Hell, maybe he'd even have the case solved by the end of next week.

CHAPTER 30

Nick drove down Route 12 through the town of Groton, Connecticut; a town that had grown around the naval submarine base and the many military personnel that were stationed there. The detective was always amazed by the town, its ability to survive by digging it's claws into the submarine base, whether in economic prosperity or depression. Nick always felt a sense of depression whenever he drove through Groton, as though a giant rain cloud hovered just above the town limits, blotting out the sun as he drove into town, and disappeared as he reached the outer limits. The town was remarkably dreary, no matter how many new businesses came through. No matter how much expansion tried to make the town seem more prosperous, this part of Route 12 in particular could not help but look cheap. However, as the detective reached the point where Route 12 became Route 1, he realized that he was not entirely correct about Groton. There was much more to the town of Groton, Connecticut than the submarine base and the retail district that clung to it like a leach; there was the older part of Groton, a part that was beautiful in a way that fit perfectly with coastal New England. Once past the middle school and the public library, the area became much less congested and as he made his way up past the town high school he found himself on a quiet suburban road with beautiful houses on all sides and the shoreline narrowing just beyond them.

Nick was amazed that Jenn lived out here in this beautiful, and most likely expensive part of town. He checked the address she had given him several times, as well as the directions he had printed off the computer web site, until he reached a point when he was certain he was heading in the right direction and just enjoyed the view in the setting sun. The detective had to remind himself that he would not be able to afford the house he was living in if it were not for the fact his grandparents left it to him after they died. The detective inside of him was questioning everything, but for tonight, he decided to put that on hold and just enjoy the company. Nick turned right onto a small road that led past several houses until he reached the mailbox with the numbers Jenn had indicated and pulled into the gravel driveway. Nick shut off the car and stepped out, immediately noticing the sound of the surf all around him. He could see just beyond the driveway where the grass began to fade and merge with sand, and beyond that where the sand became beach and then water. The house itself was amazing, the perfect beach house overlooking the water.

Nick rang the doorbell and tried to peer through the screen door without looking as if he were trying. He heard Jenn's voice from somewhere off in the house beckoning him in. Nick turned the latch on the screen door and pulled, then slipped himself inside.

"You really should answer the door personally," Nick suggested. "What if I had been a burglar?"

"Most of the burglars I know don't ring the doorbell first," Jenn fired back. "Besides, I would have just mopped the floor with you like I did last weekend."

"Don't remind me," Nick said. "Hey, this is a beautiful home. How'd you find a place like this?"

"You mean, how do I afford this on my salary," Jenn said, correcting him as she came out of the hallway, into view. Nick couldn't help but smile, she looked beautiful and what amazed the detective the most was the fact that she wasn't even trying. "That question sounds like one I would expect from internal affairs. You're not switching departments are you?"

"Not at all," Nick said. "I don't care how you afford this place; I just want to know who your realtor is."

"This isn't really my place," Jenn answered. "The house itself belongs to my best friend. She's a hotshot doctor specialist who is never here. She split up the house when she bought it, the upstairs is her apartment and she invited me to move in downstairs. She charges me a very modest rent, which I insisted on paying, and she knows that her home is always and watched over."

"A beautiful arrangement," Nick commented.

"No, it's a nice arrangement," Jenn corrected him. "It's the view that's beautiful."

With that, she led him over to the far wall, which was almost entirely made up of the sliding glass doors which overlooked an enormous porch, which looked out over the beach and the water. Beyond the beach and the water was the western horizon, where the sun had finally gone out of view but had left brilliant colors of pink, red, and orange in its place. As Nick looked higher into the sky, the colors faded and mixed with blue and purple of the encroaching night.

"It is beautiful," Nick said in awe of the scene. "I don't know how you force yourself to come to work in the morning."

"It's tough," Jenn said with a smile. She then took Nick's hand and pulled him close, something Nick had not been prepared for. She pressed herself up on her tip toes and her face inched closer to his. They had not kissed yet, though Nick had thought about how he might close the evening with one. He leaned back into her and lowered his head just a little, enough for her to reach his lips, and they kissed. She held it there for a moment, then pulled away slowly and looked at him. "I've been wanting to do that for a while. Now what's for dinner?"

Nick took her to a small, hole in the wall, Italian restaurant that he knew of back in Groton. He had remembered it as he had been driving through town, and though he hated to spend any more time in the town than he had to, this little restaurant served the best Italian food he had ever tasted. The restaurant boasted that it had first opened five years after World War II by an Italian American soldier, who returned home from the war with nothing more than a high school diploma, and had found success as a chef. Nick could not be certain whether this story was true, though the restaurant did reside in one of the older buildings on the street, nestled nicely between the naval base and Electric Boat. Nick was certain that the restaurant was a big success with the lunch crowd and had been introduced to it himself during a case a few months ago. The staff was all family and shouted Italian around the restaurant, making the patrons feel as though they were just part of the family. Nick found a parking space on the street a few blocks up and together, he and Jenn walked down to the restaurant and were seated immediately.

Jenn asked about the case between placing orders with the waitress. Nick did not know whether she asked because she was genuinely interested in the case, or because she felt it was the right thing to do. Nick skimmed over the case, not giving out many details, almost as though he were talking to the press again. The fact of the matter was, he was not sure about the case, and though he knew about Allun's past, he was not sure where that fit into the murder and therefore was not ready to talk about it. Nick was certain Jenn could tell that he was leaving parts out, but said nothing, just listening to him as he spoke. She asked questions here and there, and when Nick was finished, he felt a little better. She said nothing, just went onto different subjects, asking about his family and things about his past. *This is a date*, Nick thought to himself. Here were two people who were getting to know each other a little better, finding out about what made the other person tick. Dinner came and before they knew it, their plates were empty and cleared and they still sat there, drinking their wine and talking, coming closer with every word. Nick had never been on a perfect date, never been so engrossed in another person that he forgot about the world around him, he never really thought it was possible. But now, staring at this beautiful woman, listening to her voice and her laugh, watching her smile he realized that this was as close to the perfect date as he had ever come.

When he drove her home, there was no uncertainty of whether the date was over; they were just moving on to a new venue. Nick found himself talking about his past in a way he had never thought of it before. In his mind, everything he had done was a step in one direction, leading him here to this point. But when he was talking to Jenn, telling her his stories, she made him realize that every one of those stories was an event in his life, a world within itself that has made him the person he is today. It was amazing to think of himself and his life this way. She invited him in and he was surprised that she had pre-set the coffee maker to brew a pot for when they returned. They talked more and more, though as the conversation began to die down, something new began to take hold. They sat together on the couch, side by side and their desire for each other began to pull inside of them. He wanted to touch her, but resisted, uncertain of her feelings. He felt like a teenager and could tell that she was thinking the same thoughts. *This is ridiculous*, he thought to himself, *she's already kissed you.* He leaned into her, and she turned her head to the side, and he kissed her.

That was all it took. That was all they needed. They were kissing, and then they were touching each other. First, he touched her arm, and then held her. She brushed her hand over his face, then through his hair, finally clinging to the back of his neck. He drew her closer to him, and soon she was nearly sitting in his lap. Their kissing grew more and more intense, she soon positioned herself directly on top of him and their desire was reaching the flash point. His hands slid over her body, and through her clothes he could feel the tight muscles of her arms, shoulders, and down her back to her waist. They were pushing against each other, their friction bringing their desire to a point of no return. She rocked against him, and he pushed himself closer and closer to her. There was a heat all around them, and at that moment he slipped his fingers underneath her thin sweater. Through their kiss, she inhaled deeply, nearly whispering a moan as her nerves registered the contact of his skin. His hands moved around her waist, and she broke the contact of their lips and simply rested her cheek against his, their bodies still pushing against each other. His hands went up her back to her neck, and suddenly she pulled back, gasping for breath as though she had been sprinting.

"I can't," she said between gasps of air. "I'm sorry, it's just too soon."

Nick pulled away, realizing that he too was gasping for air.

"It's okay," he said. "You're right. It's too soon."

"I want to," she assured him. "It's just too soon, I can't. I'm sorry."

"Stop," he said. "You're absolutely right. I got caught up in the moment. It's too soon, you're right."

Jenn relaxed and slid her body up against his, resting her head on his shoulder. Nick wrapped his arms around her as she whispered in his ear.

"I like you a lot," she said. "I really do. I just don't want..."

"You don't have to say anything," Nick said, trying to reassure her. "This was my fault. I got carried away, and I'm sorry. I like you too, and I wouldn't want to go any further if you had any concerns that this might turn into a one night stand."

That was all he needed to say, she moved her lips against his cheek and after she kissed him, she said something without verbalizing it. He felt her lips move against his cheek and he knew immediately what she was saying.

"I had a great night," he said. He made no attempt to move, just held her in his arms. For her part, she just sat there, nestled up against him, sharing something with him that even in their time talking over dinner they could not have imparted to one another. There was an understanding, they liked each other, they wanted more of each other, and they wanted something real. After sitting together there for the better part of an hour, saying nothing but revealing so much, he turned to her and whispered in her ear.

"I'm going to go now," he said softly. "I'm going to go now but I'm going to call you in the morning. I want to see you this weekend."

Jenn just merely nodded, and began kissing him on his cheek and on his neck. Nick felt something warm and wet on his skin, and realized that it was a tear. Nick kissed her cheek, where the tear had fallen, then kissed her lips.

"I'll talk to you tomorrow," he said.

"Do you promise?" she asked in a whisper.

"Wild horses couldn't keep me from it," Nick said and smiled. Jenn slipped herself from his grasp and he rose off the couch. She rose along side of him and walked him to the door. They kissed there, passionately.

"Tomorrow, you'll call?" she asked.

"Wild horses," he answered, then kissed her one final time and turned to leave, feeling her eyes on him as she watched him walk away.

CHAPTER 31

Nick was on fire. As he drove back from Jenn's home in Groton, both his mind and body felt like a runaway train. His mind was running in overdrive as he raced through his memories of the evening, trying to find any clue, anything that he might have misconstrued as a sign that she wanted more from him. However, the more he thought about the evening, the more certain he was of himself. There were no signs, she wanted him just as much as he wanted her; but something had happened, something had caused her to stop. *Did I say anything, did I do anything?* It was driving him crazy; analyzing everything he said and did when deep down, he knew that he had done nothing wrong. Jenn was right, this just wasn't the right time to go further, and the more he thought about it, the better he felt about the evening. They were on the same wavelength regarding their burgeoning relationship. If they had gone any further that night, they could have compromised what they had gained this far. Jenn made it clear that she wanted to take it slower, she wanted to build something; and Nick knew that was exactly what he needed. He needed something real, something he could count on. As he drove away, he knew that tonight's events were not a defeat, it was not the end but the beginning; and that thought gave him some measure of hope.

Unfortunately, his body did not agree. The caffeine from the coffee and the build up of desire had left him unable to relax, and definitely unable to sleep. He was not going to be able to go home, not in this condition. He needed to take his mind off of this; he needed to focus on something else for a while. As fate would have it, it was then that Nick realized that he was quickly approaching the off ramp that would lead him directly to the police department. Nick couldn't help but laugh to himself; he could never get away from it. He was certain that Dr. Tanner would have something to say about this, about how his subconscious mind had steered him here, but maybe she would note this developing romance in his life as something positive. Not that what she thought really mattered in the end, all that mattered was that he confront his demons. The off-ramp was a hundred yards ahead and, giving in, Nick eased the car into the far right lane just as he came to the end of the Goldstar Memorial Bridge. At the next fork in the road, he kept to the left and headed into downtown New London. From there, it took less than five minutes for him to make his way to the New London Police Department. It was just after eleven, and Nick found the building eerily quiet as most everyone had gone home, leaving only the night shift and duty personnel in each department. Nick climbed the stairs up to the Investigation Unit, only to be met by the cold, angry, and irritated stares of a group of uniformed officers. Nick looked back at them harshly, not really caring that they were pissed at him, but wondering what had set them off. It didn't take him long to figure it out as he was approached by the detective on duty, a short, overweight, balding man named Kenneth DeVoy.

Kenneth DeVoy was one of those police officers who wasn't really very good at his job, a person who felt that being a cop was simply a job and never really considered it a career. DeVoy had climbed the ranks just as everyone else did, but after a particularly bitter divorce, he had shut down, and now it was pretty well understood that this was the place where he would end his career. He had not actually run an investigation for well over two years now, though he had worked on some, mostly doing grunt work. He made no complaints, and when not working under another detective on an investigation, he was manning the unit after hours, making sure the few officers who worked those hours did their jobs. Giving him reign over the night shift was purely just for show, a sign of respect from Lt. Hollings for his years of service. There was nothing behind the power, however, and everyone knew it, especially DeVoy.

"What's going on?" Nick asked as DeVoy approached. As second in command of the Investigation Unit, Nick was clearly DeVoy's superior officer, but Nick hated throwing his weight around, especially when he had to work with these people, and usually gave DeVoy an undue amount of respect.

"We've been drowning in phone calls," DeVoy answered. "Ever since the press conference we've been getting calls from people who have a lead on who Father Allun's killer might be."

"Any of interest?" Nick asked, now understanding why all of the uniformed officers seemed so upset. He had created a feeding frenzy, then did not bother to stick around and see what panned out. Nick knew this was going to happen; there would be hundreds of calls, if not more. Less than a tenth of those would be forwarded to him, as possible information pertaining to the case, and he was certain none of them would lead him to a killer. However, he had bought himself and the department some time, and that was all that mattered right now.

"There are twenty five that we did not just dismiss out of hand," DeVoy stated. "Each call is recorded and then transcribed. We take the information and run down any possible angles, just as you instructed. We have eight run down so far."

Nick took the eight bundles of paper and made his way across the squad bay to his office. Once inside, he closed the door and pressed the play button on his CD radio, and as he eased into his chair behind his desk, the sound of Fleetwood

Mac filled the office. Nick read each transcribed call twice, then read the report, and finally re-read the transcribed calls. There was the remote possibility that there was something underlying each call, something that the investigating officer might have missed. In each case, the officer was right on, and none of the cases seemed very interesting in the end. Of the eight paper clipped packets of paper, Nick put only two aside for Wilkins and Mitchell to follow up on. He left his office and returned to the squad bay to leave the papers on Wilkins' desk. Just as he did, a uniformed officer called out to him.

"Detective," the officer called out. "There is a call for you, someone who states he has a tip regarding the case and will only talk to you."

Nick sighed, slightly annoyed. This too, he knew would happen. There were going to be a lot of kooks who came out of the woodwork, probably some "psychics" who believed that they could see who killed Father Allun. Others would claim that God was telling them who the murderer was and all of them would only want to speak to Nick directly. Nick picked up the telephone receiver and pressed the flashing red button.

"This is Detective Grenier," he started. "May I ask who I am speaking to?"

"I thought all information would be kept confidential," replied the voice, almost playfully. There was a strange metallic sound to the voice that Nick immediately recognized as being dubbed through a voice synthesizer. The only thing Nick could identify from the voice was that it was male based on the deep quality of the tone.

"All information is confidential," Nick responded. "We just give each caller the opportunity to give identifying information should they choose to."

"Are you tracing this call?" asked the person on the other end of the line. Nick was quickly becoming frustrated. There was no need for this amount of secrecy regarding a tip that would most likely lead nowhere.

"No sir," Nick assured him. "We don't have the capability to trace all the incoming calls. As I said, everything here is confidential."

"Good," replied the man on the other end. "Then I want to tell you how extremely disappointed I am in you detective. I thought you would have figured out more about Father Allun by now."

"Is there anything you want to tell us?" Nick asked. There was a steadily building knot in his stomach as he started to feel as though this caller might actually know something about the case. Nick snapped his fingers at DeVoy, then pointed to his phone hoping that the detective understood him enough to start tracing the call.

"First and foremost, detective, Michael Allun was not the saint you made him out to be on the news this afternoon," the man said. "Allun was a sick, twisted individual who thought he could bring everyone closer to God. I'm rather surprised you haven't come upon his debauchery yet. I would have expected more from a man with your reputation."

"What kind of debauchery are you talking about?" asked Nick, trying to get the caller to reveal a little more about what he knew, and hopefully, who he was.

"More than you could imagine," the caller answered. "Do you even know that he has a home in Norwich? Perhaps you should spend more time investigating this case and less time worrying about what some reporters are saying."

"Sounds to me like you've been to his home," Nick commented. "Were you one of Allun's sexual partners?"

"Of course not," answered the caller, enraged. "He could never have convinced me to join him with his ridiculous..."

The caller stopped short, realizing suddenly that Nick did indeed know about Allun's home, and more importantly, about the victim's private life.

"Very good, detective," the caller said after a brief pause. "How long have you known about Allun?"

"Longer than you think obviously," Nick responded. "Almost since the beginning. Once we started digging, it wasn't that hard to find."

"And how much of this charade was meant to draw me out?" asked the killer. There was no point in his pretending to be a concerned citizen with a tip any longer. Nick had played this perfectly, and the killer knew it.

"You were making a statement when you killed Allun," Nick said. "I understand that, though I don't know what the statement is. I knew that you would want to set the record straight. I understand that you are not just some crazy person on a killing rampage. There is method and intelligence to your work. Everyone here appreciates that fact."

"Thank you for that, detective," the killer answered. "But I don't quite believe you. I underestimated you this time, and I'll be sure not to make that mistake again."

"Look," Nick began. "This doesn't have to be a long drawn out thing. I'm going to find you, there's no doubt about that. You obviously want the world to know about Allun, he obviously hurt you somehow. You killed him, but there had to be more than that, you had to kill his image. If you turn yourself in the prosecutor is willing to cut you a deal, and during that time you will have all the opportunities you want to tell the world what kind of person Allun really was."

"Turn myself in," responded the killer with an astonished snort. "I am nowhere near finished. I have important work to do, and it is obvious that you have underestimated me just as much as I have you. You really have no understanding whatsoever about what is truly going on here."

"Why don't you tell me," Nick suggested.

"Allun was on a crusade," the killer said. "A sick crusade no different than those crusades and inquisitions his employer attempted hundreds of years ago. I too, am on a crusade, detective, but mine will be so much more successful. I will show this state, and in the end, the world what true justice really is. Do you know what real evil is, detective? Well I do, I have seen it for myself, and now I will purge it from the earth, starting here. These evildoers that I target and those like them around the world will feel fear for a change, and soon everyone will understand why."

Nick knew at once that this conversation was coming to an end. This killer was making his statement and then would hang up, leaving Nick with absolutely no questions answered. He had to find a way to prolong this; he had to find a way to find out more.

"I guess I was wrong," Nick said. "You are just a crazy nut. No one will understand you, especially if you don't bring yourself in. I will hunt you down and no one will understand why you've done this. You'll just be another pathetic killer."

"Nice try detective," the killer answered. Nick could almost feel the killer smiling on the other end of the phone. "But you won't be able to bait me this time. I am going to enjoy having you hunt me; it will keep me on the top of my game. I've also enjoyed this talk; we will have to do it again."

Nick heard the familiar click of the call being terminated, then looked at the receiver for a moment before setting it back down in it's cradle. There was so much going through his mind now that he could not latch onto one coherent thought.

"Please tell me you were tracing that call," Nick said to DeVoy, who was staring at him along with the rest of the officers in the bay.

"Did you tell me to?" DeVoy asked sarcastically, answering the detective's question. He then imitated Nick's snaps and hand gesture. "I don't know what that was supposed to mean. As for the call, we can have the phone company trace where it originated from."

"Do that," Nick ordered. "And have whoever's transcribing this call type it up quickly and bring it to me with the audio recording."

Nick snapped at DeVoy again and pointed at his watch.

"That means now!" he yelled. "Just so there isn't any confusion."

Nick watched DeVoy sulk off and then picked up the phone and quickly dialed a number. Immediately, Hollings answered, her voice slow and hoarse as though she had been asleep.

"Hey boss, did I wake you?" Nick asked sarcastically.

"What the fuck do you think?" asked Hollings, quickly waking. "It's almost midnight. I take it you weren't able to close the deal if your date ended so soon. I hear they make a pill for that kind of problem now a-days."

"Yeah well, maybe I can use that twenty dollars you owe me to get myself a prescription," Nick fired back with a smile on his face. "The killer just called, and according to him, this is just the beginning."

CHAPTER 32

Run, run, run away. The little girl's inner voice repeated the words she had told herself for years. Now a young woman, she still saw herself as nothing more than that scared little girl. Now the girl sat on the hard plastic toilet seat cover in her bathroom, the shower running cold water at full blast. She couldn't afford to run the hot water if she was not standing in the shower. The girl pressed a plastic bag of ice wrapped in a kitchen towel against her face, though she could already feel the left side of her face beginning to swell. The ice was of no use whatsoever. She would probably have to call out sick from work tomorrow if the swelling was bad tomorrow night. She would probably be fired soon; this would be the second shift she had missed in less than two months. Then she would have to deal with him. He would find out that she had been fired, that was inevitable. He would tell her that she was a loser, that she was useless. He would unleash a constant barrage of insults to keep her self esteem at the lowest possible point. He would tell her that she was too stupid to hold down even the most menial job; then he would beat her, again. The irony was not lost on her.

Why do I stay? She could not help but ask herself this question every time she found herself sitting here on the toilet, holding back the tears and trying in vain to keep the signs of abuse from showing. *Why don't you run away?* The answer to that question was simple. She had no where else to go. She had not been as fortunate as her college schoolmates. She did not have a home to return to when school was out. She did not have anyone, it was just her, and that was how it had always been. She had always felt all alone when she was

189

living in the dorms, even though she had a roommate. She was not the same as all of the other girls; they all had a caring family unit. They all had confidence and self esteem; they could make friends and have boyfriends and had an inner strength that would not allow them to be subjected to this kind of abuse. The girl had none of these things. She did not have a mommy or a daddy to return home to during winter or summer break. She stayed there alone in the dorm, just as lonely as she would have been if classes were in session and she was surrounded by her fellow classmates. That was when he found her, during the winter break of her second year. She could remember the first time he talked to her; she was so scared of saying something stupid that she almost vomited. She was terrified of him, but in a different way than she was now. He was the most charming and attractive man she had ever met, and for some reason that she could not begin to fathom, he was interested in her. He lavished her with money, gifts, and affection. Most importantly of all, he lavished her with his attention; the very thing that she was in need of the most.

His name was Chris, and he knew exactly what it was the little girl needed; he preyed on it. The little girl was damaged, and Chris could spot that a mile away. He used his knowledge and understanding of her condition to get her, very much in the same way he used his charm to get her; get her into his bed, get her into his apartment, get her to help him in college, and to get his frustrations out. It wasn't her fault that she got better grades than he did; God knows she tried to help him as much as she could. The fact of the matter was there was so much he did not understand, and it had been going on for so long now that he was lost whenever she tried to help him. It was like trying to talk to someone in another language, there was no area of common ground, there was no Rosetta Stone. Chris's inability to keep up with the little girl only served to make him angrier. She could not help the fact that she did not need to study as hard as he did, and she definitely could not help the fact that she was smarter than he was. She made the mistake of saying that aloud once. She missed school and work for an entire week. *Yes,* she thought to herself, *the answer was very simple.* The fact was, this was his apartment, though she paid all of the bills, and if anyone was going to have to leave, it was going to be her. This thought only led her back to the same conclusion; she had nowhere else to go.

She told herself she could go back to the dorms. This was tricky though; there was a waiting list and if he found out she had signed up to move back in, he would make life a living hell until she got away. Then there were his words that haunted her every time she found herself on this line of thinking. He had once threatened her, threatened to kill her if she ever tried to leave him. There was something in his eyes that told her he might actually try it, though at this moment she could not help but wonder how death could be any worse than the hell in which she was living now. *Run, run, run away.* That was what her brain continuously tried to tell her as she sat there with the ice melting in the plastic bag, waves of pain washing over her face. That was when she started to cry. She did not cry when he beat her anymore, she would not give him the satisfaction. It was only when she was sitting here all alone, when her mind was telling her to do the thing she had done all of her life, it was then that she cried. It hurt for her to cry, physically and emotionally. She shouldn't have to run away, she had done nothing wrong. She was tired of running away from situations that were not her fault, but what else was there for her to do. She couldn't stay and endure this for much longer. She had come so far, and the thought of losing all that she had accomplished nearly broke her heart. She had run away from her uncle's home, losing contact with almost everything from her former life. She only stopped running when she was taken in by the sisters, and though they were hard on her, they taught her discipline, and most of all, they loved her. No one from her family had come looking for her, not even her mother.

She breezed right through high school. The discipline had been helpful in teaching her how to live her life, but the main reason she strived to do so well was because of how much the sisters had done for her. She did not want to let them down, and she could not understand that there was no way that she could let them down. They loved her, and they always would. The little girl received a full scholarship from the state university, but turned it down for a partial scholarship from a college on the other side of the country. She was willing to work day and night to pay for it if it meant that she was far away from that home that had caused her so much pain. Yet now, here she was, contemplating running away again, leaving behind everything she had accomplished. When was it going to be her time to stand? She looked at her watch and knew that Chris would be home in a couple of hours. His temper would have died down by then and he would be apologetic and caring, making promises that he would never touch her again, making promises that he would never keep. She had once believed it, the first time that he had hit her. She hoped it was true the second time, and by the third time she knew it was just something that he felt as though he had to say. He would remain sweet and caring for awhile. How long he would stay that way depended on how long she could keep from making a mistake in his eyes. It could be a few weeks or a few days, there were no set rules.

Run, run, run away. This time she told herself no, and the moment she did, an idea formed in her mind. She could call the police. She could file a report and maybe Chris would get the help he needed, and even if he didn't, he might be scared straight enough by spending a short time in jail that he would never do it again. The more she thought about it, the more plausible the idea seemed. Even if nothing happened and Chris was released that night, she could make up an excuse. She could say that the police told her that they were called because they heard a fight. Perhaps, a neighbor called when they heard the screaming and the police forced her to file a report. Chris was smart enough to know that this was not the way it worked, and she knew that it was a lie, but Chris thought she was stupid and naïve and maybe he thought she was just dumb enough to believe whatever the police told her. It could work, and the worst thing that could happen was he gained nothing from it and just kept on beating her, and that was going to happen anyway. She was not going to run away this time. The little girl was not going to give up all that she had accomplished, not this time.

Suddenly, she heard a noise that jarred her thoughts back to the present. Someone was at the front door; there were keys in the lock. This was impossible; Chris was never home this early. She knew that he had not had enough time to decompress; he had not had enough time to cool down. Immediately, the little girl experienced a flash of déjà vu, not from the many times Chris had come at her, the expectation of what was to come. No, her flash backs came from her memories of her uncle coming down the hall, the little girl desperately hoping he would think she was asleep. She heard the front door open and knew that Chris was coming for her, and all she could think was *run, run, run away.*

The killer opened his eyes and the images were gone. He looked back and forth down the street to make certain that he had not been spotted as he stood there daydreaming. He had heard the little girl's stories so many times now that it seemed like his own memory. The little girl had been so scared, she had been so weak. In some ways, Chris had been right. So long as she stayed there with him, she had been pathetic. The killer was not pathetic, however, he was a hero and soon everyone would understand that. He was here to wipe clean the stain that had been these men's belief that their behavior had ever been acceptable. He would visit onto them the pain they had inflicted on others. The world would come to see that it did not have to stand for this anymore. He would give the girl the justice she so rightly deserved. He would be the avenger.

CHAPTER 33

Jack Brenner sat in an old, rickety wooden chair, behind the worn wooden desk that he had purchased with it over ten years ago and stared out into the small space that was his office. He didn't turn the lights on very much; the walls were grimy and faded just like the rest of the store, and what few customers he had were not very interested in having much light on them. He sat there in his chair, listening to the sound of the emptiness, as his emotions began to slide down the slippery slope of depression. This had been something that had been going on for awhile, something he seemed unable to control. At times like this, when it was quiet, the voices in his head seemed so much louder. There were times when he wanted to press his hands against his ears and scream, but he knew that it would not help. Jack thought of his drugs, yearned for them and their effects. He would take them with three extra strength sleeping pills and wash them down with wine. The wine was cheap, usually the lowest price bottle on the shelves of his local liquor store; he did not drink as a sign of status or taste, simply for effect. He would take the drugs, which usually seemed to be very slow acting unless he combined them with the sleeping pills, and within thirty minutes his mind would be numb and he would drift away. The voices in his head would slowly diminish, becoming softer and softer until he could barely hear them. It was the only time when he was truly alone; it was the only time they would leave him alone. He would barely be able hear his mother telling him how she wished she had a son she could be proud of, how he was such a disappointment. His father's voice would be scarcely more than a whisper, telling him how he wished he had never "knocked-up" his mother, how Jack was a pathetic waste of life. Unfortunately for Jack, his drugs weren't here; they were at home, and he was going to have to endure the voices for a little while longer.

When Jack was younger, his drug of choice had been cocaine. Even now, years since his last hit, he could still remember what it felt like to be high. There were no voices in his head when he was high, there was no one to be disappointed with him, there was only pure bliss. That was what he missed the most; the pure bliss. It was the pure bliss that released him from morality and the thoughts of consequences. Nothing mattered when he was high; he was in his own little world, *his world*. No one could bother him there; no one could make him feel bad. He could and would do whatever he wanted to. He was older now, though that was not the reason he did not get high anymore. The simple fact of the matter was that he could not afford to get high now, he did not have the economic freedom he once had. Now he was reduced to Zoloft and sleeping pills, and they were far from pure bliss. With the cocaine, he was removed but his mind was still there, sharp and alert. With the Zoloft, he felt as though he were trying to climb out of a wet sack. There was a muddled, often mind numbing sensation that came with taking the drugs. That was why he took the sleeping pills; he simply could not bear to be conscious in such a state. He would zone out in front of the television, sometimes he would put on one of his movies and recite the lines and sensations until he fell asleep.

Unfortunately, Jack was here in his store and at least one hour from achieving any sort of peace of mind. He was sitting here alone, with not one customer in the entire store. Even his one employee had called out; this was the third day in a row. She probably wasn't coming back. The dazzle of working for him had long since faded away. Working for Jack must have seemed cool at first, but then she got to know him and realized just how pathetic he really was. He was alone, and as he thought about it for a moment, he realized it really wasn't very much different from the rest of his life. Jack was one of those people who could be standing in the middle of a crowd and still feel alone. His parents always told him that he would never make anything of himself and that they would always be disappointed in him. They were only half right; Jack did make something of himself. In fact, in Jack's business, there was a time when he was as big as they come. As for disappointing his parents, he knew that nothing he could have ever done would make them proud, so he might as well not even try. Jack decided to go into the most appealing and lucrative field an eighteen-year-old boy could dream of, the adult film industry.

Jack swiveled his chair around to look at the rows of shiny statues and awards that lined the shelves that barely clung to the wall behind his desk. This was Jack's legacy, this was the only proof that he had ever existed in this world. Jack Brenner had once been known as Jack Hammer, adult film star. At one time, he had been one of the biggest stars in the industry, which was quite an achievement in a field where ninety percent of the interest was focused on the "actresses". For almost twenty years, Jack Hammer commanded one of the highest salaries per picture; and what part of that he didn't put up his nose went to lavish parties meant to keep the focus on him and reinforce his ego. However, in the mid eighties, the industry began to change dramatically. Many actors and directors saw where adult films were headed and changed a little bit at a time to keep up, but Jack was unwilling to accept change and tried everything he could to keep things the same. Change was hard to accept when you were at the top. However, when the nineties turned into the 21st century, bringing with it DVD's and the internet, there were no more adult "films". The movies deteriorated until they were nothing more than different scenes with a corny plot inserted around it. The internet changed everything even more, until it was all just individual scenes. The time of Jack Hammer, the star, was coming to an end, and if he was going to survive, he was going to have to make some drastic changes.

Using his notoriety and what was left of his money, Jack turned his attention to the internet, making short scenes that he sold with a membership to his site. Jack was immediately amazed at how easy it was to shoot these scenes, and relatively inexpensive when compared to the amount of money he raked in with membership dues and extra bonus features. There was no real overhead; Jack shot all of the scenes out of his home. All of the plots were basically the same; a young, shy, innocent girl influenced to open up sexually until, at the end of the scene, she was a raging sex-aholics. He was also amazed at how easy it was to find stars for his scenes. There were always young, desperate women in need of fast and easy cash, and the male stars were even easier than the women. When reality television began to take hold, people's desire to see everything uncensored at the click of a button caused Jack to realize a new dream. His dream of twenty four hour, real time porn captured live became a reality for Jack. Jack found that he was making more money than ever before, and he was again a respected giant in the industry. It was when he was the giant again that Jack learned a startling truth. It's easiest to slip when you're standing at the top; and when you fall, you fall hard.

Jack fell hard. His first problem came when he was arrested for starring an underage actress in one of his online scenes. Though the girl wasn't forced, she was still a minor and Jack found himself buried under a mountain of charges, with more and more charges continuously leveled against him for, what he considered to be, this one "mistake". Just when he thought there were no more charges to be drawn up, the police found out how the girl got her starring role in the scene. Jack was convicted of statutory rape and promoting the sexual performance of a minor. Because her performance was over the internet, federal charges were leveled against him as well. There was barely enough time for Jack to hide some money before the government seized all of his assets and sent him to jail for six years. When Jack got out of jail he planned on starting up his websites again, but this time was going to be different. He was going to be smart and not get dragged down by anyone. However, he never really got off the ground. Six months after starting up a new site, one of his actresses tested positive for HIV, and after testing all of his stars, they all came back with HIV and Jack was shut down for good. That was two years ago, and now Jack was running a small store in New London, selling adult movies, erotic toys and novelties. Everything Jack Hammer had been was gone. Very few people knew who he was; even fewer actually frequented his store. The only people who came in now were lonely, pathetic middle aged men and those few porn aficionados who actually remembered who Jack Hammer had been. They all left disappointed, just as his parents had been when they departed this earth, disappointed. His parents had won, and he knew they were looking down on him and laughing.

Jack tried to remember what it was that drove him to all of this in the first place, and the moment he thought of it he wished he hadn't. He had gotten into this life because of his own first sexual experience. She had laughed at him, told him that he was exactly what she had expected, short and far from sweet. She told him that commercials lasted longer than he did. She constantly insulted and berated him, and in his naïve mind Jack thought he was in love with her. She had been his first, and he knew nothing about love or the world. She hurt him over and over again, cheating on him regularly and telling him that he was worthless. It wasn't until he realized that everyone he loved thought he was worthless that he decided to prove them wrong. Unfortunately, they were all long gone by the time Jack Hammer was a success. Now, he was just Jack Brenner again, the pathetic, withered end of what had been something great. Everything his parents had said was right, he was so much a disappointment that even Jack couldn't stand himself. He had to self medicate and drink to even feel remotely comfortable in his own skin. This is what Jack Brenner thought about all day, everyday. However, at night, when he was all alone, these thoughts seemed to overwhelm him. He lowered his head and closed his eyes, wishing with all of his heart that he might have the courage to take his own life; but Jack knew that he didn't. Jack was the same weak child that sat there and smiled as his girlfriend insulted him and cheated on him. Jack hurt so much that he wanted to cry, but he didn't even have the energy for that. Jack opened his eyes and looked back through his office out to the front of the store. That was when his world changed suddenly, violently pulling his consciousness from its introspection. Jack almost fell out of his chair in terror. He opened his mouth but found himself unable to speak. There, standing before him, was a figure cloaked in all black, looming over him ominously. The figure just stared at Jack, as though looking at a creature in the zoo. It remained standing there, as if hovering just above the ground, until finally it's curiosity waned. Then, with lightning speed, it approached him. In that moment, Jack knew that his pathetic life would soon be over, and yet something inside Jack Brenner told him it would not end soon enough.

CHAPTER 34

Jack Brenner had once heard stories from people who beat the odds, survived death when they should not have. He had once heard them explain how in their minds they knew they were going to die, but their bodies just could not accept defeat. That must have been the conflict inside himself because though Jack's mind was certain that he was about to die, his body was telling him to run. His body started to move, pushing himself up from his chair and moving subtly around the desk just as the figure came at him. Jack then sprinted away towards the front of the store, the two bodies passing each other practically in mid-air. Jack's attacker must have realized at that moment that his prey would not be so easy to catch. The figure reached out for Jack just as the two bodies passed each other, gripping Jack's shoulder and pushing him down hard. Jack stumbled precariously under the sheer force of his attacker's grip but was able to keep his footing and remain standing long enough to get loose and make his way to the front of the store. The attacker had all his momentum going forward, and careened into the desk. He rolled at the last second, pushing off from the edge of the desk to give him more speed as he pursued his victim out into the main store. The attacker lunged out at Jack, catching hold of his leg for just a moment, pulling his prey off of his feet and down to the floor hard.

Pain surged through Jack's leg and up his back. He had felt something on his lower leg and then suddenly found himself heading face first into the floor. Unable to brace himself for the impact in time, Jack's right knee slammed into the tile floor, the pain so intense that a queasy feeling immediately formed in his gut. However, survival was the only thought on Jack's mind, and he squirmed from side to side until he was able to shake his foot loose from his attacker's grip. Jack clambered around on his hands and knees for a few seconds as he tried to get back to his feet. His leg was in so much pain that he had to limp with every step, slowing him down considerably. His attacker was back on him in seconds, throwing him down forcefully on the floor and pinning Jack down with his hands and knees. The attacker removed a small, plastic device from the waistband behind his back and pressed the open flat end against jack's skin. Pushing the device down hard, the attacker snapped back up to his feet and pressed the button. Immediately, 10,000 volts of electricity surged through Jack's body, causing his muscles to seize and spasm as a bright white light with electric blue dots flashed in front of his field of vision. His mind, however, was still intact as he tried to will himself to fight back. The spasming of Jack's muscles caused his legs to jerk involuntarily, catching between his attacker's legs and throwing him backwards and away from Jack. It took less than a few seconds for Jack to gain control of himself again and continue his escape. He fumbled around, sliding himself backwards as he knew his attacker would be on him soon. His arms reached out for the racks of videos, pulling them down to delay his impending doom.

Just as Jack began to roll himself over, his eyes caught the light through the tinted window from the outside streetlamp. Suddenly, something new surged in Jack's mind; hope. His store was almost two blocks away from the New London Police Department; if he could get outside, into his car that sat right on the curb, he might be able to get away alive. He couldn't imagine his attacker feeling comfortable enough to pursue him once he was out on the street in full view of anyone driving or walking by. Just then he heard cursing, the voice muted and strange. What Jack noticed most was the fact that the voice was not that far away. Time was against him, and he had to move quickly. Jack pushed himself upright, limping quickly towards the door. He tried his best to put as little weight as necessary on his bad leg, keeping his mind off of the pain and focused on the exit. As Jack approached the doors, he knew that something was wrong, though he could not put his finger on it directly at first. Finally, as he closed in, he realized what was wrong. The outer gate was pulled down over the doors. The gate pulled down vertically over the doors and was usually the last step in closing the store that Jack performed on his way home. Both fear and doubt spread through Jack's mind as he attempted to understand how his attacker could have closed the gate. Whoever pulled it down had to have the key to unlatch it from it's position above the door and then lock it again at the bottom. He could not imagine how this person got a key, but worst of all, Jack now knew that he was really going to die. There was no escape now except through the back entrance where he received deliveries, and he knew there was no way he was going to get back there in time. Jack's momentum carried him right into the right hand glass door of the entrance. The door gave just a little, less than an inch, and though Jack tried to force his hand through the gap to pull on the gate, he knew there was no hope. Jack turned just in time to see a small whip of mist come up in his face, and then a burning and blinding sensation engulfed his sight and all he could do was sense the approach of the end.

However, Jack's time was not over, not quite yet. When he opened his eyes next, he was lying face down over some hard surface. There was a slight pressure against his wrists and ankles, though he barely noticed it at first. Jack turned his head from side to side in an attempt to get his bearings and orient himself with his surroundings. He could not remember losing consciousness, or how he got into this position. Jack tried to push himself up, but the moment he moved his arms up, his legs were pulled forward. Immediately, he knew exactly what was going on. His wrists were bound to his ankles, the ties running underneath the table. Using what little slack he had, Jack felt around with his hands, finally grasping a wooden object near the corner. There was a groove carved into the wood, and after a few seconds of feeling around with his fingers, Jack knew exactly where he was. He was in his office, tied face down on his own desk. Jack also knew what was about to happen. This is how he cast his stars many years ago, forcing them to show off their talents while face down, degraded.

"Do you remember now?" asked a strange voice. Jack knew without seeing the figure that it was his attacker.

"You don't understand," Jack cried out. "It's just how things were done. It was the porn industry for God's sake, what the hell were they expecting?"

"You treated them all like dogs," the voice remarked. "You pinned them down, painfully having your way in some sick right of initiation. I doubt your own initiation was half as degrading. You are trash, Jack Brenner, and I am going to take you out."

Jack screamed, he screamed before anything happened, though he really didn't know why. This was revenge, this was someone's vengeance, and for what little life he had left, he could not understand why. He was Jack Brenner, formerly Jack Hammer, and though he had since faded from the spotlight, he was still someone. This wasn't supposed to happen to him, he had never imagined that anyone would have wanted to hurt him.

"Don't worry so much," the voice said, coming from a different part of the office. The attacker was moving around Jack. "After tonight, you are going to be Jack Hammer once again. After tonight you are going to be the star."

CHAPTER 35

By eight the next morning, Nick already had everyone involved in the Allun murder investigation working at full force. Nick sent Detective's Wilkins and Mitchell off to run down the leads that came from the anonymous tips. By the time Lieutenant Hollings got in, Nick and Kevin were going over Nick's telephone conversation with the killer for the third time. Nick was certain that there was some clue in the phone call, something that would help him to figure out who the killer was. As for Kevin, he felt as though this call reinforced his theory that the killer was related in some way to Father Allun's sexual experiment. When Hollings was settled at her desk, she called Nick and Kevin in and wanted to replay the tape of the conversation, she then wanted to hear their thoughts on what the next step should be. Hollings listened to the recording twice, first to hear the conversation between the detective and killer, then to listen to the killer himself. Unfortunately, the digital synthesizer the killer used to mask his voice was going to make identification impossible. It also was making it hard for the detectives to pick up any clues in the killer's voice or manner of speech. The only time any emotion actually came through was when Nick asked the killer about his part in Allun's sex life. In that brief moment, it was clear that the killer knew Allun in some form or another.

"So," Hollings began after pressing the stop button on the tape recorder. "I guess we can all agree that the killer knew Allun, probably well, but at least well enough to know about his sex life."

The two detectives nodded, and Hollings could tell by the look on Nick's face that he was concerned about where she was headed with this train of thought.

"What are your thoughts?" she asked, looking expectantly at them. "Where do we go from here?"

"We have to interview all of Allun's sexual partners," Kevin jumped in, as if bursting at the seams. "This proves it. The killer was so enraged by the fact that we were calling Allun a moral pillar of the community that he had to to set the record straight. It's got to be a sexual partner, or someone related to them."

"I don't think so," Nick said softly. "You heard what the killer said. When I asked whether he was one of Allun's partners, he said no."

"How many killers have you investigated that tell the absolute truth?" Kevin asked, shocked by the detective's seeming naivety. "He lied; he was trying to make you understand that there was more to Father Allun without spelling it out for you, then was caught off guard when you asked him the question so abruptly."

Hollings was nodding her head, following Kevin's line of thought. Nick could tell it was making sense to her becuase it was making sense to Nick too. That was the problem though; it was making too much sense. It was too easy. Sarrucci's interpretation of the killer made him out to be an intelligent person, someone whose motive would not be so easy to uncover.

"I have to agree with Detective Smith on this one, Nick," Hollings said. "It makes sense, it all fits together."

"But when the killer said no about being Allun's partner," Nick started. "He said no quickly, off the cuff, without thinking about what his answer would signify. He didn't stop tp think about lying; it took him a few seconds before he even realized that I knew about Allun."

"Maybe the killer didn't think that he was lying," Kevin offered. "Maybe he's told himself the lie that he wasn't a partner so much that it became true in his mind, and he answered quickly because he believes it is the truth."

"This is getting a little too deep for me," Hollings said.

"So we have a killer that goes to all the trouble to make devices of torture almost identical to those used during the Spanish Inquisition," Nick started. "He takes his time with the victim, obviously took his time making the torture devices, all for a motive that we solve within days. There's more to this guy than just a revenge killer. And if that's all it was about, then why continue? Why kill someone else? You heard what he said at the end of the call; he is going to purge the 'evildoers' from the earth."

"But he didn't say anything about actually killing someone," Hollings pointed out. "He just said he was on a crusade."

"You've got to be kidding me," Nick said in frustration. The tension in the room was reaching its peak.

"What the fuck do you want then?" Kevin asked, pushing himself off of the wall he was leaning on. "I'll tell you what you want. You want this guy to be another Nemesis. You need him to be another Nemesis."

"Fuck you," Nick said under his breath.

"All right, all right," Hollings said, pushing herself forward. "This is getting us nowhere."

Kevin was already nearing the door. His frustration with Nick, and the case as a whole, had reached the breaking point.

"You know, I might not be the great Nicholas Grenier," Kevin said, stopping as he opened the door to Hollings' office. "But I've been a homicide detective for years. I have solved most of my cases, and I've done it by following the clues and the facts. The facts in this case say that we are dealing with someone who is familiar with Allun, familiar enough to know about his little experiment. We follow these clues instead of hoping he's this intelligent psycho-killer you want him to be."

Kevin then walked through the door into the squad bay, slamming the office door behind him. Nick stood, leaning against a filing cabinet, staring at the floor. Hollings watched him for a few minutes, neither of them saying anything.

"You know I have every respect in the world for your abilities," Hollings started.

"Don't say it," Nick interrupted.

"Sometimes a duck is just a duck," Hollings continued. "Now I have to agree with Smith on this one. You seem to have clues pointing you to a whole list of suspects, and you are the only person who believes there is something more."

"This guy wants us looking at Allun's partners," Nick said. "It takes the focus off of him, long enough for him to kill again."

"Jesus Nick," Hollings said. "There is no evidence he is going to kill again. There is no evidence that this is anything more than what it looks like. Smith is right; you do want this guy to be another Nemesis."

"How many times have I been wrong about a killer, about a murder?" Nick asked.

"Oh come on, Nick," Hollings muttered.

"How many times?" Nick insisted.

"Never," Hollings said. "Not once. But guess what, nobody's perfect. Nobody's right all the time. That doesn't make you any less of a detective. Not everyone is right about everything all the time."

Nick pushed himself off of the filing cabinet and began pacing back and forth in front of Hollings' desk. Hollings knew that she needed to redirect his attention for a little while, let him cool down long enough to see the way things really were.

"I'm not wrong," Nick stated, though not necessarily to her.

"You never told me about your date last night," Hollings said. "Who is she?"

"Just someone I met recently," Nick said, smiling suddenly as he thought about Jenn.

"So you're not going to give me her name. She must be a cop," Hollings said. Nick looked at her for a moment, surprised by her instant deduction. "I'm a detective too, you know. Just because I sit behind this desk doesn't mean I haven't ever solved a case."

"The date was nice," Nick said. "We had a nice quiet dinner. There is something about her, we understand each other. I don't know, I think I blew it. She cooled off at the end of the night. I think I pushed her too fast."

"Hey, hey," Hollings said. "That's more than I needed to konw. I'm not your shrink. Have you called her since last night?"

"No," Nick said. "Speaking of which, I promised to call her this morning."

"Well go," Hollings said, waving him away. "Call her."

Nick exited the office feeling better than he had just a few moments ago. It bothered him that Smith and Hollings felt that he wanted this killer to be another Nemesis. However, he couldn't help but feel as though there was more to this killer than met the eye. It was too easy to pass him off as being connected to Allun. This killer was methodical, exacting, and most of all, patient. Sarrucci was right about this killer, Nick was right about this killer; there was much more to him than it appeared. Nick just had to find the clues to lead him there. Nick entered his office and closed the door. He walked around his desk and sat down in his chair, then punched Jenn's number into the phone and listened to the dial tone. Jenn picked up after the second ring.

"Hey, it's Nick. I wanted to make sure that we were alright after last night."

"We are now," Jenn said. "I'm glad you called. I'm sorry about how I reacted. It's just that I'm afraid of having a one night stand, not that I think that's what you want. It's just that…"

"You don't have to explain," Nick assured her again. "It was too fast, and I'm the one who should be apologizing. I just hope you feel comfortable enough to go out again."

"Of course I do," Jenn said. "And it means a lot to me that you called today, especially with what's going on right now. I have to be honest with you; I didn't expect you to call after I saw the broadcast."

"What broadcast?" Nick asked, suddenly confused. "What are you talking about?"

"Haven't you been watching the news?" Jenn asked. "Anderson says he has a tape of Allun being murdered. They've been showing bits and pieces of it for the last fifteen minutes."

"What?" Nick asked, jumping out of his seat with the phone still glued to his ear. "They've been showing the murder on television?"

"No, just bits and pieces of the beginning," Jenn said. "They've shown Allun bound to what looks like a chair, they're mostly just showing his face. They are also focusing heavily on the date on the tape, as if the date proves this is authentic."

"Oh shit," Nick said in shock. "I have to go, I'm sorry. I'll call you tonight, I promise."

Nick hung up the phone and rushed out of his office to Hollings's office. As he approached, he saw her and Kevin leaning against her desk, looking across the room at what Nick knew was the television. He walked in without knocking and focused his attention on the screen. After a moment, he turned to look at Hollings, and when she turned her attention on him, he could tell by the look on her face that they were all in trouble now.

CHAPTER 36

The shit has hit the fan. That was the first and only thought that went through Nick's mind as he began to watch the news broadcast. The first fact that interested Nick was that the station did not restart the clip where they had the first time fifteen minutes before. As the station showed a frozen image on the tape, the screen turned green and there was a distorted face in the image; and though frozen in terror it could still be made out as Father Allun's face. The killer had used a camera with a special night vision capability to film Allun in the dark. The broadcaster continued to focus on the time and date stamp on the lower right hand corner of the screen, marking the tape as having been recorded last Saturday, exactly a week ago. There was a sense of urgency about the studio anchors, they were trying to make it extremely simple to understand, they wanted to make sure everyone knew the tape was authentic. Nick was surprised at the insistence with which the anchors continued on, and how everyone seemed to be playing catch up, as if this were an event happening live. Nick tried to sort it out in his head, tried to understand why the news anchors were not at their professional peak, and then something occurred to him. He was going to tell his thought to Lt. Hollings when her phone rang and she picked it up. She immediately went into subordinate mode, making her tone lower in deference. Nick knew that she was talking to the brass, and he knew that it was not going to be good unless they came up with some answers fast. The police department as a whole ran the risk of taking a big hit.

Nick stepped out of the office to make a phone call, leaving Kevin alone watching the television report as Hollings tried to cover herself on the phone. As for Kevin, he watched in amazement and disbelief, hundreds of questions running through his mind. He had never suspected that the killer would have taken video of the murder, though he started to feel as though he should have. What more perfect revenge than to tape the murder of the man who sexually humiliated you, taping it for his own pleasure. This was perfect, this was undeniable. There was absolutely no doubt in his mind now that he was dealing with one of Allun's sexual partners. The detective was tired of Nick's way of investigating. Though he respected the other detective, Kevin felt the best way to investigate a case was to follow the leads. He did not have a sixth sense as Nick seemed to that enabled him to see the murders. He had to rely on what evidence was left over, and that evidence was telling him something far different than what Nick's heart was telling him. Nick wanted this case to be more than it was, and his lack of logical reasoning was starting to wear on Kevin. The fact of the matter was that this was a Norwich homicide and Kevin was more than willing to go it alone if he had to. Kevin had already talked to his chief, and though the governor's office would not let Kevin officially take over the investigation, the chief was willing to let Kevin investigate it on his own. Kevin did not want it to come to that, but he was being left with no choice. Hollings hung up the phone and sighed heavily.

"Where's Nick?" she asked sharply.

"He stepped out," Kevin answered. "Was that your chief?"

"Oh yeah," Hollings said. "He has already received calls from the governor's office and the state attorney general's office, all wondering if there was anything in this tape that could prove we were lying during the press conference."

"Everyone's playing the 'cover their ass' game," Kevin remarked.

"What the chief wants to know is whether this tape was shot using Allun's equipment, maybe in his own home," Hollings said, staring at the television screen and shaking her head. "How could the station be so wreckless as to show such a thing on the air?"

"What I want to know is, if this tape is authentic why would they wait so long to air it?" Kevin asked, as if to the screen itself.

"Oh, it's authentic," Nick said, entering the office. "I just got off the phone with the station manager and he's got quite a story for us. He says Anderson called in less than an hour ago, requesting a live feed. The station granted the request, having no idea what was going to be shown. They thought he was here at the police department, wanting to do a live feed on site. The manager states that they had no idea Anderson was going to roll any footage, and when they realized what they were looking at, they froze the tape at this image and cut the live feed. I thought it was weird the way the anchors were acting, and now I know why. They were trying to cover the station and not lose face at the same time."

"I am going to have someone's ass," Hollings screamed. "I want Anderson brought down here for questioning, and I want you to ride him until he breaks down and cries."

"Don't worry," Nick said. "He's already on his way down, with his cameraman and the station's attorney. The manager assured us that he will be bringing the original copy of the tape and that they will cooperate with us fully. The station is caught in a feud here, between Anderson and us. I doubt they knew about it beforehand, and they don't want to alienate us, not when they get so much information from us."

"So the question becomes, how long has Anderson had this tape?" Kevin asked, bringing them back on focus. "We need to call some tech guys down here to authenticate the tape with us, and to do their tech thing to find any possible clues."

"I'll get them up here," Hollings said. "You guys prepare to take on Anderson. When are they going to be here?"

"Any minute now," Nick said, turning his attention to the squad bay as if he expected the three men to come walking through the doors right on cue.

Any minute now became fifteen minutes later, when in walked three men with smug looks on their faces, as if they ruled the world. Nick had a plan, a way to make them feel a little less self-assured. He had instructed two uniformed officers to separate Anderson and his cameraman the moment they came in and take them to different interrogation rooms. There was only one attorney for the two men, but Nick knew that he wouldn't be frazzled by the change up. The attorney simply waited outside the interrogation rooms, waiting for the detectives to come and question whichever person they wanted. As Nick watched them go by, he decided that he was going to start with the cameraman, whose name was Paul, and make Anderson sweat a little. Nick walked into the interrogation room, followed by Detective Smith and the station's attorney. The two detectives walked around the table to the far side of the room, where Hollings could see the look on the cameraman's face through the one-way glass.

"You are in a world of shit my young friend," Nick started.

"Detectives," the attorney began. "I am not going to let you intimidate my client."

"Why don't you pipe down there mouthpiece and listen to what the good detective here has to say," Kevin said, stepping up to the lawyer as if he were going to physically assault the other man. Kevin Smith was an intimidating figure even when you did know him, and he was even more intimidating when you didn't.

"Do you know what obstructing a police investigation is?" Nick asked. "That's when you withhold evidence from law enforcement. That was what you did when you did not inform us you had that tape."

"You can't pull this Gestapo shit on me," Paul said, smiling up in the detective's face. "Confidential informants; reporters have them all the time, doesn't it fall under journalistic shield."

"You can only charge him with obstruction if you have evidence that he withheld the tape, and that he had it for any length of time," the lawyer said, regaining some of his confidence, though his eyes danced back and forth, fearful of Smith.

"It became obstruction the moment you knew what was on that tape and did not alert the police," Nick said.

"Whatever," Paul said, rolling his eyes. "Either charge me or leave me the fuck alone."

There was a tap at the window and then the door opened. In walked the NBC station manager, followed by Lt. Hollings.

"This is Mr. Andres, the station manager," Hollings said, introducing him to the detectives. Andres shook hands with both detectives, and then turned his attention on Paul.

"I like you Paul," Andres started. "I've always liked you. When Mark Anderson came to us and wanted to be a reporter, I thought of you immediately. I thought, here is a reporter who has all the ins and outs in the police department, here is someone who can get you both to the big time fast. You see, I was thinking of your career. There were plenty of more senior cameramen who were up for the position, definitely ones more qualified. But I saw something in you, and I wanted you to do well. You've disappointed me though; you put the entire station at risk with your stunt."

Paul looked over at the lawyer for a second, which enraged Andres, causing him to slam his hand down on the table hard.

"Don't look at him! You look at me!" Andres shouted. "He's my lawyer; he's the station's lawyer, which means he defends you at my discretion. You disappointed me, but I know you're going to make it right. You have ten seconds from the moment I stop talking to tell these detectives everything they want to know and if you don't I'm going to have to suggest you get your own lawyer because you won't have my help, you won't have the lawyers help, and I assure you that you won't have a job with us. You put the station at risk for lawsuits if not having our license pulled by showing tape of a man being murdered..."

"But I didn't know," Paul cried out. He was broken, tears flowing steadily from his eyes, his entire body shaking. "I swear I didn't know. He called me and..."

"Who called you?" Kevin interrupted, his voice forceful and commanding.

"Anderson," Paul stammered in fear. "Anderson called and told me to hurry down, that he had something that was going to scoop everyone and put us at the top for good. When I got there, he said we were going to do a live feed and to set up quickly. It took all the time I had just to get the van set up before we went on the air."

Andres cocked his head to the side, as if to suggest he did not believe the cameraman.

"I swear, here look at my cell phone," Paul said, pulling out his phone and opening it up. He scrolled down a list to the second set of numbers. "It logs the time, look at the time. I live in Old Saybrook; I barely had time to get there before we went on. Anderson said later that there were hours on that tape. I didn't have time to see any of it. I swear if I had

THE DEVIL YOU KNOW

known what was on the tape I wouldn't have linked up for the feed, I swear."

The detectives left the room with Andres and Hollings following. Paul was left in the room crying, with his head down on the table. The lawyer was still inside, patting Paul on the back as if trying to console the man but stay professional at the same time. Needless to say, he was doing a terrible job.

"Jesus you should have been a cop," Kevin said, turning to the station manager. "I've never seen a man break that fast."

"You almost made me cry," Hollings said under her breath.

"Whether he knew what was on the tape or not," Andres said, deflecting the praise. "He never would have had enough time to view it. Plus, he has always been loyal to me and the station; I doubt that he would have aired it if he knew."

"Will you still fire him?" Nick asked, noting a fatherly concern coming from the manager.

"No," Andres said, shaking his head. "He'll do the obligatory penance, filing video reels in archives for a month or two, at least until we are certain there will be no fall out from airing what little of the tape we did. Then he will have to work his way up a little, but he won't be fired. I don't want my employees thinking I'm that big a bastard. It would look really cold hearted if I didn't show any compassion for my own nephew."

"Damn," Kevin muttered under his breath. "Your nephew."

"What about him?" asked Hollings, pointing through the one way glass at Anderson. "Can we expect the same sort of cooperation?"

"I'm afraid that you're in a whole different league there lieutenant," Andres said, and everyone there knew what he meant, perhaps even more than Andres did himself. "But we'll give you all the support we can."

"What do you think?" asked Kevin. "Good cop, bad cop?"

"No," Nick answered. "I think I should go in alone. He says this vendetta is between him and the lieutenant, but I think it's really between him and me."

Before Nick could move, Detective Wilkins brushed by all four of them and walked up to the door to the interrogation room.

"Not today," Wilkins said. "Today this is between an ex-cop and his partner."

"But you haven't been briefed..." Nick started, but before he could finish Wilkins was in the interrogation room alone with Anderson, slamming the door behind him.

CHAPTER 37

Detectives Grenier and Smith watched in shock as Wilkins stepped up to the table in the interrogation room and dropped his notebook case on the table. Nick looked over at Hollings to say something, but then stopped when he saw the look on her face. There was a type of knowing smile there, as though she knew something like this was going to happen. Nick turned back to the window and watched, knowing that there was nothing more he could do now. Wilkins was not up-to-date with the facts on hand, but Nick was not going to blow it now by interrupting them. This was just something that was going to have to play out, and Nick would deal with whatever happened. Nick flipped the switch on the speaker and listened in with everyone else. Seated at the table, Anderson was already spewing his venom. There was a lot of pent up anger inside of him, and at times like this, when he let his bitterness loose, it was hard to believe that he had ever been a cop, much less a homicide detective. Wilkins just listened at first, as if Anderson's caustic remarks did not faze him.

"Did Grenier really think that by sending my old partner in here that I'd really open up and tell him everything he wants to know?" Anderson asked, mockingly at the one way glass. "Or maybe he's too afraid to deal with me directly. Maybe he's afraid that I'll prove he's not as great as everyone thinks he is."

"No," answered Wilkins calmly. "I'm just here because I'm the only one who will talk to you. I'm the only one who isn't so angry that I want to throw you through that glass. Everyone else out there, they're pissed."

"Who's everyone else?" Anderson asked, rolling his eyes.

"Well, there's Nick and Lt. Hollings who are just floored by the fact that a former police detective could act this way," Wilkins began. "Then there's the station manager who is furious that you put the station at risk for lawsuits so irresponsibly."

"The station manager isn't here," Anderson said, doubtfully.

"Mr. Andres," Wilkins began. "Balding, glasses, medium height and build with an expensive suit. You better believe he's here and all of them are together, spitting fire. You should be thankful that you have me to deal with."

"Oh yeah," Anderson said, sarcastically. "Real thankful."

"So, how long have you had this tape?" Wilkins asked. "How long have you been holding out on the police, making us look bad when you had a crucial piece of evidence in your possession?"

"Hey," Anderson said, leaning forward and pointing a finger at the detective. "I just got that tape today. As for making the department look bad, you guys are doing that all on your own. When you lie to everyone and just sit on your asses hoping the killer will come forward, what do you expect people to think? As for the tape, I got it today and that's all I'm saying until I talk with my lawyer."

"Did you know what was on it prior to playing it for the public?" Wilkins asked. Anderson said nothing, just looked down at the table. Wilkins knew that he was not going to get anything out of Anderson unless he mixed it up a little. "I'll take that as a no. So it was the cameraman who decided to play the tape live, and you just went along with it."

"Hey!" Anderson shouted, coming alive again. "Paul does what I tell him to, not the other way around. He didn't even know what was on the tape until we were broadcasting it live."

"That's good," Wilkins said, pleased with Anderson's reaction. "That corroborates what he told us, that you called him over and told him to play the tape and that he had no knowledge of its contents prior to the broadcast."

"You talked to him before you talked to me?" Anderson asked, now at the height of his fury. "You kept me waiting here, me and talked to some lowly cameraman first."

"I want to know everything that has happened from the time you got the tape until now," Wilkins said, ignoring Anderson's outburst. "I want a detailed accounting of everything that has happened."

Anderson said nothing, silenced by his own anger. He had been played by his old partner, played by his need to prove he was not subordinate to anyone. That need had supplied Wilkins with the information to prove the cameraman's statement. Wilkins understood where he now stood with Anderson. There was no bond between them, not that there ever had been. However, Wilkins had been Anderson's partner, and he had respected that until now. Now they were playing hardball, and there were some issues that Wilkins had been waiting a long time to get off of his chest.

"You know," Wilkins started. "I never did mind being your partner. I knew that you weren't a great detective; hell I knew that you weren't even a good one. I dealt with your hatred and bitterness of anyone and everyone who was better than you, for one reason; you were my partner. I didn't agree with you on some matters, I didn't agree with you on many, but I kept my feelings to myself because you were my partner. My partner! I gave you more respect than you deserved because of your rank and seniority. When people talked about you, I was the one who defended you. All because you were my partner. However, you are not my partner anymore. You left, throwing a temper tantrum because Grenier was better than you. I thought that a transfer would be the best thing for you; you could retire and enjoy the rank and privilege that came from it. However, you started this vendetta, and now you've proven who you really are. No cop would put his own interests above a murder investigation. No cop would tarnish the reputations of his fellow officers, no matter how he felt about them. A lot of things could be said about you, and time and again this department has chosen not to sink to your level. No, you're not a cop, you're just a bitch with a grudge and that's all you'll ever be."

Anderson said nothing, and for a time, neither did Wilkins. The detective needed to know if there was anything of the old cop left in Anderson. He needed to know if there ever was anything in Anderson. Wilkins had listened to the lies and half truths that Anderson had been spewing for a long time. He had heard from Nick and Lt. Hollings about the things that Anderson was doing to discredit the department, and though he saw a lot with his own eyes, he still could not believe that a police officer would hurt his own colleagues to settle a grudge. However, now he knew that Anderson was just out for himself. His bitterness had twisted whatever decency he had left in him, enough to cloud him from the obvious. Enough to make him think that showing a videotape of a murder was perfectly justified if it got him what he wanted.

"The tape came in the mail this morning," Anderson said finally. "I opened it and there was a note from the killer inside. Immediately I put on some leftover latex gloves I had, and treated it like a piece of evidence. Still, it had been addressed to me and I felt as though I needed to know what was on it. I viewed the tape and then called Paul, my cameraman, and told him to come over. I wanted to get it out on the news before someone else found out about it's existence."

"At least you had the foresight to preserve the chain of evidence," Wilkins said, tugging at the bag with the videotape, the envelope and the knife Anderson had used to open it.

"Hey, it was the police that lied to the public," Anderson pointed out. "You said that Allun was a saint. You didn't bother to mention his abundant sexual life."

"How do you know about his sex life?" Wilkins asked. "That wasn't part of the tape."

"It wasn't part of that one," Anderson said with a smile. He reached into his jacket pocket and pulled out another tape, also in a plastic bag. "This one is of him and a man and a lot of leather straps."

Wilkins reached out and ripped the bag out of Anderson's hand.

"I might be holding a grudge," Anderson said. "But it does me no good to lose the one job that will give me the opportunity to exact my revenge."

"Trust me when I say you won't have that chance," Wilkins said, rising from the table to leave.

"What about me?" Anderson asked. "Am I free to go?"

"You know the drill," Wilkins said over his shoulder. "First we verify your story, then we see about letting you go."

Wilkins exited the interrogation room and closed the door behind him, leaning against it to support his weight. This interrogation had been the worst for him. He had been forced to pit his knowledge against a man that he had trusted with his life, even though he had not liked him very much. For the police, partners were like brothers, and there was a bond that was not easily broken. However, Anderson had found it easy to break the bonds of brotherhood that had been forged through years of working side by side. Wilkins had not found it so easy, and still didn't; but this was a homicide investigation and Anderson's willingness to use that to his own advantage broke with everything a cop is taught to believe in. Wilkins looked up suddenly, expecting all eyes to be on him, but found that he was alone in the hallway. Everyone had left, and immediately he realized that he could be in serious trouble for jumping in on Grenier's investigation. Wilkins made his way through the squad bay and noticed that all eyes were on him now. He was the center of attention, and apparently everyone was waiting to see if he was in trouble too. Wilkins entered Hollings' office.

"Lieutenant," Wilkins started, but she just held up her hand.

"Save it," she said. "Nick is your immediate superior and you need to go through him. Chain of command."

Wilkins turned and made his way to Nick's office, uncertain whether Nick would understand why he needed to do what he did. It didn't really matter though. Wilkins had broken with procedure and could have possibly made things worse.

"Well, what did you find out?" Nick asked, his face blank to whatever emotion was going on inside.

"Anderson viewed the tape," Wilkins said. "He knew what was on it, but he did preserve the chain of evidence and that should help. He also handed over another tape, one of Allun's homemade sex movies. Anderson knows, but as to how long he will keep our secret is unknown."

"He'll keep it until he needs it," Nick said. "Then, when he sees the chance to use it to his advantage, he'll use the information against us."

"I need to explain my actions," Wilkins began, unable to hold it any longer.

"No you don't," Nick said. "I never considered how hard it's been on you, watching your partner break with his duty as a cop, pulled between your own duty and your bond to your partner. I owe you an apology for not seeing it sooner."

Nick came around from behind his desk and stood face to face with the other detective.

"I've never wanted to be anyone's boss," Nick said. "I've never thrown rank around. It's just not like me. However, I am your superior officer and I think I need to let you know

224

that I have never been more proud of one of my detectives as I am today. You kept your head, didn't play his game and still came out with the information we needed. And hopefully, you found some peace yourself."

Nick extended his hand, and Wilkins shook it without thinking. He had not expected this response, but was grateful to not be in trouble. The two detectives walked out of the office together and stood before everyone in the squad. There was a sense of relief that everything was back to normal, emotionally at least.

"So where do we go from here?" Hollings asked, exiting her office.

"Detectives Wilkins and Mitchell will take the tapes to the tech guys and hold their hands while they pull every little scrap of evidence out of it," Nick said, smiling at them both. He then turned his attention to Kevin who had been oddly quiet since the tape hit the press. "Detective Smith and I will be interviewing Allun's sexual partner."

Everyone was quiet for a moment, shocked that Nick had finally conceded to the interviews. Nick smiled at Kevin.

"Hey, you have to go where the evidence leads you."

CHAPTER 38

Nick and Kevin spent the rest of their Saturday conducting interviews with Father Allun's sexual partners. The interviews were bad; there was just no other way to describe them. Most of the people, though aware of Allun's murder, had no idea that they could be linked back to him. Many of them had not even known he was a priest until they saw him on the news reports. None of them knew that they had been videotaped. They felt violated, first by Allun taking away their privacy, and now by the police, whose very presence threatened to expose their relationship to the victim. None of them wanted to talk to the detectives. Some did because they felt compelled to, while others were barely willing to tell them anything at all. Some told them nothing, demanding the detectives leave the moment they knew why they had come. Worst of all, the entire day had been as Nick expected and feared. They had spent all of these hours talking to the partners and were left with nothing new. They had no valuable information, no viable suspects, and only a few bits of information that created alibis for those few who were willing to speak to them. Kevin had done most of the driving, and Nick was acutely aware the other man had not spoken a word since leaving the home of the last person they interviewed.

"What are you thinking about?" Nick asked, unable to deal with the drawn out silence any longer. The lack of conversation was almost suffocating in the small confines of the car's interior.

"I'm thinking about what a colossal waste of time this was," Kevin answered. "I'm thinking that it's about time for you to say you told me so."

"Look," Nick said with a shrug. "You said it yourself; we follow where the evidence leads us. This was where it was leading us."

"You don't have to patronize me," Kevin stated. "This was a wild goose chase."

"Like I said," Nick repeated, turning back to the window. "We followed the evidence. Besides, it's not like we had anything else to do. This was the only lead we had left."

"Are we in agreement that none of the people we interviewed are suspects?" Kevin asked, keeping his eyes peeled on the road, though it was obvious that his mind was elsewhere.

"For the most part," Nick said. "I'll have Mitchell follow upon the little facts we do have, but I doubt any of them had anything to do with it. Don't lose hope though; there are a couple more people we'll check out tomorrow."

"I can't fucking wait," Kevin muttered.

The next day was Sunday, and it followed the same pattern as Saturday afternoon. There were five more people to check, and the detectives talked to them all. However, there was a little twist in the day. Four out of the five people demanded the videotapes be handed over, obviously with the intent of destroying them. They all threatened legal action, and Nick wondered why he hadn't considered this reaction before. In fact, the more he thought about it, the more he was surprised that all of the partners had not demanded the same. They probably would, once they had time to go over every course available to them. From what Nick could tell, none of the partners knew anything about being recorded. The detective could imagine that they were all in shock; first from finding out that Allun was a priest, then from the fact that there was a lasting memory of the event. The two detectives finished the interviews just after noon that day, and when they parked to go to their separate cars, the same heavy quiet hung in the air.

"I just want to get this out of the way," Kevin finally said. "You were right and I was wrong. There, just so we're clear."

"There is no right or wrong," Nick said. "We were going to have to do these interviews at some point, and the information we gathered was going to be the same one way or another. At least we know."

"Somehow, that doesn't make me feel any better," Kevin said.

"Can we both agree that Allun was murdered because of his secret sex life?" Nick asked, exasperated. It was hard enough keeping his own spirits up, but to have to support Smith's emotional well being was beginning to take its toll.

"Yeah," Kevin answered. "That much is obvious."

"Well, these interviews were about his sex life," Nick explained. "We weren't going to be sure until we talked to them, and now that we have we can focus on the next avenue."

"And what would that be?" Kevin asked. "The next avenue?"

Nick paused before speaking, thinking about how he was going to answer that question. He had been thinking about that very thought the entire drive home from the last interview, and he had come up with only one answer. They would have to find out every person who knew anything about Allun's sex life. If the killer was not one of the partners, then there had to be someone else who knew about the priest's night life. The killer knew about it, and he had to have found out from somewhere, so there had to be a way anyone could find out.

"We focus on anyone who might have known about Allun's sex life," Nick finally said. "First we find out how the killer learned about Allun. We check out every detail of Allun's life, and we go from there. And while we're at it, we ought to find out where the wax stamp came from."

"You're obsessed with that wax stamp," Kevin said. "You don't talk about it, but everyone can tell you are always thinking about it."

"There has to be some connection between the stamp and the killer," Nick said. "Whoever has the stamp, whether it was Allun or the killer, has to have some connection to it. There is some significance and I just can't figure it out."

"It's stuck in your craw," Kevin said absently.

"Again, I don't know what a craw is," Nick started, shaking his head. "But I don't think I want anything getting in there."

"You don't," Kevin said bluntly. "It can be a bitch to get out."

The detectives separated and Nick decided he could not go home feeling so empty handed. Nothing had been accomplished today and he had the feeling that if he went home like this, he was only going to be depressed for the rest of the night. Nick decided that he would pay Jenn an unannounced visit, and maybe would be able to determine what direction their relationship was taking. That at least would be some sort of progress and he could go home feeling as though he had finally accomplished something for the day. He had worked the entire weekend, and having no time off, he was not going to be in his best form for Monday morning. Nick drove out to Jenn's house, thinking about an excuse for dropping by while driving. However, when he pulled into her driveway and saw her running out to greet him, he realized that he did not need an excuse. She was just happy to see him, and even more pleased that he felt comfortable enough to drop by like this, especially after how they both might have been feeling since the other night.

He and Jenn made dinner together, taking their time while eating, just talking and feeling comfortable with each other. Afterwards, they cleaned up together and finally found themselves on the couch together; Nick sitting on one side with Jenn lying across the couch, using his legs as a pillow. The television was set to a 24-hour news station, though the sound was muted and Jenn just lay there staring up at him. Nick did not notice however, his mind was focused on his case. He was becoming deathly afraid that this would become his first unsolved case. Every detective had them; it's just that Nick had been lucky so far. Now, he was running out of leads, and unless something happened soon, he was going to become like all the other detectives, normal, and that was unacceptable to him.

"What are you thinking about?" Jenn asked, her voice reeling him back in from his thoughts. He looked down at her and smiled.

"Nothing," he answered. "The case. I'm sorry, I'm not being attentive."

"You don't have to be," Jenn said. "I just like being here with you. This is the best time we've had so far."

"I agree," Nick said, desperately wanting to lower his head and kiss her. "I feel more at peace right now than I have in a long time."

Jenn smiled, and in her eyes, there was something more.

"Ask me what I'm thinking," she said softly.

"What are you thinking?" Nick asked, lowering his tone to match.

"I'm thinking you should stay the night," she said, raising her head and turning, bringing her face close to his.

"Are you sure?" Nick asked, a little weary. "Are you sure we're ready for that?"

"We don't have to fool around," Jenn said with a smile. "Not if you think that's moving things too fast."

"What do you think?" he asked, surprised by her sudden directness to the subject.

"I think I'll know when I climb into bed with you," she answered.

That night turned out to be great. They did not end up having sex or making love. They just spent the night in each other's arms, touching each other's body, their lips almost never separating. There was a language that passed between them, as if they were having a conversation with each other in their minds. There was no awkward moment, no second guessing or doubt. There was only the two of them, closer to each other than they had ever been; mentally, physically, and emotionally. There were no more doubts about where their relationship was headed.

The next morning, Nick could hear the sea's rhythmic pounding of the shore, could sense the sun snaking in through the blinds of the windows, but made no attempt to get up. Jenn lay there with him the whole time, and he guessed that she must have a later shift that day. As for Nick, everyone in the Unit knew that he had spent the entire weekend working, and no one was going to make a fuss about him coming in a little late. However, at a little after nine in the morning, his pager went off. Nick turned it off without looking at the number and rolled over and put his arm around Jenn. Five minutes later, his pager and cell phone rang and he grumbled as he turned over to retrieve them.

"Whoever this is is in some real deep shit right about now," Nick said into his cell phone.

"Is that so," Hollings said from the other end of the call. "Well I hate to interrupt your beauty sleep, as you are in such desperate need for some, but we have another murder, and I need you on the scene."

"I'm already investigating a murder," Nick said. "Give it to someone else and I'll check up on them later."

"Nope," Hollings said. "This one's all yours, now get your butt out of bed and get over to this address."

Nick made a mental note of the address and hung up the phone, reminding himself that all good things come to an end. He rolled over and watched Jenn sleep for a few minutes, then kissed her lightly on her shoulder.

"Do you have to go?" she asked. She had been awake the entire time, but like him, had simply been enjoying the company of the other beside them.

"Were you pretending to be asleep?" Nick asked, only slightly surprised.

"Whatever will keep you in this bed," she answered, turning her head up to look at him.

"I'll come back to this bed," Nick promised. "Or maybe you could make your way over to mine and we'll see if you are as comfortable at my home as I seem to be at yours."

Nick climbed out of the bed and looked around for his clothes.

"That sounds good," she said.

"I'll call you later," he said, slipping his pants on and grabbing his shirt.

"You promise?" she asked.

"Wild horses," Nick said, walking away. It was all he needed to say.

CHAPTER 39

Nick drove to the crime scene trying to maintain the façade that he was irritated about being woken by the call, but deep down he was euphoric. It had been such a great night, just lying there in bed with Jenn, sleeping beside her, waking up beside her. They were now at a level in their relationship where they were beyond the games, beyond the image and the self doubt. They had been intimate, close, together and yet alone. Nick did not know how to explain what had happened last night, but at the same time, he did not feel as though he needed to. It had just been perfect, and best of all, he was no longer unsure of where they stood. There were no questions now; there was just the two of them. That was all he needed to know. As he was nearing the Gold Star Memorial Bridge on I-95, he remembered he and Kevin were supposed to meet and go over the case in a few hours. Nick called the other detective and explained the situation with the new homicide, and Kevin understood completely. All homicide detectives have had more than one open case at a time throughout their careers, and Kevin told Nick that he would start doing some preliminary work on Allun's background as they had discussed the afternoon before. Nick hung up the phone and felt as though this were for the best. At this point in the case, it did not require both of them to be working on it, and Nick felt as though he needed to get away from it a little and come back fresh.

Nick made his way to the address given him by Lt. Hollings and as he pulled his car to the curb just down the street from the crime scene itself, he realized just how close to the police department he really was. As he neared the scene, Nick was amused by the audacity of the killer, striking so near to the police department without fear of getting caught. The detective was even a little bit impressed. As Nick approached, he flashed his badge at a uniformed officer standing in front of a police barricade and ducked down underneath the yellow police tape that was tied to it and down the sidewalk to a barricade on the other side. There, standing in front of the store was Detective Mitchell, waiting with a hot coffee in his hand.

"Is that for me?" Nick asked, reaching out for the cup.

"No," Mitchell answered and quickly pulled it back to his body. Nick laughed and shook his head, wishing now that he had stopped for a cup himself.

"Why have I been called down here if you both are on the scene?" Nick asked, hoping the junior detective could shed some light on the lieutenant's frame of mind.

"I don't know," Mitchell answered. "Mine is not to question why."

"What do we have here?" Nick asked. Mitchell opened his fancy notebook and flipped through the pages.

"The victim is Jack Brenner," Mitchell began. "A.k.a. Jack Hammer; apparently he was some sort of famous porn star in his day. Anyway, he's found dead in his office, and according to the M.E. inside, he's been dead for several days."

"Who found him?" Nick asked, shocked that an ex-porn star had a store just down the street from the police department and Nick had never heard about it before now.

"An employee," Mitchell answered. "Her name is Emily. She came by looking for her check, and found the place a mess. She went back to see if it was a break in, and found her infamous employer dead. Apparently, it wasn't a pretty site. EMS took her to the hospital, said she's in shock."

Nick was about to ask another question when Wilkins came into view at the open double doors and waved them in. He had been inside, waiting for CSU to do a preliminary scan of the scene, enough to make room for the detectives to come in. Nick and Mitchell made their way to the front doors, donned the plastic booties and stepped inside.

The store was in shambles. When Nick was a teenager, his mother used to tell him that his room looked like a tornado hit it. It was her favorite expression. Her words came to mind as he viewed the mess that surrounded them. The detectives had to step gingerly around the videos, shelves, and display stands that littered the floor. As Nick tiptoed carefully around everything, he could not help but snicker at some of the titles of erotic films on the floor.

"Remember detective," Mitchell warned. "We're supposed to be professionals."

"Yeah, but this goes above and beyond," Nick said, passing the by the videos. There were boxes of sexual toys spread across the ground, and there was an item in particular that the detective could not identify. "What in the hell."

Nick stopped and kneeled down for a closer examination. He did not dare touch the box or the video that was lying on top of it; he just craned his head to the side a little to get a better view of the box. Mitchell turned back and carefully retraced his steps until he found the spot where Nick had stopped. Mitchell bent his body to the side to get a better look, and then sighed.

"They're anal beads, detective," Mitchell said, amused by Nick's seemingly inability to understand the toys concept.

"You've got to be kidding me," Nick muttered.

"Please don't make me explain it to you," Mitchell pleaded, then turned and continued on back towards the victim's office.

"I must be leading a sheltered life," Nick commented, following Mitchell. They finally reached the back office where they found the body of the victim.

Already a smell was emanating from the dead body. Nick put his hand up to his face, looking away from the body until the Vapor-Rub was passed around. Nick found the gel to be a helpful tool during times like this; a little placed on the upper lip just beneath the nostrils helped to alleviate the stench of death. It helped, but didn't totally block out the smell. After Wilkins and Mitchell applied the Vapor-Rub, they passed it to Nick and after applied, Nick took his first full deep breath since entering the office. He was now able to devote his full attention to the dead body.

The body of Jack Brenner was tied to a wooden desk, faced down and naked. There was blood around the body, as well as on the legs and arms. Even from where he stood at the entrance to the office, Nick could see a phallic shaped object protruding from behind the victim. Nick just shook his head and sighed, then walked around to view the front of the body. Blood covered the face of the victim, and in his open mouth was what looked like an award of some type, secured in the open mouth with a long silk scarf. There was something about the placement of the body that struck Nick; he just couldn't put the right words to it. Mitchell bent down to examine the body as Nick looked over at the shelf full of awards to read them more closely. They were all adult film awards, and Nick read the words on each one.

"Our boy was hog tied," Wilkins said from across the room.

"That's it," Nick said, snapping his fingers as he turned. "He looks like one of those pigs with the apple in his mouth, what do you call them?"

"Like a roast pig?" Wilkins asked.

"Just like that," Nick commented. "I guess someone really didn't like this guy."

"I really don't see how this guy was the stuff of legend," Mitchell remarked. Nick turned to see Mitchell examining the dead body. "Wasn't he supposed to be a big porn star?"

"I've heard size doesn't matter," Nick said.

"Is that what all your girlfriends tell you," Wilkins joked.

"Yeah man," Mitchell added. "They were just trying to make you feel better."

"Maybe the little detective isn't all he's cracked up to be," Wilkins said. Mitchell started laughing.

"Get it," Mitchell said. "Dick is short for detective. He made a joke."

"How about I leave you all here with stinky the pig to figure out the case by yourselves," Nick said, taking the brunt of the jokes.

"Ah come on man," Wilkins said. "We all have our shortcomings."

"Nice," Nick said, walking around to the left side of the body. "Real nice. What do you see down there detective?"

Wilkins could tell by the tone of Nick's voice that all joking was over. They had all had their fun, and it was only natural given the crime scene and the circumstances. Nick understood that in their line of work they all needed an outlet of some sort. However, the CSU team was making their way back to the office again and it was time to show some professionalism.

"I can't see that much without rolling him," Mitchell started. "But there are little spots of dried blood all over the body and on the desk, and..."

Nick and Detective Wilkins both immediately registered the fact that Mitchell had stopped talking in mid sentence. They both turned to the detective examining the body.

"Shit, I think these are splinters," Mitchell said, pointing to little fragments jutting out of the body.

"So he was raped here before being killed," Nick said. "He was assaulted so hard that little bits of wood lodged in his skin."

"This place is a nightmare," said one of the CSU techs. "There are probably tons of fingerprints and God knows how many types of bodily fluids all over this place. We'll be lucky if we find anything useful."

"Do what you..." Nick started. That was all he remembered saying. In fact, that was just about all he remembered. Nick moved his hand against the desk to steady himself as he kneeled down on the other side of the body, and just as he did, the detective heard a high pitch scream from somewhere off in the distance. He suddenly felt feverish and weak, and then he was blinded by an intense white light, which then gave way immediately to pitch blackness. There was the sensation of falling, endlessly falling and then he was swallowed up by the darkness. In that moment, Nick knew that he was losing consciousness, though all his mind could do was wonder where the screaming was coming from.

CHAPTER 40

Nick did not know where he was, did not know what was going on, only knew that the ear piercing screams were driving him insane. He could see nothing, could not even be sure that he was actually able to move. There was no point of reference, no difference to the unending darkness. However, the screams died away as did the darkness, and something started to materialize before him. Nick found himself staring at an office, not unlike the one he had just been in. The desk was the same, though as he looked around, he realized that this office was far more densely furnished with cheap, yet plush furniture. It was the type of furniture a kid might pick out if given unlimited resources and no self control. Nick felt himself moving around the desk, not so much physically as his perception of the room changed. Nick knew exactly what was going on, this was his vision, this was his vision of the crime, and he prepared himself for what he was about to see. Suddenly, lights began to flash in his eyes like strobe lights, and then beyond that, Nick saw bright halogen lights shining down on him. An image began to materialize before him. Two people in front of the desk, a man, a younger version of the victim Nick had just seen was standing over a much younger woman who he was forcing face down on the desk. She was squirming, trying to regain control of the situation but he was too powerful. He had the advantage of size, strength, and position.

Then, as Nick watched unsure of what was going on, another image appeared right next to the first. This time, it was Brenner assaulting another young woman. Multiple images appeared and as they did, Nick found that the screaming returned.

They were the screams of the women he abused. The room filled with these images, bodies moving but seeming as real as smoke, like ghosts. The images and screaming began to take its toll on the detective's mind, and he was forced to look away. However, there was no where to look that did not have a scene of Brenner mistreating and abusing young women. The sense of pain and fear seemed to surround Nick, while the arrogance of expectation seemed to exude from Brenner. Nick felt his anger rise as he was forced to witness scene after horrific scene. Whenever one scene would fade away, another would replace it. In all, there must have been fifty scenes of abuse, women crying and screaming, Brenner yelling and laughing, grunting and sweating all over them. Image after image, scene after scene, Nick was forced to watch what was happening, only hoping that a clue would emerge from this horrible vision. Nick began to understand why he was forced to view this over and over again. It was because Nick's visions were images of crimes. This is what Nick saw, whether it was murder or rape, shoplifting or assaults. This room, the desk in particular was the setting for so many crimes.

Finally the scenes of sexual violence faded away, thankfully not replaced by any others. The screaming died off and Nick was left in the room, alone. After what seemed like a few minutes, the image of Brenner sitting in his chair formed in front of him. Brenner was far different now; old pitiful and alone. There was something oddly rewarding about the man Brenner had become, after seeing how much he had taken from the lives of others. Nick felt no pity for this creature, no desire to help him, only justified smugness. Nick felt himself turning to examine the room, but it was the detective that almost screamed in his own vision when he found himself suddenly face to face with the figure he knew to be the killer. Nick felt a strange sort of pain overwhelm him as the shock hit him, the shock of not only seeing the killer, but realizing that this was the same person who had killed Michael Allun. It wasn't just the fact that the figure was wearing the same clothes as Allun's killer; it was the eyes. Nick could see the killer's eyes and immediately recognized them. Nick turned back to see the look of fear and surprise on Brenner's face, and as the figure came at Brenner, Nick stepped aside instinctively as though he were part of the unfolding events instead of just witnessing them.

Nick watched, shocked by the speed in which Brenner was able to move his own body. Brenner was still fast, inspired by the thought of self preservation. Nick had been surprised that the older man had put up any fight at all. Nick watched the events play out, taking in every detail, understanding now why the crime scene looked as it did. He watched as the killer incapacitated Brenner and dragged him back to the office. Nick watched as the killer sexually tortured Brenner, screaming at him though Nick could not hear the words. Nick felt as though he could not breathe as he became overwhelmed by what the killer was doing to Brenner, though a feeling of justified revenge accompanied his disgust. When the killer was finished with Brenner, he bent over and strangled the unconscious body. There was some twitching from the victim, but no struggle. Finally, the body went totally limp and the killer turned and stared straight ahead, as though he were looking directly at Nick. Though the knit mask was again pulled down over the face, Nick couldn't take his attention away from the killer's eyes.

"Detective," Nick heard a voice call out. It was the first sound he had heard since the screams that filled his ears.

"Detective," the voice repeated. The figure reached out, and Nick began to tremble in fear. He had never been a part of a vision before, and he was now truly terrified.

"Detective!" screamed a voice and suddenly Nick was jolted back to the crime scene, Wilkins and Mitchell standing over him. "Nick, are you alright?"

Nick flung himself from side to side suddenly, disconnected from himself. He was back in the crime scene, back in Brenner's office. The putrid stench of death was recognizable again and Nick tried desperately to remember what happened before his vision.

"What happened?" Nick asked, in a deep guttural tone.

"You passed out," Mitchell said. "You were having some kind of seizure. Are you alright, do you want us to call an ambulance?"

"No," Nick said. "No, that's not necessary. How long was I out for?"

"Just a few seconds," Wilkins said. "Any longer and I would have called the ambulance anyway."

"I saw the crime," Nick said. "I saw all of them."

"What are you talking about?" Mitchell asked, grabbing Nick by the shoulders to steady him. "There was more than one crime?"

"This desk," Nick began, slowly raising himself up. "This desk has been the scene for countless rapes, and this murder. It was why the killer picked this spot. This was revenge, revenge for everything that Brenner did."

"Everything Brenner did to who?" Wilkins asked, trying to follow along. Though he had witnessed Nick's trances before, he had never been certain that he actually believed that Nick saw the crimes play out before him; and he had never seen Nick have an attack like this.

"Women," Nick said, exiting the room. "Young women; would be stars in his films. He forced them to have sex with him, taping the event for his films and his own pleasure. There were flashing lights and big halogen bulbs shining down during the vision, he was filming the entire time, and so was the killer."

"How do you know this?" Mitchell asked, though he knew the answer would not hold up in a court of law. However, Nick just ignored the question and made his way out into the store. Nick ordered the CSU tech to take samples around the door, saying that some type of pepper spray or mace had been used there. Nick then made his way back to the office where Mitchell and Wilkins were waiting for him.

"Maybe we should take you to the hospital, just in case," Wilkins suggested.

"He was sitting in the chair," Nick said, ignoring the comment. "He saw the killer and ran, getting past him and out into the store. The killer caught him twice, stunning him with a taser right here."

Nick stopped directly over the spot where the two had struggled.

"Brenner got away again though," Nick said. "It's ironic that the greatest effort this man ever made was at the end of his life. He ran for the doors but was trapped, the gates were down. Did that woman who found him, did she mention whether or not the gate was down?"

"I'll have to check my notes," Mitchell said. "She didn't say exactly."

Nick just waved off the answer as though it did not really matter.

"The killer dragged Brenner back here and did to him what he had done to all those countless women," Nick said.

"Except the killer didn't stop with rape," Wilkins reminded Nick. "This time he went all the way."

"This whole scene," Nick said, waving his hand around the room. "Even the murder itself was made to send a message. It's just like Allun's murder, it too was meant to send a message."

"You're not thinking..." Mitchell started.

"Yes," Nick said, nodding his head. "It's him. It's the same killer. He's out for justice, just like he said on the phone, he's on a crusade."

CHAPTER 41

Nick left Detectives Mitchell and Wilkins at the crime scene to finish up with the preliminary reports and to supervise the crime scene unit, not that they needed supervision. The truth was, Nick needed some time to himself. He was feeling very strange after this most recent vision, and he was left with a lot of questions. He had never experienced anything like that before, never viewing multiple crimes all at the same time. It was all very overwhelming, and what bothered Nick the most was that out of all of the crimes committed there on that desk, the only one that he would be able to solve was the one in which Brenner was actually the victim. Fate seemed rather cruel in this particular case, as he knew that there were many women out there who would never get the true justice they deserved. Brenner should not have been the victim; he should be facing justice in jail, receiving the same kind of punishment behind bars that he inflicted on those confused and helpless young women. Nick felt his anger building up inside of him until he reached a point where he knew that he would no longer be of any use at the crime scene. That was when he decided to head back to the Investigation Unit. It took all of two minutes to pull his car away from the curb and drive the whole block and a half to the department. Again, Nick was astonished by the lack of concern the killer expressed for his own safety by committing the crime so close to the New London police headquarters. Downtown New London was relatively small compared to other cities, but it's main streets were very rarely quiet. The killer must have known that there was a good chance that he would have been seen, or that someone would have heard something; and yet he got away without there being any witnesses. Nick felt as though there was something very disturbing about that fact.

As Nick parked his car and went inside, he felt as though he were being eyed suspiciously by everyone he passed. Suddenly, he wondered whether the news of his momentary loss of consciousness had already filtered through the building. Nick was certain that one of his detectives had alerted Hollings the moment he crossed the street to retrieve his car, and it was very possible that someone had reported it while he was still on the scene. Nick did not want to spend his time explaining to everyone that he was all right, and definitely did not want to fight Hollings about taking a day off to be checked out by a doctor. As Nick climbed the steps to the second floor of the building, he decided to try to sneak into the unit and to his office without being seen. He held no illusions about whether or not this attempt would actually work, but he would try anyway. However, he already had a back-up plan should he need to make any explanations. Nick pushed his way through the door to the squad bay, and immediately all eyes flashed on him, then noticeably snapped back to their work as if everyone was trying their best to make it seem as though everything were normal. That was when he was certain that the word had already spread along the grapevine, and he could not imagine now how big the story had become. Nick did not walk down the main aisle between the rows of desks, but instead tried to remain inconspicuous by turning off and skirting along the wall past the far right end of the rows of metal desks.

"Nick!" screamed Hollings from back in her office. Immediately, Nick knew that all of his efforts had been for nothing as he turned and walked back towards her office like a child caught red handed by a teacher. Nick entered the office, looking at his lieutenant as though nothing had happened. "Oh you can wipe that look off of your face right now. What happened at the crime scene?"

"Victim was Jack Brenner," Nick said. "He was the owner of the local adult video store."

"I already know all about that," Hollings said, frowning. "I knew all that before you did. I want to know what happened to you."

"You know," Nick said, not wanting to actually verbalize what had happened. "I saw what happened, you know, the murder."

"You never passed out before," Hollings said, trying to prod him along to tell her more.

"This was different," Nick said. "Brenner was a sick man. He had raped many women on that desk. All of the crimes committed there came to me at once. It was a little overwhelming."

Hollings remained silent for a moment and just nodded. Nick had never been able to fully describe what he experienced when he would go into a trance and see the crime play out in his mind, but from what Nick had been able to explain, she understood that there was much more than just watching it. Nick experienced it in a way that was more vivid than a dream, and yet his mind was still fully conscious the entire time. Hollings never considered Nick's ability to be a gift, though it had never failed to help the Unit solve a case. She could not imagine what it must be like for Nick to have to witness gruesome crimes and not be able look away because it was all happening in his mind. However, she was more concerned about him now than she ever had been before because to date, he had only been forced to view one crime at a time. Now he had seen multiple rapes and abuses, all leading up to a particularly heinous murder. Suddenly she felt guilty for assigning him the case in the first place.

"I'm sorry," she said, causing Nick to glance up suddenly. He had never heard her apologize for anything before. "I assigned you this case because I thought you could use a break from the Allun murder. Knowing who Brenner was and how he earned his money, I thought that this would be a 'comic' departure. I never thought that there would be so much more to it."

"It's not your fault," Nick said with a smile, appreciating her concern. "No one could ever know what happened, and I can't be afraid that I am going to be overwhelmed by every crime scene I happen to walk on. This was a learning experience and hopefully I will be able to handle it better next time. As for this case being a departure from the Allun case, I think you should hold that thought for now. The person who killed Brenner killed Allun too."

Hollings sat up straight in her chair now, leaning forward over her desk. Nick knew that he had her full attention now.

"How can you be sure?" Hollings asked. "I thought you said you could not identify the person who attacked Allun in your vision."

"I couldn't," Nick admitted. "Nor could I in this vision, but the killer was wearing the same clothing and the eyes were the same."

"The eyes were the same?" Hollings asked, letting out a sigh. "That could mean anything, and the fact that they were wearing the same clothes doesn't mean a thing either."

"It was more than that," Nick said, having anticipated the resistance he would get from his superior. "There was a feeling about the killer. I got the same feeling when I saw the murder at St. Patrick's. This is the same guy, I'm sure of it."

Hollings returned to a reclining position in her chair and looked down at the desk, as if preparing her next remarks.

"What?" Nick said. "I'm not over-reaching here. Don't say that I'm too focused on the Allun case because I'm not."

"Nick," Hollings began. "I'm the first person to back up your beliefs, but it's not like we can run an investigation by them. We have a hard enough time getting hard evidence during a case, and most of the time your 'visions' help us to find it. But these last visions haven't led us to anything, at least nothing that wasn't circumstantial. 'Wearing the same clothes, has the same eyes', that doesn't help us at all."

"Look, I'm just telling you what I saw," Nick said. He was getting angry now. He never wanted to have these images popping into his head, but he had dealt with it and it had helped solve many cases. He did not appreciate her questioning him and his ability the moment things weren't going right.

"Don't look at me like that," Hollings warned, as if reading his mind. "I'm not turning on you; I'm just playing devil's advocate. You said it yourself that these last two were not like your usual ones. Is it possible that you really passed out and what you saw was a dream?"

"A dream of Brenner raping maybe fifty women?" Nick asked incredulously. "Oh yeah, that must have been it because I so often dream about people I don't even know. Then there's the murder, I guess that was just a dream too."

Hollings was just staring at him now, her expression was a clear indication that he was about to step out of line. Nick took a deep breath for a moment before continuing.

"This was definitely a vision," he said. "The biggest difference between my dreams and my images of crimes is the fact that when I see a crime, I know what it is I'm seeing. My mind is still conscious of what is going on around me. It's not like in a dream where it all seems real because I don't really know that I'm dreaming. There were things that I saw in the vision, things that I pointed out to the CSU guys. Can you at least stay on board with me until the forensic report comes back?"

"I'm not jumping ship," Hollings said. "I just want you to be open to other possibilities. The last thing I expected was for you to tell me that both murders were related. The victims are the extreme opposite of each other, one a priest and one a porn star. Tell me, when you first entered the scene, did you think that they had been committed by the same killer?"

"No," Nick admitted. "But now that you mention it, the two victims were more alike than we think. They both had very active and bizarre sex lives. They could easily both be considered sexual deviants. Perhaps that is the only thing that binds them, but I'll take it and run with it because it's the only thing that makes sense in both cases."

"You're thinking about the phone call with the killer," Hollings guessed.

"It's about the sex," Nick said, a light shining in his eyes. Something had clicked in his brain, and he was seeing things in a whole new light. It always amazed Hollings when she saw him go into this mode. It reaffirmed her belief that Nick was born to be a detective. "It's the sex that the killer can't stand. It might not be sex in general, but the..."

Nick stopped for a moment and just shook his head back and forth, as if clearing his mind. He was on to something, he knew it and Hollings knew it, and she knew well enough to stay silent and to let it come to him.

"No, not the sex, it was the trust," Nick said, snapping his fingers. "Both Allun and Brenner abused the trust they were given. Brenner took these girls who he knew were scared and nervous enough at the thought of having sex on camera, and he had to humiliate them and break them. He had to take away every bit of power they had. As for Allun, he picked up unsuspecting men and women, and his natural charisma probably inspired a lot of trust. Then he takes them to his home and using the trust he's gained, convinces them to

THE DEVIL YOU KNOW

go a little bit further until he has them tied up and being videotaped."

"It sounds very possible," Hollings said, following the detective's line of thought, but obviously not certain. "You still have a long way to go to put it all together."

"It's consistent with the stories from Allun's partners," Nick said. "It shouldn't be hard to find a couple of the women that Brenner raped."

"It's a start," Hollings admitted. "It looks like those interviews that you were so dead set against might just be useful after all."

"Don't tell Smith," Nick said. "I'll never live it down."

Just then, there was a knock at the door and Nick turned to see Wilkins and Mitchell standing in the doorway. There was a look on their faces that told Nick that the detectives had already found something interesting.

"You guys are finished with the scene already?" Hollings asked, suspiciously.

"CSU is almost done," Mitchell said. "We left instructions and some uniforms to keep an eye out. We had to come back to show you something we found."

Mitchell handed a file over to Nick, who read it and then looked up suddenly at the detectives to be certain that he was interpreting it correctly. Mitchell just smiled and nodded.

"What is it?" Hollings asked. "What are you looking at?"

"An arrest record," Nick said. "It seems that Jack Brenner was arrested for statutory rape and promoting the sexual performance of a minor. He pled out."

"What's so interesting about that?" Hollings asked, knowing her detectives wouldn't leave the scene of a crime early without a good reason.

"It's the arresting officer that's so interesting," Nick answered. "The arresting officer was a Detective Mark Anderson."

CHAPTER 42

Mitchell and Wilkins spent nearly two hours getting all the pertinent information from Brenner's arrest records of seven years ago. Nick needed to know more about the victim, Brenner himself if he expected to be able to draw any link between the murders. Nick was certain that he would have a clear picture of who Brenner was by the end of the day, and with any luck, they might even have a suspect in mind. Nick knew that it wasn't usually that easy, and this killer had not been easy so far, but somewhere there had to be a connection between Allun and Brenner. The killer had to know them both somehow, had to know about their past and their private lives to incorporate so much into each murder. The killer had to know something about Brenner and how he raped women on his desk to recreate the scene the way he did. The killer also had to know about Allun's private life, the phone call between the detective and the killer already proved that he knew what had gone on at Allun's home. Nick's first thought was that the killer was a victim himself, possibly of both men. That is the only thought that Nick could logically use to connect the men. There was no way Allun would have spent any time with a person like Brenner, not publicly at least. There might be some private connection, though Nick doubted it. However, the police would soon pick through Brenner's private life and hopefully learn everything there was to know about him.

The two detectives returned with two cardboard boxes full of papers, manila folders, brown accordion style folders, and typed transcripts. Nick had not realized how big Brenner's bust had been. Wilkins and Mitchell dropped the files down on Hollings' desk and sighed, both obviously exhausted after searching for the records. Nick looked at them, ready to tell them to take a break, when he noticed the gleam in their eye that told him they were ready to get down to work on this case. Whatever preliminary information they had unearthed just in finding the records had jumped started their engines, and now they were eager to begin.

"Where do you want these?" Wilkins asked, looking back and forth between Nick and the lieutenant.

"We need to do this somewhere private," Nick suggested. "Anderson has been getting information from somewhere in this department, and I don't want him to know anything about us pulling the records from his old case. We'll never live it down."

"I agree," Hollings said, not wanting to see her investigation broadcast on the local news again. "We're here; the records are here, why don't we all just stay here."

The three detectives and their lieutenant all reached into the boxes and retrieved some files, placed the files in front of them and began to read. Nick knew that not all of the information they would need was going to be here; the tiny details that meant more to Nick, like gut feelings and impressions, Brenner's attitude when arrested and all of those other emotional things would not be able to be gleaned from these files. Nick could only hope that there would be enough information that he would not have to ask Anderson for his opinion of the case; that he would not have to ask Anderson for any help. Anderson's help was something Nick could not bring himself to ask for.

Nick began to read the arrest report, the first piece of paper that began an investigation that turned Brenner's life upside down. As Nick read on, he began to understand why there was so much paperwork relating to this particular case, and he began to see a side of Mark Anderson, the detective, that he never knew existed. There was something between these two men, some intense obsession or hatred on the part of Anderson that made the detective work himself like a dog to put Brenner in jail for good. According to the paperwork, it all started the day a sixteen year old girl was dragged into the Investigation Unit in New London by her mother. According to the girl's mother, she had found her daughter with eight hundred dollars and demanded to know where it had come from. After a huge argument, the mother had learned that the girl had received the money as payment for starring in a sex scene. The mother demanded to know where the girl had gone to shoot the scene, and after finding out, had brought the girl to the police. Anderson caught the case, and this is where it started.

Something in Anderson had been enraged by this particular case. Here was a detective who had seen his share of gruesome murders, had investigated all sorts of crimes, but this case had been the one that he could not let go. According to the records, Anderson dragged Brenner down to the police department with no hesitation. Anderson sweated Brenner for almost twenty four hours without letting up. After twenty four hours the police would have been forced to arrest Brenner or let him go. Two hours before the police would have to make a final decision about Brenner, Anderson offered him a deal, though in was unclear whether he was authorized to make any deals. There was no evidence that the prosecutor had yet been brought in on the case, but Anderson offered to drop the charges to a misdemeanor if Brenner was able to destroy any tapes of the young girl and made sure that she would not appear on the internet. It was too late, however, and though there had not been any scene sold on DVD or video yet, the girl's scene had already been posted on the internet, and was probably already being viewed by it's members. Even if they took out the scene with the girl from the site, it would still have been accessed by someone, and would still be out there somewhere. It seemed as though this was the point where Anderson had crossed the line from anger to hatred.

Brenner was picked out of a line up five minutes later, by the victim, as the man who had hired her. From there Brenner was arrested and arraigned the next morning. Anderson was there in court, insisting that the prosecutor push for no bail. Though the prosecutor did everything he could, the judge denied his request for remand and released Brenner on bond, which was posted easily. Brenner did not even have to shut down his site; all he had to do was take the scene with the girl off of his web site. Before he did, however, the site posted record hits and for twenty eight hours, this girl had been his main attraction and had brought him in ten times more money than he had paid her just to star in the scene. This was when Anderson became obsessed. The detective hounded Brenner, following him wherever he went, pulling him over for the most minor traffic violations, dropping by Brenner's work, checking the ages of all of the actors. The case against Brenner was continuously becoming less important to the prosecutor, as there was nothing to go on. There was some question as to how the girl found out about Brenner and then there turned out to be a fake I.D. The girl had a fake driver's license that made her out to be eighteen. The case was slipping away, and without something big and damning, it began to look as though Brenner was going to be able to plead his way out of trouble.

It was during one of Anderson's unannounced visits to the set that the detective found the damning evidence he so desperately needed. He found Allun auditioning one of his new actresses alone in his office, bent over that same desk. The woman was eighteen and there was no crime there, but Anderson immediately knew exactly what was going on. The detective went straight to the sixteen year old girl and demanded to know if Brenner had done the same to her, and when the detective found out the truth, Anderson had everything he needed. Brenner was arrested for statutory rape, and all the dominoes began to fall from there. Anderson was even able to talk to a friend in the FBI and convince him that there were some federal issues due to the fact that the minor had been viewed having sex on the Internet. Anderson did whatever he had to do to make Brenner stay in jail. Brenner was convicted within hours of closing arguments and was sentenced to twelve years in prison. Anderson visited Brenner in prison regularly, taunting and having his fun with Brenner. Anderson got one of the guards to let it slip to the general population that Brenner was a child molester, in an attempt to make life as miserable as possible. After six years, Brenner came up for parole, and despite Anderson's efforts, Brenner was released. That did not stop the detective from harassing Brenner on a daily basis, though. In fact, it was in part due to Anderson's continued persecution that Brenner made certain to stay on the up an up. Brenner had his actresses and actors tested for sexually transmitted diseases on a regular basis, and that was when they found out about the transmission of HIV between all of them. That was the end for Brenner.

Nick closed his file and placed it down in his lap. The other detectives were still reading, though they were all coming to the end, and coming to the same conclusion. There is always one case, at least one case, which stays with a detective his entire life. Whether justice is done or not, there is something that stays with a cop, something that will keep him awake at night, make him wonder if there was anything he missed, if there was anything else he could do. This had been that case for Anderson; this had kept him awake at night. Anderson had poured himself into this case, never giving up, never ceasing to search for new ways to keep Brenner down. Something about Brenner disgusted Anderson, made him never give up on ending Brenner's career for good.

"We have to bring him in," Hollings said, jarring all the detectives from their thoughts. "There is more to this story. Anderson knows much more about Brenner than is in these files. If Brenner had enemies, Anderson would know."

"I agree," Nick said, nodding his head. "I don't like it, but if there is anyone who knows everything about Brenner, it's Anderson."

"He's not going to give up his information freely," Wilkins pointed out. "I don't even know if he will come down here."

"He'll come down here," Hollings assured the detectives. "When we tell him we need his help with a case regarding Brenner, he'll fly down here."

"We'll still have to tell him that Brenner's been murdered," said Mitchell.

"He won't be so eager to help once he knows that," Wilkins said, finishing his partner's thought. "I doubt he'll care less who killed Brenner."

"Anderson's not in the good graces of the station manager," Nick mentioned as he looked up at his lieutenant. "If we offered him the exclusive on this case, made him look good with his boss again, I think he'd help us."

"Only to screw us later on," Hollings said, conceding to her detectives.

"I'll call him," Wilkins said. "As his former partner, I'll take the hit."

"No," Nick said. "I'm the lead on this case, I'll call him. If there is any groveling to be done, he'll appreciate it more if it comes from me."

Nick rose from his seat in front of Hollings' desk and turned to leave the office.

"Where are you going?" Hollings asked. "You can call him from here."

"No thanks," Nick said shaking his head. "If I'm going to have to kiss his ass, I'd prefer to do it in the privacy of my own office."

CHAPTER 43

When Mark Anderson stepped into the squad bay everyone could see that his entrance was somewhat less triumphant than his last visit. Anderson was weary and cautious, his eyes darting back and forth over the faces of the officers and detectives sitting behind their desks, fastidiously working their individual cases. Detectives Wilkins and Mitchell had been waiting for Anderson to arrive, and when he did, they greeted him as warmly as possible and escorted him to an interrogation room. There was no misunderstanding amongst them, the police needed information and Anderson was the man who could supply them with that information. To his credit, Anderson was not being the pompous ass that he had been last time. Nick had already surmised that this would be disconcerting to Anderson, but it could not be helped. There was no other room big enough to fit the three detectives and Anderson comfortably and privately except for his lieutenant's office, an idea that she was firmly against. Hollings made it clear to Nick that Anderson would never set foot in her office again as long as she was in charge of the Investigation Unit. Nick understood her feeling, but was still left with the dilemma of how to transform one of the interrogation rooms into a conference room that might make Anderson feel more comfortable about giving up information about Jack Brenner's arrests.

Nick decided that a conference room atmosphere was exactly what he needed. While they were waiting for Anderson's arrival, he had huge chalkboards wheeled into the room, as well as great big dry erase boards and easels. Nick stacked all the files Wilkins and Mitchell had pulled regarding Brenner's original arrest on the rectangular metal table in the middle of the room and added the noticeably thin murder file to the top. Nick played strategy in his mind as he tried to conceive the best possibly way to make Anderson open up. The detective had no illusions about how difficult this would be. Anderson did not trust the department, and the department definitely did not trust Anderson, but all the feelings of ill will had to be put aside to apprehend a killer; Nick knew this meant his ego had to be put aside as well. There was a quick knock at the door, and when it opened; Wilkins stepped in followed by Anderson and Mitchell. Nick immediately offered Anderson the seat at the head of the table, also nearest to the door in an attempt to make Anderson feel more in control. They offered him food or drink, both of which he declined.

"I'd just like to know why I'm here," Anderson said.

"Of course," Nick said, taking a seat himself. The two other detectives followed his lead. "First, I'd like to say that all of yesterday's garbage is put aside for time being. We have a case that involves Jack Brenner, and in reviewing the files, we found that you were the investigating detective who arrested him seven years ago. We are having difficulty pinning down any real useful information on Brenner, and it seems that you might be the person who knows the most about him."

Anderson studied the faces of all the detectives before answering, looking for any doubt in their faces that might lead him to believe they were playing him. When he looked at each man, he found only the look of sincere interest.

"I probably do know the most about him," Anderson agreed cautiously. "But certainly not by choice. A mother brought in her sixteen year old daughter one day over seven years ago, charging that Brenner had shot a sex scene and she wanted him, and the man she had sex with in the scene charged. It was a scam and everyone knew it. The mother was a known drug addict who was pimping her daughter out for easy money, but a crime had still been committed. The thing that pissed me off was how arrogant and cavalier Brenner was about the entire thing. I pushed and pushed, following him around, showing up at his work. Around this time, we found out that there really wasn't a case against him. The mother had paid for a fake I.D. for her daughter so that she could go on the shoot, and then when the girl didn't end up making all the money that her mother thought she should, she dragged her daughter down to us hoping that she might have a civil case in the end. As it turned out, the guy in the scene was only seventeen, the girl was sixteen and we found our case falling apart. The girl was the real victim, but her mother was more of a problem than Brenner, and Brenner knew it the whole time."

"But then you found out about the rape," Nick said, taking down notes, listening intently.

"Yeah," Anderson said, shifting positions in his chair as he made himself more comfortable. "I went over to his work, where he shot his pictures, to give him some shit. When I got to the door, I could hear screaming, and I naturally thought that he was hurting someone. I bust in there and find him and some young woman going at it. He's screaming at me about my harassing him, and I'm looking at this woman who is obviously not enjoying herself and something starts to spark in my brain. I asked this woman if she was alright, she had been crying and screaming for him to stop. I asked her if she wanted to press charges and she says no, that he promised her a starring role in one of his scenes. That's when I realized what was going on; this was Brenner's way of auditioning his talent. I was pissed; I dragged him down here, even before I knew for certain that he had raped the girl. Once she confessed, it was all easy from there."

"It seems like this guy really got to you," Wilkins said.

"He did, though I don't really know why," Anderson answered. "It was just that he was so smug, thought that he could do anything with these girls because they were willing to have sex on camera. I don't know, look, can I get something to drink?"

Nick decided that they should take a break at this point and they ordered food and drink from a local restaurant and ended up trading stories of cases as they waited for their food to arrive. For a while, it seemed as though this were a team, and everyone felt comfortable with everyone else. When the food arrived, Nick decided that this was the time he was going to have to put all of his cards on the table.

"Look, we haven't been completely honest with you," Nick began, immediately catching Anderson's attention. "Brenner was murdered last night, and the reason I didn't tell you right away was because of our history and your past history with Brenner. But, you deserve to know the truth, and if you don't want to continue helping us, I think we all would understand."

Anderson regarded Nick for a moment, chewing on a french fry as he decided whether to continue. After a minute, he sighed and nodded.

"I can understand that," he said. "But what about the Allun case?"

"We're still investigating that," Nick said. "But to be honest with you, this Brenner thing is not a high priority. We're just covering our asses right now. We need to do some preliminary ground work so that it looks like we did some investigating. Hopefully it will give us enough time to focus ourselves back on the Father Allun murder. I know I don't have to explain it to you."

It almost made Nick nauseous to have to explain himself to Anderson, to make it seem as though they were friends and there was no history between them. Nick didn't know whether or not he was buying the act, but Anderson was definitely feeling more and more comfortable around them. The four men spent the next two hours going over possible suspects, looking for anyone who might have a grudge against Brenner. Unfortunately, the list was long. Anderson immediately suggested the obvious, any of the women who Brenner had raped and mistreated. Then there were all the actors who contracted HIV from their encounters together on the set when Brenner was in prison. Secretly, Nick was trying to draw ties to the Allun case while listening to Anderson's theories. The fact of the matter was, the killer of both men was a male, and most of the possible suspects in the Brenner case were female. Nick could not count out the possibility that a man had acted on one of the women's behalf, but the level of rage present in both murders suggested someone who was directly wronged by both men. The only problem was finding that person who was a link between them. The detectives were making lists and charts, drawing lines on the chalkboard between victims and Brenner. It was really beginning to look like a working case, though Nick knew there was more beneath the surface that Anderson would never know. Then came trouble.

Suddenly, there was a knock at the door and Detective Smith entered, followed by Lt. Hollings. Nick introduced the two men, knowing that each already knew of the other, but had not officially met. There was something in Smith's eyes, something that Nick had never seen before. It was the look of a predator closing in on his prey, and suddenly Nick's tension level jumped five notches as he tried to anticipate Kevin's reason for being here. Nick looked over at Hollings, who just put a finger over her mouth and pointed to the Norwich detective, indicating that Nick should listen to what Smith had to say.

"I'm running the Allun murder investigation in Norwich as I'm sure you know," Kevin started, trying to remain friendly. "Did you know the victim?"

"Who Allun? Not really," Anderson said. "Only what I read about his working through the Norwich diocese. I didn't know him personally."

"Just wondering," Kevin said, as if it didn't matter. "He was doing a lot of charity and fundraising, getting money from influential people to help the poor. I've been doing some digging on Allun and some interesting information has come up. I know that you've been covering the case for the local news, and I figure Nick here has a deal with you for an exclusive in exchange for whatever he's working on, so I think we can all feel comfortable talking about this stuff together."

Kevin looked around the room at the other detectives who just nodded uncertainly, but were listening carefully. They trusted Hollings and she had given the signal that they were to follow along, so they did. At that moment, Anderson began to relax again, as he eased back down in his chair.

"I was reading here that Allun grew up in Boston, and then realized you grew up in Boston," Kevin said, looking up at Anderson. "You lived like three blocks away from Allun. Did you know anything about him or his family?"

"No," Anderson repeated. "A lot of people live in one block, detective."

"That's the truth," Kevin said nodding, his smile almost disarming. "You guys even went to the same school. It's funny that two people can drift past each other so closely and never really know each other. Not to mention that they both end up here in Connecticut, no more than fifty miles away from each other. Coincidence can be a crazy thing."

Warning bells started to ring aloud in Nick's brain as he began to crunch all the facts together with the information he knew about the Allun case so far.

"Well anyway," Kevin said, as if moving on. "Here's something that might help all of us if it got out on the news. Allun was an altar boy at Our Mother of the Immaculate Heart, one of the big cathedrals there. Do you know which one I'm talking about?"

"Yeah," Anderson said, slowly, not following the detective's line of thought. "I was actually an altar boy there too."

"No kidding," Kevin said. "So you would have been there at the same time as Allun. Did you know of any strange things going on?"

"I don't know what you mean," Anderson said, almost stammering. Something had begun to agitate him, he was starting to get suspicious of the detective. "Let's make it clear. I was five years older than Allun. We weren't altar boys at the same time, there was just a year's overlap between the time he was there and the time I left for high school."

"Oh," Kevin said, nodding his head as though he understood. "So then, you did know Allun."

CHAPTER 44

Anderson's eyes widened as he realized that he had trapped himself. His breathing became rapid and his eyes darted back and forth around the table as he tried to come up with a response. Something was happening here, something that he did not believe the other three detectives knew anything about. There was a sense of anticipation, as if everyone there were holding their breath, waiting for him. Smith had Anderson in his sights, Smith knew something, but Anderson could not think clearly enough to give him the advantage. Smith was trying to direct him somewhere, make him say something but Anderson did not know what the Norwich detective was looking for.

"So you knew Allun," Kevin prodded, repeating his question.

"No," Anderson answered quickly. "I said that I knew of him."

"No," Kevin said, correcting the other man. "You said you knew of him through the Norwich diocese, you said that you never knew him in Boston."

"Okay, yeah," Anderson stammered. "I knew of him in Boston. We probably passed each other in the halls at school, or even at church. But that was it."

"No, you knew him better than that," Kevin said with a sigh. The detective reached into his cushioned binder and brought out a small video cassette, placing it face down on the table. The words "Anderson and Allun initiation" were written on the label. "It was a long time ago, but people still remember that you and Allun were close friends. I've talked to them all, there are witnesses."

"They're mistaken," Anderson spat. "Like you said, it was a long time ago."

"It's true," Kevin said softly, not reacting to the other man's outburst. "It was a long time ago; memories fade or change, people forget. But video doesn't lie."

Kevin lightly tapped the top of the tape as it lay there on the table. Anderson stared at it, shaking, as though it were a weapon that could physically hurt him.

"We can get a television in here," Kevin said. "We can all view what's on this together. I don't want to do that, though. I don't think you want to do that either."

There was a long pause here, where no one said anything. Everyone watched Anderson who was still staring at the tape as though he and it were the only things in the room.

"I need to say something to you," Kevin started, speaking slowly and softly. "I know what's on here, and no one else has to. From me to you, what this priest did to the two of you was wrong, it wasn't your fault. It was the priests, he was sick, both mentally and physically, and his sickness hurt both of you. I can understand why Allun became the person he was, and I have to say I have all the respect in the world for you, for not becoming like them."

Anderson looked up at Kevin and as he did, a tear slipped past his lower right eye lid and rolled down his cheek, following the crease in his jaw until it stopped just under his chin. The emotion had now reached the point of pure pain, a pain that everyone in the room could feel as they too began to understand what Anderson had endured. There was guilt, sorrow, fear, shock, sadness, and anger; every one of them experiencing each emotion for different reasons. A voice inside Nick's mind was screaming; it was his own voice, his inner voice. He was screaming for Mark Anderson, for the child who had been raped by a priest, by the person he was supposed to be able to trust. He was screaming for the detective who was filled with rage, but never had the opportunity to express it, to get over it. He was screaming for the man who was alone in the world, who no one could ever understand without having gone through the same pain. Nick was screaming for the unfairness of it all, of what Anderson had gone through, what he had done, and what he was going to have to face. Nick understood now, he understood how all the pieces came together. It wasn't a vision, it was simply understanding. He looked over at Hollings who was shielding her face, hiding her tears. Nick looked over at Wilkins who was staring down at the floor, unable to look his old partner in the eyes because of the guilt he felt for never really bonding with Anderson the way a partner should. Mitchell stared at the man with pity and compassion, the only one of the New London detectives who could actually look Anderson in the eye; and then there was Smith who had figured it out all on his own, who had taken on the horrible task of confronting Anderson with the truth, the outsider who had the most sympathy of all. He took pity on all of them; the detectives included, and simply did what had to be done.

"I can't imagine how hard it must have been," Kevin continued. "You took on the shield to fight crime, to stop those like the priest who had hurt you. All those horrible crimes you've witnessed in your time, your restraint was...heroic."

Anderson just sat there, staring at the tape, his eyes now full of tears, little red streaks lining both cheeks. The man was broken, his armor peeled away, vulnerable in front of the very people he had convinced himself he could trust the least. There was nothing but the emptiness, threatening to swallow his mind and soul, threatening to collapse under the sheer weight of his pain.

"You saw him there," Kevin said, almost in a whisper. "You saw him at the Norwich Policeman's Charity Ball; it was an event to raise money for PAL, the Police Athletic League."

Anderson started to shake his head weakly, his last defense against the truth.

"Don't, not now," Kevin said, almost pleading with the other man. "You've come so far, you've let it out. Don't deny yourself peace now. You got a special invitation to the ball because you had been a cop and are now a reporter. You could cover the event from the inside. That was when you saw Allun."

"He was just standing there," Anderson muttered, staring off into space as though in shock, as though he were all alone in the room. "He was smiling and talking casually with someone, as if there were no pain inside of him. Then I saw what he was wearing, I saw his black clothes and his white collar; he was a priest. Of all things, of anyone he could have become, he became a priest. I walked right up to him, I confronted him. He seemed shocked, but then pleased to see me. As though we had been best friends for the entire time instead of just those years as altar boys. I was furious, and he told me that we would have to get together later."

"You and he went out," Kevin continued. "You went to catch up, you went to understand."

"Yes," Anderson said, letting the memories flow out of him. "I had to know how he could have become a priest. He tried to explain it to me, tried to make me understand but his answers were ridiculous. His story made no sense."

"You paid for dinner that night," Kevin reminded him.

"Yes," Anderson continued. "I couldn't let him pay for me. He tried to insist, but I wouldn't let him. He said we were friends, he said for old time's sake. But I couldn't, his money came from...sin. I didn't want anything to do with it. I didn't want it to feed me, nourish me, cloth me. I didn't want it to have anything to do with me."

"You went home and stewed on the events of that night," Kevin said as if seeing the same memories that Anderson saw.

"His answers did not satisfy you; in fact, they just served to make you angrier. Allun had not just taken on the robes of your abuser, Allun had taken his place. You knew that he was hurting people, maybe not the same way that the priest hurt you, but he was hurting people nonetheless. You had to stop him, you had to kill him."

Anderson snapped back to reality, his eyes filling with the light of comprehension, color filling his face once again.

"I didn't kill him," Anderson said.

"No one here blames you," Kevin assured him. "There isn't a person in this room who doesn't understand what you did. You attacked him and your anger got the best of you, and you gave him the justice he deserved."

"I didn't kill him," Anderson insisted.

"I thought it was strange how you were always a step ahead of the police," Kevin began. "You always knew more about the case than we did. You always had more answers, and were able to make us look bad. When we held the press conference, I saw the anger in your eyes, you kept asking us questions, like little hints that you knew Allun was not the good citizen we were portraying him to be. The only way you could make justice known was by introducing the tape of his murder, and there was only one way you could get it out there and still look good to your boss's."

"But we weren't playing ball, we weren't playing your game," Nick interjected, knowing that it was now his turn to take the reigns. "You got the tape to us, but you knew that we weren't going to show it to the public and they would never know what kind of man Allun truly was. Then there was your own pain, the pain that did not cease with Allun's murder. Killing Allun did not take away your anger, and you had to turn your attention elsewhere. That was when you remembered Brenner."

"I didn't kill him," Anderson repeated, more forcefully. "I didn't kill either of them."

"You remembered what Brenner had done to that girl, to all those women," Nick continued, ignoring Anderson's outburst. "You thought that by killing Brenner, this one case you never got out of your system, maybe then you would have peace. Like Allun, you gave Brenner the justice he deserved."

"Before you say anything else," Hollings said, having regained her composure. She opened a folder and pulled out a piece of paper, placing it down on the table in front of Anderson. "This just came in from the forensic examiners. Mace was used to incapacitate Brenner. Samples taken from Brenner's skin had the same chemical composition as police issue mace. Brenner was also hit with a stun gun, and marks and bruising on his flesh match it with the same issue given to police officers. Finally, fibers and plastic from under Brenner's nails match those that were caught by knicks in the wood of Brenner's desk, and they all matched police issue gloves. Unless you have an alibi that firmly places you somewhere far from these two crime scenes, I'm afraid there is no other conclusion for us to reach."

"This is a frame up," Anderson said, jumping to his feet. There was an anger and intensity to the man that Nick had never seen before. In the last few days, Nick had witnessed the steady deterioration of Anderson's ability to keep his anger in check, but now he looked like nothing more than a cornered, wounded animal. "You're trying to shut me up for good, you're framing me."

"Mark Anderson," Smith began, rising to his feet. "As a detective of the city of Norwich, Connecticut; I am placing you under arrest for the murder of Father Michael Allun. You have the right to remain silent, anything you say can and will be used against you in a court of law. You have the right to an attorney, and if you cannot afford an attorney, one will be provided for you by the state of Connecticut. Do you understand these rights as I have read them to you?"

"I did not kill them!" Anderson shouted. "I did not kill them!"

"Mark Anderson," Nick said, stepping forward. "You are under arrest for the murder of Jack Brenner. You have the right to remain silent..."

"Fuck you!" Anderson said, spitting in Nick's face. "Fuck all of you."

Wilkins and Mitchell were already around the table, attempting to restrain Anderson as he fought to get free. Nick continued reading Anderson his rights, though the other man was not listening; only spewing forth curses, obscenities, and wild accusations. Anderson fought even after Mitchell managed to get the handcuffs on him. He bucked up and down, trying to break free of the detectives' grip. Nick watched for a moment, as though he were watching a dying animal in his last throws of life, then shook his head as shock began to overwhelm him.

"Detective Mitchell," Nick said aloud, the last thing he could hear before the rhythmic beat of his blood surging past his eardrums deafened him to all else. "Book him."

CHAPTER 45

Nick quickly walked back to his office, feeling the emotions inside of him beginning to boil, nearing the point at which he would explode. He knew people in the squad were looking at him. They had just seen Anderson dragged out in handcuffs, ranting that he was being framed. Everyone would want to know what had happened in the interrogation room; the rumors would begin to fly. Nick did not care about that now, though. He only knew that if he did not get to his office where he could be alone, he would explode at someone who did not deserve it. Nick reached the outer office of his ex-assistant, then passed through it into his own office, closing both sets of doors behind him. He had just arrested his killer, he should have been happy. There was no happiness here, however; there was only confusion and anger. Anderson had been right in front of him the entire time. Nick had brought him down to interview and get information about Brenner, never once suspecting that he could have been Brenner's killer. It was so obvious now as he put it all together; Anderson hated Brenner, had devoted so much time to making Brenner's life miserable. It made sense to Nick, it fit in with what he had thought the killer's motivation really was. Anderson had hated both men because they abused the trust of those they had sex with. Brenner raped and mistreated the women who came to him for a job, forcing them to have sex with him, many times actually using force to get what he wanted. As for Allun, he had gone from the victim to the abuser, becoming the very monster he hated as a child. Nick did not blame himself for not seeing the connection between Allun and Anderson before; that would have taken the kind of research that Smith had devoted himself to for the last night and day. However, now presented with all of the evidence, it was clear that Anderson had means, motive and opportunity; and apparently he did not have an alibi. It all fit perfectly, as though Anderson was the missing piece in the puzzle. And this thought bothered Nick.

Nick was not really sure what it was that bothered him so much about this at first. Anderson killed two men, and he deserved to be punished for his crimes; but Nick could not help but feel pity for the man as well. Anderson deserved justice for himself, and that was something that he would never have. Whoever had abused him as a child got away with it. The man was on the tape, Nick was certain of that, but he was also certain that nothing had ever been done to stop this man from abusing these two boys, and most likely dozens of others. Child molesters very rarely stopped after one child, in fact, most of them did not stop even after being arrested. When released, the number of molesters who re-offended was staggering, causing many states to look into different methods of diminishing or eliminating the urges of these sexual predators. So far, nothing has worked successfully. Nick could only imagine the anger and rage that had built up inside of Anderson over the years. Nick was actually surprised that Anderson had not snapped years before. Seeing the heinous crimes that he witnessed in his years as a detective, must have fueled his anger. Nick wondered if this situation could have been avoided if someone had only befriended Anderson. It was ironic that the man who needed a friend more than anyone was the man who would not let anyone close to him, a man who drove others away by the pain and anger that had been building up inside. Anderson was as much a victim as the two dead men; none of them would ever have any peace. This sorrow began to solidify into anger as Nick continued to think about what Anderson must have gone through. He did not need to see the tape to see what depraved acts were committed against these boys.

Anderson could never tell anyone as a child, no one would have believed him. He could imagine how much Anderson must have hated going back to the church, working there in such close proximity to the man who was abusing him. He could see the priest smiling at them when they passed each other in the hallways or in the main gallery of the cathedral. That condescending look of superiority, as though the priest had done nothing wrong. Nick could imagine the sheer terror that must have seized a young Mark Anderson when he heard his name called to visit with the priest in his office. He could only imagine what lies and backward logic the priest must have used to explain what he was doing to the boys, what he wanted the boys to do to him. Nick found himself shaking with anger, heat washing over his body. Nick felt as though he were trapped in a tunnel, between the terrible images of Anderson's past and the anger that was threatening to explode from within him. He could see the young boy Anderson had been, crying in the darkness of his room at night, knowing that there was no place safe for him. Nick had carried the overwhelming pain all the detectives had felt for the other man, from the interrogation room into his office, and it did not take much for that pain to become anger and hate. He could understand why Anderson had done what he did; he could understand how easy it was for him to kill those two men after taking that step over the line. It was becoming too much for him, those feelings of pity and compassion combined with Nick's anger and guilt with himself for not trying to understand the man better. Nick felt the familiar sensations of the angry beast within him, breaking through his resistance, overpowering Nick's inner will to suppress it.

Suddenly, the phone rang; and though it surprised the detective it did not cause him to jump. Instead, it was the last thing Nick could deal with now, and that thought was all the incredible anger needed to break through the wall Nick had put up inside of him to keep his angry beast inside. Nick picked the entire phone unit off of his desk and tossed it across the room, screaming. Nick heard a snap as the phone cord was violently ripped from the wall and the unit crashed into the wall on the far end of his office, smashing into different pieces. It was all Nick could do to keep from going crazy, tossing everything around his office until the beast had no energy left for destruction. A psychopathic doctor named The Nemesis had once suggested that Nick was a killer. There was a killer's mind inside of Nick, and though he had been successful for so long in keeping his own anger and pain inside, the killer was there nonetheless. It was this monster within him that enabled the detective to understand the crimes he investigated with such accuracy. It was this understanding that had enabled Nick to solve every case he came across. Hollings was right; it was his gift and his curse. Nick had come this close twice before to letting the killer lose, once in a standoff between drug dealers, and then the other time when he actually captured The Nemesis. Both times he had been taunted by the beast within him to take that step, that one little step over the line that would change his life forever. Thankfully for Nick, he had friends and people who cared about him who saw the signs of the struggle within and were there to help him through it. Unfortunately Anderson had been all alone; there had been no one there for him. Anderson's transformation from the law enforcing police officer to the revenge seeking murderer was simply a matter of time. It was like a demon inside, constantly gnawing away at your will, constantly telling you to take those little steps until one day the demon is all you hear and the voice of reason is silent. Nick wondered how loud the demons inside Anderson must have gotten before he took that final step.

"It wasn't your fault, you know," Hollings said, standing in the doorway to Nick's office. The detective did not turn; he was not surprised to know that she was standing there.

"It wasn't anyone's fault," Nick said solemnly. "And yet we all could have prevented this by simply sticking it out, by not giving up on him."

"Everyone goes through their share of bad shit," Hollings said, her voice cracking as she strained to keep her emotions intact. Nick could tell that she felt just as guilty as all the rest, more perhaps because she had been Anderson's supervisor. She felt as though she had let him down. "You know, ultimately, it comes down to the choices we all make."

"We're not so different, Anderson and I," Nick said. "I can't help but wonder where I'd be if it hadn't been for the support and understanding you showed me during my first homicide case."

"You're wrong," Hollings said, forcing a smile. "There is a world of difference between you and Anderson. You did not kill anyone, even when you were at your darkest point. The Nemesis taunted you, even made you think that he had hurt the woman you loved, and still you were able to keep from losing yourself. Anderson killed those men, he gave in to his anger, and you never did. You are nothing like him, you're stronger than him."

"Doesn't make me feel any better though," Nick said, turning and facing his lieutenant.

"I doubt any of us will for a long time," Hollings stated. They both looked out Nick's office window into the squad bay where all eyes seemed to be nervously flickering back and forth from their work to Nick's office. It took a moment, but his lieutenant's words finally sunk in and the detective suddenly realized that he was not alone in his grief.

"Do you mind if I make a command decision regarding all of us?" Nick asked her. Hollings just shook her head and smiled, knowing what he was thinking. Nick approached her and brushed past as he made his way out to the squad room where his two detectives and Smith were waiting for him.

"I'm sorry I didn't get to warn you ahead of time," Smith started. "You were already in there with him, and there wasn't a chance to get you out without making him suspicious."

"You don't need to apologize," Nick insisted. "You did the right thing. In fact, you were the only one who was able to see Anderson for who he really was. It's me who should be apologizing for not giving your theory about the sexual aspect of Allun's private life enough credence."

"We were both right," the Norwich detective said, extending his right hand. "And we were both wrong. I'm just glad we got him in the end."

Nick smiled and shook Kevin's hand, realizing this might be the last time they worked together for some time. Allun's murderer had been apprehended and there wasn't that much more for them to do together. Most of the leftover work could be done by phone.

"It's been a pleasure working with you," Nick said.

"Let's do it again sometime," Kevin said with a smile. "But not too soon."

Nick laughed, as did Wilkins and Mitchell and the detectives could all feel the ice breaking a little. The tension level was easing down, and their emotions were coming back to normal. Nick turned to the two detectives.

"I know you guys feel guilty," he said. "You're wondering if there was anything you could have done. I'm wondering the same thing, but the lieutenant is right, there's only so much you can do. There is only so much you can give, and you couldn't make Anderson open up to you. He chose this, whether consciously or by just giving in, but it's not our fault."

Nick paused for a moment, looking both men square in the face until he was certain that they understood him.

"I think Lt. Hollings will agree that we need some time to ourselves, to get our minds right," Nick began. "We all worked ourselves hard through the weekend, and I'm taking the rest of the day off, and tomorrow too. We'll come back Wednesday morning, fresh and ready to wrap up this case and hand it over to the prosecutor."

Nick then turned and looked at Hollings, who simply gave the final approval by nodding and giving him a "thumbs up". They all said their good byes to Detective Smith, and then gathered their belongings and made their way out of the squad individually. Nick had wanted to suggest that they meet up at STP's for a beer, or maybe several. However, he knew that each one of them needed some alone time to get some perspective on what had happened today, Nick most of all. He drove home, blasting the radio and hoping the music would drown out his thoughts. When Nick got home, he changed his clothes into a pair of athletic sweats and made his way down to the basement, where an old, worn leather punching bag hung from the braces. Nick donned his boxing gloves and went to work on the bag, punching it without rhythm or control, just wailing away on it. He let his frustration and pain pour out of him, letting the demon loose in a controlled setting. He kept at it until tears poured from his eyes; he kept at it until his pain and frustration were gone and only the emptiness of grief remained; he kept at it until he had no energy left to move his arms or to stand. He finally just collapsed under the weight of himself, tears streaming from his eyes, but unable to cry, unable to do anything but sit there on the floor. That was where Jenn found him hours later, sitting there collapsed on the floor. She rushed to him, tried to get him to respond, to talk to her, to tell her what was happening. Nick couldn't though, he did not have the energy for any of it; he just took her in his arms and held her, realizing that what he needed more than anything was just someone beside him.

CHAPTER 46

Hours later, Nick found himself in the shower, the hot water cutting through the tension and frustration of the day. The water washed over him, the constant sound of the water drops hitting the tile floor blocking out everything, allowing his mind to wander and drift in and out of his memories of the day. However, unlike when he was pounding on the leather punching bag, here he was able to remain calm and serene, here he was safe. He knew Jenn was out in the kitchen, cooking. She was concerned about him, but knew that he just needed time to sort things out in his mind. He was amazed at how well she understood him in such a short amount of time. They had been dating only two weeks, and yet there was something about her that just fit with him. The only thing that did concern him was what she might think of him after what happened downstairs. Nick would have to explain it, he would have to explain everything and he really did not want to go back over every detail of his feelings again. He had replayed it enough already. Unfortunately, Nick was certain that many different versions of the day's events had circulated through the department until now it barely resembled the truth. He was going to have to tell her, he was going to have to explain himself.

Nick climbed out of the shower and toweled off. Once he was dry and dressed, Nick opened the door to the bathroom and was immediately overwhelmed by the delicious smell of grilled meat. Nick made his way to the kitchen softly, trying to surprise her. He sidled up behind her and kissed her gently on the back of her neck, and the moment he did, he knew that she had known he was coming. She was not in the least bit surprised by him, and in fact, she pressed herself against him as he wrapped his arms around her waist.

"I didn't think you were going to come out of there," Jenn said, dividing the food between the two plates.

"Are you kidding me," Nick began. "The moment I smelled this feast nothing could keep me away. To what do I owe this fine banquet?"

"Someone told me the way to a man's heart is through his stomach," Jenn said with a smile. Nick reached down to pluck a crisp, stir fried vegetable from the plate. She smacked his hand and he dropped it immediately. "I'm just playing to my strengths."

Nick turned her around to face him and looked into her eyes.

"You've been playing very well then," Nick said softly, trying to let her know what she meant to him without having to say it. She knew what he was saying though, and kissed him softly.

"Go sit down," she ordered. "And tell me about your day."

"You go first," Nick said, grabbing two wine glasses and a bottle of merlot and making his way to the table. He wanted to delay the inevitable, and though it was a pretty transparent attempt, but he had to try. "You're the guest of honor."

Jenn told him about her shift, which was pretty boring for her. She mostly spent the day with her partner Socha, giving out traffic tickets and responding to two automobile accidents. She also had a report of shoplifting, but the thief was gone by the time the patrol car reached the store. It was all basically routine events on a pretty routine patrol. Jenn told Nick that he had made a pretty big impression on Socha, who had become a different person since their last encounter. Nick could sense that Jenn's story was coming to an end, and knew that he would have to tell his own story soon.

"So," she started, anxiously. "Are you going to tell me what was wrong with you down there, or are we going to pretend it didn't happen?"

"Do I have a choice?" Nick asked, trying unsuccessfully to be funny.

"Not really," Jenn said. Nick sighed and rose from the table to open a new bottle of wine. "Well?"

Nick went over to the counter and grabbed the corkscrew, then retrieved a bottle of white wine from the refrigerator and began to uncork the bottle. He looked up at Jenn, who was staring at him as though her heart were going to explode in anticipation.

"There was a murder in New London," Nick began. "The owner of that adult video store down the street from the department, Jack Brenner was killed."

"Really?" Jenn asked. "What a terrible loss for the world."

"Yeah well, it's more complicated than it seems," Nick continued. "His death is connected to the murder of Father Allun. It was the same killer."

"How can you be sure?" Jenn asked, shocked by the detective's certainty. "I mean, you just started investigating."

"Hey, I'm good," Nick said, trying to lighten the mood. Unfortunately, he was unsuccessful again. "There were clues that helped us to link the two crimes."

"What clues?" Jenn asked, her interest piqued.

"Well, not so much clues as..." Nick hesitated for a moment before continuing. "Well there was the same feeling to the case; the type of murder was the same. It doesn't matter; we know who the killer was. It was Mark Anderson."

"As in Detective Mark Anderson?" Jenn asked, unconvinced.

"As in ex-Detective Mark Anderson who is now in lock up," Nick answered. "It seems that Anderson had a connection to both of the victims."

"But that could mean anything," Jenn stated. "Degrees of separation, everyone is related to everyone else in some way or another. I might know someone who knows someone who knows someone else. That's a connection but not enough to get arrested for."

"Anderson was intimately connected to each of the victims," Nick explained. "He has a history with both men, a rather sordid history. He also had means and opportunity. Let me assure you that we were on quite solid footing when we arrested him."

"And the murder weapon?" Jenn asked. "You have it with Anderson's prints on it?"

"Not exactly," Nick answered. "It wasn't that kind of weapon. The murder weapon was a weapon of opportunity; Brenner was strangled with a silk cloth that was sold in the store. There are fibers and other clues that helped us to put two and two together."

"Sounds awfully circumstantial to me," Jenn said, rising and taking the plates over to the sink.

"Perhaps I should run the evidence by you, counselor. Are you sure you want to be a prosecutor, you're beginning to sound like a criminal defense attorney," Nick said. He had meant it to be funny, understanding that her lawyer's mind had kicked in and she was doing what lawyers do, tearing the evidence to shreds. However, her constant criticism was grating at Nick's already raw emotions, and his frustration had come out in his voice.

"I'm so sorry," Jenn said, turning to him with an apologetic smile. "I didn't even realize that I was doing it. I'm sure that you are right about him. It must have been tough arresting him, even though he's been a prick to you guys lately. Once a cop, you know?"

"That's not even the worst of it," Nick said. "Anderson is a victim himself, he was abused sexually by a priest when he was a boy. That's how he knew Allun; they were altar boys at the same church."

"My God," Jenn gasped.

"It always seems to come down to those two words," Nick said with a forced chuckle, though his face gave away his true feelings. "I find myself making the same comment and not realizing how sick it really is in light of current events. This case, it's just not going to end the way I want it to. I'm not going to close this case feeling good about it, no matter what happens."

"I can imagine," Jenn said compassionately, and stroked his arm. She then turned and began rinsing off the dishes. After a moment, she turned and looked him square in the eyes. "Do you think that you could excuse yourself from this case? Maybe you could site a conflict of interest."

"What are you talking about?" Nick asked, laughing off her comment. "The case is practically closed. All I've got to do is hand my reports over to the prosecutor."

"Look what it's doing to you though," Jenn pointed out. "Why don't you let one of the other detectives finish it up, as you said, it's almost done."

"No," Nick said with a sigh. "I've arrested an ex-cop. If we're going to see this the whole way, this case should have the force of either the lead detective or the head of the Investigations Unit firmly behind it. Hollings can't sign off on it because of their history; we have to keep any hint of bias out of it. We all may have a personal beef with Anderson, but I have the least real history with him and with our evidence, this should seal the deal. Speaking of deals, it won't surprise me if Anderson takes one when he comes to his senses."

"The evidence is that strong?" Jenn asked, as if surprised.

"As you said, it might be circumstantial, but there is a lot of it," Nick said. "If it walks like a duck."

Nick pulled Jenn away from the dishes and together they made their way into the living room. They sat together, mostly lying together on the couch, each listening to the breathing of the other, fully content in each others company. Nick had not felt like this in a long time, like he was able to just let the rest of the world slip away and live in the moment here with her without thinking about what was outside his door. This was contentment, and it was exactly what Nick was looking for. Later that night, in bed, Jenn lay with her head on his chest. They hadn't said anything to each other in a long time, and they didn't need to. Their bodies said everything that needed to be said, and what passed between them was understood immediately by the other. Jenn traced the outline of the muscles on Nick's chest and he could feel her breath on his skin as she exhaled.

"Get off this case Nick," she said, almost pleading. "Let someone else finish it up."

"Don't worry," Nick said, and kissed her on her head. "It's almost over."

"I hope so," Jenn whispered. "I hope so."

The next morning, Nick awoke alone in bed. For a moment, he wracked his mind trying to remember if he might have done anything wrong. Everything seemed so right, as if they had been speaking the same language, although unspoken. Something slipped off of the pillow beside him, and he reached over and picked up a folded half sheet of paper. Jenn had written him a quick note, knowing that he would be concerned when he woke up without her. She said that she had an early shift and would call him later. Beneath it she put a heart and her name. They were getting closer to that point, he could feel it, and he didn't know if it should feel so natural, so easy. Underneath her name she wrote a short line "Don't do what you're thinking of doing, take the day off." Nick smiled, continuously amazed at how well she knew him. However, the detective could not ignore the call, the yearning of his soul. He showered quickly and dressed, knowing that he was hopeless. There was nothing else for him, there was no day off; he was a homicide detective.

CHAPTER 47

Nick could not help but replay Jenn's words in his mind over and over again, something about them stuck like a tape in a revolving loop. She kept telling him that the case seemed very circumstantial, and of course, she was right. There was very little physical evidence that linked Anderson to the crime, and even though Nick knew good prosecutors who had convicted criminals on less than what the police had, the detective knew everyone would feel much better if they had real evidence linking Anderson to the two crimes. However, even though a part of Nick was a detective who wanted justice, he was also a human being. The thought of sending Anderson to prison for the rest of his life just did not sit well with Nick, and he knew why. Anderson broke the law, and he should be punished; but Anderson was also a victim who never saw justice for the crimes committed against him. There had to be some type of balance, some way to make it possible for everyone to sleep at night, for everyone to feel as though justice had been done.

Nick contacted the district attorney who would be prosecuting Anderson, trying to see where the prosecutor stood on the idea of a plea bargain. The prosecutor had been thinking along the same lines, though more concerned that Anderson may engender sympathy amongst the jury. Not wanting to take the chance that Anderson may walk away from the charges entirely, the prosecutor had contacted Anderson regarding a deal, but had not even heard back to schedule a sit down, much less been able to spell out terms of the plea. Nick knew what was going on in Anderson's mind. The ex-detective turned reporter saw the way his ex-colleagues had reacted when they found out the truth about him, and Anderson must have known that if he could get that kind of sympathy out of people who did not necessarily like him, then he had a real chance with a jury who had no preconceived ideas about the man. This would make the prosecutor work harder than ever to portray Anderson not as a victim, but as a cold blooded murderer who deserved no mercy.

Nick needed evidence now more than ever. Ironically, Nick was now searching for evidence of a crime to save Anderson from himself. If the police could bring credible evidence to the prosecutor, and the D.A. could make Anderson see what a jury would think of that evidence, then maybe Anderson would do the right thing and take a deal. So the question now was, what evidence would do the trick, and where was that evidence. Leaving the house, Nick knew that he needed the perspective of a person not fully involved with the case, but informed as to the methods of this particular killer. Nick needed advice from his friend Sarrucci again, and after letting her know that he was coming, he drove quickly to her house, wanting to get right into the case again.

"Where's that handsome detective you were hanging out with?" Sarrucci asked as she answered the door. "If I had known you were coming alone I would have thought about it a bit longer."

"That handsome detective is wrapping up the case his own way," Nick responded, then smiled. "And it's nice to know where I stand on your list of friends."

"Oh don't worry," Sarrucci said, brushing off Nick's feign at insult. "Detective Smith is just eye candy. You and I, we have history."

"I need your evaluation of another case I'm working on," Nick said, getting right to the point. "I have my own opinions regarding it, but I am interested in hearing what you think."

"You're going to have to put me on the payroll," Sarrucci said, taking the Brenner case file out of his hands and examining the contents. She looked quickly, but committed as much to memory as possible, examining it professionally just as she had the first time Nick visited her. "Very interesting."

"What do you think?" Nick asked, leaning forward in anticipation.

"Well, you know this is the same killer, right?" Sarrucci asked, not really looking for an answer to her question. She knew Nick well enough to know how good a detective he was. There was no doubt in her mind that Nick had brought this material to verify what he already knew. "There is the same pattern of rage here, the same use of objects to make a statement, the same patience and determination. He probably kept Brenner alive for a long time, hurting him and subjecting him to all kinds of physical and mental tortures before killing him. In fact, I'll wager it's the mental and physical pain that does it for this killer. Killing the victim is secondary to revenge, to making the victim pay for what the killer perceives as his crimes."

"What do you mean?" Nick asked, beginning to think along a new line of thought. "Are you saying that this killer did not intend to kill at all?"

"No," Sarrucci said. "Only that this killer gets more thrill out of the torture than the killing. He only kills the victim when he feels there is no more satisfaction to be had from the torture. If the killer could restrain himself a little more and draw out the abuse longer, there is no telling how long he would keep his victims alive. However, in this case, the killer can not control himself enough to not let his rage get the better of him. The killer inflicts the pain, the harshest punishment he can think of, and after a while the victim breaks and goes into shock. When there is no more response, be it fear or his reaction to pain, the killer feels as though he has no more use for the victim and kills him. In this case, the killer seems to be able to control himself for up to forty-eight hours before he has to kill his victim."

"So this killer abused Brenner all weekend," Nick said. "Once Brenner's senses shut down, the killer lost interest in him."

"Yep," Sarrucci responded. "However, your killer is getting worse instead of better. Most killers learn from the first murder, they start to get better at it over time. That's not the case with this killer, though. This killer is losing control more and more easily with every crime he commits. Take the first murder; he abducts Allun, takes him to a safe place, and using instruments of torture, takes his time and then deposits Allun back at St. Patrick's. In this case, he attacks Brenner at his work, most likely staying in the shop with his victim the entire time. The killer uses items he finds there on the premises to torture and kill Brenner with. Then there is the evidence left behind."

"What evidence?" Nick asked.

"It's obvious to me from this murder that the killer is or was in law enforcement," Sarrucci said. She could tell by the look on Nick's face that he had been keeping that little fact a secret for a reason. "Don't look at me that way, I can read what it says here in the report. The fibers that matched police issued cold weather gloves, the taser marks on the body. The killer is a cop, and this cop is getting more and more angry. That anger is blinding him and causing him to make mistakes. What you need to be looking for is a cop who has a connection to both of the victims."

"We found the very person," Nick informed her, feeling more and more validated in his thinking by her perspective on the case. "Did you ever know a Detective Mark Anderson?"

"Only enough to know that he is a prick," Sarrucci said, her entire demeanor changing when Nick mentioned Anderson's name. "He used to lie on the stand to paint a more vicious image of the criminals he arrested. Usually his lies pertained to discussions he and the criminal had alone in interrogation. No one could ever prove that he was lying because he made sure no one was there during the interrogation. He would tell the jury that the guy confessed or some crap like that. Did you know that he even threatened me once not to testify because evidence I turned up exonerated the person he thought committed a crime. He's a real creep."

"I'm not arguing with you on that point," Nick said. "However, we've proven his connection to both victims and there is quite a background between him and Allun. We know it was him, and we were able to arrest him, but there just isn't a lot of physical evidence that would make this a slam dunk."

"There's something else," Sarrucci said, reading the emotion on the detective's face. "You're hesitant about something."

"It's just that Anderson was a victim himself at one point," Nick said with a sigh, hating to go over it again. "He doesn't necessarily deserve the maximum sentence, but he also doesn't deserve to go free. I need to find the evidence that will make him see that a plea bargain is the best way to go in this case."

"I don't know if I agree with you on that one," Sarrucci began. "But if it's evidence you need, it looks as though you have everything you're going to get from the Brenner crime scene. Unless you come across the exact taser he used, or the exact set of gloves that left these fibers, then I think you've gone as far as you can. Anderson knows enough about forensics to know that he needed to get rid of both of those items the minute he was done with the crime. The taser and the gloves are probably in some plastic bag with a cement brick inside on the seafloor of the Long Island Sound."

"What about Allun's murder?" Nick asked, switching gears immediately. "What evidence might we be likely to find there?"

"That murder was different," Sarrucci said. "That murder was far more exacting. The killer was good enough to leave no physical evidence of his presence at the crime scene. What you need to do is find the torture devices he used on Allun, and you need to find the wax."

"That's it," Nick said, snapping his fingers. "I forgot about all of that. If we could find that stuff, then we'd have an open and shut case. Anderson would be crazy not to take a deal then."

"You're a better person than I," Sarrucci said, shaking her head. "Anderson would not hesitate in sending a person he perceived to be guilty up the river for life, whether this person were really guilty or not. I've seen him do it, he's an animal Nick. He doesn't care about anyone."

"But I'm not," Nick said. "Anderson is the way he is because of crimes committed against him. He never saw justice for those crimes, and it's only natural to see why his view of justice is so skewed. He probably has so little faith in the system that he believes he had to lie to see that justice was done. I'm not excusing his actions, but sending him to prison for the rest of his life isn't going to change the person he is now, only compassion will."

"He didn't show compassion to Allun or Brenner," Sarrucci said.

"It's got to start somewhere," Nick said, rising from his seat in Sarrucci's living room. He was getting drawn into a debate, and that was the last thing he needed at that moment. Sarrucci had probably been choking on her own anger for the way Anderson had threatened her, and she had every right to be angry but Nick couldn't change that now. He had to look to the future, and he felt compelled to do something for

Anderson now. "Anderson may be a prick and a creep. He may be a murderer and a monster, but I'm not going to let myself become an angry bitter person like him by doing nothing. It's never too late for a person to change, but they can't do it alone. Trust me, I know."

CHAPTER 48

When Nick left Sarrucci's home, he headed straight for the Investigations Unit. Sarrucci had been absolutely right; he needed to find the torture devices Anderson had used on Allun. That was the best way to close this case for good, and the best way to make Anderson a little more receptive to the thought of a plea bargain. Nick spent the entire drive making a mental list of where to search for the devices, and by the time he arrived, he felt confident about this new avenue in his investigation. When he walked into the Investigations Unit, no one seemed the least bit surprised that he was here on a self-designated day off. Nick was concerned he would have to cut through the normal drivel with one or two people, explaining politely why he was here even though he did not owe anyone an explanation. However, when he entered there were only one or two pairs of eyes that even looked up, and no one really seemed overly interested. Nick went to his office and gathered his laptop and some other items related to the case, then made his way back to the interrogation room they had set up as a conference room when Anderson had come in. It still had the charts they had made and all the reports still sat on the desk, and most of all, it was quiet. It wouldn't take anyone too long to forget that Nick had come in, and he would be left alone to get some work done.

Nick plugged his laptop into the power and DSL outlet in the wall and turned the unit on. While he waited for the computer to come to life, he focused his attention on solving the issue of where he should begin. Sarrucci seemed certain that because of the nature of the wounds the devices of torture must have been exact replicas of the original devices used in the Spanish Inquisition. She was also certain that the killer would have built the devices himself; deriving pleasure just from the thought of what pain lay in store for his victim. This was a problem for Nick, giving rise to a dilemma in his mind. If Anderson did build the devices himself, that suggested a level of determination and focus that Nick had not thought about before. This preparation beforehand was the very definition of premeditation. This made Nick hesitant about helping Anderson, this man who had so cleverly planned this torture/murder of another human being; making him question whether Anderson deserved any compassion at all. Though Nick was not certain what he would do now, he did know that he was going to need the information anyway, and set his focus to finding the devices. What he would do with the information was something he would have to deal with later. Nick got online and within minutes was weeding through tons of information about torture. He realized immediately that he was going to have to narrow down his search parameters. Soon, Nick was reading articles and looking at conceptual drawings of these devices. After two hours, Nick was no closer to finding the devices, but he definitely knew a lot more about them.

Just after noon, Detectives Wilkins and Mitchell came in, dressed for business, ignoring the offer of a day off just as Nick had. They walked into the interrogation room and found Nick staring at a computer screen, jotting down notes.

"I knew you couldn't stay away," Wilkins said, making his way across the room. "We really need to find you a girl."

"I've got a girl," Nick said without looking up from the computer screen. "Besides, you're here. What does that say about you two?"

"It says we're pathetic," Mitchell said. "Or that we've been infected by your non-stop work ethic."

"It could be worse," Nick said with a shrug. He looked up at both men who were leaning against the wall directly across from where Nick was seated. "I talked to the prosecutor; he's offering Anderson second degree murder on both Allun and Brenner, sentences to be run concurrently, twelve to twenty years. With good behavior, Anderson would be out in no more than fifteen."

"Jesus, it's a gift," Wilkins said, amazed at the level to which the prosecutor was willing to lower himself just to clear this case from his desk. "How long did it take Anderson to think about it?"

"About ten seconds," Nick said, leaning back in his chair. "He refused the deal and said 'I did not kill those men'. He says he wants his day in court."

"You've got to be kidding me," Mitchell said. "Our case may be strongly circumstantial, but a jury is going to have no second thoughts about convicting him on what we have. What is he holding out for?"

"Anderson thinks that the jury can be swayed by sympathy," Nick said. "Sympathy for his situation. I can't say that I entirely blame him for thinking that, I mean, just look at how we all reacted when we found out. And we didn't even like him. That's why I'm here today. I want to find the evidence that would convict him hands down, no questions asked, no deliberation. If we can show Anderson that we have this evidence, then he may be more willing to plead out."

Both detectives simply nodded and said nothing. If they had any problems with this plan, as Sarrucci had, they were not going to make it known. Nick started by explaining what information he had so far and what he was looking for. Soon all three men were seated around the table, scribbling furiously on legal pads as their computers hummed softly. Each man slipped into the zone quickly, and soon they were all quietly working on their assigned tasks. A few hours later Wilkins was able to give the approximate dimensions and plans for each of the torture devices. Immediately, all three men knew that they had to find out what Anderson had in his home. Fortunately for them, the Norwich police had already searched Anderson's home as Detective Smith was now trying to wrap up the Allun investigation from Norwich. The Allun case was, in fact, theirs and Nick was left with the Brenner investigation due to jurisdiction. Norwich had agreed to roll the charges into one for a plea arrangement, but that still left Kevin in charge to tidy up the case. Nick called Kevin to ask what he might have found at Anderson's home. Nick had no intentions of letting Kevin know what he was working on or why. Kevin had about as much sympathy for Anderson as the rest of the detectives did, but it was already common knowledge that he was unhappy about the terms of the plea. Kevin answered all of Nick's questions, thinking that his questions were related to the taser and the police gloves. Nick did nothing to change Kevin's assumptions and by the end of the conversation, he knew that there was nothing at Anderson's home that would give them the information they needed.

"There was nothing," Nick said as he disconnected the call on his cell phone. "The torture devices weren't there and there was nothing that suggested he had a place where he might have kept them. I want you two to do a background and credit check on Anderson, find out everything he was paying for lately and where he was going. I want everything. He has to be keeping those torture devices somewhere and I can't believe he's destroyed them after putting so much exacting work into building them in the first place. They have to be somewhere."

The two detectives left the room to start their search, and just as they exited, Sarrucci popped her head in.

"Hey," she began hesitantly. "Do you have a minute?"

"Yeah sure," Nick said, rising to his feet and offering her a chair. "What are you doing here?"

"First, I want to apologize for the way I acted before you left," Sarrucci said. "I think it's great that you want to help Anderson, I just got caught up in my feelings about him. You were right though, he does deserve compassion and we all have to find a way to sleep at night. I've also been thinking seriously about Anderson and how he fits my impressions of the killer."

"Me too," Nick said. "There are some things that fit and others that don't."

"I know, and I didn't know how to reconcile him as the killer and my impressions of the killer until it hit me," Sarrucci said, pausing for a moment as if for effect. "I think this killer has a split personality, and after I reviewed the murders under that thinking, everything made sense. Anderson must have multiple personality disorder."

"A split personality," Nick repeated, suddenly concerned. "Are you saying he didn't know he killed those two?"

"I'm not saying that at all," Sarrucci said with a smile. "In fact, I think his feelings about both men played into the split in his personality and the reason they were targets. First, I don't believe he is a fully split personality, or that such a thing exists. The definition of multiple personality disorder is two separate and distinct personalities, both operating at different times, almost always unaware of the other personality. However, any psychiatrist who believes in MPD also believes that the disorder stems from a hugely traumatic experience, usually in childhood. Now I don't subscribe to MPD because I don't believe an event so traumatic as to create a second personality in a person can cause that second personality to be unaware of the first. I do believe, however, that an event can be so traumatic as to cause the creation of a second personality, but that that second personality draws it's polar opposite behavior from the first."

"I don't get it," Nick said, shaking his head. "You don't believe in multiple personalities, but you believe Anderson has one."

"No, I don't believe Anderson didn't know what he was doing," Sarrucci corrected him. "Let's look at Anderson's personality for a moment, the personality we all know and love. He's hot headed, he's rash, he's angry and he's impulsive. This does not fit with the personality of the killer. Our killer is focused and determined, our killer is patient. However, we are left with two inescapable truths. There is a relation between Allun, Brenner, and the killer, and the killer is losing his ability to remain patient, to draw out the satisfaction of torture. Now you said that seven years ago Anderson began stalking Brenner, bothering him at home and at his work. When Anderson found that his means of intimidation were not working, his anger rose. He thought that Brenner was going to get away with what he did to that girl and those feelings of anger merged with his anger about what the priest did to him when he was a child. This hatred built up until it began choking Anderson's mind and eating away at his morality. This is when the split occurred, and now we are left with two distinct personalities. Anderson the hot headed police officer, who looks for justice but wants to get it any way he can; and then there's Anderson the killer who has no qualms about killing, with viciously taking the lives of those he believes are guilty. However, there is a commonality in the backgrounds of the people he kills. The killer personality does not kill at random, and because of the targets he chose, leads me to believe that if MPD does play a part in this case, the killer personality is feeding off of the primary personality."

"Which denotes that the two personalities are aware of each other," Nick said, completing her thought. "Which means he knew what was happening, even if Anderson the Prick wasn't doing it."

"Exactly," Sarrucci said. "Anderson's frustration and anger become rage, and that rage reaches the boiling over point, at which time Anderson the Killer is personality comes forth. With this personality, Anderson can do whatever he deems necessary without remorse."

There was a sudden knock at the door and Mitchell entered with a folder of papers in his hand.

"Sorry to interrupt," he began. "I couldn't find anything that might lead us to a place where Anderson might be keeping his torture devices, but I did remember something. Michael Allun had a storage facility somewhere out towards Exeter, Rhode Island. It's in the backwoods somewhere, just outside of Voluntown, Connecticut. Allun bought it off the original owners when they went bankrupt, and according to his financials, Allun's not leasing it out to anyone."

"Could the devices be Allun's?" Nick asked, looking over at Sarrucci, who seemed just as surprised as he. Suddenly, a young uniformed officer burst through the door, nearly knocking Mitchell of off his feet. The officer was panting and his face was red, and it looked as if he had been running a marathon.

"There's this guy on the phone asking for you," the officer said, looking directly at Nick. "He says he's your killer."

CHAPTER 49

Suddenly, the atmosphere around the detective seemed to go from calm and collected to sheer panic and confusion as everyone around him reacted differently to the news that the killer was on the phone. Nick alone said nothing as he tried to wrap his mind around the possibility that Anderson might have set this up. Nick made his way down the hall from the interrogation room quickly, followed by the other detectives and Jessica Sarrucci.

"This is impossible," Wilkins ranted. "Anderson is still in lock up, downstairs in this very building. This is a prank."

"This is a set-up of some sort," Mitchell said, also trying to comprehend the possibilities of the phone call. "This is some friend of Anderson's who is trying to cast suspicion off of him."

The moment Mitchell said it though; they all knew it was not true. Anderson had no friends, he had no one to confide in; he had no one who would come to his aid in a time of need. This was something else.

"Calm down, everyone," Nick ordered, knowing that he had to get control of the situation. Whatever was going on, he was going to need his complete concentration on this phone call. "Wilkins, go downstairs and find out what Anderson is doing right now. Mitchell, get a trace running and I want this call recorded on our end. Jessica, follow me, I want you listening in."

Nick made his way to Hollings' office, sat down on the corner of the desk, and pressed the speaker and hold button at the same time, then he spoke down into the phone.

"This is Nicholas Grenier," the detective began. "Who is this?"

"You know who this is," replied the electronically altered voice. "Or at least you're afraid of who this is, which is why you kept me on hold for so long."

"If you are implying that you are the killer, then I don't believe you," Nick said.

"You know," the voice began. "Each time I call, I'm doing so because I am disappointed in your lack of abilities, or is this, too, a test? Tell me detective, would you arrest an innocent person just to bait me, just to draw me out again?"

That clinched it in Nick's mind. This person was either the killer, or someone who was closely related to him. If Anderson was in fact the killer, then he had to have someone on the outside that he was feeding information to. This was a theory that did not track with anything Anderson had done, ever.

"Are you tracing this call, detective?" asked the voice.

"You bet we are," Nick answered, seeing no reason to lie. "Why do you call me, why put yourself out there to be caught when there is a perfectly good scape-goat here in police custody."

"Whose going to catch me detective, you?" asked the voice, the incredulity coming through the electronic filter clearly. "It is precisely because you have a scape-goat that I have to call you. If I didn't, you would hang these murders on whoever you found the most convenient. What are you going to say and do when I kill again?"

"Is that why you kill?" Nick asked. "Because I haven't caught you yet?"

"No, detective," answered the killer. There was no question about who this was now. "I know that at some point I will be caught and this will all come to an end. I kill because I am forced to deliver the justice that the police were unable to deliver in the first place."

"What crime did these men commit?" Nick asked. "Allun may have been a sexual sadist, but his victims were willing participants. As for Brenner, he comes as close to the line of rape as anyone can, but no one came forward, no one filed charges. Their crimes are moral ones, not legal ones."

"The fact that you can make that distinction is criminal," the killer spat. This was Nick's plan all along, to catch the killer off guard and get a little more information out of him than he had planned. Nick had to keep this guy rolling just a little longer.

"So are you going to kill me now?" Nick asked. "Does my thinking that there is a difference between moral and legal crimes warrant a visit from you?"

"No detective," answered the killer, obviously regaining his calm. "I have no issue with you. You are a good man, from what I understand. I simply pity you. However, I going to kill someone, if only to get you to release your scape-goat."

"That's not necessary," Nick began.

"Oh, but it is," said the killer. "You have not caused me to deviate from my plan any, just to move my timetable up a little. I would have killed this one anyway. You see, detective, the crimes these men commit go far deeper than just rape, or sexual sadism. Their true crime was in that second where their victims went from having a sense of security to the understanding of despair. Don't forget, these men are only getting what they deserve, they are only repayed what they have taken."

"Until the point when you kill them," Nick interjected.

"Their deaths were necessary," the killer said. "It was closure for their victims. Do you think that a victim would feel any less violated if they saw him out on the street? No, they would just relive their despair over and over. Allun and Brenner's death is the most crucial part of this justice."

"I will find you," Nick uttered, not knowing anything else to say. "I will stop you."

"Of that, I have no doubt," the killer replied. "In fact, I'll even give you a clue so that you can stop me and release an innocent man. There are waves and waves of potentials to bring to justice. I will surf for the one who is the most fitting, the most deserving of my attention. In fact, I know the perfect one; he was just brought to my attention recently. He will not die until eight o'clock tonight. He will receive a visit from me at seven thirty. I will not deviate from my plan, whether you are there or not. If you figure out who my next victim is, you can save a life and stop me in the process. If not..."

With that, the killer hung up, leaving Nick and Sarrucci standing there, waiting with baited breath. After a few seconds, Nick realized that the killer had ended the call, and that every moment he stood there, he was wasting time. Nick exited Hollings' office, followed by Sarrucci, and began pacing in the squad bay, waiting for Wilkins to come back up from the lock up downstairs, but also to begin strategizing and bouncing ideas off of everyone. Mitchell stood at his desk, removing earphones from his ear.

"Did we get the trace?" Nick asked him.

"They're running it now," Mitchell answered. "We'll have it in a few minutes."

"Why give us these clues?" Nick asked, clearly questioning Sarrucci though he did not look at her directly. "Why make a game out of it? If he wants us to know who the next victim is, why not give us the person's name?"

"He's absolving himself of guilt," Sarrucci replied. "He's giving you the opportunity to stop him, to save the next victim. However, he's only giving you so much information. When the time runs out, and he kills his next victim, he can put the blame on you for not catching him in time. It's actually an interesting insight into this killer."

"Anderson was in his cell the entire time," Wilkins said, panting and out of breath as he had run up the steps to get back to the Investigations Unit. "I had a conversation with the smug bastard, or tried to at least."

"Your killer is not completely at peace with the notion that he kills his victims," Sarrucci said, continuing her prior thought. "You killer feels guilt and remorse for crossing the line, for killing these men. Yet clearly, he feels as though it is absolutely necessary to do so; for the closure. He feels remorse for the killing and he can't bring himself to let an innocent man go to jail for a crime he did not commit."

"This is all well and good," Mitchell said, as he moved away from Wilkins, who was listening to a recording of the call through the earphones. "But it doesn't bring us any closer to catching this guy, or stopping the murder that happens in four hours. The trace says the call originated from a pay phone across the street from the Fitch Middle School in Groton."

Nick hung his head and paced back and forth even faster now; trying to find the clues the killer left and arrange them in some kind of order.

"Waves and waves of potential victims," Nick muttered under his breath. "I will surf for the most deserving one. One has been brought to my attention, die at eight, visit at seven-thirty."

Nick looked up at the other detectives.

"He still plans to torture the victim for thirty minutes," Nick said. "He's letting us know that everything will still go according to plan."

"But what's the clue?" Wilkins asked, coming in on the conversation after listening to the call.

"Waves, surfing," Nick said. "Surfing, surfing the net, the Internet. Surfing was the clue, he plans to surf the net for his next victim, or he found his next victim on the internet. But how do you find a criminal online?"

"These aren't just any criminals," Sarrucci interjected. "Their 'crimes' are sexual in nature. I'll bet you the killer feels that his victim's are sex offenders."

"And sex offenders have to register with the state," Nick said, finishing her thought. "There are online registries of sexual offenders."

Mitchell had already taken off on the detective's thinking and had grabbed the nearest computer and begun typing away. He got online and typed in SEX OFFENDERS, CONNECTICUT into the search bar as everyone else gathered around him. In a few seconds, the results flashed up on the screen.

"There are hundreds of sites," Mitchell said, surprised by the total number of pages he had to search through. "How are we supposed to know which one is the site the killer is using?"

"The first one," Nick said. "The official Connecticut state sex offender database, that's the only one he'd use."

"How can you be sure?" Wilkins asked.

"Because the database is updated by people in law enforcement," Nick said. "Because our killer is a cop, it's the only database he'd trust to use."

Detective Mitchell clicked on the website address and clicked back and forth until he reached the page for the database itself. A giant red warning flashed at him, informing the reader that using the information to harm a sex offender was a punishable offense. However, Mitchell did not have time to comment on the irony and within 60 seconds was scrolling through a huge list of names and addresses.

"Jesus Christ," Sarrucci exclaimed. "I had no idea there were so many."

"We have to narrow it down to this area," Nick said.

"Why?" Wilkins asked, unconvinced. "The killer has a little less than four hours before he attacks the next victim. You could get anywhere in this state in four hours."

"But the killer still needs prep time," Nick said. "Besides, all the other victims were in this general area. Our killer is giving us a clue; he's not going to dash out hopes of intervening by killing someone in the northwest hills."

"I found him," Mitchell called out, surprising everyone. "I found the next victim. His name is Andrew Cooper."

"How can you be sure he's the right guy?" Wilkins asked, knowing his partner. Mitchell rarely committed himself to a statement unless he was certain of it. That didn't make Mitchell slow or indecisive, it actually meant that Mitchell could process information at a faster rate and when he made a statement, he was usually right.

"Andrew Cooper's name was just updated and highlighted by the state because he failed to meet with his parole officer for the last two visits and he was just flagged as non-compliant," Mitchell explained.

"That would bring him to the attention of our killer," Nick said. "What was he convicted of?"

"He was convicted of sexually molesting thirteen girls at the school where he worked as a teacher," Mitchell answered. "He was released from prison four months ago and listed his mother's home as his address. He's missed two appointment's with his parole officer and upon investigation, his mother claims to not know where he is living or working now."

"That would fit as a potential target of our killer," Sarrucci stated. "A teacher who abuses the bonds of trust he has with his students. He would be a prime candidate, but it just seems too easy."

"I agree," Nick said, turning his attention back to the detective seated in front of the computer. "You're telling me that you are absolutely certain this Cooper guy is our man."

"Oh, I'm certain," Mitchell said, turning around in his chair to reveal a big smile. "You see, Cooper was a teacher at Fitch Middle School."

"Holy shit," Wilkins exclaimed. "The school across the street from where the killer called us. He was leaving another clue."

"Alright," Nick said, clapping his hands together. "I'll call Hollings; we'll need her to back us up. Wilkins, you get every available man together, call them in if you have to. I want a task force ready to move the moment we know where Cooper is. Jessica, you work with Mitchell. I want you two to scour every avenue to find Cooper. Use any psychological workup necessary, call his PO, threaten his mother. We just have to find him."

"What do we do with Anderson?" Wilkins asked.

"He stays where he is," Nick answered. "Until we're certain. The killer has left us holding the bag on this one, and I'm not ready to let this one explode in our faces."

"How do we explain the manpower?" Mitchell asked. "If we find Cooper, what are we going to say?"

"When we find Cooper," Nick corrected the junior detective. "We'll bust him for violating his parole. All the manpower may be overkill in the end, but I think we're all in agreement that the killer has left too many clues for it to be a coincidence. Cooper may be a child molester and he may deserve to rot in jail, but nobody gets to arbitrarily decide to kill another person. Don't confuse yourself, the killer is not doling out justice, he's seeking revenge. We can't let another person die, no matter who he is or what he's done."

Everyone just stared at Nick, even those officers who were not initially part of the conversation. This was a task that everyone was going to have to help undertake. Nick had not meant to give a speech but he could understand the conflicting emotions that must have been running through each of them, because they were running through Nick too. The fact of the matter was, this killer was committing murder; no more, no less.

"Find him," Nick ordered, then went into Hollings' office and closed the door.

CHAPTER 50

As the hours passed Nick became more and more nervous. The tension level in the Investigations Unit was reaching the flash point as everyone feared that their time to find and save Andrew Cooper would expire. Detective Mitchell worked quickly, with focus and purpose; never succumbing to the nervous atmosphere that was enveloping everyone else. Jessica Sarrucci helped Mitchell, first by supplying a psychological background, through the little information they were able to come up with in such a short period of time, then by trying to guess the killer's plan for Cooper. Wilkins spent his time first putting together teams of uniformed officers, and then drawing up strategy plans that could be improvised at a moment's notice once they located Cooper. He had also contacted all the local police departments for cooperation. As the deadline loomed ever closer, it was more and more obvious that they would need the assistance of any nearby police department to secure Cooper's safety. Nick envied Mitchell and Wilkins; they both had a job to do, something to take their mind's off the steadily ticking clock. As for Nick, there was nothing to do but wait and be all the more conscious of the fact that he was running out of time.

Cooper's parole officer, simply known as Parker, came down to help supply information and to be present for the bust should it go down. According to Parker, Cooper had been a model parolee since being released from prison, which Nick knew was a rarity in itself. Cooper had done everything he was ordered to do upon release; he had registered as a sex offender, stayed away from children, met his curfew, and gone to all of his court mandated therapy sessions. Cooper had never missed, or been late to, a meeting with his PO, nor had he been a second late in checking in on his nightly phone checks. Parker admitted that even he had been mildly surprised when Cooper missed his first appointment two months ago. Parker had not been too concerned about it, as Cooper had been responsible in meeting all his other obligations, but when he missed his second appointment Parker began to get suspicious. The parole officer contacted Cooper's therapist, who said that Cooper had missed his last two appointments as well. When Parker checked Cooper's work and last known address and found that his parolee had gone missing, he knew immediately that Parker had gone under the radar.

Apparently, prison had been especially hard on Andrew Cooper. There was an honor code even amongst criminals, there were degrees of fear and respect accorded to individuals by what they were convicted for. However, there was no fear or respect given to child molesters, and everyone wanted a piece of Cooper. He spent most of his time in the infirmary or in solitary confinement. Nick had heard that time in the hole was hard time, but he could imagine that it was better than being beaten and raped on a daily basis. There would have been no one to protect him, no one to watch his back. Cooper would have been alone and vulnerable. He went in as a slow moving, slightly overweight man who did not know how to defend himself; he would have been easy pickings. When Cooper got out of prison, life had not improved much for him. His conviction voided his teaching license, and being forced to register on the sex offender's database kept him from getting any jobs that might bring him anywhere close to children. He was red-flagged every time a potential employer did a background check. This had forced him to get menial jobs, for which he was over-qualified, and which he understood little about. He made next to no money, and he had no time to himself. When he was out of work he was monitored constantly; going to therapy sessions, meeting routinely with his parole officer, and checking in by phone several times a day. After a while, it was enough to make any person go a little crazy and want some freedom. Cooper had complained that everyone in his neighborhood knew what he had done, and living there had been unbearable. He had tried to get an apartment of his own, but his lack of money was a problem and when the landlord did a credit check, his time in prison was the first thing they saw. In the end, Cooper had been forced to live with his mother, a situation that was less than ideal because she hated him.

Wilkins had gone over to Cooper's mother's house personally to question her. Unfortunately, the detective came back with nothing. Wilkins questioned her, then threatened her, sweated her, and even tried to intimidate her. It became evident that she truly did not know where her son was. When Wilkins returned to the Investigations Unit to report back, Nick knew immediately what little information he had gotten from Cooper's mother. She had been harassed and victimized over what her son had done. She had lost her home and was now renting a house in an older, more rundown section of New London. All of her friends stopped speaking to her, she lost her job, and everything she had worked towards for so many years was gone. Nick was certain that the only reason she had let Cooper stay with her was because he had nowhere else to go, but having him back in the house must have been torture. He must have been a constant reminder of everything she had lost. Sarrucci was the first to point out the easiest answer, that Cooper was already dead. It was a shocking thought to Nick, but not an unbelievable one. It made sense when he asked himself why the killer would give the police this opportunity to stop him. It was the killer's way of making the police look bad. In the end, Nick dismissed this thinking, feeling as though the killer would not stoop to something as low as that. The killer wanted to rub it in the their faces that he was better than the police, that no matter how close they got to him they would never be able to stop him. Besides, the killer had not lied to them yet, there was no reason to, he was in complete control. The killer must have felt very confident in that fact.

Hollings had been forced to come in to oversee the investigation and to cool off the brass. The chief of police had been called back to work, something he was less than happy about, and Hollings was reporting to him every thirty minutes on where they stood in finding Cooper. The whole thing was a mess; their prime suspect, Anderson was downstairs in lock-up and the police were now playing catch up in an attempt to disprove the fact that the person on the phone was the killer. However, Nick knew that it had been the killer on the phone, and that the police had made a big mistake with Anderson. There had been so much evidence pointing to Anderson, that even though he had not put it together before Smith had come into the interrogation room over twenty four hours ago, it made sense when Anderson was put into the equation. Unfortunately, that was the very problem, there was too much evidence pointing towards Anderson, and Nick started to feel stupid for not seeing this for what it was, a set up. Someone had set Anderson up, and if the killer was really a police officer, that would narrow down the suspect pool considerably. Hollings was furious though, and when she wasn't reporting to the chief of police, she was strategizing damage control. Nick couldn't help but feel sorry for her, it hadn't been her fault. It hadn't been anyone's fault; everyone would have done the exact thing that she did. Everyone would have looked at the evidence and arrested Anderson in a heartbeat, and everyone would have been wrong. Unfortunately, what everyone would have done isn't remembered and Hollings was worried that she would have to fall on her sword. Nick was determined not to let that happen, but it wouldn't be easy. When Anderson was released, he was going to make their lives hell. It was automatically assumed that he would wage war with the department, filing a lawsuit and using his position as a television news reporter to tarnish the reputations of everyone who had a hand in his arrest.

"It's not your fault, you know," Nick said, repeating the words she had said to him just over twenty four hours ago. "I remember you saying that to me just yesterday."

"But this time, it is my fault," Hollings replied. "We arrested Anderson and it looks like we were wrong."

"Everyone makes mistakes," Nick offered. "Anyone in your shoes would have made the same decision and you didn't have anything to do with Detective Smith arresting him. Anderson would be in jail whether we arrested him or not. He lied to us, he's lied since the beginning, and I'm still a little interested in how there can be so much evidence pointing to him."

"It's called an orgy of evidence," Hollings stated. "And there are very few times when there is so much evidence pointing to one person. I should have been wary of it from the start; it just seemed to make so much sense."

"I know," Nick agreed. "I can't believe that he wasn't set up by someone."

"That's what we should be focusing on next," Hollings stated. "Who would have set up Anderson, who would have a connection to the victims?"

Nick just nodded, knowing that his lieutenant was going through the motions now. She was worried that the blame for arresting Anderson would be laid directly at her door. He knew that she now regretted being pushed into having Nick oversee the Allun investigation in the first place. She was back peddling, and it was not something that she was very good at. Nick needed this to work tonight; he needed to save Cooper and to catch the killer at the same time if it was possible. If the police could come up with a win now, it would overshadow the fact that they had arrested the wrong person. There was a quick knock at the door and Mitchell entered, not waiting to be invited in.

"I've found him," Mitchell said. "Cooper is using his middle name, and has re-applied for a driver's license and social security number under the new name."

"Has he made it legal?" Nick asked, surprised that he had remained under the radar so long with such a simple plan.

"It doesn't matter," Hollings said. "Do you know where he is?"

"He's renting a place in Gales Ferry," Mitchell said. "He's also got a job with the Groton Public Library."

"That's a violation," Nick said. "There is no way he'd be able to get a job at the library, with such close proximity to children if they knew who he really was."

"Have the Groton police move in now," Hollings ordered. "Have them secure the house and him as well."

The three detectives got into an unmarked car and headed off to the address where Cooper was now living. There was now less than a half an hour until the deadline expired, and if everything went according to plan, the police would get to Coopers house in the next five minutes. They just had to hope that Cooper was at home, though Nick had a sneaking suspicion that he wasn't. Wilkins had just pulled the cruiser into the far left lane of the Gold Star Memorial Bridge when the call came in informing them Cooper's house was empty. Nick had been expecting this news and his mind had been looking for alternative places where they might find him. Hollings ordered everyone to meet at the middle school, going off of the advice from Sarrucci. It was Jessica's feeling that the killer would use something significant to Cooper's past at the murder. The only thing that they could think of was to kill him at the place where Cooper had committed his crimes. Nick, however, felt that this was not the right thinking. Nick knew that the killer's timetable had been moved up, and he would not be planning the same drawn out type of torture and murder that he had been able to get away with when he attacked Allun and Brenner. This was a different type of murder; this was the killer's way of thumbing his nose at the police, his way to show how much better he was.

"He's not taking Cooper to the school," Nick said. "He's going to kill him somewhere public, somewhere we would not expect."

"Where are you getting this?" Mitchell asked from the passenger seat. "That doesn't fit with the profile."

"This murder is the killer's way of showing us that we can't follow any profile," Nick said. "He's going to kill Cooper right under our nose, publicly. He's going to try to kill Cooper and get out without anyone knowing he was there."

"We have orders," Wilkins said. "We can't just disobey Hollings' orders. If you're wrong and Cooper is killed at the school, Hollings will kill us."

"I know," Nick said. "But the killer is not going to strike at the school; he doesn't have time to plan that. Trust me, he's going to kill Cooper somewhere public, somewhere we should have thought of but never expected."

"So, where is this public place?" Mitchell asked.

"The public library," Nick answered, a thin smile spreading across his face as he became certain he knew what this killer was thinking. "The killer is going to kill Cooper at his own workplace. He's going to kill Cooper during operating hours, with people all around. A quiet space, a clean quick murder; we need to hurry, there's not much time left."

CHAPTER 51

Nick jumped out of the car the second Mitchell pulled it up alongside the curb. Standing outside, Nick found himself facing the front entrance of the Groton Public Library. The detective turned to survey the area. The parking lot was expansive, filled with cars an hour and a half before closing. This, however, was the end of the summer and school was still out, so the building would be packed with parents and children. This was not the ideal place for something to go wrong. The sun was beginning to set far off in the west, but the dog days of summer still had it's teeth deep, and the weather was hot and there was very little wind. Nick's shirt clung to him as the humidity and the anticipation made him sweat a little more than he regularly would. Nick made his way onto the sidewalk and towards the entrance of the library. Mitchell and Wilkins followed close behind as they crossed through the two sets of automatic sliding glass doors and into the air-conditioned lobby. Inside, Nick came to a halt to get a better appreciation of the layout of the building. The Groton Public Library was not necessarily one of the largest buildings, but there were still plenty of nooks and crannies where the killer could be lying in wait. There were plenty of quiet and secluded spots where he could attack his unsuspecting victim.

Mitchell stepped over to the check out desk and whipped out a picture of Cooper, asking the young woman at the counter whether she knew him. She immediately stated that she did, and that Cooper was working tonight back in the stacks, shelving books. Nick did not wait to overhear any more of the conversation, but he knew that Mitchell was telling her to make a general announcement telling everyone that the library was closing early. Mitchell would not make the mistake of telling the young woman what was going on, the last thing the police needed now was a panic. Nick scoffed at this thought, realizing immediately that the three detectives were less than an imposing force against a killer who did not want to be caught. They were alone against this man, and there wasn't going to be any back up within the next five minutes. Hollings had everyone stationed at the school, but Nick was certain now; if Cooper was here, then the killer was here too. Nick stepped forward, quickly scanning every face that he passed. To the right of him was a large open space where DVD's were open for browsing, as well as an area where people could sit comfortably and read. To his direct left was another open area, with a few racks of magazines standing for perusal. In front of him was the real problem, the information desk, which was really a series of counters in a diamond formation, behind which several librarians answered questions and helped people search for information. Beyond that was an area of computers lining the far wall of the building, and directly behind the information desk were the stacks of books, four rows deep. From where he stood, Nick could tell that the lighting was less than optimal for a search at the head of every row. Nick would have to go in; he would have to go into the stacks to find Cooper, hopefully before the killer did.

The announcement came over the intercom system, causing everyone in the quiet building to jump. A woman came on and, very politely, asked the patrons to collect their belongings and exit the building as quickly and orderly as possible. She explained that there was the indication of a gas leak towards the back of the building, and that the police had asked everyone to return to their cars and leave, as the parking lot and exit were completely safe. Nick was pleased with Mitchell's quick thinking, creating a cover story that would get no flack from anyone, especially parents. However, there was still the note of tension in the woman's voice, and it was apparent to everyone in the library. People started to rise from their seats and gather their books and papers. There was some anticipation in the air, but the tone of fear in the woman's voice had only served to hasten the patrons desire to leave. Everyone could tell that there was something wrong and they were not going to stay to find out what. Wilkins waited at the automatic doors, watching everyone as they left, searching each face for Cooper. As patrons passed the detectives, Nick could hear them commenting that they could smell no gas, but none of them seemed to not believe the story; it was perfect.

Unfortunately, none of the people passing Nick looked like Cooper. This meant that he was somewhere still in the building, and it meant that Nick was going to have to go in and get him. The stacks of books were situated in an area shaped liked a huge rectangle. Looking in, as he began to pass the information desk, Nick realized that he was on the long side of the stacks. This meant someone could hide further down inside the stacks and move on as Nick passed, without the detective knowing. He was not positioned strategically, not that anything about this was planned strategically. Nick knew that he was going to have to move to the shorter end, minimizing the chances that he might miss either Cooper or the killer. As Nick moved to the right of the stacks, he found himself in another open space where rows of desks had been set up and spaced apart for patrons to study and work quietly. Nick turned to his left and faced the first walkway into the stacks. There was no one present in the open corridor, and Nick crouched over slightly to get a better view in that small space between the tops of the books and the bottom of the shelf just above. However, he could see no bodies, faces or obstructions. He couldn't see anyone in the stacks, but he knew that this was just the beginning. The killer had been confident about his abilities, just as he had been confident about knowing where his victim would be. Nick could only hope that Cooper had managed to get passed him, towards the front, and hopefully Wilkins or Mitchell had him. However, Nick knew that if his colleagues did have him, they would have called out by now. No, Cooper was still in here somewhere; and if the killer stuck to his plan, he was still alive, for now.

Nick slipped his sidearm from it's holster, clipped to his belt, and raised it up in front of him. Nick side stepped down the length of the next stack of books to the next corridor. There was no one inside here either. The lighting seemed as though it got progressively worse as he neared the back of the stacks. Perhaps it was Nick's mind playing tricks on him, the anticipation making everything seem a little off. Nick kept staring carefully in the space between the books as he side stepped down again, to the third corridor opening. There was only one other entrance at the far end, but Nick felt certain that this was the best place for him to enter the stacks. If the lighting was off, then it was better he enter here, closer to the forth row, where he was closer, but still be somewhat in the middle with the best light ahead of him. The detective was not certain about the validity of his logic, but he knew Cooper was inside there somewhere, and Nick was no closer to saving him standing here on the outside of the stacks. Nick took a deep breath, and stepped into the rows of books.

Quickly, he jerked his head from side to side, making a quick look of each side to ensure it was clear. Nick took a second glance down the corridor to see if there was anything he could make out, and once certain that nothing and no one was moving, he took another step forward to the next intersection between shelves and the corridor. He repeated his motion, checking up and down the aisles to be certain that he had accounted for everything. At this pace, it was going to take an hour for him to check the entire row; and it was still possible for him to miss seeing Cooper somewhere in a blind spot. Nick stepped quickly to the next intersection, and just as he swept the area clear with his eyes, there was a chime from his watch. Nick jumped, and then remembered that he had set it. Nick pressed the glow button and read the time indicated on the watch, 7:30p.m. At that moment, there was a blood-curdling scream from somewhere deep within the racks, and then darkness descended all around the detective.

CHAPTER 52

She stood there, in the middle of her living room, staring at the door. Her boyfriend was pounding away, screaming for her to open up and let him in. She closed her eyes, hoping and praying that this wasn't happening to her, that he was not on the other side of the door about to hurt her. However, when she opened her eyes, she realized that her prayers had been in vain and that there was no escaping what monster lay on the other side. She just stood there hesitantly, hoping that one of the neighbors would do something. She could never understand why no one would come out and stop him from beating on her, or call the cops. There was no way that they didn't hear her screams or his yelling, especially the neighbors with whom she shared a common wall. Even if someone just came out and said something, maybe he would realize that everyone knew what was going on. Instead, they enabled him, acting calm and polite when they passed him in the hall, and yet looking sympathetically at her as if to impart that they knew what she was going through. They did know what she was going through, they heard it every time and yet they did nothing. And here he was now, standing behind the door, pounding and shouting away. All her neighbors knew what lay in store for her tonight, and yet they were not going to do anything to stop him.

She was jarred from her thoughts by a new sound of pounding at the door. Her boyfriend had gone from pounding with his fists to throwing all of his two hundred pounds against the door like a battering ram. It was only a matter of time now, only a matter of time before he burst into the apartment and found her standing there shaking. Then he would be more angry, he would become enraged, and for the first time since she knew him, she had the feeling that he might just kill her. It was an impossible position; open the door to him and face the brunt of his anger, or wait for him to bust through and be the object of his fury. She could not understand why he was home so soon. There were usually three levels to his drinking, or more accurately, three levels to his drunkenness. The first level was the bruised ego self pity. He would sit at the bar and focus on how he had been mistreated by everyone and how nothing was his fault. His anger would build and build until he reached stage two, which offered itself as outward anger and aggression. When he kept drinking, he would usually pass on to stage three, emotional need. At this point, he would come home and be apologetic for what he had done, trying to explain how it wasn't his fault and how he needed help in dealing with his anger. However, help would never come, and they would land right back where they were now. Her boyfriend was quiet obviously still in stage two, and he was now here to vent his aggression on her again.

She noticed the space between the door and the frame becoming wider with every strike against it. It would only be a minute or two now before he would be in her face. She started thinking up an excuse for not answering more quickly. If he got in and saw her standing there, his rage would become like a force of nature, unleashing upon her until all his energy was spent. Suddenly, a voice entered in her brain, softly as if calling out from far away. It was not the same voice that told her to run away, though it seemed to come from the same place. *Stand and fight*, it said. She almost laughed out loud the moment she registered the thought. What was she going to do, she weighed all of one hundred and ten pounds and she had no idea how to defend herself. He would come at her, swinging his fists and all she could do was to curl up and turn away from him. There was no defense, there was no way to stand and fight. There was nothing she could do. She took a step forward, and then another. She reached the door much sooner than she had wanted to and felt her fingers on the deadbolt, twisting it open. It was as though someone else were in control of her body, turning the door knob and opening the door just a crack. She held her breath in anticipation for what was to come.

He burst through the door with the force of a locomotive, coming to stop quickly as he realized that she was nearly cowering behind the door.

"What in the hell took you so long?" he demanded.

"I was in the bathroom," she whimpered. "I couldn't get out until now."

Her boyfriend seemed to think about this excuse for a moment, then turned to survey the apartment. He was not as upset as she would have expected, though she could still feel the rage seeping from every pore in his body.

"Who's here with you?" he asked abruptly.

"What?" she asked back, not understanding the question.

"Who else is here?" he demanded, nearly shouting at her. "Who else is here in the apartment?"

"Nobody," she answered. His paranoid mind had never posed this question before, and suddenly she wondered if he thought she had been cheating on him. "There's nobody here, check for yourself."

It had been more of a statement than an offer, but he looked around and decided to take her up on the suggestion. He walked around the apartment quickly, pausing only briefly in each room. She followed closely behind him as he made his way back to the bedroom, wondering what it was that he hoped to find. It was only as he passed her, brushing her aside that she realized that he was bleeding on one side of his upper lip and his left cheek appeared to be slightly swollen.

"What happened to your face?" she asked, shocking herself with the level of true concern that exuded from her voice.

"I got into a fight," he answered, offering no more explanation than that.

So that had been the reason he was home early. He had gotten into a fight at the bar and been forced to leave. Other than beating on his girlfriend, he wasn't very physically assertive. If he did get into a fight with another man, he most likely lost. That was why he was home now, that was the reason he was so angry. He needed to regain some of his ego. After a cursory search of the apartment, he stopped and turned on her.

"There was no one else here?" he asked, trying to stare her down.

"No," she promised. "I've been in the bathroom the whole time. Do you think I want anyone seeing me like this?"

That was it, that was all the attitude he needed from her to unleash his rage upon her. She knew she had made a mistake the moment she heard herself say it.

"What's that supposed to mean?" he asked, almost yelling. She backed away, fear filling her eyes once again. "What the fuck is that supposed to mean!"

"Nothing," she said, almost in tears. She was already cowering, preparing for his first strike. "I didn't mean anything; I just wanted you to know that I was alone."

"Of course you were alone," he said with an arrogant smile. "Who the hell else would want you?"

With that, he let his fists fly. His first punch caught her in the stomach, causing to her double over for just a moment before she lost all energy in her legs and fell to her knees. The second punch was also meant for her stomach, but since she collapsed his fist caught her square in the jaw. Little blinking lights flashed before her eyes and a wave of nausea passed over her, almost causing her to vomit. She choked it back, feeling the burning acid and bitter taste of her own bile sliding back down her esophagus. He pulled her up to her feet and started smacking her roughly, shaking her in between strikes. He was saying something, though she could not hear him. She just retreated in her mind to the only safe place she knew, turning her face and as much of her body away from his blows as possible. She heard the voice again, *stand and fight*. It was still soft, but every time she heard it, every time he hit her, the voice became a little louder. His fists must have been getting sore or his palms hurting because he had gone to mostly shaking and screaming at her. Finally, he became frustrated by her lack of response and threw her from the back of their bedroom into the bathroom. She collided with the wall, grasping for anything to keep from bouncing off of the wall, and dragged the cheap plastic towel holder down from the wall as she hit the ground. She could hear him screaming now, she could feel his presence growing closer. He was not done with her, not by a long shot. The voice was calling out now, much louder than before. *Stand and fight. Stand and fight.* He was screaming now just for the need to hear some noise. He reached down and grabbed her by her blouse. *Fight!*

She turned as he lifted her off the ground and swung out with her free hand. Her nails caught his skin, pulling small patches off. He cried out and staggered back, giving her some room between the two of them. She slowly brought herself to her feet, never taking her eyes off of him. He was cursing at her, screaming now that he was going to hurt her, how she had brought this all on herself. She didn't move, she didn't say anything. She did not try to defend herself at this point, did not make any excuses as she knew there was nothing she could say that was going to keep the inevitable from happening. He came at her in a blind rage, unable to fully comprehend the look on her face. *Fight!* She raised the towel bar up and behind her and as he approached, she swung with all of her might, catching him on the left side of his head. He staggered again, backing up and that was all the opportunity she needed. She came at him in a rage, all the pent up anger from years of abuse coming to the surface. Abuse by all the men in her life who should have loved her, and instead hurt her and molded her into the creature she was about to become. She pounded the bar against his body, screaming at him. She didn't know what she was saying, and certainly did not know what she was doing. It was as though she were suddenly free; free from the voice in her head, no longer female, no longer even sounding human, screaming for her to strike again and again. Her boyfriend started with cursing, then begging her to stop, then crying and whimpering. She did not let up, however. She continued her attack until she heard him scream in an even higher pitch. Her viscious assault had broken his arm when he had attempted to shield himself from what had seemed like a never-ending assault. She liked his screams, she liked his fear. The piercing sound that came out of his voice was like music to her ears. His trembling, whimpering made her feel powerful. She continued her assault until she was certain that she had broken his leg and a few of his ribs. He lay there now sobbing, unable to move, curled in a ball and trying to cover his fractured extremities. She stood over him, satisfied with herself until she caught her own reflection in the mirror. She could not see herself; she could not even distinguish the sex of the figure. All she knew was that it was evil and powerful. Something about this sickened and excited her at the same time. She dropped the towel bar and stepped over him. He turned away defensively as she passed. She went to the telephone on the bed stand and dialed 911.

The killer opened his eyes and the image of the memory that was not even his own melted away into darkness. He was no longer there, in that bathroom; he was here in the present, in the library. The killer was suspending himself by the water pipes that ran above the ceiling tiles just over the stack of books. He was waiting there, waiting for Cooper, waiting for his next victim. Suddenly, there was an announcement over the intercom. An anxious woman trying to hide her concern told the patrons of a possible gas leak and asked everyone to gather their belongings and exit the building. The killer smiled, to himself. Grenier was here; he had figured out the killer's clues and was here to save Cooper. The killer had to admit Grenier was a worthy opponent; the detective had surprised him again. He had assumed that Nick would not be able to put his clues together in time to save Cooper, and in fact, he hadn't. It was still too late, no matter what. Now Grenier would see first hand the power of vengeance. Vengeance did not need a particular time or place, vengeance did not need to be organized. Vengeance could strike anytime, anyplace; and from now on, vengeance would do just that. Grenier would soon see how truly ineffective he was in stopping vengeance. *I am vengeance,* thought the killer. *And vengeance is mine.*

CHAPTER 53

Andrew Cooper pushed the double leveled cart into the stacks of books, guiding the cart slowly down the aisles between the bookshelves. The cart was heavy, nearly overflowing with books, making it difficult to steer the cart effectively. Cooper sighed, lifting one of the heavy books from the cart and sliding it into place beside other books of the similar subject resting on the shelf. He then turned his attention to the next book on the cart and read the number, then pushed the cart down the aisle a little further. He kept his head down for the most part, looking up only occasionally when he needed to read the numbers that were taped to the spine of the books. There was a pattern here for him, and he followed it to a tee. He would load the cart in the back, first loading the fiction books, then the non-fiction, and finally the reference books. There were very few of the reference books to put away, and the non-fiction books never came close to equaling the number of fiction books so when he was finished with the reference and the non-fiction, it always seemed as though he were halfway through each cart. It was one of the little idiosyncrasies Cooper had developed to make the time go by a little faster. Everyone had them, everyone at every job had a way of making the time go by, and this was his. He just kept his head down and focused on his work, and if he followed this routine, no one would harass him; no one would even notice him.

Keep your head down, he thought to himself. *Mind your own business.* He had to run these thoughts through his head over one hundred times a day. It was the only way he was going to make it through, the only way he was going to survive day to day. Cooper had not wanted to violate his parole, but he had been given no other choice. One of the conditions of his parole was that he register as a sex offender. This had never bothered him, he knew he had committed a terrible crime and he knew that there were going to be repercussions for him long after he was released from prison. What he had not expected was how his registration would keep him from getting any type of job that would afford him any kind of lifestyle beyond that of an impoverished citizen. He couldn't live that way, not with the demands and obligations that he carried with him from his previous life. He had college loans, debts that he had been unable to pay due to his incarceration, bank foreclosures and creditors. The only dream that had sustained him through prison was the idea that he would strive to get his life back together, and that was something that the system made impossible for him. The system set him up to fail, and there was no way for him to meet his obligations without violating his parole. He had become the very thing he had dreamed of not reliving; he had become a criminal again.

As Andrew passed a man scanning the books on the shelf, he reminded himself again to keep his head down. It was this kind of thinking that had saved his life in prison. He had been a marked man from the moment he entered the gates. Someone had leaked it to the guards that he was a child molester, and they had made certain that it was well known throughout his cell block. Andrew was beaten constantly, raped over and over. There was nothing he could do; there was no refuge for him except solitary. Andrew had quickly found that the only safe place in prison was in the hole, and Andrew did anything he could to get sent there. He picked fights with convicts smaller and meeker than himself; he threw punches at the guards every now and then, all to get himself sent to the hole. Everyone knew what he was doing, and Andrew was always careful to not strike a corrections officer. They knew why he was doing it, and after a year they actually felt sorry for him and gave into his feeble attempts at being sequestered. When he came up for parole, his fights and fake attacks on the guards were never mentioned. Everyone could tell that there was something about him, something worse than being in prison. Andrew imprisoned himself emotionally, beating himself down over what he had done. He had never understood it; all he could do was be sickened by himself and punish himself as much as possible. That was why he did nothing to fight back when he was beaten and raped by other inmates because in his mind he believed that he deserved everything he got.

Keep your head down, the voice said as he passed the man. The man searching the books did not even seem to notice that Andrew was there, but he made certain not to make his presence known anyway. Ever since violating his parole he was flagged on the sex offender database, and he ran the risk of being spotted by any over-protective parent or wanna be cop who had the website saved to their internet favorites menu. There were those who visited the site daily, sometimes more, looking for anyone they might recognize. He could understand the parents' desire to search the database for anyone in their town who might be listed, but it was the wanna-be cops, the guys who wanted to be in law enforcement but could never pass the entrance exam who were the real threat. They were the ones who felt as though they were doing the police work without the restraints of having to follow the law. Andrew knew that he deserved far worse than what he had gotten in prison, but these guys were just vigilantes, and he was scared of them the most. *Just keep your head down and mind your business*, he reminded himself. If he followed these simple rules, no one would notice him; no one would make a fuss. Andrew had no desire to repeat his crimes, and he certainly had no desire to go back to jail.

As Andrew pushed the cart again, he passed an older teenage girl and could not help but admire her figure. He screamed at himself not to look, but at the same time he had to scoff at his own thoughts. There was no way to stop his desire, no way to quell the urges that fought to get free. There was only the daily struggle with himself, the continuous disgust he held for himself that only doubled every time he looked in the mirror. Andrew had no idea why he was the way he was, why he felt this way. Andrew had had a lot of girlfriends in high school, had been sexually active in the early part of his freshman year. He had loved sex, as all teenage boys do; his raging hormones causing him to think about it so much that he could not even escape sex in his dreams. When he had gone off to college, he had continued to date high school girls, usually juniors and seniors. However, as the years of college passed, he stopped dating these girls because of the way it would appear to others, and because he was beginning to notice a sick trend. He had very little interest in women his own age, and no interest in woman just a few years older. It was in younger women that he was attracted, and that horrified him. He stopped dating for a long period of time, only going out once in a while with women his own age to see if anything had changed in him. Unfortunately, nothing had changed. To this day, Andrew could not be sure whether he chose teaching because of his love of knowledge or to be closer to the teenage girls. To be certain that he did not let his urges get the better of him, he opted to teach middle school students; not wanting to deal with the temptation of high school girls. He knew he did not have the patience to teach elementary students. However, the middle school girls became a problem too. They began developing earlier and earlier, and they were dressing more and more provocatively in an attempt to imitate young celebrities on MTV and in the movies.

Stop, he screamed at himself. He knew he had to stop himself from letting these thoughts get away from him. He suppressed his urges, hoping that the disgust he felt for himself would be enough to keep him from giving in to the desires that burned within him. Andrew had not opposed the harsh sentence put down against him; he had pled out and asked for no special treatment. He had served his time, and he had spent six months doing everything possible to become an upstanding member of society. He spent his time with the court appointed shrinks, and read every psychology book he could find dealing with the subject of child molesters and sex offenders. But they had offered no real help to him, given him no real solutions. In the texts he could find only suggestions; hormone therapy and chemical castration. In his sessions with his shrink he found himself being set up on a daily basis. His shrink focused their time on making Andrew relive his crimes, trying to make him derive satisfaction from his memories so that she could find an excuse to violate his parole and send him back to prison. She was of the mind that there was no cure for sex offenders and that they should be locked up for life, she felt that they would always pose a threat to society. Andrew couldn't help but feel as though his therapist's feelings came from a dark and sordid past. She would get Andrew all worked up and then tell him that their time was up, leaving him so aroused and angry that without any control, he would possibly jump the first fifteen year old girl he came across. However, Andrew would not give into his urges, and he certainly would not give her the satisfaction of being right. The whole system was against him, there was no way else for him to feel.

As Andrew stopped the cart at the end of a bookshelf, scanning for a certain number which he kept repeating in his head to keep from forgetting, he heard an announcement over the intercom. It was the young woman volunteer, a foreign woman who married a service man and came to volunteer at the library in hopes that she would be able to improve her English. It had worked apparently, as it was nearly impossible now to tell that English was her second language. She relayed the information that there was a possible gas leak and asked everyone to prepare to evacuate the building. However, there was something in the tone of her voice that caused Andrew to second guess her explanation. He sniffed for a few seconds, trying to see if he could pick up the scent of gas. He could not quite believe that the building used gas heat, and the more he thought about it, the more certain he was that someone had mentioned something about the heating being supplied by an oil furnace. There was something else, there was something wrong. However, the powers that be wanted the library closed, and it was his job to follow along.

"Excuse me," Andrew called out. "Young lady. We need everybody to get their things and head for the exit."

Andrew used his professional voice and the patrons did not question him as they slid the books back onto the shelves and made their way out of the stacks. Andrew then turned and walked down the aisles, looking for any stragglers. There was an intensity that was starting to build as more and more people headed for the main exit. Andrew found two other people lingering and pointed them to the doors, and once he was satisfied that the stacks were clear, he headed back for his cart. He found it right where he had left it and got behind it, pushing it back up to the front. As he reached the intersection of one of the aisles, the lights snapped off. Andrew whipped his head from side to side, trying to adjust to the darkness. Suddenly, there was a searing pain in his shoulder that shot bolts of light into his eyes. He screamed out unknowingly, and tried to move away. He had no idea what was directly in front of him, and he could not shake the feeling that he was in some kind of grip. Suddenly there was another pain, more intense than the first, causing him to cry out again and collapse underneath himself. It was only then that he became aware that he was not alone in the stacks, and it was at that moment that he felt truly scared. It was the first time since prison that he felt as though he were going to die.

CHAPTER 54

The killer shifted his weight to his legs to maintain his balance as he waited for his prey, suspended just inches above the ceiling tiles, just a few feet above where his victim would be. The killer had been thrown off just a little by the presence of the police, surprised that Grenier had been able to figure out the clues in such a short amount of time. Grenier really was one of the best detectives out there, and the killer knew that he would not be able to elude the detective for much longer. He just needed time; time to allow everyone to understand his purpose. Grenier had been remarkably efficient in keeping the sordid details of the victim's private lives a secret, making it nearly impossible for the masses to truly understand. The killer found it ironic that by making the mistake of arresting Anderson, his time table had been moved up. There would have been far less pressure on him had they not had such an easy suspect from the start. The police would have continued their investigation, probably taking days to turn up leads. However, they had immediately focused on Anderson because of his connection with Brenner and the previous arrests. What connection Anderson had with Allun was not entirely clear to the killer, but Anderson was now under arrest, charged with crimes he did not commit. The killer could not let that stand; he could not be a party to the downfall of an innocent man. That would detract from what he was trying to do here. So now the killer was here, forced to move up his timetable and the secure nature in which he brought about his vengeance. Grenier and the rest of the police needed to know that the killer was not afraid of them. He needed them to know there was no place he could not strike.

However, Grenier had found Cooper. How he had done it so fast was beyond the killer, but he did not have time to think about that now. There had been a general anxious commotion since the announcement to clear the building, but that did not matter to the killer. All that mattered was that he complete his task, that he kill Cooper. There would be no satisfaction from this murder, no torture that brought about repentance. Grenier may have been able to get the people out of the library, but that did not matter. This murder would still be public, and it would still be high profile. There was no way that the police would be able to keep it out of the press now, and once Anderson was released, everyone would know about the private lives of his victims. Only then would everyone truly understand, only then would the killer have peace. That did not necessarily mean he would stop hunting, but it would bring a peace to his mind that he had not had in many years. The killer hovered just above where the aisles intersected each other at the back of the library. The killer had experienced a moment of fear and concern when he saw Cooper walk by hastily through the small slit in the adjusted ceiling tile. Cooper had abandoned his cart full of books, and for a moment, the killer had been concerned that his prey had fallen for the ridiculous story the police had concocted.

The killer's concern quickly dissolved away as he could hear Cooper ushering people out of the stacks. *How gallant,* the killer thought. It wasn't enough to impress the killer, though. It wasn't enough to make the killer think twice about what he was planning to do. Cooper would come back for his cart, and that was when the killer would strike. As he shifted his weight again, the killer used a free arm to pull the ceiling tile out all the way, giving him the ability to slip down from the darkness when Cooper was disoriented. The device the killer had installed on the power lines would cut the power, just like it had in the church. Cooper would be disoriented and would not even notice the opening in the ceiling just above him. Then the killer would strike, it was all mapped out so perfectly. Even his escape plan was perfectly arranged. The parking lot could be crawling with police cruisers and still no one would notice him leaving.

The only loose string was Grenier. The killer had no idea where the detective was in the building, but he had to assume the worst. The killer knew that Grenier was not one to be underestimated, and the killer knew that he was going to have to make every second count. The loss of power would throw everyone off, but Grenier would quickly realize what was going on and adjust accordingly. The killer heard the soft pad of Cooper's feet as his soon-to-be victim made his way back to the cart. Cooper spotted it quickly, passing by the removed ceiling tile and killer just above it. The killer watched as Cooper started moving the cart forward, each step bringing his prey closer to him. Though Cooper moved without hesitation, each step seemed to become slower and slower, as if time itself were slowing down. The killer hoisted himself forward, causing his back to arch outward unnaturally as he used both legs and feet to maintain his balance. In a few seconds, all he would have to do was let go, and the killer would slip right out of the exposed square and onto his target. Right on cue, the lights cut out and the slight squeaking of the wheels on the cart stopped. This was the moment; this was the time to strike.

The killer released his grip on the pipes, causing his head and torso to slip through the hole in the ceiling as he used his legs and feet to steady him. The killer quickly took hold of the back of the bookshelf and climbed down silently, like a spider. He could hear his victim mutter something under his breath, as Cooper attempted to orient himself with his surroundings. Though it was not completely dark, the already secluded nature of the bookshelf placing caused only a small amount of light to filter through. Cooper never saw the killer as he turned away, and the killer knew that this was it. Pressing his outstretched index and middle fingers together, the killer jabbed them hard into Cooper's back, directly hitting a pressure point. Cooper screamed out in pain as the nerve endings fired, shooting pain through his body and stemming up to his brain. The killer then supported all of his weight on his left arm and swung his body around like a gymnast. He came down on his feet silently and shot his fingers out again, hitting a different nerve this time. This caused Cooper to stumble and fall to his knees. Quickly, the killer flipped himself up and over his victim, drawing a small double edged straight blade from a soft canvas sheath that was secured to the underside of his left arm. Time was crucial now. The killer had to kill Cooper quickly and slip away into the faint light before Grenier spotted him. Cooper's scream would have brought Grenier running, and the killer could feel the detective's presence growing closer in his mind. Using his left hand, the killer pulled back on Cooper's hair, causing him to cry out again, this time much weaker than before. Then, with expert precision, the killer slipped the blade underneath Cooper's chin and drew it quickly across the skin of his exposed neck. All of Cooper's strength gave out suddenly, and the dead weight of his victim pulled the killer down on top of him.

"Freeze!" a male voice called out. The killer almost jumped with fright. Though he was certain Grenier was close, he still was not prepared when they finally confronted one another. "Put your hands in the air and stand up."

The killer did just as Grenier instructed. He knew that the detective's sidearm was pointed at him, and he knew that everything he did from this second on would have to be perfect if he had any plans of escaping. The knife was still in the killer's right hand, though turned downward so as to keep it shielded from view. The killer rose slowly, tensing the muscles in his legs and lower back as he drew his body upright. He closed his eyes and listened, listened to the sound of the overhead ventilation, the sound of his own heart beating, the sound of Grenier's excited breathing. The situation was tense, and both the killer and the detective were running on adrenaline.

"Take two steps backwards, towards me," the detective ordered. The killer's eyes were still closed, but he did as he was instructed. He was forming a mental picture in his mind of what distance and obstacles were between the detective and himself. The killer could hear Grenier breathing, hear him ordering him to move backwards and stop. He had a clear image in his head where all the bookcases were in relation to the two of them, he knew everything.

"Now turn around slowly and face me," Grenier ordered. That was his mistake, that was what the killer had been waiting for. He had been waiting for the detective to make his fatal error.

The killer started to turn slowly, continuing to appear as though he were following the detective's instructions. However, under the mask, he wore a knowing smile. Just as his shoulder came in direct line with the detective, he threw the knife in the detective's direction. He knew that Grenier would see it coming, he had no intention of hurting the detective, and this was merely the distraction he needed to get away. The detective, in fact, did see the knife as it left the killer's hand. The knife struck the detective's gun hand, and just as Grenier moved out of the way of the knife, he discharged one shot. However, the killer was already in motion, and the detective's aim was wide, sending the bullet off and up to the right. In the time it took to readjust his vision from the muzzle flash, the killer had clamped down on the detective's gun hand like a vice. Twisting the weapon and his hand away, the killer was able to rip the weapon right out of Grenier's grasp. Finishing the movement, the killer raised the weapon in his hand and lashed out at the detective with the butt of the pistol, striking the detective on the side of the head.

Grenier, however, was faster than the killer had expected, and twisted his body with the movement of the killer so as to catch as little of the oncoming strike as possible. The butt had been originally aimed to land directly on Grenier's forehead, but he had deflected and the glancing blow struck just behind his right temple. Grenier swung out with his left hand, the only free hand he had, but the killer simply ducked though he was forced to release his grip. Grenier then swung with his right hand, his dominant hand and arm, but the action was so delayed that the killer simply swatted his arm away. Grenier stepped back to get some room between him and his attacker, but the killer anticipated this and simply stepped in closer. This crowded the disoriented detective, and the killer struck out with his right leg, connecting with Grenier's abdomen. The detective rolled into the kick and grabbed onto the killer's leg and wrapped his right arm around the killer's waist, lifting him up and slamming him into the bookshelf directly behind him. The killer was unfazed, however, and allowed the detective's force to carry him as he lifted his left knee and connected with the detective's jaw. Grenier stumbled and released his hold on the killer, striking out with his right arm again. This time the killer grasped the detective's wrist in his hand and rotated his entire arm forward, using Grenier's own momentum against him and slammed him hard into the bookshelf, face first. That took almost all of the fight out of the detective, and though he lashed out with both arms, he was having difficulty standing up on his feet and soon fell. Grenier still refused to give up, reaching out for where he thought the killer was, swearing and threatening the other. The killer took two silent steps backward and watched the detective flail around on the ground pathetically. The killer felt sorry for him for just a moment, and then remembered that one day the roles would be reversed and Grenier would most likely show no mercy. Still, Grenier had done the best he could, and the killer's mission was accomplished; at least for today.

The killer heard voices from all directions, and suddenly realized that Grenier's companions were closing in. The killer quickly jumped forward and, using shelves of the metal bookcase like rungs of a ladder, propelled himself up and back into the open square in the ceiling. Once he was balanced on the pipes again, he felt around quickly and located the missing tile and replaced it. He then pulled himself along the pipes in the direction of the bathroom. He heard voices calling out now, at least four or five voices, and knew that more backup was on the way. Stopping only seconds at a time to reorient himself, he made his way to the bathroom where he had originally come in, dropped himself back down out of the ceiling, and retrieved the clothes that he had carefully folded and hidden. He smiled as he took a good look at the policeman's uniform lying neatly folded in a canvas bag behind one of the toilets. This was how he planned on escaping. He quickly donned his uniform and slipped out of the bathroom and into the throng of uniformed officers coming in and out of the building. It took just a second for him to fall into step with two other uniformed officers who had arrived on the scene as back up.

"Is the bathroom clear?" asked one of the officers, suspecting nothing. In fact, the officer had just assumed that the killer had been in there checking the area.

"All clear," the killer answered, confidently. The two other uniformed officers walked off towards the information desk, while the killer simply side stepped and walked out of the building. In a second, he was outside looking very official as he made his way across the parking lot with purpose. The next second, he had stepped around the young officer who was blocking off the area, keeping the patrons back who were now stepping up to see what was going on. The second he was beyond the throng of bystanders mulling around, he was gone.

CHAPTER 55

Nick sat on the floor, his back propped against the bookshelf, alone in the darkness. There on the floor he fought off waves of nausea by focusing on the pain that flooded through his body, and fought unconsciousness by focusing back on the nausea. It was a vicious cycle, but it was the only way the detective could cope with the state that he had been left in. It took only a few minutes after firing his weapon for Wilkins and Mitchell to find him, but so much had happened in that time. Nick could scarcely remember what had happened, only truly understanding that he had just been pummeled. A copperish smell was now filling his sinuses, which was only serving to make his nausea worse. It was the smell of death, the smell of Cooper's blood as it permeated the carpet around the dead body. He had tried to get up on his feet a few times, but had been unable to rise beyond his knees and quickly fell back into a seated position. That was where Wilkins and Mitchell found him, bleeding and fighting to remain conscious. The killer was gone, long gone, and Nick knew it the moment he slipped away. Nick had no idea where the killer had gone, or how he had slipped by all the people out in the parking lot. As Mitchell helped Grenier to his feet, Nick could hear the library fill with authoritative voices, all spreading out across the building to search for any sign of their killer. The two detectives helped their wounded colleague out of the stacks and over to the information desk where they could see better. The emergency lighting had kicked in, but the light did not penetrate the heavy concentration of books in the stacks of the library. Only here in the open space, were the police better able to assess what had happened here.

Andrew Cooper was dead. Despite the best work of the New London Police Department, Nick had been unable to stop the killer from striking, unable to put the clues together fast enough to keep this from happening. It did not matter that they had been given too little information and an impossible deadline; no one was going to care about that. All anyone would remember was that the police arrested the wrong person and were too focused on him to prevent another murder; Anderson would make certain that was all the public knew. Lt. Hollings arrived just as the coroner's office staff was rolling out a stretcher with a black body bag on top, containing Cooper's lifeless body. No one needed to tell her anymore than what she saw; they had failed. When she stepped up, two EMT's were attempting to convince Nick that he needed to go to the hospital.

"What the hell happened?" she asked angrily. Nick shot her a look while he grabbed an ice pack from one of the tech's and gingerly placed it on his head.

"What the hell does it look like," Nick answered. There had not been enough time for him to calm down, and now he was going to have to deal with his lieutenant's attitude as well. "We were too late. The killer was just too many steps ahead of us to stop him."

"I didn't mean about the murder," Hollings said, explaining herself. "I meant what happened to you."

"I got the shit kicked out of me, that's what happened," Nick said, trying to rise to his feet. The senior EMT tried to warn the detective to remain seated, but Nick just pushed him lightly out of the way and slowly made his way back to the stacks where Cooper had been killed.

"Did you confront the killer?" Hollings asked, hoping for anything positive she might be able to take from this tragedy. "Did you get a look at him?"

"Not at his face, if that's what you mean," Nick began. "He was wearing a mask. He's quick though, and strong. I tried to subdue him and he barely had to exert any energy to stop me."

"How long had Cooper been dead when you got here?" Hollings asked.

"He wasn't dead when we arrived," Nick said. "There was still about five minutes left. I went back to the stacks here, but then the lights went out and I heard a scream. I found the killer standing over the body a few seconds later, tried to arrest him, and got my ass handed to me in the process."

"Shit," Hollings exclaimed. "We were so close."

"I just don't understand how the killer escaped the building unseen," Nick said, trying to understand everything that had happened.

"It doesn't matter," Hollings said. "The killer obviously had this whole thing planned out from the beginning. He's just playing his games, making us chase our tails until we look incompetent."

Nick listened to his lieutenant continue on, though he was not sure that he completely agreed with her opinion. Hollings was looking for any way she might make this event look better than it was. The truth was, it was a nightmare, and soon the brass would be looking for someone to blame. If they did not find someone to blame, they would start looking for someone to sacrifice. Hollings was trying to get out in front of the issue, ready to put a positive spin on tonight's events, even if it was for only long enough to catch the killer. The moment Anderson was released from jail, he would begin attacking the police department right and left, suing any and everyone he could think of, and whipping the media into a frenzy. Nick, however, could not concern himself with these thoughts. Mistakes had been made, but there was nothing he could do about them right now. All he could do was focus on the case at hand, find the killer, and bring his murder spree to an end. Hollings had been right though, the killer had planned this whole thing out. There was no other way that he would have felt comfortable enough to change his methods and kill Cooper in such a public place. The killer usually abducted his victim, spending time torturing him and causing as much pain as possible. Tonight had been different, though. Tonight had been nothing like the first two murders.

"What time is it?" Nick asked, his brain latching on to something that he had just been thinking about.

"It's seven fifty," Hollings said, checking her watch. "Why do you ask?"

"The killer said he would attack Cooper at seven thirty," Nick said, reminding his lieutenant of the killer's promise when they had spoken on the phone. "He said Cooper wouldn't be actually dead until eight o'clock."

"So what?" Hollings asked, unsure of where the detective was going with his thinking.

"Cooper was going to die tonight no matter what," Nick said. "The killer knew that he was going to kill Cooper whether we got here before eight o'clock or not. The killer probably did not expect us to get here in time, thinking that he would then have enough time to do what he wanted with Cooper."

"What could he have done here in this public place?" Hollings asked, unconvinced.

"That's the point," Nick said. "That's why this location was chosen in the first place. The killer has made it clear in our two telephone calls that he is looking for validation by the public, stating that he is committing these murders to get justice, to protect the people. However, we have been pretty tight lipped about the murders, keeping the bad stuff to ourselves so as not to shock anyone. By keeping these secrets quiet, we have kept the killer from getting the notoriety he has been looking for. His only chance now was to kill someone publicly, to get everyone's attention focused on him and the murders. He knew our tactics; he knew what we would do. He knew that even if we did figure out who Cooper was, we were likely to run the numbers to find him, starting with his mother's home and the place where he abused his victims, and working our way out from there."

"He did not expect you three to show up before he killed Cooper," Hollings said, continuing the detective's thought. "When he realized the police were here, he had to accelerate his time table, not waiting until eight to kill Cooper, but killing him right away."

"We need to put a lid on this situation," Nick said. "We need to get the coroner's boys back in here immediately. We need to get Jessica Sarrucci back down here, seal off the area and keep anyone from talking to the press until we are ready."

"What are you thinking about?" Hollings asked. "There is no way to keep quiet the fact that someone died here. Everyone just saw them wheel the dead body out of here."

"They may have seen a body bag with a dead body," Nick began. "But they did not see how Cooper died. It will be impossible to keep Cooper's identity a secret, but then again, we don't have to. We'll stick with the original story, there was a gas leak and the library had been forced to evacuate. In the excitement, someone had a heart-attack and died at the scene."

"What about the blood?" asked Hollings, unsure of why they were talking about this, but getting caught up in Nick's momentum.

"This is where Cooper died," Nick explained. "He probably fell here and hit his head on the bookshelf, causing him to bleed until his heart finally stopped pumping."

"That's a lot of blood," Hollings pointed out.

"No one's going to see the blood," Nick reminded her. "We just need a plausible story to explain the dead body."

"And to what end are we concocting this cover up?" Hollings asked, finally getting around to the most important question.

"Time," Nick answered in a word. "Time to put all the clues together. The only thing we, as the police, have going for us is the fact that we have been able to keep the true motive for the killings a secret. The killer thought he could force our hand by killing Cooper publicly, but if we can give the press an explanation other than the truth, we may be able to do the only thing we can to foil the killer's plans."

"So you want me to go out there and lie to the press," Hollings said. "Tell them that Cooper had a heart attack and only hope that they don't dig into Cooper's past a little and figure out who he is."

"No," Nick said. "Tell them the truth about Cooper. Tell them that he was a convicted pedophile who just recently violated his parole and that the reason the police were here was to bring him in. It was when we got here that the staff and police realized that there was a gas leak and while the building was being evacuated, Cooper spotted the police and panicked, resulting in the heart attack."

"What's to keep the killer from coming out and telling the press that Cooper was really murdered?" Hollings asked.

"Secrecy," Nick answered in a word. "The killer's only true power comes from the fact that we don't know who he is. The killer is the only one who would gain from letting the truth be known, and the minute he does is the minute we'll have him caught."

"So he'll keep his identity a secret for as long as he thinks he can keep doing his work," Hollings said, rationalizing the detective's thinking. "To expose the police as liars and the victim's private lives would mean exposing himself as the killer. You're thinking he's not willing to do that yet."

"Not yet," Nick said. "But he's going to be pissed about this. This murder was to be his failsafe, take the focus off of Anderson and turn it back to where it belongs, on him and more importantly, the victims. Expose the victims for the scum they are, making him look good in the process. If we are successful, he's going to be looking for his next victim very soon."

"So what are you going to do?" asked Hollings.

"I'm going to try to get out in front of this guy," Nick answered, placing the ice pack down on the shelf. "We have been led around by the nose for far too long. We only act when the killer gives us a little tidbit, and I'm tired of investigating this case that way. There are clues all around us, I just need a better way to look at them to figure this out."

Nick sighed and turned to leave. He felt satisfied that Hollings could handle everything from here. There would need to be a statement made to the press, and the higher the ranking officer the better. In the meantime, Wilkins and Mitchell could carry on the investigation privately here, searching for any clues that might have been left. Nick needed to get some air, he needed to start this case at the beginning, thinking it through until he had all the pieces and had fitted them together.

"Where are you going?" asked Hollings, hoping to get an idea of what the detective had planned from here.

"To higher ground," Nick said sarcastically, over his shoulder. "I'm going to get a better view of this case."

CHAPTER 56

Nick stood under the hot, powerful stream of the shower as he let the searing water burn at his skin, the heat sink deep into his aching muscles. It had been hard for him to drive home because his muscles tightened and became more and more painful. When he finally pulled himself out of his car, it had been nearly impossible to move without pain shooting through his entire body. When he undressed and took a look at himself in the mirror, he found huge bruises starting to form all over, with pockets of swelling here and there. Nick climbed into the shower and just stood there for well over an hour, looking for any kind of relief the shower might provide. Hollings had told him to take his time, and that was precisely what he planned on doing. This case had gotten out of hand, and the police were no closer to solving it now than they were after the first murder. Nick had been playing catch up with this killer the entire time, and he was sick of it. Nick had to get ahead of this killer somehow, had to turn the tables on him, and Nick did not plan on leaving his home until he had figured out a way to do just that. No one would be surprised if he did not show up at the Investigations Unit the next day, everyone there would be picking up the pieces of the latest disaster; Andrew Cooper's murder. Nick only hoped that Hollings was able to sell the story that they had decided on before he left, hopefully giving the police a precious second of time before the press found out the truth and starting hounding them for results.

Jenn had called him on his way home, checking to see if he was alright and wanting to come over. Nick knew that he should focus on the case right now, but could not bring himself to tell her to stay away. In fact, the more he thought about it, the more he felt like he needed a little break. He needed something to take his mind off of the case, and he could always use some alone time with Jenn. She told him that she would be over as soon as her shift was done, which gave Nick some time to himself, to recuperate both mentally and physically. The physical part was going to take a few days. His head still pounded from where the killer slammed the butt of his own gun into his temple. Thinking about his wounds reminded him about the fight he had with the killer, which only served to make him feel worse. The killer was fast, adept at self defense. Nick was no expert at fighting, but his police training had taught him many self defense moves, and his home workout sessions had put him in good physical condition. Nick replayed the fight over and over in his mind, seeing every move he made as if in slow motion, trying to understand how the killer got the best of him. Nick soon realized that the killer had the best of the fight from the start. Nick had made the stupid mistake of ordering the killer to turn and face him. Nick let his anticipation get away from him, feeling as though he had to know who the killer was. He felt as though he had to look into the face, into the eyes, of this man who had murdered three people, torturing two of them. It never occurred to the detective that the killer might still have the murder weapon, and that should have been his first thought.

The more Nick thought about what happened, the more embarrassed he became by his actions. This embarrassment led to humiliation, until he could no longer stand to think about it. However, these thoughts were not so easy to turn off, and Nick found himself replaying every move; watching in his mind as the killer easily brushed off the detective's attacks. It was as though the killer knew what Nick was thinking all along, and now it felt like the killer was laughing at him. Nick's bruised ego could not take much more of this self deprecation, and by the time Jenn arrived, Nick's mood had gone from bad to worse. She could sense his attitude the moment she entered the house, though he tried his best to cover it with a smile. She held him softly in her arms, then stepped back and appraised his condition. He knew he looked worse now than he had when he got home, even though the shower had helped to easy the pain a little. She softly kissed the bruises on his face, telling him how glad she was that he was alright. She told him that she had arrived on the scene late, having been posted to check out the school and be there when Hollings arrived. She explained how Mitchell had called for back up the moment the three detectives had arrived at the library and confirmed Cooper was there. By the time she had arrived on the scene, the killer was gone and the police first had to fight their way through the crowd of people who had been evacuated from the library. Most uniformed officers had been ordered to secure the premises, which was why Nick had not seen her on his way out.

Nick told her all of the events of the day, telling her about the phone call and their desperate attempts to find Cooper in time. Soon Nick was telling her about the fight, not realizing his anger had started to rise and flare with each new telling of the story. Jenn watched him, concerned and confused. She had never seen him act this way, never seen him get so emotional. Nick went on and on about what he should have done, how they would have had the killer in custody right now if Nick had not been so anxious and had followed procedure.

"This isn't your fault," Jenn said, trying to reason with him. "There is no following procedure on a case like this. Maybe things could have happened differently, but there is no way you can say that the end result would be any different than it is now."

"That fucker was fast," Nick said, as if not even hearing her. "It was like he knew what I was going to do before I did it. It was like he spent no effort to stop me."

"Nick," Jenn began. "This guy has killed three people. Two of them he took his time with, torturing for days before he killed them. He quickly overpowered all of them, he's obviously well trained. There is no way one person could have brought him down, especially in the conditions you were faced with."

"What do you mean?" Nick asked.

"You were in the dark with no back up," Jenn said, reminding him of all the details. "You did what any good cop would have done and you secured the scene, trying to minimize the danger to all of the other patrons. You went into a dark area alone; you never had the upper hand in this matter. The killer knew the layout and had a plan; he had the advantage from the beginning. Nobody else would have done any better against this guy."

"It just kills me, you know?" Nick said. "Knowing that this guy is probably having a good laugh right now, knowing that he killed someone right under my nose. If we hadn't gotten there, Cooper would probably have been found by some patron looking for a book. Imagine this killer slipping into the library, killing a grown man, and slipping out unseen. Which is exactly what he did."

"It's not like you had a chance to stop him," Jenn said, becoming mentally exhausted from trying to lift Nick's spirits. She was beginning the think it had been a mistake coming here. "You had an impossible deadline with only two clues to go on in the first place. The fact that you actually figured out who the next victim was going to be, and found out where he was only goes to show what a great detective you are. No one else would have gotten so close."

It was then that Nick realized how much he needed her, how good it was to hear this kind of thing from a person who cared about him. She was right; the killer had controlled the events of the evening from the very beginning. It was only blind luck that Nick and his colleagues were able to put the clues together as they had. This killer was smart, strong, and quick. Nick may not have been able to stop him this time, but that did not mean that this was over; not by a long shot. Nick sighed and smiled.

"Thank you," Nick said finally. "I needed to hear that. You know, it wasn't until today that I really came to understand how truly lost I am in this case. I mean, I was totally on the wrong track with Anderson, being overwhelmed with the circumstantial evidence and my feelings towards Anderson. I totally blocked out the fact that the killer might be someone else."

"That was not your fault," Jenn pointed out. "You were following Smith's lead on that. It was Smith who was wrong about Anderson; he was the one who led you down the wrong path. After the way he connected Anderson, it was only natural that you would see the evidence you had in the way that you did."

"But the killer was still out there," Nick pointed out. "And he is still out there now. He has been leading me around with a trail of crumbs, leaving only the clues that he means to. I've got to get ahead of this guy; I've got to figure him out. I need to be more prepared for him. Maybe I should take your class."

"It's a class for women," Jenn said, with a smile. She rose from the chair she was seated in at the kitchen table and walked over to the bruised detective. "But I guess there is always room for one more."

"Oh yeah?" Nick asked. "Wouldn't that be breaking the rules?"

"Not when I make the rules," Jenn said. She stepped right in front of him and looked him in the eyes for a moment. Nick had second guessed himself many times since their first date, but there was no second guessing now. He leaned forward and kissed her, pressing himself into her. His entire body was in pain, but he ignored it, breathing deeply and taking her smell into him. He put his arms around her and suddenly they were locked in each other's embrace. They clumsily made their way up the stairs, not wanting to break from each other. Nick's excitement was getting the best of him, his need to be together with her causing him to rush. She slowed him down, however. She lovingly undressed him, being slow and carefully aware of his aches and pains.

All Nick could do was watch her, watch her and submit. At first, he had felt as though he were on fire, feeling as though he could wait no longer. However, she had changed suddenly, and she had become more loving than he had ever seen her. When she kissed him, something about the way she touched him slowed everything down. The minutes seemed to drag out in the best of ways. She touched him, massaging him, kissing every muscle, tracing each contour on his body. She never closed her eyes, and neither did he. They stared at each other the whole time, as if entire conversations were passed between them in the slightest glance. He began to feel her more deeply than he had ever felt any woman before, as if their emotions were one and the same. He undressed her as slowly as she had done him. He kissed every hollow and dimple of her skin, he softly traced his fingers along her spine and down her back, causing her to shudder with anticipation. When they were together, it was slow and luxurious, as if there was no one else in the world but them. Nick could not hear or sense anything else but her. They made love for hours, and that was what it was; love. They were together in a way Nick had never experienced before, and suddenly he felt as though he understood. He had never made love to anyone before now; he had never truly felt this way about anyone until now. In that moment, he was scared, exhilarated, sad, and hopeful all at the same time. They fell asleep together, holding each other, still connected. When Nick woke up, barely an hour had gone by, but he felt as though it had been half the day. He said nothing, just closed his eyes and drifted in and out, totally content. He would become aware of Jenn every now and then, feeling her waken and roll back into him. He would feel her touch him, then fall asleep again. There was one point when he woke to her kissing him, softly on his neck and face. He did not open his eyes, just lay there feeling her lips against his skin. She pressed her lips against the skin just before his ear and whispered the words 'I love you". Nick said nothing, unsure of whether he was supposed to respond or not. He wasn't even sure that she knew he was awake, but could not help but smile just a little.

A few hours later, Nick found himself lying with Jenn's head on his chest. He was stroking her hair, both of them awake but saying nothing. There was nothing they needed to say.

"Are you hungry?" Nick asked, drawing his head close and whispering.

"No," she said, turning her head up to face him. "I'm totally satisfied."

"Is that right?" Nick asked. Jenn merely nodded, her chin rolling on his chest as she did. "I'm sorry about my attitude earlier."

"I'm not," Jenn answered. "It's my job to make you feel better. It's you and me, and that's what I'm here for."

"That shouldn't be your job," Nick said. "But you're right, it is you and me."

They stayed together for a little while longer, and soon Nick became aware of the time. It was almost eleven o'clock, though Nick could not believe that it was still the same day. It felt as though they had been together for days, as if there had been nothing else in the world but them. Nick apologized but explained that he wanted to see the late news before they went to bed. Jenn understood, and in a few minutes they were both dressed again and downstairs in the living room, watching the television. Nick wanted to see how the press conference had gone, and sure enough, the library story was the first story aired. The cover story had stuck and apparently the press was buying it. The reporter explained the situation as the police had explained it, then cut away to Hollings' statement. Everything had gone perfectly, and for now, the story was contained. Nick sighed; satisfied with the knowledge that he had a little more time. Suddenly, he felt some pressure as Jenn pushed him up and began to rise.

"What's wrong?" Nick asked.

"I can't believe this," Jenn said. "You guys are lying again."

"What are you talking about?" Nick asked, shocked by her sudden change in attitude.

"You guys are covering up the story again," she said, her anger rising. "You're burying the story, and you are lying to everyone about what's really going on."

"We're not burying anything," Nick said. "We need more time. More time to find this guy."

"And that justifies lying to the public?" Jenn asked. "They have a right to know what's going on. They have a right to know that there is a killer out there. And what about Anderson, has he been released yet?"

"He'll be released first thing in the morning," Nick assured her. "We just have to conclude that there is no involvement between he and Cooper, and we can't get him into court until the morning."

"But you knew," Jenn said, stammering. Her anger was getting the better of her, and she was having trouble speaking coherently. "You knew since the killer called you that Anderson was not guilty. It's unforgivable to keep an innocent person locked up for a moment more than is necessary."

"We couldn't be sure at the time," Nick said. "I don't like this anymore than you do, but there is procedure. We can't get a judge into court until the morning, it sucks but that's the facts."

"But you could go to a judge's home and get a warrant signed if you really needed to," Jenn pointed out. "This entire case is a pack of lies. You lie about the so called 'victims', you lie about the killer, you lie to yourself about your only suspect and for what. You have nothing to show for it but more dead bodies!"

Jenn was screaming now. Nick had never seen her like this before. It was like watching Dr. Jekyll transform into Mr. Hyde.

"Where is this coming from?" Nick asked, trying to calm her down.

"We're supposed to be better than this," she said, turning and walking to the door. "Cops are supposed to protect people; we're supposed to tell the truth. You can't seem to do either. Funny thing is, the killer is not a liar, and he is protecting people. The killer has taken three guilty people, three people who have hurt many, many others and stopped them the only way possible. What have you done? What have you done but put an innocent man, a victim himself, behind bars. I thought...I don't think I really know you, Nicholas Grenier."

Jenn turned away from him and opened the front door, stepping through without looking back. She slammed the door leaving Nick standing in the hallway; confused, alone, and most of all, heartbroken. This is not the way he had anticipated the evening ending when they were together in bed. She was angry with him, for the first time since they had started dating, she had been truly angry. What hurt him more what that she was disappointed in him, and the more he thought about it, the more he realized that she was right. He was supposed to be better than the killer; he was supposed to protect the innocent. He had failed miserably at both. He had arrested Anderson for two murders he did not commit; he had lied to the public, in effect endangering them. What hurt him the most was that she was right about everything, especially the fact that the only thing he had to show for this case was more dead bodies.

CHAPTER 57

After Jenn left him standing there alone, Nick was left with nothing to do but to go to sleep. Sleep was elusive to him, though, his mind unable to focus on anything or nothing else but their fight. It had not even really been a fight, as the entire conversation had been virtually one sided. Nick could not understand what had set her off so, or even why she felt so passionately about it. Nick had lied, and Jenn had been right; this was not the first time. In fact, Nick had not even thought twice about lying to the press, and through them, the public. The thought had come to him as quickly as second nature, without pause or hesitation. Nick was not sure what bothered him the most, that he was so quick to go to the lie as a back up, or that no one but Jenn called him on the fact; especially not Hollings. Jenn was removed from the case, and Nick could see how it helped her to have a more objective opinion. Nick was so far into this case that his objectivity was becoming clouded. His ability to see right and wrong, to see the motives and purpose for each murder was being eroded and, in the momentum created by the killer was causing him to jump to the wrong conclusions. Nick needed to get a hold of himself, reset himself in this case before he lost his place entirely, and the case along with it. Jenn's words had stung him, cutting him to the quick, and Nick knew that it hurt because it was true; he had lost his focus, lost his calm collected demeanor that came from being able to see the murders the way he was usually able to. In the morning he would start again, in the morning he would start anew.

Nick drifted in and out of sleep, his dreams taking him back to the murder scenes over and over again. The images in his mind seemed to focus on the dead bodies specifically, causing Nick to wonder whether there was some clue that he had missed. He woke periodically, feeling as though he had not found any therapeutic level of sleep, causing him to feel more tired and frustrated every time, as if he had never fallen asleep in the first place. When Nick finally did fall asleep, he fell hard into a deep sleep that carried him through until late the following afternoon. He did not hear the repeated phone calls from Lt. Hollings, nor did he hear the call or subsequent message left by Jenn, apologizing for their fight. When he finally opened his eyes and focused, the sun was setting through his windows facing the western horizon, and Nick just lay there for hours, slipping into and out of consciousness until he could lie in bed no longer. When he finally climbed out of bed, he immediately wished that he had not even tried, as his muscles were stiffer and more painful than they had been before. Nick popped a handful of Motrin into his mouth and slowly made his way down the steps to the kitchen where he fixed himself some dinner. The sun was now gone, with only the darkness remaining, filling the lower level of his house and causing him to stumble many times as he came down the stairs. After eating a little, Nick decided that he was not going to get any work done that night. He swallowed three sleeping pills and settled in on the couch, watching television, just waiting for the late night news before he went to bed. He never got that far, however, as the pills took affect and he was asleep again within thirty minutes. There were no images of bodies or crime scenes this time, as he fell into a deep, dreamless sleep.

When Nick awoke first thing Thursday morning, he felt refreshed and ready to take on the case anew. The detective felt like an entirely new man. Though his muscles were still a little stiff, he felt a fire burning inside of him, and he could no longer lie around doing nothing. He quickly showered and dressed, planning to spend the entire day scouring the case file for clues until he was certain that he was on the right track. Before getting down to business though, he knew there were a few things that he needed to take care of first. Nick listened to all of his messages, and decided to call Hollings first and get any new information. Unfortunately, there was none. There had been no clues left at Cooper's murder scene; the killer had even maintained the presence of mind through his fight with Nick to gather up the knife he had thrown at the detective before fleeing the scene.

"So you've got nothing new for me then?" Nick asked, incredulously. The police, forensics, and the medical examiner should have been working on the case for twenty four hours now; there should have been some new information.

"Not regarding the case," Hollings answered. "But I do have some information regarding Anderson."

Nick took in a deep breath, in anticipation of what was to come. He knew that once Anderson was released, all hell would break loose and he kicked himself now for not being able to stay awake long enough to catch the evening news.

"Alright," Nick said with a sigh. "Lay it on me."

"Anderson was released yesterday morning," Hollings began. "And though all charges were dropped with both the court's apologies and our own, he left threatening everything under the sun. He said that he would be suing all of us, of course, and also said that he was going to destroy us in the press. By us, I assume he means you and me. However, he has been conspicuously quiet, and nothing has been leveled at us so far."

"But," Nick said proddingly, hearing the tone in her voice.

"But the chief of police has been working overtime trying to come up with a response to any accusations he lobs our way," Hollings continued. "While most of the brass seems to be holding their breath, the chief is determined to not let us be caught with our pants down."

"So, we're making up excuses," Nick said, feeling his anger rise a bit. "We are looking for ways to cover our ass when we should be saying that had Anderson told us the entire truth from the beginning, he never would have been in the position he was in."

"If the shit hits the fan, the chief wants it to fall back onto Detective Smith and the Norwich Police Department as a whole," Hollings said.

"That's bullshit," Nick exclaimed. "We're not going to lay the blame on another cop when it should have been laid on Anderson's doorstep. If he had told us the truth, none of this would have happened."

"I know, and I agree with you," Hollings said. "However, Anderson is a victim, and the chief feels as though the department is going to look like a big bully if we lay it back on Anderson, even if that's where the blame belongs."

"I won't let him do it," Nick said with conviction. "I will not blame another cop for something that was not his fault. We backed Smith's play, we went along with him because it made sense. All the clues pointed to Anderson, and no law enforcement agency anywhere would have done any different."

"I told you that I agree with you," Hollings stated. "But unless we are able to come up with something else, the chief is not going to change his mind on this."

"Then I'll change his mind for him," Nick said. "I'll give him no choice. He won't have the opportunity to blame Smith after I'm done."

"Don't even think about it," Hollings warned. "I know what you're thinking and I won't let you do it. I tried to reach Smith all day yesterday, but he won't answer. Apparently, he's pissed with us for keeping him out of the loop about Anderson and he's in deep shit with his own chief. It's already not looking good for him. I did leave a message, warning him about what the chief had planned, but I haven't heard back from him. You need to come up with something, and you need to come up with something fast."

Nick hung up with Hollings and placed a quick call into Mitchell, telling him to call if things got any worse. He then stared down at the phone, knowing that he had one more call to make before he could focus all of his attention back on the case. Nick dialed Jenn's number, unsure of what he was going to say when she picked up the phone. He was relieved when her answering machine came on, and just said the first thing that came out of his mind.

"Listen," he began. "I'm sorry that I upset you the other night, and you were totally right about what you said. I investigate cases a certain way, but this case has really thrown me for a loop. There's a lot I'm trying to juggle with this and it's obviously too much. You were right, we shouldn't have lied, and I'm going to make it right one way or the other. I don't...I don't know what else to say other than you were right, I was wrong, and I would really like to talk to you about it when you're ready."

Nick hung up the phone, unsure of what he had just said, but only knew that it had come from the heart and waiting was all he could do now. He turned and stared into the living room, where the case file lay on the living room coffee table alongside a fresh legal pad. The case was still unsolved, the killer was still on the loose, and the shit was about to hit the fan politically. Nick needed to come up with some answers, and he needed to come up with them quickly. He sat down on the couch and opened the file for the hundredth time, taking the first report off of the top of the stack and reading it as though it were the first time. He read the entire file through as if he was doing so through new eyes, taking notes on anything and everything that struck him. Nick made outlines of clues that the police had followed, and what new information had just floated to the surface that he might not have had time to look at before. Each murder had its own clues left behind, whether the killer left them on purpose or not. The only exception so far was Andrew Cooper's murder, though the forensics team was still picking the library apart looking for any evidence that might have been left behind. Something stuck out in Nick's mind as he reviewed the case again, and the first thing had come from his conversations with the killer; the last call in particular, where the killer scolded the police for being on the wrong track. There had been something the killer had said about the way he found Andrew Cooper. Nick had been unable to dissect the killer's words thoroughly because of the urgency in finding Cooper before the killer did. Now, however, Nick felt as though he had something he needed to investigate a little more closely. Then there was the wax seal left in Father Allun's thigh. There was some kind of significance to it, something that Nick did not understand, but needed to. Finally, there was Brenner's murder. It had seemed so obvious to the police when Anderson had been arrested, the fact that there had been so many links to the police had just helped to solidify their case. But now, Nick knew that Anderson was innocent, which begged the question of where the glove fibers, the mace and taser came from. The mace and taser could have come from anywhere, though the forensic analysts seemed certain that both matched the type used by the police. However, police uniforms were not easy to get your hands on, especially not authentic uniforms. The killer had to know where the police got their uniforms, unless...

The doorbell rang suddenly, and Nick was jolted from his thoughts to reality. Nick looked around quickly, and then turned his attention to his watch, which read ten minutes past nine in the evening. He had been working all day and night without a break and he had not even realized it. Nick rose from his place on the couch and walked to the door. He opened it to find Jenn standing on the other side of the door, tears streaming down her face. Nick smiled and pulled her inside, taking her into his arms and kissing her tears. She kissed him back and in a few seconds they were locked in each other's arms as if afraid to let the other one go. There was nothing to say, nothing they needed to say. This was their way of apologizing to the other in the most pure and simplistic form each knew how. Nick lifted Jenn up in his arms and carried her upstairs where they spent the rest of the night making love until they fell asleep in each other's arms. They were more passionate now then they had ever been, as if the thought of not talking to the other again had reminded the other of how precious their time together really was.

When the morning came, Nick awoke to the sound of the telephone. He groaned and turned to look at the clock on the nightstand, and though it took a few seconds for him to focus, he was finally able to read the number that read two minutes after six in the morning. Nick picked up the phone and pressed it to his ear.

"Hello," Nick said.

"It's Mitchell," the detective said quickly. "I'm sorry to call so early, but I thought you'd want to know that the shit is about to hit the fan just as you predicted."

"When?" Nick asked. He had been preparing for this all the previous day, though he had hoped it would not happen.

"At ten this morning," Mitchell said. "Whatever you're going to do to protect Smith, you need to do it quick."

"I'll call you back in ten minutes," Nick said, and hung up the phone. Jenn was stirring and turned over to see the expression on his face. All he could do was look at her and realize that she had never looked more beautiful than she did at that moment.

"Is everything alright?" she asked, her voice still hoarse and her vision still caught up in a sleepy haze.

"It will be," Nick answered. "Tell me, would you still date me if I were suddenly unemployed?"

Jenn turned over fully now to look at him squarely.

"Would you get a job at some point?" she asked, unsure of what was going on in his mind.

"Oh yeah," Nick said playfully. "At some point. I'd probably get a job at a fast food restaurant."

"Could you get us free food?" Jenn asked, attempting to sound serious.

"I could try," Nick said, picking up the phone again and dialing in a number he knew by heart, though had never needed to dial before.

"Then yes," Jenn said. "I'd still date you."

She pushed up on her stomach and planted a kiss on his unshaven cheek. Nick smiled, his vision instantly locking on to the way the white sheets slid down her naked back and stopped just above her hips.

"That's good to know," Nick said, then turned his attention to the phone. "Yes, this is Detective Grenier; I need to speak to the Governor please."

There was a pause, as Nick listened to the secretary's automatic excuse in handling incoming calls that asked for the governor directly.

"I understand," Nick said. "Could you at least pop your head in and tell him that Detective Grenier is on the phone and says it's urgent. If he can't talk to me then, I'll understand."

The secretary seemed a little put off by the detective's persistence, but did as he asked. She knew that if this was something truly important and she did not get the governor's answer, it could spell the end of her job. In a minute she was back on the line and asked him to hold for two seconds as she forwarded the call to his office.

"Nick," said a gruff male voice that the detective immediately recognized as the governor's. "Is everything alright?"

"No sir," Nick answered. "It seems that I need a favor."

CHAPTER 58

Nick experienced a sense of déjà vu as he watched nearly one hundred men and women scurrying around hurriedly preparing for the press conference that was set to begin in less than ten minutes. He tried to study the faces of the reporters in an attempt to ascertain whether Mark Anderson was among them. Nick wanted to believe that Anderson would not show up, the press conference taking place so soon after his release from police custody. However, it was no secret that the press conference today was being held to stem the tide of questions that were now surfacing around the rumors that the death in the Groton Public Library might actually have been a homicide. There were also rumors that there had been an arrest made in connection to the Father Allun murder, but that the police had released this person. Nick had no doubt that the reporters before him already knew that Anderson had been arrested, though they probably did not know why and were not willing to report publicly until they had solid information. As for Anderson himself, Nick knew that he would not miss an opportunity to humiliate the New London Police Department, especially now. At the department, everyone above Hollings had been holding their breath, waiting for Anderson to make a public announcement or file a lawsuit against the department. Nick knew there would not be a public announcement though; it would force Anderson to disclose why he was considered a suspect in the first place, and it would force him to explain his relationship to both victims. That was something Nick did not think Anderson was prepared to do.

Nick felt a gentle tap on his shoulder and turned to face the Connecticut State Attorney General, Alexander Masterson. Masterson was an imposing figure, standing over six feet six inches tall with a huge muscular frame, Nick could understand how the man had gotten as far as he did in life. Masterson had been a legal wizard, joining the district attorney's office in Raleigh, North Carolina straight out of college and never looking back. He rose through the ranks of the DA's office by his intimidating demeanor and remarkable legal acumen. Masterson had grown up with Governor Haisley, and when the governor was elected into office, he invited Masterson to come north and fill the position of the State's Attorney General. Masterson had been an asset for state prosecutors and police alike. His understanding of the difficulties faced by law enforcement, combined with his determination to reduce crime state wide had helped to solidify all the different local law enforcement departments and had done just what he and the governor had promised, giving Connecticut the lowest crime rate in New England. When Nick had phoned the governor earlier in the morning, he had not expected to get this much help so soon, and he certainly had not expected such legal muscle to reinforce him. But here he stood, looking up at the State's Attorney General, feeling reassured that his decision to pre-empt the New London chief's press conference was the right one.

"I don't usually get called down to stand in support of a local detective at a press conference," Masterson explained. "You must really be in the governor's good graces."

"I hope that I can stay there," Nick said. "I do appreciate you coming down though. There were nasty rumors going around that we have to nip in the bud with our statement here."

"What is it you want me to say here?" asked the State's Attorney General looking beyond Nick's shoulder at the sea of reporters who were getting more prepared and anxious by the minute.

"How much you want to say is really up to you," Nick answered, expecting Masterson to have been a little more prepared than he seemed. "I can handle the details, and since we don't have much good news it would probably be better for you if I did most of the talking. All we really need is for you to open the press conference and show you support the department."

Masterson looked down at the detective, surprised by his candor. The State's Attorney General then smiled and chuckled softly.

"Are you trying to protect my political image, detective?" he asked.

"No sir," Nick answered, only then realizing how his words must have sounded. "I just don't want you to get boxed in with questions you might not be prepared for."

Masterson just smiled a knowing smile and stepped past Nick, taking the step up to the podium and tapping on the microphone to get everyone's attention. Suddenly, all the commotion out in the crowd stopped and all eyes focused on the State's Attorney General. Masterson addressed the group of reporters, thanking them for being there so early and laying out the rules for the press conference. Masterson then introduced Nick as the lead detective in the investigation of the death at the Groton Public Library and stepped back as Nick took the hot seat.

"Thank you for coming," Nick began, having just realized that Masterson was much better prepared than Nick had imagined, and probably better prepared than Nick was himself. "Two days ago, police from the New London Police Department went to the Groton Public Library in search of an ex-convict who had just recently violated his parole, and because of his offenses, was deemed to be a public threat and needed to be found and arrested quickly. The parolee's name was Andrew Cooper, though he had falsified his name and records to get employment at the library, which was just one of his many parole violations. Upon reaching the scene, police found the library full of patrons, and not knowing whether Cooper was armed and dangerous, they decided to have the building evacuated. The story that there was a gas leak was authorized by me, and was meant to remove the threat to the public quickly by evacuating the building with no questions asked. While the building was being evacuated, police spread out and searched for Cooper. It was only a few minutes after the building was empty that the police found Cooper dead, the victim of a homicide. The killer had been hiding, and an attempt was made to detain the individual, but he assaulted the officer and escaped."

Nick paused for a moment, allowing the reporters who were taking notes to catch up and for the information to sink in with everyone. He was not concerned that anyone would jump the gun and ask any questions, as Masterson had been emphatic about the rules.

"There were some rumors that Cooper had a heart attack and had died as a result of that," Nick continued. "Since the investigation was in its infancy, and the victim's family had not been contacted, it was my decision to allow the rumors to continue until more solid information could be gathered. Let me state officially; there was no cover-up. The story of the gas leak was used for public safety, though the department did nothing to correct the inaccuracies of the rumors of Cooper's death, there was no outward attempt by the department to make his death look anything different than what it was. After two days of investigation, it is now clear that the murder of Andrew Cooper was committed by the same person who murdered Father Michael Allun and Jack Brenner. Though there are no social links between the three victims, there are commonalities and evidence which links the killer to all three men. As I stated earlier, the killer did get away. However, the police have several people who we will identify as 'persons of interest' and an arrest is forthcoming.

Lastly, I want to assure everyone that the public as a whole is not in any danger, women and children are not in danger. There is no need to panic or to drastically curtail any family or individual plans and activities. This killer has an established profile, and has not and will not deviate from it. All the police ask is that the public exercise common sense when going out, especially alone, and be aware of your surroundings at all times. As I have said, an arrest is imminent, and the threat will soon be removed. The New London Police Department has been working in conjunction with the best detectives at the Norwich Police Department, and our combined investigation is producing solid leads that will end with an arrest any day now. The department has been running this investigation by the book, making certain that the heads of all departments on both the police and state's prosecutors sides have been fully briefed before taking any steps so as to ensure a clean conviction once we arrest this killer. I thank you for your patience and will now open the floor up to any questions you might have."

Nick took a deep breath as every hand flew up into the air and his name was called out over and over, each voice louder than the next in an attempt to get his attention. Nick scanned the faces of crowd, mostly looking to make sure that he did not call on Anderson if he really was out there; he did not want to get ambushed. Nick pointed to a female reporter and everyone became immediately silent.

"You say that an arrest is imminent," the young woman commented. "Can you give us any more information, how soon do you plan on making this arrest?"

"An arrest will be made in the coming days," Nick answered. "As I said earlier, the police want to make sure that there are no legal loopholes this killer can slip through."

"You said the public is safe," started another reporter. "Can you tell us how you can make that statement when the killer is still on the loose? What is the profile the killer is using to choose his victims?"

"I'm not going to elaborate on the killer's profiling because we are talking about a mind that sees things with skewed perception," Nick answered. "However, though the profile seems strange, the killer seems to be sticking with it to a tee, which makes the department confident in our statement that the general public is not in danger. However, I will again emphasize that everyone should use basic common sense when out in public, at all times, especially while our killer remains on the loose."

"Can you give us the identities of those 'persons of interest' you spoke of earlier?" asked a voice from the far left.

"I will not comment on an ongoing police investigation," Nick answered. "Next question."

"Isn't it true you had a person in custody at one time?" asked a voice from the back. All commotion seemed to cease and the reporters turned to search out the person who asked the question. The crowd seemed to part somewhat as all eyes landed on Mark Anderson. Anderson took a few steps forward and both men stared at each other, hard. "Is it also true that you had to release this person because you had acted too rashly? What can you tell us about that, detective?"

"It is true that we had a person in custody at one point," Nick answered, his gaze never breaking from Anderson's. The detective had prepared himself for this exact possibility. "The evidence had pointed to an individual who had connections to Brenner and Allun. This person, who I will not identify until he comes out and makes himself public, had acted suspiciously and had subverted the police's every attempt to ascertain the truth. While I am sorry this person was arrested and held wrongly, it should be known that it was his own actions that led to his arrest. Had he simply been truthful and forthcoming during questioning, these events never would have happened. In fact, it is because of the actions of this individual, that countless hours of police work were misdirected when they could have been out searching for, and even possibly identifying and capturing, the real killer. The police department has apologized to this person, and I will even do so publicly. I am sorry that this person was arrested and detained when it is now obvious he was innocent. I also hope he understands that it was his own actions that led to this, and no one else's."

Everyone waited with baited breath as all eyes shifted to Anderson, waiting for a response. Everyone there knew it was Anderson the two men were talking about, and that this was his way at getting some kind of revenge. However, Nick had once again shut him down, minimizing the damage and now they waited for Anderson's response.

"Attorney General Masterson," Anderson called out, using the last trick he had. "Do you still feel comfortable with Detective Grenier leading the investigation when he has made such a drastic mistake already? Don't you think that this case should be put in more capable hands?"

"The only mistake made in this case was by the man who was detained for a short amount of time," Masterson said, stepping up to the podium. His already massive body and imposing demeanor only seemed to increase as he stepped forward. Nick was not sure how far he would go in backing him up, but was appreciative of Masterson's official defense of the police without hesitation. "While unfortunate, the circumstances leading to the arrest of this individual could have been avoided, and he has only himself to blame. As for your second question, there is no one more capable of solving these crimes than Detective Grenier. I only wish that all our detectives, both on the force and those recently retired, were as capable as Detective Grenier."

That last comment was a slap in Anderson's face, and everyone knew it. What was worse, Masterson had verbally slapped Anderson down on live public television. Anderson stood there seething in his anger, nearly trembling with hate. It was as if steam was going to start rising off his body at any second. As for Masterson, he just kept his gaze locked on Anderson, as if his stare alone could cause the other man to ignite into flame. For a moment, Nick thought there might be more than just words between the two men. However, Anderson took a step back as if physically pushed back, then turned and walked away in his anger. That spelled the end of the press conference and all the reporters hurried away to get their story into the news room for the noon airing. Masterson turned and walked past Nick, stepping down off of the makeshift stage and heading off towards his awaiting car. Nick watched him walk away for a moment, and then followed quickly.

"Thank you for that," Nick said. "That was not expected."

"I didn't say anything that wasn't true," Masterson said without stopping or looking over his shoulder. "And it's you who should be thanked, for saving the reputation of another officer."

"Well, thanks anyway," Nick said, unsure of what he should say next. "It helps to keep the press at bay when they know that we have the support of your office."

"You do have the support of my office," Masterson said, turning and stopping in front of the detective. "And that of the governor, for now. However, the longer this case takes to close, the thinner our support will be stretched. I think you understand what I'm saying here. Close this case, and do it quickly, or else you might find yourself standing all alone at your next press conference."

With that, Masterson shook Nick's hand, though the detective was not really offering it. He was still processing the fact that his job and his reputation had just been threatened.

"What are your plans now?" asked Masterson.

"Well," Nick began. "I think I need to see my doctor and get a prescription for a little perspective, and then I'm going to solve this case."

CHAPTER 59

Nick placed a quick call to Detective Mitchell and then swung by the department to pick up the new additions to the case files that he had requested before driving up to Norwich, Connecticut. Nick knew that now would not be the time to show his face in the Investigations Unit, or anywhere in the building for that matter. The chief would be out for his head, and though he was leaving Hollings exposed, he knew she could handle it. Hollings was probably a little irritated by Nick's decision to go over everyone's head and call the Governor, but he knew she felt the same way as he did about hanging Smith out to dry. The brass had been terrified of what Anderson might do from the moment he left his holding cell, and feeling as though they could not lay the blame on Anderson because he had been a victim once himself, they looked for another scapegoat. Nick could not allow that, not because he was overly friendly with the Norwich detective, but simply because it was wrong. This was not the blue wall coming into play to protect one of its own; this was simply a matter of doing the right thing. Anderson needed to know that he was not going to be able to use the New London Police Department as his target anymore. Nick had no illusions, he knew that one press conference had not quelled the vendetta between Anderson and the police, but it was a start.

Right now, however, Nick had much more pressing matters to focus on. With Masterson's words still echoing in his head, Nick was now more acutely aware than ever about the need to close this case. He needed an avenue to explore, some place to begin looking. That was the real problem, though; there was no place to start. Every time Nick thought he had a place to start and began digging, he found himself further and further away from an answer. He needed to break the case down to its simplest form. There were three victims, and there was a killer. Nick now needed to expand from there, using everything he learned as a cop and put it toward the case until he had a viable suspect, until he had anything resembling a lead. As Nick made his way up to Norwich, he could not help but feel as though he needed to talk to Smith about the case. This had been Smith's case from the start, but there had been a lack of confidence from the beginning that shifted Nick into the unenviable position of running the investigation. The lack of confidence was not in Smith as a detective, but simply stemmed from the fact that Smith had never been involved in a high profile case. The governor wanted somebody the press and public knew, someone they felt comfortable with. Once Brenner was murdered, all the weight of the investigation had been shifted to New London. Nick realized Smith had a reason to be put out; having been second guessed as a professional, having the person he suspected turn out to be innocent, and having the department ready to turn on him. However, he was still a police detective with an unsolved homicide, and Nick was going to have to appeal to Smith's professionalism if he was to have any chance of putting an end to this. Nick placed the Bluetooth earpiece in his ear and entered Smith's cell phone number into his phone and pressed SEND. The call went directly to Smith's voicemail.

"Listen, its Grenier," Nick began. "I know that you are pissed off, and I know that you've gotten the short end of the stick on most of this case and all I can say is I'm sorry. I didn't hold that press conference this morning to get in your good graces; I did it because it was the right thing to do. Now I understand your ego is bruised, but there are more important issues than Kevin Smith's ego. There is still an open homicide; the detective in you still has a homicide to investigate. So when you get a hold of yourself and get back to being a detective, give me a call."

Nick pressed the END button on the cell phone and returned his full attention to his driving. He hoped the call would get Smith's attention, reminding him that there was more than his ego to deal with. Nick got off the interstate at exit 80 and negotiated the familiar back roads until he was pulling into the parking lot of a brick walled building that housed several medical offices, including Dr. Nancy Tanner. He had missed his scheduled appointment with her last week because of his investigation, and he had promised Hollings that he would keep this one, and here he was. Being honest with himself, Nick actually looked forward to this appointment, knowing that he needed someone to talk to about his recently unpredictable life. He wanted her to know that he had made some changes, especially in the relationship department. Mainly, he wanted her to know that he had not missed their last appointment because he was putting it off. He wanted her to know that he was doing well and that he was not afraid of these appointments, though inside he was still a little apprehensive. Nick climbed the steps and took the first door on the right as he reached the landing to the second floor. As he stepped through the doorway, he immediately found himself staring into the smiling face of Tanner's receptionist. Space had been tight in Tanner's office, and since there was only one room beyond the waiting area, available space had to be maximized, which meant a very close reception area. The receptionist informed Nick that Tanner was ready to see him immediately, and the detective followed her back to the door of Tanner's office. The receptionist knocked and opened the door without waiting for a response, and Nick entered and took his normal seat in front of Tanner. When the door closed again, they began.

"It's good you could find time in your busy schedule for our appointment, detective," Tanner said, opening with their usual banter.

"Are you sure it's wise to be laying a guilt trip on a person who is seeing you for therapy?" Nick fired back, hoping his response would prove that he was unfazed by her comment.

"I suppose you're right," Tanner replied. "I saw the press conference on the news this morning, you looked pretty good up there."

"Really," Nick replied, as if truly appreciative of her comment. "You know they say the camera adds ten pounds."

"Are you here for a therapy session or are we going to have another fight?" Tanner asked. "I only brought up the press conference because you looked more in control today than I have seen you in a long time. I was particularly pleased with the way you responded to the reporter who was attacking you with questions. There seemed to be some animosity between the two of you."

"There is," Nick answered. "But his anger is more directed at the police department as a whole. As for looking better, I do appreciate the comment. Things have been going well in my personal life, even if my professional career is questionable."

"Why do you feel your professional career is questionable?" Tanner asked. "It looked as if everything was under control at the press conference. You even had the State's Attorney General in your corner."

"There's been a lot of behind the scenes shit going on," Nick answered, being purposely vague. "It has to do with a case."

Tanner could sense there was more to the story than Nick was saying, and she felt that it might even be therapeutic for him to talk about it. However, she could also sense that Nick was holding back for a reason, and felt that it would be better if she led him back to the subject later, making it seem as though he came back to it on it's own.

"Tell me what's going on in your private life," Tanner said, jotting some words down on a pad and circling it.

"Well," Nick said, hesitantly. "I've been seeing someone. It's only been two weeks now, but I feel as though we have a strong connection."

"That's great," Tanner said. "That's a real step forward for you. Are you dating this person, or do you feel as though you've moved beyond that to the next stage?"

"I think we've moved beyond that," Nick answered. "It was strange at first. There is a mutual physical attraction, but there is also an emotional connection that has really developed. There is a sensitivity to her that I don't think I've found in another person before."

"Well, that really is great," Tanner remarked. "I did not expect something like this to happen so quickly for you. When we spoke last, you were concerned that your career might put any potential love interest at risk. What has changed your mind about that?"

"Well," Nick said with a sigh. He turned his eyes up to the ceiling as if looking for the best response. "As it turns out, she is a police officer too. She doesn't work in my unit, though she does work out of the same department. As for any fear of endangering her, I know that she knows how to take care of herself. Hell, she can kick my ass. But more importantly, she understands what it is to be a cop. She understands the fears, anxiety, and frustration. I guess I'm trying to say that we can relate to each other."

"So you feel you can talk to her about your work," Tanner said, steering the conversation along. "Can you talk to her about this case?"

"Yeah, I..." Nick hesitated just a moment. "I can talk to her for the most part. She has her set ideas, so sometimes it's difficult for her to agree with certain tactics or decisions, but on the other hand, I have gained a lot from her insight. She has a way of seeing the other side of the matter, and in this case it's been very valuable."

"What do you mean by *this* case?" Tanner asked.

"It's just that in this case, nothing is as it seems," Nick answered with a little chuckle. "Every time I think I'm on to something, that something turns out not to be what I thought it was. It doesn't end up pertaining to the case at all, though it does end up being a separate entity of its own. Truth be told, I feel further away from an answer than I did when I first stepped into St. Patrick's Cathedral two weeks ago."

"How is this case different?" Tanner asked.

"I don't know," Nick said, shaking his head back and forth. "There's something that just doesn't seem right about it. When I left your office after our last appointment, I was called to the scene of a murder/suicide. When I got on the scene, it just seemed easy, and not because there were two dead bodies and it was obvious. The whole scene seemed to fit, I could understand the flow, see the events that led up to it in my mind. It just fit. This case though, there is something that is just not right. Unfortunately, I have yet to figure out what that is."

"But you've said that having an outside, objective opinion has helped?" asked the psychiatrist.

"I've had a number of outside opinions, and they have all helped," Nick answered. He watched curiously as Tanner continued jotting down notes on her pad. Nick was always curious as to what she actually wrote down, and what her assessment of him really was. Just then, the pen seemed to teeter in her hand before slipping out of her grasp and falling to the floor. The pen hit the floor on its side and rolled underneath her chair. Nick pushed forward to help her, but Tanner was already up, holding up her hand. Nick realized instantly that his moving closer could mean invading her personal space, and could mean that he would get a glimpse of the notes she wrote. Nick settled back down into his seat, mildly amused at the sudden hyper-awareness of space that Tanner seemed to exude. The doctor knelt down with one knee on the floor and slipped her hand under the chair, feeling for her pen. Her back was to Nick, and the detective found himself even more amused by the seemingly growing frustration that built as she spent more time fumbling for the pen. Finally, she let out a victorious gasp as she grasped the pen and pulled it out from under her chair. She began to rise, and as she did, Nick watched entranced as he found himself slightly aroused and confused by what felt like a familiar movement. There was something about the fluid way she rose that set off a spark in the detective's brain. Tanner was suddenly aware that Nick was watching her, and turned her head towards him.

"Get a good look, detective?" she asked, injecting a slightly serious tone to let Nick know that the way he was looking at her was inappropriate. However, Nick had left the curious aspect of her movement behind and was focusing on the familiarity of it.

"Do that again," Nick said.

"Do what again?" Tanner asked, confused.

"Bend down and stand up again," Nick answered. "But stand up the way you just did."

"Yeah, I don't think so," the doctor stated firmly. "Perhaps we should devote some time to this."

"Do it again," Nick said, this time in a serious tone. Nick pulled a pen out of the inside pocket of his sports jacket and lobbed it across the floor until it came to rest beside her chair.

"This is getting a little weird," Tanner began. Nick rose and stood before her, staring at her. Her mind was screaming at her to not give in to his demand, to make it clear that this was entering an area that was inappropriate and slightly disturbing. However, she could tell by the look in his eyes that she was seeing his business side, the professional side. This was not his way of getting off, this was something else entirely. Tanner rose slightly and bent over again, trying to remember how she had been positioned when she reached under the chair. She picked up the pen in her hand and rose slowly, hoping that she was doing now what she had done before without thinking. She did not take her eyes off of the detective though, scanning his face for any type of emotion.

As for Nick, he watched her stand the way a doctor would watch a patient move during a physical exam. There was nothing sexual or entertaining about it; he was trying to place the movement she was making. His mind already knew that it had something to do with his case, something significant. It was a movement, a position that he had seen women make over a thousand times. There was nothing overtly sexual in it, just a fluid, luxurious way a woman moved that a man was not capable of. It was something that was slightly exhibitionist in the movement itself, one of those millions of little unintended movements a woman makes that captures the attention of a man. Nick tried to think if this was something that Jenn had done, something he had noticed recently that might be triggering this feeling of déjà vu. However, he immediately dismissed the idea, knowing that Jenn was too shy to move like this, no matter how unintended the gesture was. Suddenly, the answer hit Nick like a ton of bricks. Immediately, he knew exactly what he was looking at. It was the killer; it was the way the killer moved in the library when Nick ordered him to stand up. He had been bent over Cooper's body and Nick had ordered him to stand up. The movement had not meant anything at the time because Nick had been focused on trying to apprehend the killer, trying to close the case. When the killer had begun to rise, Nick had dismissed the slow, fluid movement as the killer's sudden realization that he had been caught. However, the killer was not doing it because he had come to some sudden acceptance of the inevitable, he was showing off; he was a she.

"Holy shit," Nick exclaimed as if stepping from the darkness of uncertainty into the light. "Dude looks like a lady."

"Maybe that's because I am a lady," Tanner said, sliding back into her chair. "Do you want to tell me what's going on?"

"The killer," Nick said, staring off as if he were seeing something real take place just beyond where Tanner was seated. "The killer is a woman. Of course, the killer is a woman."

"What?" asked Tanner, now completely confused.

"I have to go," Nick said, returning his attention to reality. He grabbed his jacket off of the back of the chair and slipped into it easily. "I have to go, but I want you to know that you may have just helped me solve my case."

"I think it would be best if we talked this out," Tanner said, rising. "I thing you should follow through with your entire train of thought aloud, so you don't miss anything."

"Yeah, no," Nick answered, his mind running away with the possibilities of this new discovery. "We'll finish up later. I have to go."

Nick did not wait for her to respond before bolting out of the door and down the steps. In his mind, possibilities were taking root faster than he could complete his thoughts. Ideas were stemming from ideas, and suddenly he felt as though the case had been given new life. The police had discounted the idea of a woman committing the crimes for many reasons, then the killer called and even though he had used an electronic device to disguise his voice, Nick had just assumed the killer was male. However, now as he replayed the killer's movements again and again in his mind, he knew that he was right. The killer was a female, and the police had been looking in the wrong direction the entire time. As Nick stepped out into the sunlight, he found Detective Smith leaning against his car.

"How the hell did you know I was here?" Nick asked, skipping the greeting.

"This is my town," Smith answered. "Nothing happens here that I don't know about."

"Get in the car," Nick said. "I think I found something, I think we've been wrong about the killer all along."

"What were we wrong about?" Smith asked, walking around to the passenger side and opening the door. "Where the hell are we going?"

"We have another appointment," Nick answered. "We're going to see another doctor."

"You just left the doctor," Smith stated.

"But this is a different kind of doctor," Nick said with a smile. "We're going to see our friendly neighborhood forensic doctor."

"My favorite kind," Smith said with a smile, and climbed inside Nick's car.

CHAPTER 60

K evin Smith tried in vain to get Nick to tell him what was going on in the detective's mind, but finally gave up when he realized that Nick was playing a little game of suspense. In reality, Nick just did not want to go over his new theories with Smith, just to have to revisit them with Jessica Sarrucci when they arrived. Nick also had a way in which he wanted to map out the case for them, so that there would be no questions when they finally understood what his thinking was. During the ride, Smith talked about his frustration with the case and often questioned how he could have been so wrong about Anderson. Nick reminded his fellow detective that he was not the only person to have made the judgment error as to Anderson's guilt. Smith brought up the press conference briefly, and though he did not come out and make a point of thanking Nick for his intervention on Smith's behalf, there was an understanding between the two men that everything was even. As Nick pulled into Sarrucci's driveway for the third time, he began to feel as though his days were continuously repeating themselves. The detectives quickly climb out of their car and Nick knocked on the front door. The heat and humidity of the day was beginning to set in, and both men anxiously awaited the transition into the cool, central air-conditioning of Sarrucci's house. A few seconds later, Sarrucci answered the door and just shook her head at Nick.

"The neighbors are getting suspicious," Sarrucci said with a smile. "They're going to start spreading awful rumors pretty soon."

"They should mind their own business," Nick said. "Besides, I brought you a present."

"Beware of strangers bearing gifts," Sarrucci said with a smile as she stepped away, allowing Nick to step through the threshold and into the house. The detective was followed by Smith, who greeted the forensic pathologist warmly.

"You wouldn't believe that you two have only known each other for two weeks," Nick commented as he walked into the living room.

"Oh, don't be jealous," Sarrucci teased. "You were always my first true pain in the ass."

"I wouldn't have it any other way," Nick replied. "We need to go over the case with you again. Particularly, we need to re-examine the murders from an entirely new aspect, and we need a clear psychological composite of the killer."

"Well, unless you've come up with some new evidence, I don't think there is anything new I can tell you," Sarrucci said. "The pattern is pretty clear and easy to follow."

"I've been thinking about some things and could use your advice," Nick said. "I promise I won't keep you long."

"Alright," Sarrucci agreed. "But the New London Police Department is going to have to put me on their payroll pretty soon."

"I don't think we could afford you," Nick commented.

"I know you couldn't," Sarrucci fired back with a smile. Everyone settled into the bar seats surrounding the island in the middle of the kitchen as Nick spread out the pages of his case file.

Nick started with the murders and the victims themselves. He drew amateurish charts that listed the commonalities of the crimes side by side. Michael Allun was abducted on a Friday and tortured for over a day and a half, then returned to the place from which he was abducted. The positioning of his body seemed significant, having been tied to a cross and hung upside down from the rafters of the cathedral. Nick reminded the others about the piece of wax, and reminded them that the police still did not know the true significance of it. Nick told them that he felt both the wax and the positioning of the body were meant to send a message to someone, and that only the killer knew what that message was. Nick then moved on to Jack Brenner. Brenner was also attacked on a Friday, though he was not abducted. He was attacked and tortured, probably for many hours if not more than a day, but was never taken from the place he was found. He was discovered on a Monday found by an employee, left in the exact position he had been assaulted and killed. He had been raped, as had Allun, but had died from strangling. Allun had died from massive internal bleeding, which had most likely taken many hours. Finally, there was Cooper. Cooper was assaulted in public, blitzed by the killer in the dark. The device used to cut the power was the same as the one used at St. Patrick's Cathedral. This time, however, the killer did not torture his victim, simply attacked and murdered him. It could have been argued that the killer knew the police were on the scene, and had to act quickly. This was most likely the case, but Nick still felt it was necessary to point out the discrepancies. Most killers, especially multiple murderers, fell into a routine, a safe pattern of killing. With Cooper, the killer was trying to make a point; that he was still out there and the police had the wrong man in custody, and to let the police know how truly impotent they were.

From there, Nick turned his focus to the victims in particular. Michael Allun was a priest who had been sexually abused by another priest when he was a child, and was now participating in rough and experimental sex with both male and female partners. It was speculated that the killer murdered Allun because of the priest's relationships. It was easy to understand how others might find Allun's actions morally reprehensible. However, Nick pointed out that Allun was not committing a crime, nor was it apparent that he was going to commit a crime in the near future. From the video footage Allun took of his partners, he had a profile of the particular person he lured back to his home, and stuck to it. When it came to his reasoning, everything seemed logical and straight forward. Whether Nick actually believed that Allun was participating in a sexual "experiment" or not, Allun did not do or participate in anything that actually broke the law. As for Brenner, he had broken many laws, most of which he had gotten away with. Brenner had forced many women to have sex with him, and some of them had been underage, though he had only been caught the one time. He had also infected many people with HIV, though it was unclear if he knew he was infected at the time. This fact aside, the differences between the two cases were clear and staggering. Jack Brenner had obviously broken the law many times, whether he was aware of it or not. Whether he saw his actions as forcing himself on women or not, in the eyes of the law, it was still clearly rape. Lastly, there was Cooper, a convicted child molester who had been released on parole only to go slip back under the radar and put himself in a position to molest children again. Though one could not be certain that was the reason Cooper violated his parole, he still broke the law.

"I don't think I understand where you are going with this," Smith commented.

"You're not trying to say that Allun wasn't killed by the same person as Brenner and Cooper are you?" Sarrucci asked. Nick sat back in his chair and smiled.

"I'm not saying that at all," Nick assured her. "In fact, I believe the killer used the same device to cut the power at the cathedral and the library just to prove who was responsible. Remember, the main reason the killer was provoked into killing Cooper so soon was because we had Anderson in custody, and Anderson was innocent. Our killer believes that these murders are some form of justice, and he could not allow an innocent man to be held or get the credit for murders he did not commit."

"So then why are we reviewing this crap?" Smith asked as his frustration mounted. "It's all the same stuff we've looked at before."

"We are looking at it because the only murder that does not truly fit is Allun's," Nick answered. "There was no ceremonious positioning of the body in the other two cases; there was no abduction. Allun's murder was cool, composed, calm and methodical. Look at the other two, what do you feel from the other two?"

"Pain," Sarrucci answered, staring down at the photos of the victims. "Anger, hatred, but mainly vengeful pain. You're right, Allun's murder is different. It suggests a different feeling towards him than towards the others."

"But you just said you were sure..." Smith stammered for a moment and then smiled. "Unless you don't think the killer ever intended to murder Allun."

"I think murdering Allun was someone else's idea," Nick said, continuing along the other detective's line of thought. "I think that someone knew our killer, knew what was going on in his head. I think he set the killer on his task, convinced him that Allun was an evil person and convinced the killer to start his spree with Allun. However, because he was detached from Allun, because this was someone else's idea, the killer did not reach the level of rage in killing Allun as in the other two murders."

"Making him able to torture Allun longer," Sarrucci said, nodding her head. "It took longer for the killer to reach a point where he could no longer wait to kill him. In fact, since Allun bled out from internal wounds, our killer may not have reached his rage climax at all."

Smith looked over at the pathologist curiously, though the look in his eyes betrayed his disgust in the very point she was reaching.

"Yes, detective," Sarrucci said with a devilish smile. "It's very much like sex. The rage he felt for his victims is very much like lust, the anticipation building inside, his screams like moans of pleasure, so much pleasure derived and yet a feeling that you don't want it to ever end. You want it to go on, you want it to last, but you reach a point when your mind can not hold you back any longer and you have to bring it to a climax, you have to kill. Then you look down, spent and exhausted, and realize that the moments of sheer bliss were just before the end. Like an orgasm, you realize that you have to start all over again, and for the killer it means finding another victim."

Both detectives just stared at Sarrucci, though Nick was far less shocked by her explanation than Smith. Nick had been used to it, the dark side of her mind. It was what made them such good friends; they both understood the darkness that existed within the other. Hers was a darkness of observance, understanding a killer in the way that he killed. Nick's was a darkness of deed, understanding the killer because he felt there might be one inside of him. Everyone was silent for a few moments, and Sarrucci began to get nervous that she had gone too far with someone who she did not know so well. Very few people knew of her dark streak, it was not something that she flaunted.

"I don't know whether to be aroused or disgusted," Smith said, finally breaking the silence.

"Probably a little of both," Nick answered, having felt the same sensation many times before.

"So who's responsible for getting the killer to murder Allun?" Sarrucci asked. "Who really wanted Allun dead?"

"We'll get back to that in a moment," Nick answered. "First, I think it would be beneficial to get a psychological composite of the killer. We have someone who can be controlled, someone who needed that little encouragement and push to go over the edge and kill his first victim. After that little push, our killer begins rolling. He's angry, someone caused him pain and that makes him want to inflict pain on others. He could not get the full appreciation out of Allun's murder, but he was able to prove that he has control, that he has the stomach to inflict a great deal of pain for hours. If he got anything out of Allun's torture, it was the pleasure of causing pain for so long. Then there was Brenner, a particularly nasty murder. With Brenner, our killer can not contain his anger. There is something about Brenner that causes him to react more viciously, more violently than before. Something about the crime that Brenner committed cuts deeper into our killer's core, and he is unable to maintain the control over himself that he showed with Allun's torture. Brenner was tortured for up to eighteen hours at most, while Allun was kept alive for well over a day. With Brenner he got the full appreciation he was looking for. The killer attacked him, causing fear. He beat, raped, and tortured Brenner; causing him to cry out in pain, plead for mercy. Finally, he kills Brenner, choking him to death. Choking is an intimate act; you have to get close, very close. The killer listened to Brenner's last breath, listened to him gag, and could see Brenner's eyes roll back in his head. With Brenner, our killer got everything he was hoping for and more. Then there was Cooper. Cooper was quick, efficient; he never saw the end coming. Just like Cooper's victims never expected to be betrayed by the person they automatically put their trust in. I wonder just how satisfying it must have been to know his cut sliced both carotids and jugular, to watch the life quickly drain from Cooper's body. No, the last two deaths were very personal to our killer. Imagine a man who was abused as a child, possibly by someone who should have loved him. Imagine a man who was abused and mistreated all of his life, a man who felt as though there was nothing better out there. Now imagine that our killer is a woman."

Suddenly, Nick caught the attention of both Smith and Sarrucci, whose eyes had been closed picturing the killer in their minds. Instantly, their eyelids shot open and their eyes were wide in sudden understanding of where Nick had been going with his theories the entire time.

"Oh my God," Sarrucci said, almost inaudibly as she began to compute the ramifications of his words.

"But that's impossible," Smith said. "You're trying to tell me that a woman overpowered three healthy men, tortured them, and killed them. It's just not possible."

"It would not have taken much to overpower them," Nick explained. "And fear can be a powerful demoralizer. The victims probably never knew their killer was even in the room until the last moment, and I'm sure the last thing they thought was that it was a woman. Our victims were paralyzed with fear, and you don't have to be a man to commit murder."

"What about Allun?" Smith asked. "It would have taken tremendous strength and force to maneuver the dead body onto the cross and then get up in the rafters and hoist the body up, upside down. And you want me to believe that a woman did all of this?"

"The person who attacked, and overpowered me in the library was a woman," Nick stated. "I have no doubt about that now."

"It fits," Sarrucci stated all of a sudden. "It fits better than a man as the killer would. This was probably a girl who was molested by someone close to her, a family member; hence the murder of Cooper. He molested his students, and this was the killer's form of revenge. As a teenager and a young woman, she probably fell easily into relationships with boyfriends who abused and exploited her because she did not know that there was anything better out there. She did not know that she should be treated better. That's why she killer Brenner, he raped and mentally abused the girls who wanted parts in his movies without even the slightest hint that it was wrong. They were so used to being used that it did not register that they had the right to say no.

However, I still think that there is some kind of splinter in your killer's personality. She does not disguise her voice because she is afraid of being identified, she does it because that voice is how she sees herself, or hears herself. The voice sounds strong, it sounds confident and devoid of fear. When she was being abused, most likely from the very beginning, her mind would go to a place where she felt safe, a place where she did not feel what was happening to her. I admit, it isn't real, but to her it was. It had to be, it was the only way she could get through it. In time, her mind created someone who would be there for her, someone who could never leave her; an alternate personality. I'm not talking about a split personality, it's not a total split because the created personality knows what is happening to the woman. The personality is most likely male, someone more able and apt to fight off her abusers."

"So you're not talking about schizophrenia, are you?" Nick asked, having had the same thoughts that Sarrucci was explaining now. "You're talking about something else."

"She created a safe haven," Sarrucci answered. "And from that safe haven in her mind, she created a hero; an avenger. He is the one who is killing; he is getting revenge, getting the satisfaction for her. This is probably someone you would never suspect, a highly functional individual who only thinks of herself as this man, this other personality when she kills."

"The devil you know," Smith muttered.

"What?" Nick asked, turning to the other detective abruptly.

"It's always the devil you know," Smith answered. "It's always the person you would least suspect."

"Who would we least suspect?" Nick asked.

"I don't know," Smith answered. "But whoever she is, someone else knows who she is. Someone who convinced her to kill Father Allun, that is, if you're theory is right. It might be easier if we try to figure out who put her up to it, and then go from there."

"I did come across a little tidbit of information that may or may not help you out," Sarrucci stated. "I couldn't get that wax seal out of my head. It's been driving me crazy, so I did a little research. Have you ever heard the saying, 'your fate is sealed'?"

Both detectives nodded absently, trying to understand where she was going with her question.

"The saying comes from a tradition that was common from the middle ages up until one to two hundred years ago," Sarrucci continued. "When a prisoner was sentenced to death, the sentence was written down on parchment and was only official when it was sealed with the wax seal of the magistrate and town or city officials. However, in the middle ages, the magistrate or town officials would have been..."

"The local priest," Nick answered, immediately understanding. In fact, it was as though a light had gone on in his mind, and suddenly all the missing pieces of Father Allun's murder were coming together.

"I don't know if that information helps you out any," Sarrucci commented.

"It answers all my questions. It makes it clear who put our killer up to murdering Father Allun," Nick said, shaking his head. "I know the who and I think I know the why, but getting him to admit it on the record is going to be difficult. This is not someone who will crack under pressure, this is not someone who will fold under the "Good Cop, Bad Cop" routine."

"What do you mean you already know who set the killer up?" Smith asked incredulously. "Do you already know who the killer is too?"

"I wish," Nick answered. "I've suspected Allun's murder to be something more than it seemed ever since we arrested Anderson. Now that we've laid the case out, I'm more certain of myself than ever. I just needed to hear other opinions, especially regarding the killer being a woman."

"You haven't sold me on that yet," Smith said. "I'm still unconvinced."

"By the end of the day you will be," Nick said, rising from his chair. "You will be convinced."

"Where are you off to now?" Sarrucci asked, sensing Nick's urgency.

"We're off to church," Nick answered. "We're after some absolution. The church says one can only receive absolution after confessing their sins. Well, I know someone who has a lot of confessing to do."

CHAPTER 61

Nick made a few quick calls on his cell phone, then slipped it back into his pocket and joined the quiet, somber mood of brooding that seemed to have enveloped the two men. The two detectives sat in their seats while Nick drove back to Norwich, each weighing the consequences of the actions they were about to take. Their meeting with Jessica Sarrucci, while productive might have been pointless because they had no proof. They were riding around, playing out theories that came up without the benefit of any evidence, and one day it was going to come back and bite them. In fact, it almost had in the case of Anderson, and ironically the only thing keeping them on the case at all was Anderson's hatred of the police force. The fact of the matter was, the killer was good. She, if the killer was in fact a she, knew how to cover her tracks and leave little to no evidence. At this point, Nick wasn't even sure if the clues linking the killer to a police officer were even real or made up. The only thing Nick was really certain about was the fact that the killer was a woman, and he was willing to stake his entire career on it. It was easy for Nick to believe that the killer was a female because he had seen her, been close to her, possibly fighting for his life. However, Smith was still finding the entire idea a little harder to believe.

Detective Kevin Smith could not be sure that it was not sexism that was driving his thought process, or whether there were any facts that were holding him back from believing in Nick's new theory. He had seen women kill before, and he was certainly not so naïve as to think that a woman could not defend herself against a man. What's more, Smith knew that women could be capable of emotional rage and taking that rage out physically. He had seen this aspect of women both professionally and personally. What held the Norwich detective back from totally buying into the theory was something else entirely. He could not help but focus on the differences in the murders themselves. Father Michael Allun had been displayed, tied to the cross and hung upside down from the rafters. The killer went to a lot of trouble to display Allun this way. As for Brenner, he too had been displayed, but there had not been the extreme effort to do so as there had been with Allun. Brenner had been left tied to his desk, where he had violated so many women and girls in the past. Smith could understand the meaning behind it, could understand the purpose of torturing both Allun and Brenner the way he did. Smith just could not get beyond the fact that there was nothing that linked Allun's private life to the way his body was displayed. Nick was right about one thing, there was a message being left there, and the police had to find out what it was. Nick had an idea that there was something more behind the murder of Allun, that the killer was driven to kill the priest by someone else. Smith was not sure about this thinking, and he was certainly not sure how they were going to get any information by going back to St. Patrick's Cathedral, but he was beginning to see where Nick was headed.

"You know he's not just going to open up and confess," Smith said finally. "He's not going to incriminate himself, even if he is the person who put the killer up to it."

"I know," Nick agreed. "And I'm not even sure that he did anything illegal. However, you must agree that there are differences between the murders of Allun and those of Brenner and Cooper."

"Of course I do," Smith answered. "But each murder has individual differences between the other two, I'm just not certain that the course of action we are about to take is going to bring about any new information. In fact, we could be burning a few bridges while we're at it."

"Well, you're more than welcome to stay in the car," Nick said. "But this is the only avenue I can see open to us, and we have got to come back with something solid or else."

"No, I'm coming with you," Smith assured his fellow detective. "I just want to make sure that you know what you're doing before you go in there."

"I hope I do," Nick answered as he pulled his car up to the curb in front of the steps that climbed up to the cathedral. Both detectives climbed out of the car and made their way up the steps, into the cathedral and back to the administrative part of the church, through the dark halls and quiet rooms that they had been down just two weeks earlier. Nick found one of the nuns who acted as the secretary for Bishop McAllister, and asked to see the bishop.

"I'm sorry detective," the nun began. "He is very busy in meetings today, and without an appointment you could be waiting for some time."

"I understand, sister," Nick said, remaining patient. He and Smith would wait here all day long if they had to, if it meant proving his theory right. Nick took a business card out of his pocket and jotted a little note on the back of it. He handed the card over to the nun. "Would you please just interrupt for a second and give him this. If he says to wait, then we'll wait. I really hate to be a bother, but I think he might want to see this immediately."

The nun took the business card and pressed it flat in her hands as if to hide the message written underneath. Nick was impressed with the fact that she did not even attempt to read the message, or even look at the underside of the card. She just smiled and made her way to the large door of the conference room that Nick and Smith had been in when briefing the priests about the case, just under two weeks earlier. While so much had happened in that time, Nick felt as though so little progress had been made on the case itself. After a few minutes, the nun returned and told the detectives that McAllister was finishing up with his meeting and would give them all the time they needed if they would not mind waiting just a few minutes. Nick agreed, though Smith asked if she could have the bishop meet them out in the courtyard, stating his desire to be out in the fresh air.

"What's your plan?" Smith asked, wanting to be sure that he was on the same pages as his colleague.

"My plan is to make him think we know more than we actually do," Nick answered.

"It's a dangerous game," Smith muttered. "This plan of yours better work because if it doesn't, there's no going back."

"Just follow my lead," Nick replied with a smile. Smith just shook his head and muttered something under his breath, clearly disapproving of the way in which they were going about collecting information. After a few minutes, the bishop came out and greeted both men, taking his seat on the bench directly across from Nick, just as he had the last time they all met.

"I feel like we've been here before," McAllister joked. Both detectives smiled. "Now, I understand from your message that you know who the killer is. What else can you tell me?"

"First," Nick began. "Let me start by saying that we are here today both as detectives, but we are also here for personal reasons. We're here to help; I want you to know that."

"All right," McAllister said, nodding his head as though he were trying to understand.

"We have the killer," Nick said. "It won't be broadcast to the press until this evening, as we have a few loose ends to tie up. We need to know where you stand exactly, before we can help you clean up this mess."

"I don't understand what you're saying," McAllister said, his face betraying genuine concern. "What mess, what loose ends?"

"Oh come on," Smith said, as if unable to control his anger. Nick just raised his hand, and then leaned forward towards the bishop.

"The killer has a..." Nick hesitated for a moment. "A rather interesting story. It's a rather damaging one if it turns out to be true, and the only people who know it right now are the three of us. However, time is not on our side."

"I'm afraid I don't know what you're talking about," McAllister said in an assuring tone.

"Perhaps you're not hearing us, bishop," Smith said, unable to contain his frustration at the lack of progress any longer. "The killer confessed after some...persuasion. Right now, we're the only three who know what actually happened with Father Allun, but soon that is no longer going to be the case. Even as we speak, the killer's private belongings are being inventoried and taken back to the police department."

"From what we understand," Nick said, returning the bishop's attention back on him, hoping to calm the atmosphere a little. "There is a world of information on the killer's computer. We need to know exactly what to be looking for if we are going to get the church through this, if we're going to get you through this."

McAllister just looked back and forth between the two men, saying nothing. The bishop's body language had changed, though. He was suddenly more withdrawn, drawing his arms close to his body and taking short, quick breaths. His mind was running a mile a minute, trying to determine just how much information to reveal.

"We get it," Nick continued. "Really, we understand. Allun was causing problems from within. He came here and expected to be given free reign, thinking that because he was Michael

TIMOTHY LASSITER

Allun, he would be instantly elevated to some position in here of respect and power. He was causing problems and day after day things were getting worse."

"Then there were his...predilections," Smith said, going from bad cop to compassion in the blink of an eye. "Allun was out there, having his private life, putting the church in line for one more scandal. He was getting sloppier in his attempts to keep his private life private, but he thought he had not been caught yet, he thought no one knew. It was that thinking that made him more arrogant here. It was only a matter of time before the word got out, and you had to do something."

"You could not let another scandal ruin the church," Nick said. "Especially not here, where there are so many people who need this place. There are so many people out there who depend on the church, and Allun was making himself quite the public figure. It was only a matter of time before it caught up with him. We understand that you did what you did to protect the church."

"You don't understand," McAllister blurted out, unable to contain himself any longer. "If this had happened before the casinos, before the attention, no one would have even noticed. But now, when there are so many poor people, so many undocumented workers here to make money off of the casinos, there are so many people who need the church for support. We don't just supply religious support anymore. For so many people, we supply food, clothing, help with housing and jobs, educational assistance. Allun was so selfish, ingratiating himself with the people, taking all the glory for himself. He thought that by making himself popular with the people, it would not matter if his private life was found out. He also used his works with the public to solidify his place here. I mean, it's not as though I could just have sent him away when he had just raised all of this money for the church."

"What should we be looking for?" Smith asked, trying to move the conversation along. McAllister sighed, and then looked down at the gravel path that led through the courtyard.

"A couple of weeks ago, I received an e-mail," McAllister said. "There were two pictures attached, Allun in an intimate embrace. One was with a woman; the other was with a man. The message said that I should keep a shorter leash on people who could be so damaging. I didn't believe it at first, and I just deleted the message. However, the following Monday I got another message, this time there were twenty photos, this time of Allun with another man and another woman. There were date stamps at the bottom of the pictures. The dates indicated that Allun had been with the man on the Friday and the woman on the Saturday. I had not suspected anything like that before the e-mails, so I decided to keep an eye on him the following weekend. It was true; he met men and women at clubs in Hartford, and then brought them back to his home. I was shocked; I did not know what to do. He participated in Mass that Sunday as though he were clean, as though he had any right to look down on the masses and give them absolution.

On Monday, I received another e-mail with pictures of Allun with the two people I had seen him with, but there was more. This time, there were pictures of me watching them. The message was kind, said that now I knew for sure. It said that there was someone out there who could stop Allun, bring compassion to the church. I agonized and agonized..."

"How did you contact the killer?" Nick interrupted. Nick could understand what the bishop was saying, understand what the bishop was feeling, but he was not going to listen to the man describe how difficult his decision was to have someone else end the life of a fellow priest.

"The e-mail included another address," the bishop answered. "It was different than the sender's address, told me to forward the e-mails I had received, with a note explaining my reasons to the e-mail address provided. I sent them, and the following Friday, Allun was attacked and was missing."

"And when you saw that his car was still in the parking lot, you drove it to his house and had someone bring you back," Smith said, putting the pieces together.

"Father Thomas has always understood the precarious position the church was in," McAllister said. "He understood it before I did. He saw through Allun's façade long before I did. Then we found Allun's body early Sunday morning, before anyone else did. I didn't know what to do, he was mutilated. We could not just leave him there like that. We found the cross in the basement; it had been a decorative fixture on the altar fifty or more years ago. The rope had been from the original light fixtures, when they were candles. Father Thomas and I bound Allun to the cross and hoisted him up with the old pulley system to the rafters."

"Giving you just enough rope to hang yourselves," Smith muttered.

"What?" McAllister asked, looking over at the other detective.

"We will be seizing your computer," Nick said. "We need to trace those e-mails to the killer, and to the person who got you in contact with the killer if they are indeed two different people."

"I deleted the messages," McAllister said, warily. "I didn't want anyone finding them."

"You can never really delete something," Smith informed the bishop. "There is always a footprint left behind. We'll get what we need."

"But you have the killer," McAllister interjected. "What do you need my computer for?"

"Forgive me father, for I have sinned," Nick said, an evil smile spreading across his face.

"Yeah, we kinda lied about that," Smith said. "We don't have the killer, though your confession will help immensely."

There was a look of panic and confusion as McAllister looked back and forth between the two detectives. Suddenly, understanding flooded his mind and a look of anger washed over his face as he realized that he had been set up all along.

"I won't cooperate," McAllister said, bolting to his feet. "It'll be your word against mine, and besides it's not like I killed Allun myself."

"No you didn't kill him," Nick said, rising as well. "But you did hinder a criminal investigation, tamper with evidence, and possibly assist in the commission of a felony. And by the way, it's not like we're alone out here."

Nick turned and pointed out over the courtyard, out to the street where three news vans were parked along the curb. Men and women were standing out on the street, some with directional microphones. The bishop knew what they were the moment he saw them, he had seen such devices on television. Nick then turned his attention to the two men in suits standing in the doorway to the cathedral with uniformed officers standing behind them.

"Those two men are detectives Wilkins and Mitchell," Nick said. "And Detective Mitchell there is holding a search warrant. I may not be able to arrest you for acting as an accomplice in Allun's murder, only time will tell. However, we will be able to seize anything here that we think might lead us to the killer, or to sending you to jail for the rest of your life. As for right now, you are under arrest for hindering a criminal investigation and tampering with evidence. Detective Wilkins, read him his rights please."

Nick turned to Smith, who was beaming with joy, and then both men turned to walk away as Wilkins approached to take the bishop into custody.

"How can you do this to me?" McAllister spat. "After all that we've been through."

"Consider it God's will," Nick said without looking back. "Maybe you'll find a priest in prison who will forgive and absolve you of your sins because no one here ever will."

"How did you figure it out?" McAllister asked. "How did you know it was me?"

"It was the wax seal," Nick answered. "You sealed his fate. He sealed his fate."

"Yes," McAllister whispered with a nod and a sympathetic smile. "It had been a gift to me once from the cardinal, a token of my faith. When I saw Allun hanging there, I knew that no matter what, the church would survive. No matter what horrible things came out in the course of the investigation, the church would continue on. It seemed...fitting."

"You were right," Nick said, shaking his head. "The church will survive; Allun's good works will be remembered. Unfortunately for you, the only thing anyone will ever remember about you is your fear, and how you tried to cover up something that was never a crime in the first place. Allun didn't break any laws, and he didn't force himself on anyone."

"He broke God's law," the bishop answered.

"Then so did you," Nick responded. "Which makes you no better than him."

CHAPTER 62

Outside St. Patrick's Cathedral, there was a buzz of anticipation that was almost electric. Everyone, public and media alike, converged on the scene as they all waited for the next piece of information to come filtering out of the giant building. Within thirty minutes, every local news channel had arrived and was reporting the breaking news, each telling the story of how Bishop McAllister had confessed his involvement in the murder of Father Allun to police. Because Nick had involved the press, the police were being portrayed in a positive light for once, something Nick's department desperately needed. McAllister had long since left the scene, heading straight to his lawyer's office to sort out the ramifications of his confession. Lawyers working for the Catholic Church had been sent directly to court in an attempt to corner any judge they could find to quash the search warrant. Everyone was in overdrive; everyone was trying to stay ten steps ahead of the impending fallout. Back in New London, the chief of police held a press conference with Lt. Hollings, spelling out the case and vaguely explaining where the investigation was going from there. Unfortunately, there was not much information to go on yet, but that did not stop the chief from capitalizing on any positive press. The police were finally back on the good side of the press, finally accomplishing something in the eyes of the people; and the chief was going to ride the sentiment for everything it was worth because he knew there was no telling how long it would last.

Inside the administrative wing of the cathedral, there was a more positive atmosphere. However, there was a different atmosphere on the inside than there was on the outside. Police from Norwich and New London were scouring McAllister's belongings, examining everything to get an idea of whether or not it would be useful to the investigation. Like ants in a colony, each working for the collective; every officer and technician set out with an individual purpose. McAllister's computer had long since been removed from the crime scene and taken back to the police headquarters in New London for examination by the computer experts. In Nick's estimation, the computer was the Holy Grail that he had come here for. Anything else they found was secondary to the possible treasure trove of evidence that might be found on the hard drive. Nick really wanted to be there, hovering over some poor technician's shoulder as they extracted old e-mails that might give them a clue as to who the killer really was. However, everyone could foresee Nick's presence as only serving to intimidate the technician, which could lead to mistakes, which was definitely something they could not afford with so few clues to go on in the first place. So Nick stayed, overseeing the search of McAllister's belongings as Detective Smith was outside supervising the search of the administrative files.

There was nothing for Nick to do now but wait. Everyone around him knew what they were doing and why. Nick needed to move the investigation forward in his mind, begin to focus on where he was to go from here. The first thing was a clue. He needed a clue, and most likely that clue was going to come from the hard drive of McAllister's personal computer. The police needed some sort of tip that would lead them to tracking down the person who had received McAllister's e-mail. From there, it was simply a matter of forcing the McAllister's internet service provider to give the police the personal information of the person who belonged to that e-mail address, and that was what warrants and subpoenas were for. The case could be closer to being solved then Nick believed, though there was a nagging doubt in the back of the detective's mind that told him this case was not over yet. The killer had not been so easy to track down so far, and Nick doubted the killer planned on giving up anytime soon. Nick replayed his conversation with McAllister in his mind over and over again. McAllister said there had been two different e-mail addresses. *Could this mean there were two people involved in this case, two murderers?* Nick shook his head for a second, as he knew that he was getting ahead of himself. Still, there was something about what McAllister said that bothered him. Why would the killer use two e-mail addresses? Why would he contact McAllister using one address, and then tell the bishop to forward the pictures on to another address? The more Nick tried to rationalize the killer's reasoning, the more questions the detective was left with.

Nick supervised the search for another half hour before he could not wait anymore. Finally, unable to suppress his curiosity any longer, Nick convinced Smith to come back with him to New London to see what evidence the technicians were able to pull from McAllister's computer. Nick pushed the speed limit the entire drive back, his thoughts focusing on the questions that were now become larger and larger in his mind. Nick did not dare tell Smith his concerns for fear of bringing the Norwich detective's optimism to a grinding halt. Smith was a good detective, but it took something substantial to get him moving in any one direction. Once he focused on a certain point in an investigation, it was hard to make him see anything else. Most cases were simple in that way. With most homicides, a good detective could get the sense of the motive right away and begin to form an investigation around that motive. This case was different, though. This case was something much different, and Nick had been forced to learn early as a detective to think outside of the box. It was that kind of thinking that had helped him to identify and capture the Nemesis, and hopefully, it would help him to capture this killer too, whoever she may be.

That was another issue between the two detectives. Nick knew that he had not sufficiently convinced Kevin that the killer was a female. This did not surprise Nick, as he knew that he had barely convinced Sarrucci of the same thing. However, now that the idea was out there, Sarrucci was beginning to come around to Nick's way of thinking. Though she had not been there when he had put the clues together, when he had matched the way Dr. Tanner had moved to the way the killer had moved that day in the Groton Public Library, Nick knew that the psychology of this particular killer was starting to fall in line with the idea that the killer was a woman. This forced the most obvious question, which woman? There had been no apparent links between young victims of Cooper and rape victims of Brenner. And though Allun had been removed from this equation in some ways, there was still the question of why the killer felt that Allun needed to die. Even now, detectives Wilkins and Mitchell were running down every name, every victim and or family member related to Cooper and Brenner's cases, searching for some common link or thread between them that might make sense. Since Nick had not heard from either of them, he was forced to assume that so far his detectives had not come up with anything yet. Still, there had to be something that connected these two victims, something that also linked Allun in some round about way.

"Sex," Smith said aloud out of nowhere. The two detectives had parked the car behind the police department building and were heading inside when the Norwich detective spoke up.

"What?" Nick asked, confused as he suddenly realized that neither man had said a word the entire drive back.

"I've been thinking about the case," Smith said. "I've been trying to come up with a possible name for our killer. To be honest with you, I've been trying to convince myself that the killer is a woman."

"And what have you come up with?" Nick asked.

"Well, to begin with," Smith started. "In the case of Cooper and Brenner, it's relatively easy to come with a list of people who had motive to kill them, men and women alike. However, we looked into the alibis of most of them."

"We did a cursory look at their alibis," Nick reminded his colleague. "Any one of them could be lying or have someone lying for them. We need to nail each one of them down."

"I agree," Smith answered. "But perhaps we're still looking in the wrong direction. We want there to be a link between Cooper and Brenner's victims, someone who was victimized by both of them and therefore had motive to kill them both. But maybe the link between the men isn't their victims, but the men themselves."

"Now you've really lost me," Nick admitted, trying to keep up with his colleague. The one thing that Nick was starting to become acutely aware of was the fact that everyone in this case was a victim of some sort. Allun, Cooper and Brenner were all victims because they had been brutally murdered. However, they had also created victims in the people they abused, either illegally or immorally. McAllister was a victim of Allun's way of life, wanting only to keep his world together and avoid a scandal. Anderson was a victim of the priest who started abusing both he and Allun. There was an over abundance of victims in this case.

"What links Cooper to Brenner?" Smith asked as he continued to explain his rationale. "What links the two of them to Allun? The only answer I can come up with is sex. Each man, in some aspect, exploited and betrayed the people they were having sex with. Cooper used his position as a teacher to create bonds of trust with his female students, and then pushed them a little at a time until they felt comfortable enough with him that they believed they wanted to have sex with him. Brenner did the same thing, but in a different way. Brenner forced himself on many of his 'actresses', some he basically downright raped, many others though he threatened in some form or another. It was the same thing with Allun, he gets his partners to feel comfortable enough to push the limits just a little, then a little further until they are doing things that they never thought they would do before."

"So it's not just the sex," Nick said, and for a moment, both detectives looked at each other, finally on the same page.

"It's the sex and the trust together," Smith said. "These people put their trust in our victims, and each one of them was betrayed. They were betrayed emotionally and physically, the most physical way being sexually."

"It makes sense," Nick said, nodding his head. "There are hundreds of names and profiles on the sex offender database. There surely were easier targets than Cooper if all our killer was looking for was revenge against any kind of sexual assault. However, our killer's guidelines for a next victim are quite specific; someone who abused the trust he was given to sexually abuse another person."

"Which would make sense if our killer was sexually abused," Smith said, carrying along the thought. "Someone who was abused and unable to get justice or retribution against the abuser. Now the killer stalks other abusers, hoping each time that killing the abuser will end her own pain."

Nick stopped dead in his tracks and looked up at the other detective.

"So now you believe our killer is a woman?" Nick asked, a smile slowly forming.

"Let's just say your theory is growing on me," Smith answered, unwilling to concede anything yet.

CHAPTER 63

The two detectives entered the police department and made their way below ground level to one of the many basement levels. The computer technicians were sequestered in a dark basement room with no windows where they stared at computer screens for most of their day. Oddly enough, they all seemed to enjoy the solitude and dark conditions under which they worked. Many officers did not understand these technicians or the computer crimes they worked, often making up condescending nicknames for the squad. However, the computer technicians shrouded themselves in the mystique of their jobs, causing an air of curiosity and mystery that surround the department and their particular jobs in it. Nick pressed a buzzer and heard the familiar click of the electronic lock being released, and pushed his way inside. In the early days of the computer crimes division, there had been some break-ins, some innocent and some not. Mostly, it had been frustrated officers attempting to get evidence from computers their own way, often times damaging and corrupting the evidence beyond retrieval. It was these over zealous officers who inspired the department to give in to the demands of the division to have extra security installed until the computer crimes division was basically a vault. As Nick entered, he recognized one of the technicians as Sergeant John Taylor, head of the division. The other two men were his subordinates, and though all the lights were out Nick was able to distinguish them from the light of the monitors they sat hunched in front of.

"Please tell me you have something," Nick said as he watched the three men furiously typing away. Taylor turned and smiled as he recognized the detective.

"Detective Nicholas Grenier," Taylor said as he looked at his watch. "Which, at ninety seven minutes, makes me the winner. Pay up you bastards."

The other two men groaned and reached into their pockets to retrieve twenty dollar bills, handing the money over to their superior.

"What's this all about?" Nick asked.

"I bet them that you wouldn't be able to go two whole hours without coming down to bug us," Taylor explained. "I won."

"Betting in a police department," Nick said. "That's pretty good."

"Oh relax detective," Taylor said, placing the money into a jar full of bills. "It all goes to the 'Geeks Night Out' fund. Each Friday, we take the contents of this jar and go party."

"Oh, I bet that's a real good time," Smith said sarcastically.

"You'd be surprised," Taylor said, turning around on his stool. "Now do you want to see what we've got or not?"

"Start talking," Nick said as he stepped up behind the technician.

"As you may or may not know," Taylor began. "Even though you delete something, it's never really gone. McAllister was cautious enough never to download his files to his hard drive. However, when he opened the e-mails that had pictures in it, his computer automatically used the media software originally installed to display the images. Those images were then 'imprinted' if you will, in the temporary files. Even when McAllister deleted the e-mails from his computer, he never thought to get rid of the temporary files."

"What about the e-mails themselves?" Smith asked. "Were they saved to the temporary files too?"

"Not entirely," Taylor answered. "Not the way the pictures were. However, we were able to get the e-mails from the service provider. You see, McAllister was not that computer savvy, and though he deleted his e-mails, he did not realize that they were saved to the temporary folder in his account for thirty days. I was able to pull them all up without any difficulty."

Nick and Kevin read the e-mails one by one, reading exactly what McAllister had told them. It was all there, just as he had said, someone watching Allun, using the pictures to insight McAllister to do the unthinkable. Nick looked up at the original e-mail address: ppptmstr@globomail.net. Then he memorized the address that the original sender advised McAllister forward the e-mail to: nkt331@globomail.net.

"What's globomail.net?" asked Smith. Nick had already figured out the answer though, he just needed to hear it from the expert.

"It's a free e-mail site," Taylor answered. "You can get an address anytime you like, and can check it from anywhere in the world. It's totally anonymous and, if established correctly, impossible to track. Globomail doesn't verify any information, so you could put in false personal information on the application and no one would know the difference. That's exactly what your guy here did, stating his name was Ali Baba and he lived on 40 Thieves Avenue. He got an e-mail address without any problem. Ppptmstr and nkt331 both used playful little first names and phrases to get their accounts set up. There is no way to trace them. I do have good news, though. Nkt331 checked his mail at different places every time, using free wireless access at places like the airport, coffee shops, computer cafes, however, there was a problem with the mail one time and he was forced to call in. The customer support logged in the phone number it came from. The call came from a phone number at the Yale-New Haven Hospital, from the office of Dr. Courtney Delaney."

"What do we know about Dr. Delaney?" asked Smith taking the slip of paper with the doctor's name and phone number out of Taylor's hand.

"Not much," Taylor admitted. "Delaney is a pediatric specialist at the hospital there, more than that is up to you."

"Thanks for the help," Nick said, stepping back. This was a lead, a positive lead, though something did not feel right about it. Dr. Delaney was a female, but Nick had not been prepared for the notion that his killer might be a doctor, much less a pediatrician. It did not seem to fit with his mental profile of the killer. "Keep working on the computer, I want you to suck every dirty little secret out of it."

Nick turned and looked over to Detective Smith, who was beaming.

"It looks like we are going to New Haven," Nick said. "And you're driving."

"Yes," Kevin exclaimed as he turned to walk out the door. "We're taking an unmarked cruiser and I'm going to use the lights the whole way down."

Nick followed Smith to the door laughing, astonished by how something so childish seems to come out of men when they start talking about driving at high rates of speed.

"Uh, Detective Grenier," Taylor began hesitantly. "A word about that computer game you asked me about earlier."

Both detectives stopped dead in their tracks, and Nick turned back to the sergeant confused.

"Computer game?" Smith asked, a mocking look beginning to form.

"Give me a minute, will you?" Nick asked, pushing Smith out of the door. Nick turned and walked back over to Taylor. "Computer game?"

"I needed an excuse to talk to you privately. I didn't mean to embarrass you," Taylor began. Both of his technicians stopped what they were doing and sat listening in on the conversation. "We did find something with the other e-mail address, ppptmstr."

"What did you find?" Nick asked, his curiosity piqued.

"I don't know who this ppptmstr is," Taylor began. "I don't know anything about him, but I think he's a cop."

"Why would you say that?" Nick asked.

"The server tracked back to where all the e-mails were accessed," Taylor said. "Each time it was a police department all over the state. Hartford, New Haven, Bridgeport, Groton, New London, Norwich, and many more. I just thought you should be aware of that, it could be anyone. I tried to dig further, but any deeper and Internal Affairs could be automatically alerted. They've set up spy software throughout the system; you never know where it is or when they're watching. I didn't want to risk it."

"Good thinking," Nick stated. "Who else knows about this?"

"Only the four of us," Taylor said. "And I will personally vouch for these guys."

"I understand," Nick said. Taylor was trying to impress on Nick the fact that any information the detective had could be compromised, and that whoever ppptmstr was, he could be someone he was working with. "Track the two e-mail addresses as best you can. Convince the server to contact you whenever these two log on. I want to know the moment they go on and where they are. Also, don't tell anyone about this; not Hollings, not the chief, not even my big friend Detective Smith. Tell no one, I just want this to be between the four of us. If anyone asks, you were following my orders, understood?"

"Understood," Taylor answered, appreciating the detective's statement. Nick had just absolved them of any responsibility should someone find out about the address. Taylor had always liked Nick, respected and trusted him. Nick always respected the role the Computer Crimes Division played in law enforcement, and could even see the need for the division to expand further as criminals became more computer savvy. In this matter, the two men understood each other completely. "You know what they say."

"What's that?" Nick asked.

"Watch you're back, Jack," Taylor answered, and turned back to the computer screen.

CHAPTER 64

The drive down Interstate 95 south to New Haven usually took about an hour when you factored in traffic and the never ending construction that plagued the highway as you got closer to the city. However, Kevin's skillful handling of the car made the drive in nearly forty five minutes flat. With lights only, the detective was able to keep them going at almost eighty five miles per hour the entire way, and with some alerts out to the patrolling state police; there was no interference on the drive down. Even Nick was impressed with the way in which his colleague handled the drive. There seemed to be something existential in the way Kevin maneuvered between other cars, sliding into and out of lanes. Never once was he forced to slow down, hit the brakes suddenly, or slip into the brake down lane. At one point, Nick commented that the detective might have missed his calling in NASCAR. Outside of his admiration for the other detective's driving, Nick kept pretty quiet during the drive down, thinking about what Sergeant Taylor had said to him before they left New London. There was something nagging at Nick, something trying to fight its way out of the darkness of a simple notion, trying to reach the light of understanding. There was a killer out there. Who she was and why she was killing these people was still more than a mystery to the detective. Worse than that though, there may be two killers. There may be a killer and an accomplice; there were many possibilities. The more Nick thought about it, the more concerned he was. There was no logical reason to give McAllister two e-mail addresses unless there was more than one person involved in Allun's murder. Two e-mail addresses only made it twice as likely for the killer to make a mistake, and this killer was not in the habit of making mistakes.

Nick tried to work things out in his mind, tried to come up with any logical reason for one killer to make it seem as though there were two people involved. Of course, someone might try to use this technique to throw the cops off of the trail. However, that was not what this killer wanted. This killer was proud of her handy work, she was not about to share the limelight with someone else. Nick could not understand why one e-mail address would be accessed only at safe locations where many people were accessing the same server at the same time, and have another address accessed only in police headquarters. Was the killer trying to make a statement, or was the accomplice? The fact that the bishop had been instructed to forward the e-mails on to the nkt331 address seemed to suggest that ppptmstr was the accomplice and nkt331 was the killer. Why wouldn't ppptmstr simply contact nkt331 himself? Why have McAllister go out of his way, causing a further trail that could lead back to one or the other, or both? There were too many questions, and for now, Nick needed to focus on capturing the killer, not the accomplice. The person behind ppptmstr was not killing people, not that Nick knew of. It was nkt331 that was the real threat, and it was nkt331 who had been in the Yale-New Haven hospital when she had called globomail customer service to fix a glitch in accessing the e-mail address. The call had come from the office of Dr. Courtney Delaney, and right now, that was the person that Nick had to talk to.

As the two detectives were leaving New London, Nick had called Hollings to keep her updated on the case and what information they had been able to glean from McAllister's computer. Hollings immediately alerted the New Haven police that the detective's would be coming down; a kind of professional courtesy one town would extend to another. After speaking with her New Haven counterpart, Hollings called Dr. Delaney directly to inform her that her detectives were coming down to question her. Both Lt. Hollings and Nick recognized immediately they had nothing to go on, no evidence to back them up and blitzing the doctor in her place of work would most likely only serve to make her clam up. If she knew anything at all, she was not likely to share it with Nick when he got there. That would mean two or more hours wasted with nothing to show for it. Hollings knew that the only way to gain the doctor's trust was to be up front with her and to see what happened. If Delaney did know something, or turned out to be the killer and tried to run, Hollings would know. Her counterpart had sent a detective over to the hospital to observe the doctor from a distance in case she tried to skip out. That was why the detectives were not surprised to find Dr. Courtney Delaney in her office with her lawyer when they were escorted in.

"Thank you for meeting with us, doctor," Nick said courteously as both detectives were invited to sit. "I know your time is precious and we have only a few questions for you."

"Dr. Delaney wants to cooperate with your investigation in any way she can," the lawyer began officially. "She merely called me to make sure that there were no misunderstandings, to make sure she wasn't railroaded."

"Why would we want to railroad her?" asked Smith, who was already suspicious by the presence of the lawyer.

"Let's face it," the lawyer said with a smile. "In this investigation, your department has been quick to misjudge innocent people."

The detectives knew immediately that the lawyer was talking about the incident with Mark Anderson, and Nick could not blame the doctor for being concerned. At the same time, it struck him as strange that she deferred to him for every answer. Though she did not look back over her shoulder as he stood behind her, she did not make any move to answer the questions for herself. This was uncharacteristic of doctors that Nick had met in the past, most of which were more than willing to give their opinion. Many he had met were absolutely unwilling to defer to anyone else, insisting on maintaining the image that they were the sole masters of their own universe. However, Delaney was different. There was a softness about her, something that seemed to immediately inspire trust and a feeling of safety. There was a motherly tenderness about her, something that must have made her quite endearing to her patients.

"Two and a half weeks ago," Nick began, trying to bring the conversation back on topic. "In the afternoon there was a telephone call placed from this office to the customer service number for globomail.net for help in accessing an e-mail account. Do you happen to have an account with them?"

"No," Delaney answered for the first time. "I have professional accounts with each of the hospitals to which I am affiliated with, and a personal account through America Online.

"But you are familiar with globomail.net," Smith chimed in. "You know that they provide free untraceable e-mail accounts."

"There are many services that provide free e-mail accounts, detective," the lawyer answered, placing his hand on the doctor's shoulder to keep her from answering. "Everyone knows that globomail.net is a free service."

"It can't be that untraceable if you used it to track down a call here," Delaney added, unable to maintain her silence. Nick smiled and nodded.

"That's a good catch, doctor," Nick pointed out. "I guess nothing is totally untraceable anymore. Everything leaves a fingerprint somewhere, just waiting to be found. Do you share this office with anyone else?"

"No," Delaney answered. "With the HIPAA guidelines, sharing offices puts the hospital at risk for a lawsuit. Yale-New Haven went out of their way to make individual offices for all of their specialists, no matter how cramped it might be.."

Nick looked around the office that was much larger than his own and laughed.

"You consider this to be cramped quarters?" Nick asked. "This office is easily twice the size of my own."

"Perhaps you should ask for better accommodations," the lawyer suggested. "Can we move on please, Dr. Delaney has patients to see?"

"Of course," Nick said, biting his tongue. "How many days a week are you here, doctor?"

"On a good week, maybe three days for about six hours a day," Delaney answered. "I make sure that I'm here at least twice a week."

"When you have privileges at six hospitals that must make it an extremely long work week," Smith commented. "How many miles do you put on your car in a day?"

"More than my share," Delaney answered. "I have a very tight schedule, and I need to maintain two homes in order to cut down on the travel time as much as possible. I have a condo here in New Haven and a home just outside of Mystic."

"My neck of the woods, eh," Nick mentioned. "Now for the record, what hospitals are you affiliated with?"

"I have privileges at Yale-New Haven, Hartford Hospital, Lawrence & Memorial, Backus Hospital, and Hasbro Children's Hospital," Delaney answered. "I have been fortunate enough to have success in pediatric oncology, and with it comes the responsibility of seeing patients where ever they are."

"Well, you certainly are a dying breed," Nick stated. "I've never known a doctor to put so much effort into seeing their patients. I'm sure they appreciate it. Now back to the telephone call, you're sure that you did not place the call to globomail. net."

"I believe Dr. Delaney has answered that question, detective," the lawyer said.

"Right, you use your personal account or your hospital accounts for your e-mails," Nick said, as though just remembering her answer. "Does your office here remain locked when you are not here?"

"Yes," Delaney said. "I am the only doctor who has access to the office."

"And your staff can't come in and use it when you are away?" Nick asked.

"My staff are all professionals," Delaney said firmly. "They don't play around in my office when I'm not here. Besides, they don't have access; none of them have a key."

"Were you here on that Wednesday, almost three weeks ago?" Smith asked, keeping the questions rolling, firing from every direction.

"I believe so," Delaney answered, suddenly shifting her attention to Detective Smith. "If memory serves, that was one of the weeks when I was able to be here on Monday, Wednesday, and Friday."

"So then you must have made the call to globomail.net," Smith stated.

"No," Delaney answered. "I told you I didn't call them. It must have been someone else."

"Who else could it have been?" asked Nick, causing the doctor to shift her attention again. They were getting her where they wanted her, vulnerable and on the verge of making a mistake; if she really was hiding something.

"I don't know," Delaney answered. "It could have been anyone."

"No," Nick said, waving his index finger back and forth. "According to you, you are the only person with a key to this office and your staff are professionals, they wouldn't just come in and 'play around' in your office."

"It could have been someone from the cleaning staff," Delaney stated, wracking her brain for any feasible answer whatsoever. She was becoming very agitated and it was very apparent to everyone in the room. "The cleaning crew has a key to the office."

"They clean during working hours?" Smith asked. "This call was placed at 2:31 p.m. that Wednesday."

"No, they clean at night, after everyone is gone," Delaney answered.

"So what then?" Smith demanded. "Who could have placed the call?"

"I don't know, I don't know!" Delaney screamed. She pushed back from her chair and rose, walking over to the window. She was visibly shaken, fighting back tears and her arms were trembling. Nick watched her for a moment as her lawyer walked over to her and whispered in her ear. Nick sighed as he watched her, knowing that she was not his killer. She did not have it in her to take lives, only save them. Unfortunately, the killer had been here, had placed that call from Delaney's phone.

"I believe you," Nick said, pulling out a slip of paper and placing it on Delaney's desk. "I'm sorry we upset you. By any chance, do you recognize either of these e-mail addresses?"

Delaney looked back over her shoulder at the detective, searching for some hint that he was mocking her. However, she found only compassion in his eyes, and took a deep breath and walked over to her desk and looked at the slip of paper.

"No," she said. "I don't recognize either of them."

"You're certain you've never contacted them, or been contacted by them?" Nick asked.

"No," Delaney answered. "I'm certain."

"We could subpoena your e-mail records," Smith said. "If you have anything to tell us, now is the time."

"You couldn't get a judge to sign anything," the lawyer spat back. "You've got no evidence."

The lawyer was right, and Nick knew it. If there was anything to get out of Dr. Courtney Delaney, they were going to have to get it through her cooperation. There was no evidence linking her to the telephone call or the e-mail account.

"This is our problem," Nick began, picking up the slip of paper and holding it between his fingers. "This address, nkt331 is our killer. Our killer was sitting right in your chair, using your phone to access this account at 2:31 on that Wednesday. There has to be some kind of answer, there has to be some way of accounting for that phone call."

"I don't know what to tell you," Delaney answered, exasperated. She looked and sounded physically drained. "I don't even think I was here around 2:30. My best friend surprised me by taking me to lunch; we were there until at least 3:30 if not longer."

"Do you remember whether or not you locked your office door when you left?" Smith asked softly.

"I don't know," Delaney answered, searching her memory for details. "I doubt it though, I usually only lock the door at night when I know that I'm not coming back anytime soon. I probably didn't lock it."

"So anyone could have had access to your office?" Nick asked, probingly.

"Theoretically?" Delaney asked. "Yes, anyone could have come in and used the phone."

"Our killer is a female," Nick informed her. "Physically fit with self defense training. She was most likely abused as a child, though her abuse could have come at any time during her life. She is angry, vengeful; possibly a man-hater. Does this describe anyone on your staff, anyone you know?"

Delaney's facial expressions changed instantly, as if an answer immediately popped into her mind. Nick saw it immediately, the light of understanding, then watched as Delaney's expression changed again, hardening.

"Unfortunately, I'm sure that describes a lot of women, detective," the doctor answered, as if giving a professional diagnosis. "However, I don't personally know anyone who fits your description. As for my staff, I'm afraid I don't know them that well. Now, if you'll excuse me, I have patients to attend to."

Dr. Delaney rose stiffly, as though the wind had been knocked out of her and she was only now trying to recover. However, she made it to her feet and stood solidly, and in that moment the detectives understood that the conversation was over. They rose from their seats and thanked the doctor again for her time, then made their way to the door. Just before he exited the office, Nick stopped and thought twice, then walked back over to the desk and handed Delaney a business card.

"If you think of anything," Nick began. "If anything comes to you, please call me. This woman is going to be caught, the ball is rolling and it can't be stopped now. I'm afraid; if someone else catches her, I'm afraid of what could happen. Do you understand what I'm saying?"

Delaney merely nodded, a single tear cascading down the track alongside her nose and down her cheek.

"If you think of anything," Nick stated, staring the doctor right in the eyes. "You've got to let me know."

CHAPTER 65

It was apparent to both detectives that Dr. Delaney was holding back at the end of the interview. She knew something, and it was significant. In fact, Nick was now certain that she knew who the killer was, and Delaney knew that Nick would know soon enough. The case was coming to an end, but it did not feel like it. The moment the detectives were back at the New London Police Department, the search was on. The task was to know everything there was to know about Dr. Courtney Delaney as soon as possible. That meant an exhaustive background check into her past, digging up everything there was to know about her; knowing where she was every minute of every day of her life. While that was not possible, finding out things about her past that even Delaney would have forgotten was not impossible, given they had enough time. The other task was to do a background check on everyone who Delaney worked with, especially staff. The first place they focused on was the staff at the Yale-New Haven hospital; anyone who Delaney worked with or who might have had access to her office. However, by Saturday morning they found nothing that could support the idea that a staff member might have been the killer. There was no one who met all the criteria already known about the killer. Though he did not ask, everyone stayed when Nick stayed, on through Saturday and into Sunday. There still was nothing to go off of. The police had gathered every shred of evidence on Delaney, and though the answer was there, it was still hidden.

While everyone else focused on staff members at other hospitals, any friends and acquaintances, and even the family background of her known patients, Nick focused on Courtney

Delaney herself. The answer was here, somewhere in the stacks of paper that made up her life. Nick had a copy of her birth certificate, a list of the schools she went to, every address she had every lived at, transcripts of her high school and college education, every paper and study she had every written, resumes and work transcripts; somewhere in here was the answer Nick sought. Somewhere in this was the answer to who the killer really was. Nick had not suspected Delaney; he had never gotten the feeling that she was the type of person who could deliberately kill another. However, there was a point in the conversation where everything changed; her attitude, her demeanor, and her responses. Nick needed to go back through his memory of their conversation; he needed to figure out the exact point when she knew. Nick replayed the questions and answers in his head, referring back to his shorthand notes every now and then to keep him on track. He remembered his thoughts and impressions during every question that was posed to her. He and Smith had ganged up on her during the beginning, trying to catch her off guard so that she might make a mistake. However, the more they questioned her, the more Nick was certain there was nothing to catch her in. He felt as though she had been telling the truth, she went out to lunch with her friend and the door had been left open. The call had been made at 2:31 to globomail.net. She hadn't lied or tried to make up an excuse where none was needed, she simply did not have an answer to their questions. They had pushed her so far that she had almost broken down in tears. She did not recognize the e-mail addresses; she did not even flinch when Smith threatened to get a court order to check her computer. *When did she change, when did she clam up?*

Nick slammed his fist down on the desk in frustration. He scanned his notes, looking for the answer. Delaney had changed when he began describing the killer. She had not changed when Nick told her that the killer had been there in the office, using her phone. No, it was when Nick described the past of the killer, the profile Sarrucci had described to him; that was when Delaney changed. Was it recognition of someone she knew, or was it recognition of herself? There was no evidence that Delaney had ever been abused either as a child or in a relationship. In fact, there had been no evidence Delaney had ever been in a meaningful relationship; a life always on the go seemed to put a damper on that. *What is it I'm missing, what did I say that really caught her attention?* Nick looked down at his desk again, staring at the papers strewn carelessly across its surface. A small slip of paper had dislodged itself from other papers when Nick had slammed his fist down, and now the detective cocked his head to the side to read it. It was the two e-mail addresses that Taylor had gotten from McAllister's computer. Something struck the detective as odd; e-mail addresses were usually names or nicknames, something that was associated to the account owner to make it easier to remember. Even though the killer had made this account exclusively for anonymity, there still had to be some significance to the e-mail names, they were not picked out of random letters. There had to be something there, there had to be a clue.

Nick looked at the first address, three letters and three numbers. He could not see anything there, and moved on to the second address. Nick put his pen down on a clean sheet of paper and rewrote the address with plenty of space between the letters.

P P P T M S T R

Nick tried to sound out the letters, started to put sounds together until he started to come up with something. As he continued to sound out the letters, a word formed: mister, or master. Nick began to realize that what he was missing here were vowels. As Nick tried to place vowels to create words, he finally came out with PUPPET MASTER. Nick quickly looked back through his notes and it fit. The first e-mails that were sent to McAllister were from the Puppet Master. This was the person who had found out about Father Allun, this is the person who had convinced McAllister to forward nkt331. The detective also realized that it was the Puppet Master who had been accessing the e-mails from police headquarters all over the state. The Puppet Master, whoever he was, had known about the killer all along, and had known who she was and what it would take to push her over the edge. But what about the killer then? Nick began to take the same approach with nkt331. Nick wrote out the letters as before, spacing it appropriately. Below that, he wrote out the vowels that could possibly go in between.

N K T 3 3 1

A E I O U Y ?

This puzzle was harder than the first. After Nick had figured out Puppet Master, it had not been so hard to realize this is what the account owner had wanted. The Puppet Master was not really trying to hide anything. However, nkt331 was more of a code, something that Nick could not see at first. He was still dealing with consonants, there were no vowels. Unfortunately, he could not see where the vowels would go to form a word. As he worked the problem, something started to nag at his brain; there was a code here. Nick rewrote the vowels out.

A E I O U

1 2 3 4 5

Then he wrote out what he saw there on the paper, replacing the numbers for vowels.

N K T I I A

That was when he saw it; that was when the detective solved the equation. Nick placed the vowels between each of the consonants until he came up with the work NIKITA. Nick flipped furiously through Delaney's paperwork, looking for anyone who might fit with the name Nikita. However, there was nothing; no friends, no colleagues, no staff, no family. Who was Nikita? Why use that name? Nick reclined in his chair for a moment and closed his eyes, searching his brain for anything that might come to mind when he thought about the word Nikita. Unfortunately, there was nothing. Nick snapped back to the upright sitting position and double clicked the internet icon on his computer screen. Nick typed the word Nikita into the search bar, and the answer came up as clear as day; La Femme Nikita. Nikita was an assassin, a female assassin. The same was true for nkt331; she too was an assassin. Nick shook his head and looked back down at the desk. Now the detective just had to figure out how Nikita was connected with Dr. Delaney. How did she know this Nikita? Nick picked up the enlarged picture of Courtney Delaney's drivers license.

"How do you know..." Nick trailed off when he read the card. There was something familiar, something that he had not seen before. "Oh, fuck."

Nick dropped the paper down on the table and rummaged through his files until he found another form with Delaney's personal information on it. Nick compared the two pages, the date of birth, the eye color, and the address. The detective felt as though he were sitting in a sauna, as waves of heat seemed to wash over him. Nick felt weak, as though he were suddenly drained of life, as he came to the realization that the answer had been staring him right in the face the entire time. Everything he had ever learned in the last two weeks rushed through his brain like a raging river, everything coming together at once.

"Nikita," he whispered. Suddenly, there was a sharp knock at the door and Nick jerked his head up to see Hollings standing in the doorway.

"Unless you say otherwise, I'm sending everyone home," Hollings said. "They've been at it for two days straight, taking no time off."

Nick just turned his head away, looking down at the floor for a moment.

"Nick, are you alright?" Hollings asked. "You look as though you're about to throw up."

"I'm fine," Nick said, choking back all of the emotion that was raging through him at this moment. He looked up at Hollings and smiled a partial smile. "You're right, send them home. It's all over now."

Hollings face went slack and she stepped into his office completely. She looked down at the detective and scanning his facial expression for any hint of jest.

"It's over?" she asked. "You know who the killer is?"

"Yes," Nick answered in barely a whisper. "I know who the killer is."

"The doctor; Delaney?"

"Yeah," Nick said, nodding his head. "She knew the moment I described the background of the killer. She did not know before then, but once I made it clear that we knew there had been abuse, then she knew."

"What are you going to do now?" Hollings asked.

Nick took in a deep breath and smiled completely. He rose from his desk and walked around to where his lieutenant was standing.

"The sun is setting, it's Sunday and the weekend is coming to a close," Nick stated. "I am going to go home and bask in the loving of a good woman before I close this case. Then tomorrow; tomorrow we'll end this."

"Do we have that long?" Hollings asked.

"Trust me," Nick said. "Nothing will happen between now and tomorrow. Have everyone here first thing tomorrow morning."

CHAPTER 66

Nick knew that now was not the time for him to be alone, and he knew that there was no where else he wanted to be right now than with Jenn. He drove over to her home unannounced, hoping first that she would be home, and second that she would actually want to see him. He could not imagine what she had been thinking as he had not even checked his cell phone over the last two days, much less answered any messages. He needed to be somewhere where he would not have to think about the case, and though he was not certain that would be possible, he was about to find out. The sun was setting in the sky, and if there was ever a good time to sit out and watch the sun set over the water, now was it. Nick rang the doorbell to Jenn's home and she came to the door with a smile.

"Good to see you're still alive," she said, opening the door to him. "I was about to call the police."

"It wouldn't have done any good," Nick answered, kissing her. "They're all busy trying to solve a murder case."

They went out to the deck and, with beers in hand, watched the sun until it had disappeared below the horizon, leaving a beautiful palette of colors hanging in the sky. Nick watched as the clouds slowly changed colors, feeling as though this were the last night on earth. To her credit, Jenn just watched the sunset with him, saying nothing. She simply watched the man she loved and the beautiful scene, her eyes flicking back and forth between the two. She could tell there was something hanging on Nick's heart, and she knew that he would let it out in his own time. As for Nick, tomorrow would be the day. Tomorrow he and Smith would finally close the case; they would arrest the killer and then pass the case off to the district attorney, hoping for a plea bargain. Nick had no desire to return and testify in the case later on, but with his luck, there would be no plea deal and he would have to face the killer he had spent the last two weeks hunting down, unmasked and unarmed.

"All right," Jenn said, unable to contain her curiosity any longer. "What's eating you?"

"Nothing," Nick said. "It's just that tomorrow we're going to put this case to bed once and for all."

Jenn stared at him for a moment, surprised, waiting for him to finish his thought.

"You know, you were right," Nick said, looking back at her. "I should have gotten out of this case when I had the chance."

"You can't win them all," Jenn said in an attempt to make him feel better. She had no idea that he knew who his killer was. "There was no evidence that was helpful, and you've had to deal with a lot of obstacles. Hell, this wasn't even your case to begin with."

Nick looked at her for a moment, and then smiled. She could not imagine that he could be sitting here, telling her the case was coming to an end in this way without thinking he would be more optimistic about it. Though she loved him and was trying her hardest, she really did not understand him at all. It was only to be expected though, as he really did not know much about her either. It was hard to believe that she was in love with him, and he with her though he had not verbalized it yet, in such a short amount of time. He wondered if this was really something they would be able to continue past tonight. Things would be different in the morning. Nick was going to make a big arrest, one that would turn the entire police department upside down. After that, Nick was going to begin his search for the Puppet Master, who like the Wizard of Oz was hiding behind the curtain, calling all of the shots. Whoever this Puppet Master was, he had his part to play in this case, and he was going to have to answer for it too.

"Maybe it's for the best anyway," Jenn continued, unaware that Nick was swimming in the deep end of his own thoughts. "Maybe its best that the killer just fade away, never to be seen or heard from again."

"What?" Nick asked, coming back in on the conversation on only a few of her words. He had missed the gist of her comment, but something there had caught him as an idea.

"If you're being forced to close the case," Jenn said, looking over at him. "Maybe it's for the best. I mean, even if the killer was caught, it would only serve to dredge up more victims in this case. If the killer wanted his day in court, he could make it very messy for everyone, including the Investigations Unit. Maybe it's just best that he disappear, never to be heard from again."

"What makes you think the killer would just disappear?" Nick said, his mind beginning to run on overdrive.

"I don't know," Jenn answered with a shrug. "I guess I had just assumed that since there had been no further contact from the killer, that he was basically done. It just seemed as though he was out to make a point, and now that his point is public, there is no need for him to continue."

"So you think the killer would just skip town?" Nick said, considering the idea. "You think that the killer would just fade away, never to be heard from again."

"I hope so," Jenn said, rising from her seat. "It's the only way everyone can save face. Do you want another beer?"

Nick just nodded and listened to Jenn walk away from him and into the house. For the first time in the detective's career, in his career as a police officer, Nicholas Grenier was considering an end that did not include arresting the bad guy. Nick found himself contemplating the idea of somehow getting the killer to run. Jenn was right; it was the only way for everyone to save face. Right now, there was a woman out there who had killed three people, a woman who had the trust of the police and the public, a woman that Nick did not want to see go to jail for the rest of her life. To throw this woman in jail would hurt everyone, and would damper the good she had done in her life. There had to be another way, and Nick realized that now he had it. However, there was no way for Nick to make the suggestion; she would only feel betrayed by him. It was years of betrayal that led to all of this in the first place. There was someone, though, who could convince the killer to run. Someone who could convince the killer to run and to keep running until she got somewhere where no one was looking for her; where no one would recognize her. It was a childish plan, and Nick could see it for what it truly was; denial. Unfortunately, Nick was too invested now, and he had to do what he could. Nick could hear Jenn in the kitchen, singing to herself. She was happy, they were happy together. He did not want to leave now, but he had no choice. Hopefully she would come to understand; hopefully she would see why he did what he did. Hell, it had been her idea all along.

Nick got up and stealthily slipped down the wooden steps that led to the walkway that in turn led down to the beach. Instead of heading toward the water, Nick made his way around the house and to his car. He jumped in and turned on the engine, spinning his wheels for a minute in the gravel before tearing off out of the driveway and down the street. Nick turned his cell phone off; he did not need any distractions now. He would have some explaining to do when Jenn got back and found him gone. For now, however, he had a case to sabotage if he could. Nick drove towards New Haven, not taking the speed limit anywhere near the speeds Kevin had taken it earlier in the day. It was a Sunday night and the traffic was pretty light, and Nick made good time. He took his time though, thinking about what he was going to say when he confronted Delaney. He had to convince her to see things his way; it was the only way that would make it so everyone could sleep at night. Nick had memorized Delaney's condo address from the records the police had pulled on her, and maneuvered his way to her home relatively easily. Nick climbed out of the car and found her door number and knocked hard. There was a voice from behind the door, and it opened softly as Delaney stuck her head out. She was surprised for a moment, and then shook her head.

"What are you doing here?" Delaney asked. "I've told you all I'm going to tell you."

"When I left this evening," Nick began. "I left with a plan. I think it is the only way we can all get through this without destroying ourselves. Before I left town, I swung by your home outside of Mystic. It's a nice place; it's too bad you don't get to stay there more than you do."

"What are you talking about?" Delaney asked, truly confused.

"I know who the killer is," Nick stated. "And you know who the killer is. You knew the moment I gave you the profile, it fit this person to a tee. Your friend came down to surprise you here in New Haven almost three weeks ago. You said the two of you went out for lunch, but before you left, she used your office to place a phone call. She had tried to access her e-mail account from your computer and had not been able to, and she did what any frustrated computer user would do and called the help line. She never thought it would come back to you."

"I don't know what you're talking about," Delaney spat. "You don't know what you're talking about."

"I know that this is not going to end the way you hope it will," Nick promised. "Denying the truth is not going to make all of this go away. You have to help me; you have to tell me what you know."

"I'm not going to help you bury her," Delaney said, almost whimpering.

"There are only two ways this can happen successfully," Nick said. "Either I catch her and arrest her, or your friend disappears."

"You could stop chasing her," Delaney offered. "You could close the case and let the thing go."

"It's too late for that," Nick said. "Even if that were a possibility, my colleague would not be able to do the same. Detective Smith is no idiot, and just because he doesn't know what I know does not mean he won't figure it out any minute now."

"Why can't you just let this go?" Delaney asked, tears welling up in her eyes.

"I can't," Nick said.

"Just let it go," she pleaded.

"I can't!" the detective exclaimed. "In my short time as a homicide detective I have been forced to accept things about myself that would make any other person put a gun in their mouth. I have accepted who I am, but it is very hard for me to balance one with the other."

Nick stopped when he realized that Delaney did not quite understand what he was saying. He looked at her, seeing her now in a way he had never really seen a woman before. This was a woman who was as torn as he was, torn between what was right and what she felt in her heart. Nick had not considered what a shock it must have been for her to discover that her best friend was a killer, and that she would have to make a decision that she and she alone would have to live with for the rest of her life.

"Let me put this in a way I think you will understand," Nick began. "I now have two loves in my life. One is my job; the other is a beautiful woman who I have been seeing for a short time now. Each are a part of me. If I had to choose between one or the other, I don't know how I would survive. I can't have one without the other, I can't be whole without being a cop, and I can't be a better cop without her love. To just close the book on this killer is would be like trying to ignore the cop in me, it would destroy everything. It's because of these feelings that I can't simply just let a killer walk around without trying to stop her.

I figure it must be the same for you. Your life is your devotion, your devotion to your job and patients, and your devotion to those you love. You love your friend, you want to protect her, especially after the kind of life she's had. At the same time, you can't reconcile what you know to be right with what she's done. You took an oath to save lives, but you have an unspoken oath to your friend. How can you let your friend take lives and not do something about it, how can you reconcile this in yourself?"

"I can't, okay," Delaney blurted out. "It's killing me, but I can't betray my friend."

"Your friend needs saving," Nick pointed out. "And we're the only ones who care enough to try. Everyone else wants to catch her, arrest her, or worse. I wasn't lying to you, what I said in your office today. If I don't catch her, if someone else does, I'm afraid of how it will go down."

Delaney stared at the detective for a moment and began to truly understand how invested he was in this case. At that moment, she began to understand that they were very much alike. She started to understand that they needed each other, that the only way either would get through this was with the other's help.

"You can't just walk away?" Delaney asked.

"I can't just walk away," Nick answered.

"Then maybe you should come inside so I can tell you who she really is," Delaney said, opening the door so that the detective could step inside. "Maybe then you'll understand what you're up against, what I'm up against."

Nick nodded, relieved that he had been able to convince her to let him in. This was going to be a long night, but he needed to be here. There was much more to this story that needed to unfold before he could truly put this case to rest.

CHAPTER 67

Nick sat down on the couch across from Courtney Delaney, who sat on the hearth just in front of the fireplace with a cold drink in her hand. A wire screen had been placed in front of the open fireplace, and through the screen Nick could see candles, all set at different levels, burning together to give the appearance of a fire. The doctor offered Nick a drink, which he refused on the grounds that he would have to drive back home at some point. Courtney just smiled and muttered something under her breath, giving the detective the impression that he was going to need a drink before the night was over. This was the defining moment; this was when Nick was going to learn all of the horrible things that had made his killer who she was. This was going to explain the unexplainable; this was literally the moment of truth. Nick did not really want to know what he was about to learn, but he knew that there was no other way now. He was too invested, he was in too deep. There was no going back, he was sitting inside Courtney's living room, he had connected with her on a personal level. They had become one concerned entity, and there was no way he could turn away and tell her that he could not stand to hear what she had lived knowing about for so many years.

"Let me tell you about your killer," Courtney began, summoning up the courage to proceed. "Let me tell you about my friend. She was born Erin Thompson, a pretty little blond girl who was my best friend. She came to live in the house down the street from me when she was five, and we became inseparable. However, before that, she had lived alone with her mother. Her parents divorced when she was three or four, her father just up and left one day. Her mother had to take three jobs to support them, and Erin very rarely ever saw her mother. She spent almost seven days a week with a next door neighbor who used to watch Erin for her mother. In fact, the only times Erin ever knew her mother was home was when she was crying, crying that her husband had left her all alone with nothing but debt. Erin's mother worked long hours at three very hard jobs only to get paid less than the men who were not as qualified. Erin's mother had to put up with daily sexual harassment because we are talking about a time when treating women like a piece of meat was acceptable. Then, on top of all the rest, the day finally came when her mother's boss tried to force himself on her. When her mother pushed him off of her, he struck her across the face, and then promptly fired her. Unfortunately for little Erin and her mother, that had been the night job that paid more because it was third shift; the very job her mother needed the most. Then came the day when Erin's aunt, her mother's sister came to the house and for the thousandth time told Erin's mother that they could come and stay with her and her husband. Erin's mother said the same thing she always said, that she did not want to be an imposition, but for some reason Erin's aunt would not take no for an answer. Erin's mother thought about this some, and realized that with two jobs and no rent, they would actually be making more money than when she had three jobs and rent. This is when we go from Erin's mother's nightmare to little Erin's nightmare.

So mother and daughter pack up their little orange Ford Pinto and move in with Erin's aunt and uncle. Erin's aunt is a sick woman who has developed this strange cough that never seems to go away. The only time her aunt actually feels relief is when she...wait for it...smokes cigarettes. God bless Marlboro. So Erin's aunt is home all day and can't work so her mother feels perfectly safe having two full time jobs and leaving little Erin at home with her aunt. Besides, it's only for a little while, and one day Erin will be old enough to understand why her mother worked so hard. Erin's mother works days as a secretary at an elementary school and nights at a local restaurant. Erin's uncle is a raging alcoholic who, when drunk, realizes he has a hard, long love for his little niece. He waits until his wife is asleep, a woman who can't stay awake past eight in the evening, then comes home from the bar and looks in on his little Erin. He starts with just watching, rubbing himself as he watches his five-year-old niece sleep. Except, little Erin is not asleep, she can smell the stench of whiskey and beer from the door. You see, little Erin's uncle is the man that all the parents on the street keep an extra eye on. He's the man who your parents warn you about, tell you to never be alone around. Unfortunately for little Erin, none of those parents had the courage to tell her or her mother about that. After awhile, her uncle becomes more courageous, and starts to sit at the edge of the bed and watch her sleep. Finally, he reaches the point where he can't stand it any longer, and just climbs right in, touching her everywhere, rubbing himself against her.

You see, I never understood why Erin wanted to spend so much time at my house. I thought it was because I had a better collection of Barbie's. My parents suspected though, and tried to accommodate little Erin as much as possible. Hell, as she got a little older, she was at my house more than she was at her own. I did not realize that it was because little Erin's uncle had gone from rubbing himself against her to forcing himself on her. She dealt with the abuse for almost ten years, never letting on, never saying anything. Finally, one day she was just gone. She had run away and it caused the biggest commotion I had ever seen in my neighborhood. Her mother searched high and low for her, my parents scoured the county searching for her. I did not realize, but my parents had not told Erin's mother that they were looking for her, and they had no intention of doing so. My father had always known what kind of man Erin's uncle was, but could never prove it. My father was a smart man, and he was a powerful man; but even he never found Erin again. I didn't even see or hear from Erin again until two years ago, but we'll get to that later. Erin ran away, ran to a convent that took in stray children three counties away. To this day, I don't know how she managed to get there alone. However, she got there, and they took her in no questions asked. Why ask questions, the nuns had seen this story so many times before, and they would see it long after Erin left them. They gave Erin a new name, as she refused to give them her own, and became Mary J. McKelley; apparently the nuns thought she looked Irish.

Mary McKelley finished high school in a catholic school run by the nuns. Mary McKelley finished third in her graduating class, though she would have been valedictorian had she not 'forgotten' to answer some very crucial questions on her final exams. You see, the valedictorian gets the picture taken for the local newspaper, and Mary McKelley could not risk anyone recognizing her and putting two and two together. When Mary McKelley applied to college, she was accepted every time, but oddly enough, she picked the school that was farthest away from where she had grown up, and never looked back. She moved out to college and hit the books. She got such good grades that one of her professors suggested she take an I.Q. test. Mary McKelley said, why not, and took the test. She maxed out the Stanford-Binet I.Q. test, and when I say maxed out, I mean they had to raise the bar of genius for her. She had never told me what the score actually was, but from what I have been able to understand, the score of 150 is labeled as genius, and she scored about twenty points higher. She breezed through her first year at college and started to feel as though she had escaped her past. She even fell in love; that was when her nightmare began again. Her first love was a fellow student who was so bitterly depressed because she was smarter than he, that he beat the shit out of her regularly. Apparently, book smarts don't always mean real world smart and she stayed in this abusive relationship for three years. He would beat her, and she would try to help him. He would drink, and she would cover for him. He beat her so regularly that she actually could tell when it was going to be a bad beating compared to a relatively average attack. It wasn't until the time that she inadvertently fought back, that she realized she had had enough.

Her prick of a boyfriend came home one night, ragingly abusive, and she had tried to protect herself and ended up hitting him without knowing it. Her body must have sensed that he was going to kill her, and something forced her to strike out. He was so caught off guard that when she realized what had happened, she could not stop herself. She beat him so hard that night he had to be hospitalized. She lied and said he had gotten into a fight at the local bar, and he had been too proud to tell the truth. From that moment on, she had become intoxicated by her new found power, and by the fear it caused. She abused him regularly, tortured him slowly but painfully, making him beg for mercy until he was crying like a scared child. However, she could not forgive herself for what she had done, for giving in, and she said she actually felt as though it were someone else doing it, she said she felt as though she were a man for once in her life. Anyway, she finally broke up with her boyfriend, finished college, and moved away again; changing her name for the last time.

So you see now; your killer, my friend has no true identity. She is nothing more than many different pieces of all the people she has ever had to be. She put these pieces together and came up with the person she is now; a person so distorted, so full of anger and hate that she has no idea who she ever was in the first place."

Nick rose from his seat on the couch and walked around to the sliding glass doors that looked out into the pitch black darkness. Though he could see nothing, he just stared out of the window, his mind on fire.

"This is going to sound corny, but I can't imagine what it must have felt like," Courtney said, staring into her drink. "What does it feel like to give into the darkness inside?"

"It feels like a second skin," Nick said absently, remembering the moment when he nearly gave in himself. "It feels like coming home. It feels like the place you were always meant to be, warm like a blanket. It feels like perfection, like you've found your place in the world."

Nick turned to find Courtney staring at him, shocked and slightly appalled.

"Though you can't stay there," Nick continued. "You can't stay in that place because for people like me and little Erin, our bitterness and pain fills that home up too quickly, until there is no room to maneuver. You see, we've seen what it is to be loved, we've seen what everyone else has and we want it too. So we hide our true nature, we try to control our true nature. Some of us, like little Erin, bury their pain hoping that it will die; but it never dies. It just grows and grows until it explodes and little Erin loses all control of it."

"So what do we do?" Courtney asked, looking up at the detective. "Do we turn her in?"

"You need to call her," Nick said. "You need to tell her to run. If she runs, if she flees the state, she will be out of my jurisdiction and I won't have the authority to pursue her. She can become Mary McKelley again."

"I can't tell her to run," Courtney said. "I can't tell her go back to the life she lived before. She has never been so complete since she decided to stop running."

"I can't call this investigation off now," Nick said, trying to make the doctor appreciate the position he was in. "My boss knows I know who she is. My boss is expecting me to make an arrest tomorrow. My boss is expecting me to close this case tomorrow, and it will be closed."

"I won't tell her to run," Courtney said, adamantly.

"Then I need your permission to search your home outside of Mystic," Nick said. "I have to do this officially, and if there is evidence, it could be in the house."

"I will not give you permission to search the house," Courtney said softly. "I will not betray my friend."

"My boss expects me to do whatever I have to do," Nick said, trying to explain. "I will get a search warrant and pull that place apart."

"I understand that you have to do what you have to do," she said. "I have to do what I have to do."

"If you don't call her," Nick warned. "If you don't tell her to run, the next time you'll see her will be in prison."

"I will not tell her to run," Courtney said, rising to her feet. "I will not tell her to go back to the life she had before. I will not betray my friend."

Nick smiled, as though he had known this would be her answer all along. He nodded and sighed.

"You're a good friend," Nick said, turning to leave. He paused for a moment and looked back. "I promise, she will never know we had this conversation. You can be at peace with the knowledge that you never betrayed your friend."

Nick left Courtney standing alone in her living room, crying. The drive back to New London seemed as though it would never end. Strangely enough, there was no apprehension about the next step. There was no uncertainty about the next move in his investigation. He called Hollings and asked her to locate the prosecutor he dealt with most often, and was surprised when his lieutenant called back and told him she was in her office preparing for a case. Nick thought he was the only person who voluntarily worked on a Sunday. Nick went to the District Attorney's office and made his way back to the office of Amanda Cross, a junior prosecutor who had been very helpful in getting Nick some warrants when he had questionable evidence.

"Ms. Cross," Nick said as he came to her door. "I'm surprised to see you working this late on a Sunday night."

"Oh shit," the young lady exclaimed. "Is it Sunday already, I am really screwed. What can I do for you, detective?"

"I need a search warrant," Nick answered. "It's for the home of a woman who knows my killer."

"Is there any evidence that links the owner to the murders?" asked Cross.

"No," the detective answered.

"Is there any evidence that the killer left evidence of a crime at the owner's home?" Cross asked, appraising the detective. Nick held his breath for a minute and then sighed.

"Not really," he said.

"Then there's nothing I can do for you," Cross said.

"Look, I really need a favor here," Nick said.

"I'm sorry, detective," Cross began. "But tonight, I'm all out of favors. You see this pile of shit I have spread out across my desk. This is the nightmare case that was dropped in my lap Friday afternoon as I was leaving for the weekend. I've been trying to find a way to avoid torpedoing my career for the last forty eight hours."

"What is this?" Nick asked.

"You know who Jonathan Menler is, right?" the prosecutor asked.

"The Jonathan Menler?" Nick asked. "Who doesn't?"

"That's right folks, the Jonathan Menler," Cross said, sarcastically. It was becoming obvious that the forty eight hours straight she had kept herself awake on coffee, caffeine drinks, and eye drops were begin to wear on her. "The same Jonathan Menler who brutally raped sixteen women and was convicted to...count it with me now...three hundred and thirty two years in prison. It was a big win for the prosecutor. However, at three Friday afternoon, Menler's new attorney drops an appeal off here that slowly makes its way down to me. In it, Menler claims that some of the evidence that was seized upon his arrest for rape sixteen, which was the very evidence that convicted him for rapes one through fifteen, was in the car that belonged to his brother which just happened to be sitting across the street from Menler's home. Because the car did not belong to Menler, it falls outside of the scope of the search warrant, and therefore..."

"Is fruit from the poisonous tree," Nick said, finishing the prosecutors thought.

"That's right," Cross said. "Without that evidence, the judge will be forced to drop the convictions on the other fifteen rapes, and will have to reduce his sentence according to the conviction of one rape, which with time served makes Menler eligible for parole in less than five years."

"Shit," Nick exclaimed. "Why are they having you handle the case? With all due respect, you're a junior prosecutor. Wouldn't they want a more experienced lawyer handling the case?"

"They would if they had any chance of winning," Cross said. "But as it seems Menler and his lawyer are right about the evidence being in his brother's car, they are more than willing to let the shit roll downhill. I have been crawling through law books, bending every loophole trying to keep from being the prosecutor who let the worst serial rapist in Connecticut history out of fifteen convictions."

"When do you have to be in court?" Nick asked.

"Tomorrow morning," Cross said, smiling a strangely insane smile. "I might be able to push the hearing off into the afternoon, but I can't do any better than that. Which is why I can't get you your search warrant. Sorry, thanks for playing. Do stop by again."

Nick laughed and shook his head.

"Fuck the search warrant," the detective said. "Stall the hearing until the afternoon and I'll take care of the rest."

"Oh really," Cross said, with a little cackle. "The great Detective Grenier is going to pull some kind of legal miracle out of his ass to save the day. I know you're good, but I didn't know you were that good."

"I didn't say anything about a legal miracle," Nick said. "However, I doubt you want to know about any illegal ones."

"No, I'm afraid that as an officer of the court, I don't want to know about anything illegal," Cross said, eyeing the detective warily.

"That's what I thought," Nick said, walking around a chair and sitting in front of her. "You see, I'm not good at all. I'm bad; I'm very, very bad. Now, tell me everything there is to know about Jonathan Menler."

CHAPTER 68

In Somers, Connecticut, near the northern border of the state, where Connecticut and Massachusetts met, stood the Northern Correctional Institution. Northern was Connecticut's only purely level 5 maximum security prison, housing those offenders who posed a threat to other inmates, and those who could not adjust to the prison life of general population. This is where Nick found Jonathan Menler. Menler had originally been housed in a level 4 security prison, but after being attacked repeatedly and beating his attackers to the edge of near death, it was determined that for his safety, and that of those who were housed with him, he be moved to a facility that would accord him isolation; Northern Correctional Institution was just that place. Menler now sat across a long metal conference table from the detective, the rapist's lawyer sitting just to the right of him, eyeing his surroundings suspiciously. Nick knew what the lawyer was feeling, though this was not his first time in the prison, a person never got used to being behind bars. Man was not meant to be caged, he was meant to be free and though people adjusted and adapted to any environment, even this one, no one ever got used to it. Nick had been surprised by how put together and with it Menler was after being in isolation all of this time. Menler had been convicted and sentenced before Nick ever became a police officer, and after a few years in the level 4 prison, he had been transferred to Northern in late 1995. Ten years in isolation, in a cell for twenty two hours a day made for some very lonely time. Most people went crazy after a while, those few who held it together seemed to be teetering on the edge of insanity, and then there was Menler who looked as though he were having the time of his life.

"Don't fucking smile at me," Nick said across the table. Menler was staring at the detective, leaning back in his chair as everyone just sat looking at each other.

"Sorry detective," Menler said, his smile still plastered on his face. "I'm just a normally happy guy."

"I don't even know why we're taking this meeting," the lawyer said. "We have nothing to say to you, and you certainly have nothing to offer us."

"You don't even know what I have to offer yet," Nick said, looking offended. The detective then turned his attention to the prisoner. "I thought I was dealing with you here. If you're not man enough to make decisions, if you need your mouthpiece to do all of the talking then I'll talk to him."

"You'll talk to me!" Menler shouted, banging his massive arms down on the table. It took everything Nick had within him not to jump, something that the startled lawyer was not able to hide. "I'm man enough, don't you worry about that."

"That's what I thought," Nick answered. "You sure did prove your manliness, raping those women."

"I don't know what you're talking about," Menler said with a smile. "But it really just burn you up that the stupidity of your fellow officers is going to set me free, and the statute of limitations is up for one through fifteen so I can't be retried, even if there were any evidence."

"Seems like you got it all figured out," Nick said. "I can't imagine why you would even entertain my offer. How's your brother by the way?"

Menler's face went slack, and then he looked at the detective, searching his face for any signs of deceit. When he saw none, his pulse quickened and he leaned forward at the table.

"You leave my brother out of this," Menler warned.

"Hey, hey big guy," Nick said. "We're just having a friendly conversation here. I just noticed that your family has not been up here to visit you in ten years. I just wondered if you knew what was going on with your little brother. He had to change his name, you know. He dropped out of college, is working in some local dive as a cook, making minimum wage. He has creditors up the ass, can't pay his bills, looks twice every time he passes a cop; it's just not a way to live."

"He's had it hard," Menler said, becoming obviously agitated. "You cops don't make it easy."

"Well, it can't be easy having a brother like you," Nick said. "I'm surprised he's been able to stay out of trouble. Anyway, enough about family, I'm here to put a deal on the table."

"We're not interested," the lawyer interjected.

"Oh, I think you're client is," Nick said. "He's at least a little curious. Just hear me out first. This afternoon you go to court to have your appeal heard. It sounds like you have solid evidence and the law is on your side. By the end of the day, you will most likely be looking at just five more years inside. However, I'm asking you to withdraw your appeal."

"Fuck you," Menler bellowed, laughing. "Why on earth would I do that?"

"Because," Nick began, a smile spreading slowly across his face. "Though you are a sick, twisted animal who has no impulse control around the opposite sex, you do have a heart. There is one person in this world you care about, and that's your brother."

"I told you to leave him out of this," Menler warned again.

"We finished here," the lawyer said, rising.

"I know how your mother abused you," Nick said, unfazed. "I know that you protected, shielded your little brother from her. You spared him what you went through. You had him move in with you the moment you got your first apartment.

You were the man of the house, unfortunately in more ways than one."

"You don't know shit," Menler stated.

"I know you raped sixteen women," Nick answered. "I know that even if you win your appeal, you will still be in prison. I also know that you must be fucking nuts if you think there is a cop alive who will let you walk out of here without making the rest of your life a living hell."

"I can't believe what I'm hearing," the lawyer said, astounded.

"I know you're guilty, and you know you're guilty," Nick continued. "You may get out, but life on the outside is not going to be any easier than life in here. In fact, I'm going to see to it that it's worse. Now I have a deal to offer you, one that will make everyone happy. If you take it, things will go easy. If you don't, well this is what I'm going to do.

First, you will be moved to a level 4 security prison to finish up your five years. Do you know what that means? You will be in gen-pop, that's right, general population. Everyone will know you're coming, and I personally don't care how many convicts you kill to keep your virgin ass, they'll get you sooner or later. Hell, you never know which CO's might just help to facilitate a little man love. But don't worry; you won't be alone for long. You see, I'll be going after your brother. It'll probably take a few years to get him right where I want him, two at the most, but I've got time. Hell, I've got at least five, am I right? I will hound your brother, night and day. I will bust him for littering, jay walking, talking on his cell phone in the car; I will look for any excuse to bust your brother. Sure, the first time or two he'll be slapped with a fine and sent back out into the world. However, the more often I bust him, the worse it will look. I might even need to plant a little evidence, but what's a little white lie for the cause? In the end, I'll get your brother, and all the prior arrests will catch up to him and he'll be forced to do some time. That's when we'll have a little fun.

I'm going to pull a few strings and have your brother incarcerated in Bridgeport; you know what I'm talking about. They go up to level 4 there, and I'm going to make certain that every convict on his cell block knows who your brother really is, who he's related to. Then, I'm going to sit back and watch with a smile while they rape and brutalize your cute little brother. Hell, by the time they're done passing him around, he'll have more holes than Swiss cheese."

"Understand that I will be reporting you, detective," the lawyer said, nearly in shock by the blatant threats being posed. "I will be speaking to your superiors, to the State's Attorney General, and to the Governor."

"But here's what I'll do if you withdraw your appeal," Nick continued, ignoring the lawyer. The detective was staring Menler right in the eye, both men's gaze locked on the other. "You get moved to Uncasville, level 3. You get to stay in isolation if you want, but you'll have plenty of privileges. Best of all, the DA won't oppose you being up for parole at sixty five, which you will be granted. As for your brother, he will be under my personal protection. He could get pulled over for DUI and if he uses my name, he'll get a pass. Your brother is a good guy, I don't see him getting in any major trouble, but I know if he does he won't fare as well as you. He doesn't have the fortitude for a place like this."

"You fuck!" Menler shouted, then became quiet and looked down at the table surface. "You cops, you pigs. You are all worse than the convicts in here. This is truly where you belong."

Nick rose and walked around the table, keeping his eye on the prisoner.

"We may be pigs," Nick said. "We may be bastards, but we are the way we are because of people like you. You don't like me, that's fine, I don't blame you. But you better understand that you made me. It's because of sick, degenerate people like you that there is a need for people like me. You raped and tortured sixteen women. The only reason you aren't on death row is because you did not kill any of them. No matter what, you don't get away with those other rapes. The minute you step outside this building, your life expectancy goes down by half. Every day you live after that takes a little more away. Even if another convict doesn't finish you off, someone on the outside will. You take my deal, you'll be safe. You'll be able to smell fresh air, and you will be free one day when only your victims will remember your name."

Menler continued looking down at the table, shaking his head softly, deep in thought. There was utter silence in the room, all eyes on the prisoner.

"So close," Menler whispered. "I was so fucking close."

"You're not listening to this," the lawyer said. "We are going to court today and we'll file papers of misconduct on the detective here while we're there. Grenier won't be a detective by the end of the day."

"You're fired," Menler said, looking up for the first time since hearing the deal, staring right into the detective's eyes.

"What?" the lawyer asked, incredulously.

"You're fired," Menler repeated. "You will not be working as my lawyer from this moment on. If you report Detective Grenier, I will deny any statement that you make."

"Fuck you both," the lawyer said, grabbing his briefcase and calling for the guard. "You both are nuts."

"How do I know that you'll keep up your end of the bargain?" Menler asked, turning the discussion back to Nick.

"You don't," Nick said. "But if you cooperate, I'll have no reason to make good on my threats, whereas if you don't, there's no telling what I'll do. I can tell you this, though; before last night, I had no interest in you. To be honest with you, the only reason I do is because you are a means to an end. I will have no problem forgetting about you when I get what I want, but I also will have no problem fucking your life every way from Sunday if you cross me. I have no compunctions about making the life of a serial rapist hell, even if I have to lie to do so."

"Fair enough," Menler said with a sigh. "What is it you want me to do?"

CHAPTER 69

Reporters, cameramen, and even the public crowded the street in front of the New London Police Department to see if they could catch a glimpse of the notorious Jonathan Menler. Because he had been convicted in New London County, Menler's appeal was to be handled by the same court, thus the rumor had it that he had been transferred down from Northern Correctional Institution just hours before and was awaiting his transfer to the courthouse. Security was heavy, and every available officer had been called in. Since Nick had spoken with Cross about the case the night before, it fell to him to provide security and oversee the prisoner transfer both to and from the courthouse, then back to Northern. The police were not just watching Menler, though. There was little chance of his escaping police custody; the police were more concerned about retribution from his victims or their families. The plan was to transfer Menler in a specialized armored van, cover him in Kevlar for the few seconds he would actually be out in the open, and keep to a tight schedule that got him to the courthouse and back behind bars in the quickest time possible. Since the word had slipped out that there was the possibility of an appeal, the media and the public alike had gone crazy, demanding answers. News conferences were being held every five minutes; with politicians, attorneys, and police officers all trying to keep the public calm while explaining the situation. For a while, Nick's killer was forgotten as he was forced to focus on protecting Menler.

Hollings was extremely unhappy. Usually it did not fall to local law enforcement to provide an escort for criminals. Menler was supposed to be transferred by corrections officers to and from Northern, but because Nick had involved himself in the process, everything had fallen into Hollings' lap, and she had had some choice words for the detective. It was not until after she had tried to cool off the chief of police that he explained to her what was going on.

"You're about ten minutes from not having a job," Hollings explained. "You go behind my back, show no respect for the chain of command, and put us in the middle of this nightmare. We have nothing to do with Menler, why did you have to go and make it our business."

"It had to be done," Nick answered. "We are killing two birds with one stone. We have a chance to catch our killer, and when four o'clock roles around and Menler does not show up at the courthouse, his appeal will be voided and there will be no chance for him to re-file."

"You're taking a risk, though," Hollings stated. "You're putting people at extreme risk. The police, your fellow officers, not to mention the prisoner. Do you remember what happened the last time you tried to bait a killer? You put innocent people at risk. You're playing with fire."

Nick strapped the Kevlar vest tight around him and did not look up at his superior. He knew what she was talking about, and he did not need reminding. It had been his first case, the Nemesis case. Nick had tried to corner the killer in a nightclub, but he had gotten away, only to abduct and nearly harm the woman Nick cared about.

"That's not the case this time," Nick answered.

"Explain to me the difference," Hollings said, cocking her head to the side in order to catch the eyes of her detective. "What makes this any different than the last time?"

"It's different because there are no innocents this time," Nick answered, looking her squarely in the eye. "There are only victims this time. That's the difference, that's what this entire case is about. Allun, Brenner, Cooper, they all did horrible things, but they too were victims. The killer herself, she was a victim too. Everybody's a victim; everyone has been somehow touched by this. No one is innocent, certainly not me and certainly not Menler."

"But he has nothing to do with this case," Hollings said. "It is you who are involving him, and if something happens..."

"Nothing will happen," Nick promised. He then resumed strapping his sidearm to a holster that was secured on the upper part of his right leg. Hollings stepped forward and bent down, helping him pull the strap around his leg. The lieutenant looked up into the detective's eyes.

"You involved my people in this," she reminded him. "You are responsible. You bring my boys back to me, unharmed. That includes you; this team only works with all three of you."

"I won't let anything happen to them," Nick promised. Then Hollings did something that he had never seen before. She reached up and caressed his face, only for a second, and he saw an emotion in her that he had never seen before.

"You are the only person who believes in her," Hollings whispered. "If you're wrong, if you hesitate..."

Nick reached up and grasped her hand, holding it firmly for just a moment.

"I won't hesitate," the detective answered. "They're my people too. I won't let her harm them. If it comes down to it..."

The lieutenant stared deep into her detective's eyes and she understood. He may believe that there was something good left in this woman who had become so dark, but he was not going to let her harm his fellow officers. They were brothers, Wilkins, Mitchell and Grenier. They were tested and true, she knew they would stand side by side until the end, and that was also what worried Hollings. They would follow each other into the fire, whether it meant they came back from it or not. Both Hollings and Nick rose to a standing position and faced each other. There was no more time for words. This was it, the moment of truth.

"I'll walk you down," Hollings said softly, almost in a whisper.

Nick stepped out of his lieutenant's office and the few officers and detectives left in the squad bay all rose as he made his way to the stairs with Hollings following behind. This was to be a carefully orchestrated event, but there was still the risk of something going wrong. There was still the risk that one of these detectives would not be coming home tonight. Each man who stood and watched the detective pass eyed him with awe, respect, and fear. There was something about the detective that they all wished they had, and at the same time, there was that thing that they did not want to ever understand. Nick was willing to take risks. He was willing to put people in harms way to catch his killer. He was unwilling to give up, no matter what. It's what had distanced him from women in the past; it was what distanced him from his fellow officers too. If cops and criminals were so black and white, if there was such a clear distinction between the two, then Nick was the shade of gray. He was the missing link between the blue uniforms and the orange jump suits; he was the bridge between the two. Each officer knew that it was not worth having his fame to be the person that Nick was forced to be.

For Nick, it was a long walk to the stairs, down to the front lobby where he saw throngs of people waiting for a glimpse, and finally down to the motor pool where his prisoner waited with Mitchell and Wilkins. Nick scanned the faces of the officers that watched him pass down the steps, across the lobby and down to the basement of the building. Nick desperately looked for Jenn, hoping in vain that she might be there, her smile enough to calm his nerves. However, she was not there, in fact she wasn't even in the building. Nick had heard she had been assigned to sit with the victims and their families. All the victims had been brought to a central location so as to be protected from the media and to be the first to hear about Menler's appeal. It seemed only right that the victims be the first to learn his fate. Nick sighed as he realized that there would be no momentary reassurance, as he realized that everything would go as he had planned. The pieces would fall where the may, and it would be Nick who would have to pick them up and put them back where they belonged. In other words, this was Nick's responsibility; glory if everything turned out, downfall if it went wrong. Nick made his way into the armory just outside the motor pool. The prisoner was dressed in an orange jumpsuit, but it was obvious that a Kevlar vest was underneath his muscular bulk. Kevlar plates had been fixed to his thighs and upper arms, a hood had been pulled tight over his head and a Kevlar helmet secured by a chin strap. Nick was taking no chances. His wrists were cuffed, though his ankles were not shackled. If there was a need for the prisoner to run, he would need to be as unbound as possible. Nick looked at his prisoner for a moment, searching for any area of exposed skin or unprotected clothing. However, there was none, Nick could not even see the expression on his prisoner's face. The detective then looked up and addressed his detectives.

"If any of you don't want to go through with this," he began. "If any of you don't feel as though you can go through with this, I'll understand."

The two detectives looked back at the other, and then looked back at Nick. Mitchell pulled an M-16 assault rifle from where it hung in a rack along the wall and handed it to Nick.

"You're the lead detective," Mitchell said. "You lead, we follow. Isn't that the way it's always been?"

"It's different this time," Nick said. "This is totally voluntary."

"You lead, we follow," Wilkins said, handing a fully loaded magazine to the detective. Nick took the metal clip and shoved it hard into the rifle.

"Shit," muttered Hollings from behind.

"Alright then," Nick said, ignoring the comment. "Safety's off. Let's get this over with and put this piece of shit behind bars as soon as possible.

CHAPTER 70

The killer waited in the dark. That was all that was left to do, wait. The killer thought of the little girl, the little girl who had so wished that she could just fall asleep. It seemed like many lifetimes since those horrible nights. There had been so much pain, there had been so much blood, and there had been so many bruises. That little girl had become a young lady, than a woman, than a killer. It had seemed so easy to make that step, but in fact, it had been a long road that led to this place, this time. The killer could still remember seeing that woman's reflection in the broken mirror of the bathroom the night that she had learned to stand up for herself, the night she had learned how satisfying it could be to fight back. It was his face that had been reflected, the broken shards capturing the twisted mass of pain and anger. It had not looked like her, it had not looked like a female, and it had simply looked like rage. The reflection looked like that of an angry, vengeful man, and it had been that persona that she had taken on every time she had been forced to fight back. *Forced to fight back*, that term seemed very ambiguous. Was anyone really forced to fight back? Had she ever really been forced, or had she fought back out of revenge, out of anger? Somewhere down the line, she had convinced herself that she was not involved; that it was him, the angry man in the mirror who had consumed her body and acted out. It had been the only way she could live with herself, with what she had done to her boyfriend; with what she had done to her victims.

Now she had to admit the truth to herself. She was not schizophrenic; there was no other personality inside. It had just been easier to think of the killer within as a man. People were more apt to believe a man capable of the horrors she had inflicted, hell she had believed it herself. That was why she made herself sound like a man on the phone when dealing with the detective. It was why she had built herself up to look like a man when attacking her victims. Women did not frighten these men, only the unknown did; only the certainty of despair that she visited upon them. It was this fear that was the only thing that made them truly understand, and it had been useful. Now this alter ego was needed once more, the killer was needed to keep Menler from being free and hurting more women. This was the riskiest attempt the killer had ever put together, but there was no choice. At the police station, Menler was fully protected. There was no way to do the deed and get away. However, here, when there was a moment of confusion, there was a slim chance that the killer could dispatch Menler and get away. Then there would be no need of the killer, he would be washed away and there would only be her. She would be free of the pain and anger that had so consumed her until now. She would not have to run; she would not have to become someone new yet again. A real life would be open to her, for the first time ever, she would be free. Or she would die here, either was a freedom of sorts for her.

The killer positioned herself better so that she could see everything around her. The darkness was heavy, but as she waited her eyes became accustomed to it and she could faintly make out the obstacles below her. She had set the obstacles for the police. She had no interest in harming them, her target was clear. The only way to make it out unscathed and without injuring Grenier and his men was to disable them long enough to kill Menler and slip away. Grenier, damn him, why did he have to get mixed up in this? She had no desire to discredit him, to make him look bad; especially after all he had been through. Things were out of her control now; there was no stopping what was coming. Perhaps it was fate that brought them so close together at this last moment. How many times had they looked at each other, looked into each other's eyes and not known the truth. There had been one point where she thought he might know, but surely he would have done something by now. Well, it did not matter now. All that mattered was that everything go according to plan, and then the killer would be gone for good. One black mark on his record, one unsolved case would not finish his career. Even if it did, it was most likely for the best. Grenier walked a fine line, one that threatened to consume him. Perhaps this would be therapeutic for both of them; perhaps this one event would save them both.

Finally, she heard the sirens as they drew near and then went silent. The escort cars had pulled around and created a perimeter. The armored van would be pulling up to the courthouse any moment now. She was in the basement, where Menler would be led in and unchained. Nick had thought he was smart by limiting exposure to Menler. The detective had ordered all officers clear of the basement and to set up upstairs in the main courthouse. That was where everyone waited for this drama to play out, where the lawyers and the prosecutor waited. Where the judge sat in his plush leather chair in his chambers, dreading the moment when he would have to vacate the guilty verdicts on fifteen rapes. The killer would save them all from this. She would do what had to be done; she would do what none of them could bring themselves to do. She would do it right under their noses, and they would only realized what had happened after it was too late. The killer would not be dubbed a criminal; she would be dubbed the only person capable of delivering justice. She would be noted for the fact that she spared the lives of the police and all the people upstairs, taking only one life, the life of the guilty.

The killer heard the familiar low rumble of a large vehicle and knew the time was now. Grenier and his men would lead Menler inside, into the killer's trap. It would be quick; this would all be over soon. The killer would disable the police quickly and easily, temporarily blinding them to her assault. Grenier was a smart detective; he would not lead Menler in unprotected. Menler was most likely wearing Kevlar body armor, and there was the possibility that he had even protected Menler's arms and legs. However, there was still a little gap between the vest and the Kevlar plates on the upper thigh. That was where the killer would strike, first fully removing Menler's genitals, then cutting deep into the rapist's femoral artery. That would kill the monster but also give him time to see the killer's handiwork. It would give him time to appreciate what true justice really was. This was something the Nemesis had done to one of his victim's and she had thought it only too appropriate. To borrow from Grenier's first killer to finish off this case. Then it would be done. The killer heard the doors opening and knew that the moment would be soon. Soon, Grenier and his men would lead Menler in, soon the killer would make her final move, and soon this would all be over.

CHAPTER 71

Nick pulled open the double doors to the basement of the courthouse and found the bay area quiet and almost dark. This is just how he had imagined it in his mind. Limiting the exposure of other people to his prisoner meant limiting the possibility of casualties if this thing went wrong. There were only two ways this thing could play out, there were only two ways the killer would let this thing play out. Either the killer attacked the prisoner and was caught, or the killer attacked and killed the prisoner and got away. She would not come this far only to turn back, and that was what Nick was counting on. In fact, it was the only thing Nick was actually certain of. Her hatred for those who abused others was the only thing that was true in her mind. He believed that she would give up if captured, but there was a part of him that remembered that she had always been like a wild beast, and when cornered she lashed out. It was what she had learned; it was what had set this whole chain of events into motion. When she lashed out at her boyfriend that one time, when she had finally stood up for herself, she learned something. Nick hoped that he was right, that she would go quietly, but he would not let his hopes for the killer's salvation override his need to keep his men safe. There was a line, and he had to set it himself before and know just how far he would go. Now that he was certain of himself, he set forth to complete his task.

Nick let the double doors slide open and let the sunlight filter into the dark space. Somewhere in here, this case would come to an end soon. Nick looked all around, hoping the light would illuminate the space enough to allow him to see where the killer was hiding. However, Nick had not really expected it would be this easy. He was dealing with an intelligent, dedicated person who would stop at nothing, just like him. Nick turned back and nodded to Mitchell, who adjusted the handcuffs on the prisoner and pulled him out of the back of the enormous van into the sunlight. On the outside, there were two threats, that of the public doing something stupid, and that of the killer thinking up something that even Nick could not anticipate. Mitchell pulled the prisoner inside and out of view of the outside as quickly as possible, and Wilkins followed him in, carefully watching for any movement. Step one had gone according to plan, they had delivered their prisoner to the courthouse safely. Now, however, was when things got a little hairy. Nick had ordered the handicap wheelchair be left by the bay for the prisoner's use. Police routinely used different methods of transportation, both in and out of buildings. No matter what Nick's plans were, safety was paramount, and the prisoner was to be wheeled inside and secured. Mitchell pulled the chair open from its collapsible mode, and Nick shoved his prisoner into it. The detective then bent down over him.

"Whatever happens," Nick said. "Thank you for agreeing to do this."

Nick then straightened and walked around the wheelchair and pushed as Mitchell drew his sidearm and took the lead position. Wilkins also drew his weapon and followed up behind Nick. Now they had to make it down the dark corridor to the prisoner elevator, which would then take them up to the prisoner's waiting area where prisoners were either arraigned or prepared for trial. In this case, the prisoner would be taken to his place in the courtroom where they would wait for the judge to convene the appeals hearing. Without hesitation, Mitchell made his way forward, followed by the prisoner in the chair, Nick pushing, and Wilkins bringing up the rear. This hallway seemed tailor made for just this type of event.

In fact, Nick would have to look into making the courthouse a little more secure in the future, but as for now, it suited his needs perfectly. Usually, there would be ten to twenty officers moving in and out, but this was a trap, both for the killer and for the detective. All that would determine the winner was whose mouse trap was better; who thought of that one thing the other did not. The corridor to the elevator was lit, mainly from the sunlight drifting in from the outside, but there was also light from the windows over their heads that were just a foot above the surface of the ground. There were bars over the windows, discouraging criminals to try and escape, and the light fell in swaths over the ground.

Mitchell began to pick up the pace, opening up the distance between him and Nick. He was headed off to the elevator, preparing to call for it and make his way back so that the doors would be open when the three detectives reached the end of the corridor. There was too much space, and Nick was about to say something when a searing bright light filled his eyes, cutting off his ability to see Mitchell in front of him. Nick yelled and turned back, only to see more bright white light fill his vision behind. He reached out for Wilkins but knew there was too much space between them. More phosphorus flash grenades lit up, blinding the detective.

"Flashbangs!" Nick called out, trying to warn everyone. Suddenly, the chair was pushed back hard, knocking the detective back a step and the wheelchair handles slammed into his groin. The chair moved away freely and Nick knew instantly that his prisoner was no longer in it. They were all blind; there was nothing any of them could do to see their way around. Nick dropped to the ground and tried to shield his eyes while feeling out for his prisoner. He looked up and could see the enormous silhouette of him standing before Nick. "Get on the ground!"

His prisoner, however, did not move. Nick screamed at him again, and dread filled his mind as he began to fear that he had been caught in his own trap. Nick shuffled back, scooting along the floor on his back, and that was when he saw his killer. From the far side, where the darkness was the only relief he could get from the blinding light, he saw the movement in the darkness. It was like something from a nightmare, something menacing that you could not fully distinguish, moving terrifyingly fast, or making it seem as though he were moving frustratingly slow. Nick opened his mouth to call out, but was unsure of whether he had made a sound or not, the only thing he could do was hope his prisoner was not caught unawares.

Then time seemed to slow. Nick felt as though he could sense each of the killer's steps, saw the glint of the knife as the killer pulled her arm back, felt the certainty of failure as she shifted into a crouching attack. However, Nick had not counted on the preparedness of his prisoner, who was not about to die easily. Nick watched as the man in the orange jump suit moved into the killer's attack, turning in with her instep. In that instant, Nick knew the attack was over. The prisoner wrapped his hand around her wrist, closing one loop of the handcuffs over her wrist. Nick realized instantly that Mitchell had, in fact, unfastened one of the handcuff loops when he had adjusted them prior to pulling him out of the van. Then, using his enormous bulk, the prisoner hoisted the killer up over his back and slammed her down on the ground hard. The killer had lost the knife, as she was right handed, and the handcuffs had now bound her right hand to his left. She flailed out with her left, though without the strength of the dominant arm the prisoner was able to slap her hand away. He then reached back and slapped her hard across the face; knocking her back and making her call out. Her venom had made her crazy with energy, though, and she bolted up again. This time, the prisoner merely lifted his knee and slammed it into her gut, knocking the wind out of her. He roughly slammed her down again. Nick was up by now and grabbed onto the massive prisoner's arm before he struck her again.

"That's enough!" Nick cried out. "Kevin, that's enough."

It was when he said Smith's name that the detective stopped his assault. The adrenaline and knowledge that he could have been killed had surged his mind into overdrive. Smith had momentarily lapsed into a self protection mode and lashed out as anyone would have.

"Move in!" Nick called out. "Everyone move in!"

Instantly, lights came on and officers wearing protective gear stepped forward with weapons drawn. The elevator doors opened and officers swarmed out, creating a perimeter around Nick, Kevin and the killer. Kevin pressed his foot against the killer's arm and Nick quickly unfastened the handcuffs, releasing him. Wilkins quickly moved in from behind, keeping his weapon pointed straight at the killer. The circle seemed to close, and as everyone became quickly accustomed to the interior light and the flash grenades faded away, the understanding that she was now trapped seemed to begin to set in. The killer rose slowly to her feet, gauging the situation as she looked around the room and counted the number of officers in the space. Nick knew what was going on in her mind. The black hood and mask covered her face so that all he could see were her eyes, but he knew her eyes well.

"Don't even think about it," Nick warned. "There's no way out. There's an army of cops upstairs and outside this building. There's no way out, Jenn."

That was when defeat truly set in. The killer looked around, then looked back at Nick and locked on to his gaze. She reached up and removed the mask, letting her hair fall down over her shoulders and breathing heavily as if gasping her first real breath of air.

"This was a trap," Jenn said. "You played me, used Smith in place of Menler. This whole thing was a trap."

"Just like the one you set for me," Nick answered with a nod. "Just like the flash grenades."

"I was after Menler!" Jenn shouted, pointing at Kevin. "I could have killed him. How long have you known?"

"That you were a woman, not long after you killed Cooper," Nick answered. "That it was you, only a day. Your friend who let you stay at her home, that was Courtney Delaney. We questioned her about the phone call you made to globomail regarding your account, Nikita. Once I saw her address, the home outside of Mystic, it all made sense. You were so mad that we had arrested Anderson, made such a big deal about it. Of course, now I know it was because you could not stand an innocent person being convicted of a crime he did not commit, and Anderson would have been convicted. There was the Friday night, when you left the bar on the first day I met you. You said you had a class, but you were really going to Norwich to kill Allun. For Brenner you used police issue stun gun and there were fibers from your gloves. We will match those. And then Cooper, how easy it must have been for you to slip out of the building when you donned your uniform again. I always wondered how the killer made it past so many cops. The self defense, teaching women how to defend themselves, it all came from the abuse you sustained. I understand now."

"You don't understand anything!" Jenn spat. "Don't you dare try and say you understand until you live what I lived through."

"And that makes it alright?" Nick asked. "That makes it alright to kill Allun, Brenner and Cooper?"

"They were guilty," Jenn answered. "All of you secretly wish you could have done what I did. You all know that they were guilty. Cooper would have done it again, he had violated his parole. Allun was a sex pervert, and Brenner, don't even get me started."

"But there's a difference between you and them," Nick said. "They didn't kill anyone."

"They killed their hope," Jenn said, becoming calm. "Each person lost a little bit of themselves after they were abused. Trust me, I know."

"Give up," Nick said.

"I can't," Jenn said. "But you can. You can decide what matters more to you, the case or me. You all know that justice was done. They all got what they deserved, they were animals."

Jenn turned her attention to Nick, her eyes moist with tears.

"You can't arrest me," she said. "You know I love you, and you know that it's over now."

Nick took two steps forward. Suddenly, all he saw was her that morning, lying in his bed, smiling at him. He had never found himself this close to peace before, not as he found himself at that moment. That would never come for him again, not like this. Nick had dealt with the heartbreak of coming to terms with the knowledge that she was a killer, his killer. Now Nick was stunned by the knowledge that he would never again have what he had in the last two weeks with her.

"Nick," Wilkins called out, trying to jar the detective's attention back to the present. Nick was getting dangerously close to Jenn.

"You can't arrest me," she said with a whisper. "You can't."

"I know," Nick answered.

"Nick!" Kevin cried.

"I can't arrest you," Nick said, a tear forming at the edge of his eye. "I love you. I heard you whisper it in my ear; it has kept my warm for so many days. I wanted to say it back, I wanted you to know; I just wanted it to have meaning. I wanted it to be personal. I love you."

Nick took a step back and watched as she smiled. In that one moment, there was only the two of them. It had been just then like it had been every other time they were together. There was just the two of them, and nothing else. Then Nick sighed.

"Detective Wilkins," Nick called out over his shoulder. "Place Officer Kelley under arrest, and read her her rights."

"Nick!" Jenn screamed as the detective turned and walked away. Wilkins moved forward and began reading Jenn her rights as Mitchell pulled her arms behind her back to replace the handcuffs. "You can't arrest me. You love me."

Everyone moved in to restrain and arrest Jenn. Only Smith watched as Nick walked back down the corridor and out into the sunlight. Smith followed the detective, watching him slowly walk across the grass to the road, and followed him as Nick walked all the way back to the police department alone.

CHAPTER 72

The following days were a blur for most in the Investigations Unit. Nick went directly from the courthouse to the police department to write his report and then disappear. He never knew Smith followed him back. Within an hour the press got wind of Jenn's arrest and was now fishing for any information they could find. The fact that Menler never arrived at the courthouse and that there was never a hearing on his appeal quickly took the back burner as all the focus was on the trap sprung at the courthouse. Nick's name was mentioned throughout, though no reporter was able to find and corner him for a statement. Nick wrote his report, left it on Hollings's desk while she was giving a press conference, and slipped out the back and got home quickly. He did not return to work for several days. Jenn was arrested immediately for the murders of Jack Brenner and Andrew Cooper. She was brought back to the police department and interrogated for many hours. Jenn did not answer any of the detective's questions though, only continually asked for Nick. Frustration began to set in as the detectives were not getting anywhere. Finally, Detective Smith placed her under arrest for the murder of Michael Allun, and after being asked the same questions about Nick, finally told Jenn that Nick was gone. That was when Jenn understood that she would not be seeing Nick again; he would not run in to save her. It was over. She then confessed to all three murders and told the detectives everything they wanted to know.

Nick went home and sat alone in his living room, wanting nothing more than to have let her go. He replayed the day's events in his mind, wondering to himself if he could really have ever let her run away. He had told Delaney to call her and warn her, tell her to run. Delaney had done what she knew to be right, she had done the only thing she could do. They were the only people who loved her, the only people who wanted her to be safe, and yet they were the only people who could save her from herself. Nick realized suddenly how horrible it was to be in love. The phone rang often, many times coming from the police department itself. Nick knew that Hollings was looking for him, wanting to make sure that he was alright, but he had no desire to talk with anyone right now. Then there were the calls from Norwich, his family was calling, then Tanner called. Everyone left messages, and not once did Nick dare to pick up. Finally, he realized there was only one person he wanted to be with tonight, and he drove alone to New Haven. He found Delaney in her home, crying as the television replayed images of Jenn's arrest. They sat together for the rest of the night and into the next day, just watching the television and saying nothing.

Nick did not come back to work until the following Friday, four days after Jenn's arrest. Jenn had confessed to all three murders and had taken the plea deal of life in prison without parole. She was to be housed in the York Correctional Institution, a prison for women in Niantic, Connecticut. As part of her deal, she was to be housed in solitary; ex-cops never faired well in general population. By Friday, the story had pretty much died down and everyone was moving on to other cases. However, there was still one thorn in the department's side that needed to be removed before everyone could move on. Hollings called Nick on Friday morning and left a message stating he needed to be at work by ten. Nick could sense the urgency in her voice, and when he called back, she told him this was an order. Everyone was to be there. Nick got dressed and drove in, knowing that nothing would be the same for him now. Nothing looked the same through his eyes; it was as if color had lost its vibrancy, as if everything had become dull. Nick went straight to his office, and no one said anything to him, everyone acted as if his absence had gone unnoticed. Nick began to feel a little better after about an hour, when the normal buzz began to fill the squad bay. He had no desire to jump into a case though, and just listened as calls came in.

Then everything stopped. It was so sudden, that Nick missed it for a moment. It was as if all activity had been put on hold. Nick watched through his office window for a moment, and then stepped out into the squad bay, curious as to what was going on. That was when he saw him, that was when he understood. Mark Anderson walked into the squad bay as if he were the king of the world, a smug smirk across his face. Nick immediately wanted to retrieve his sidearm and shoot the smug bastard right in the ass. Hollings stepped out of her office, and Nick wondered now if this is why he had been called in.

"I suppose you all have something to say to me," Anderson said as if speaking to everyone. His eyes, however, were firmly focused on Hollings.

"I do have something to say to you," Hollings said, holding out a videotape. Nick knew immediately what it was; the tape of Anderson's molestation. "This is the tape we uncovered at Allun's home. This is the tape of you."

Anderson's face immediately drained of color as he realized no one here would be apologizing to him today. No one here was going to say any of the things he felt he deserved.

"You know, you are such a gigantic prick that part of me would have no problem seeing that this found it's way into the hands of one of your competitors," Hollings said, admiring the tape, turning the tape over in her hand. "However, Nick said something a few days ago that has stuck with me. He said there were no innocent people in this case, only victims.

He was right, there were only victims. No matter how pissed off you make me, I just remind myself that you are an angry victim, a little boy who was horribly victimized and has never come to terms with it. Then I realize that it's not your fault that you are the way you are, and it's not my fault that you are the way you are, and I end up feeling much better about the way things were left between us.

This is your tape, there are no copies. You can take it and do with it what you will. I can give it to you and not worry about what you are going to say or do because I have come to terms with some things. I have come to terms with the fact that you are an angry, pathetic little boy who needs some serious help. I hope that one day you can find it. I know that I am not like you, that I don't need leverage over you to keep you from telling the truth. I did the right thing by not promoting you to lead detective, and I did the right thing by having you transferred. You were not a very good detective, you let your objectivity get clouded by your emotion, and you might have ended up doing more harm than good. I wish you well in your career as a reporter or whatever you decide to do from here, and I can do that because I am free of any guilt I might have had about what had happened between us.

Now, I'm going to make something clear to you. Hunting season on me and my unit is over. If you come at me or my detectives again, I will shut you down. I will not stoop to your level by bringing up your past or threatening to expose what happened to you because I am better than that. I will shut you down by exposing who you are, that angry bitter man who never was a very good cop. You do what you have to do, you be whatever type of reporter you decide to be, but know that I will not tolerate you disparaging good cops because you are angry that you never were one. That's all. Have a nice life, and get out."

Instantly, every detective, every officer, even the secretaries rose from their seat and stood, staring at Anderson. Everyone crowded in a little, with Hollings, Mitchell, and Wilkins standing in the middle. Anderson knew now that his little private war with the police department was over. The vengeance he felt so entitled to was to be denied and he knew that Hollings was deadly serious. There would never be a time that he could disparage her again, but he also knew that she would never hold this tape or his past as leverage over him. He was, in fact, quite certain that this was the only copy of tape.

"Do you need help finding the door?" Hollings asked.

"No, lieutenant," Anderson said, in barely a whisper.

"Then find it now," she said. All of the detectives watched as Anderson left the squad bay for the final time, no longer a cop, barely a man, and certainly no longer a threat to the police department. Hollings sighed as he went down the stairs and the doors to the squad bay closed behind him. She looked between Wilkins and Mitchell, who merely smiled and nodded, then turned her attention back to Nick's office where he had been standing. He was no longer there.

"Where did he go?" Hollings asked, looking back at the other two detectives.

"Oh shit," Wilkins said, immediately realizing where he was. "He's gone."

CHAPTER 73

Nick never heard the last part of Hollings' speech to Anderson, though he knew what the outcome would be. Hollings was putting the past behind her, putting her guilt behind her, and Nick instantly realized that he needed to do the same. He could not go through his life never seeing her again, never admitting to himself that he still loved her. Nick drove out to the York Correctional Institution, uncertain of what the result would be. All he knew was that he had to see her, even if she never spoke to him again. Beyond that, there was one question that remained unanswered in his mind, one questioned that ate away at him. It needed answering, and though he was not sure if she would provide an answer, again, he had to try. Nick checked in for the first time in his life as an actual visitor, someone not there on an official assignment. He was like any family member, though he had a few privileges that others did not. He found himself in a holding cell where prisoners met with their attorney's privately. He waited until they brought Jenn in, and was shocked and taken aback when he saw her. In four days she looked as though she had aged forty years. There were deep lines in her face and her hair seemed thinned and gray. She wore a grayish jumpsuit that did not flatter her figure at all, and she was already starting to show signs of weight loss. Nick had to resist the urge to take her in his arms.

"What the fuck do you want?" she asked, bitterly.

"I had to see you," Nick said, deflecting her anger. "Are you being treated all right?"

"Why do you care?" she asked. "Are you going to bust me out of here?"

Jenn laughed at that comment, a little chuckle that was more for herself than anything else.

"Do you need anything?" Nick asked.

"What could I need, Detective?" Jenn asked. "I think you're here because you need something. Do you need some peace of mind, someone to tell you that you did the right thing? Well fuck you!"

"No," Nick said. "I don't need peace of mind. I won't ever have that. I do need to know who the Puppet Master is."

Jenn immediately shut her mouth and stared at Nick for a moment.

"You know about him?" she asked.

"I know he led you to Allun," Nick said. "I know he has his own part to play in this. I know that I won't let him get away with it."

"Good luck," Jenn said, laughing again. "You don't know shit. You have a name and an idea."

"Who is he, Jenn?" Nick asked, slamming his fists down on the table, startling her. They were both so strung out on their emotions that both were about to snap.

"I don't know! Jesus!" Jenn answered. "All you care about is the case. That's all you ever cared about."

"That's not true," Nick said. "That's not true and you know it."

"Then what are you doing here?" she asked, losing her grip on her emotions. "What the hell are you doing here?"

"Wild horses," Nick said, and then tried to smile. Jenn looked at him quizzically for a moment, and then began to cry. It was a deep cry, she fell to her knees. Nick kneeled down and took her in his arms, letting her cry on his shoulder for as long as she needed to. They did not say anything for the rest of the visit; he simply kissed her before he left. He was heartbroken, and what's more, he was simply broken, he was all alone. There was no answer for him as to who the Puppet

Master was, no person to take his pain and anger out on. As Nick gathered his belongings, he fought back the tears that seemed to well up from within as he realized there were some things he was never going to have answers to. He made his way through the corridors of metal bars and thick doors until he reached the outside.

As Nick began to make his way over to his car, he saw two men standing beside it, waiting for him. Detective Wilkins and Mitchell were simply leaning against the car; waiting for their partner, waiting for their friend. When they realized that he had left the police department, they both knew where he had gone, and they both knew he was going to need their support. When Nick saw them standing there, saying nothing, their mere presence stating the reason for their presence; only then did he realize that he was not totally alone.

ABOUT THE AUTHOR

As the child of a military family, Timothy Lassiter grew up all over the world, having the fantastic opportunity to visit and learn about other cultures first hand. After his family settled in southeastern Connecticut, Timothy joined the U.S. Navy and served as a Hospital Corpsman, where he had the opportunity to work with the military police, as well as local law enforcement. After returning to New England, Timothy has continued to pursue his medical career as well as using his beloved home state as the setting for his novels. With the help of friends in local law enforcement, Timothy has been able to continue to pursue his interest in the criminal field and has been overwhelmed by the support he has received in the technical, legal and law enforcement matters that have helped him to maintain historical and technical accuracy in his novels.

Printed in the United States
202099BV00004B/10/A